PATRICK CARMAN's

SKELETON CREEK

PC STUDIO

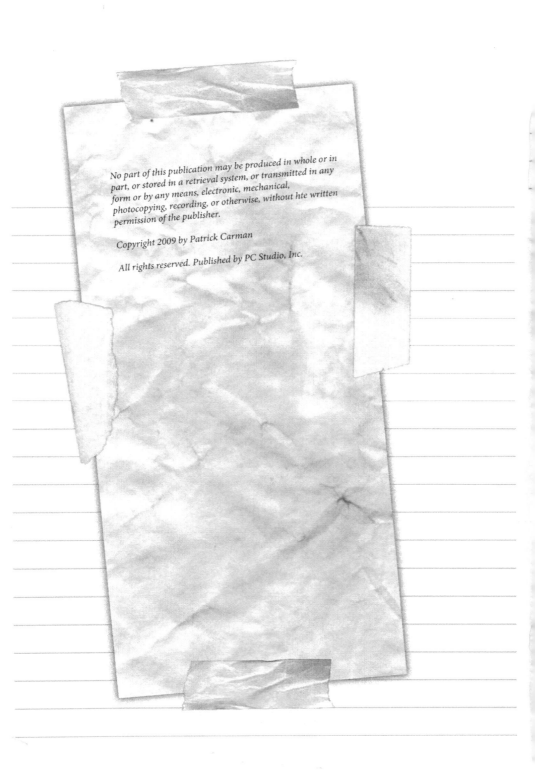

Copyright 2009 by Patrick Carman

All rights reserved. Published by PC Studio, Inc.

Monday, September 13, 5:30 a.m.

There was a moment not long ago when I thought: <u>This is it. I'm dead.</u>

I think about that night all the time and I feel the same fear I felt then. It happened two weeks ago, but fourteen days and nights of remembering have left me more afraid and uncertain than ever.

Which I guess means it isn't over yet. Something tells me it may never truly be over.

Last night was the first time I slept in my own room since everything happened. I'd gotten in the habit of waking in the hospital to the sound of a nurse's shuffling feet, the dry chalk-dust smell of her skin, and the soft shaking of my shoulder.

<u>The doctor will visit you in a moment. He'll want you awake. Can you sit up for me, Ryan?</u>

There was no nurse or doctor or chalky smell this morning, only the early train crawling through town to wake me at half past five. But in my waking mind, it wasn't a train I heard. It was something more menacing, trying to sneak past in the early dawn, glancing down the dead-end streets, hunting.

1

I WAS SCARED — AND THEN I WAS RELIEVED —
BECAUSE MY OVERACTIVE IMAGINATION HAD SETTLED
BACK INTO ITS NATURAL RESTING STATE OF FEAR AND
PARANOIA.

IN OTHER WORDS, I WAS BACK HOME IN SKELETON
CREEK.

USUALLY WHEN THE MORNING TRAIN WAKES ME UP, I
GO STRAIGHT TO MY DESK AND START WRITING BEFORE
THE REST OF THE TOWN STARTS TO STIR. BUT THIS
MORNING — AFTER SHAKING THE IDEA THAT SOMETHING
WAS STALKING ME — I HAD A SUDDEN URGE TO LEAP
FROM MY BED AND JUMP ON BOARD THE TRAIN. IT WAS
A FEELING I DIDN'T EXPECT AND HADN'T THE SLIGHTEST
CHANCE OF ACTING ON. BUT STILL, I WONDERED WHERE
THE FEELING HAD COME FROM.

NOW, I'VE RESTED THIS JOURNAL ON A TV TRAY
WITH ITS LEGS TORN OFF, PROPPED MYSELF UP IN BED ON
A COUPLE OF PILLOWS, AND HAVE STARTED DOING THE
ONE THING I CAN STILL DO THAT HAS ALWAYS MADE ME
FEEL BETTER.

I HAVE BEGUN TO WRITE ABOUT THAT NIGHT AND ALL
THAT COMES AFTER.

Monday, September 13, 6:03 a.m.

I need to take breaks. It still hurts to write. Physically, mentally, emotionally — it seems like every part of me is broken in one way or another. But I have to start doing this again. Two weeks in the hospital without a journal left me starving for words.

I have kept a lot of journals, but this one is especially important for two reasons. Reason number one: I'm not writing this for myself. I'm putting these words down for someone else to find, which is something I never do. Reason number two: I have a strong feeling this will be the last journal I ever write.

My name, in case someone finds this and cares to know who wrote it, is Ryan. I'm almost old enough to drive. (Although this would require access to a car, which I lack.) I'm told that I'm tall for my age but need to gain weight or there's no hope of making the varsity cut next year. I have a great hope that I will remain thin.

3

I CAN IMAGINE WHAT THIS MORNING WOULD HAVE BEEN LIKE BEFORE THE ACCIDENT. I WOULD BE GETTING READY FOR THE HOUR-LONG BUS RIDE TO SCHOOL. I WOULD HAVE SO MUCH TO SAY TO SARAH. AN HOUR NEXT TO HER WAS ALWAYS TIME WELL-SPENT. WE HAD SO MUCH IN COMMON, WHICH KEPT US FROM GOING COMPLETELY CRAZY IN A TOWN POPULATED BY JUST UNDER SEVEN HUNDRED PEOPLE.

I'M REALLY GOING TO MISS THOSE CONVERSATIONS WITH SARAH. I WONDER IF I'LL GET LONELY. THE TRUTH IS I DON'T EVEN KNOW IF I'M ALLOWED TO MENTION HER NAME. BUT I CAN'T STOP. I AM A WRITER. THIS IS WHAT I DO. MY TEACHERS, PARENTS, EVEN SARAH — THEY ALL SAY I WRITE TOO MUCH, THAT I'M OBSESSIVE ABOUT IT. BUT THEN, IN THE SAME BREATH, THEY CAN'T HELP BUT MENTION THAT I'M GIFTED. LIKE WHEN MRS. GARVEY TOLD ME I UNDERSTAND WORDS AND THEIR USAGE IN THE SAME WAY A PRODIGY ON THE PIANO UNDERSTANDS NOTES AND SOUNDS. BUT I HAVE A MUCH SIMPLER ANSWER, AND I'M PRETTY SURE I'M MORE RIGHT THAN MY TEACHER IS: I HAVE WRITTEN A LOT, EVERY DAY, EVERY YEAR, FOR MANY YEARS IN A ROW.

PRACTICE MAKES PERFECT.

I THINK MY FAVORITE WRITERS ARE THOSE WHO ADMITTED WHILE THEY WERE STILL ALIVE THAT THEY COULDN'T LIVE WITHOUT WRITING. JOHN STEINBECK, ERNEST HEMINGWAY, ROBERT FROST — GUYS WHO PUT WRITING UP THERE IN THE SAME CATEGORY AS AIR AND WATER. WRITE OR DIE TRYING. THAT KIND OF THINKING AGREES WITH ME.

BECAUSE HERE I AM. WRITE OR DIE TRYING.

IF I TURN BACK THE PAGES IN ALL THE JOURNALS I'VE WRITTEN, I BASICALLY FIND TWO THINGS: SCARY STORIES OF MY OWN CREATION AND THE RECORDING OF STRANGE OCCURRENCES IN SKELETON CREEK. I CAN'T SAY FOR CERTAIN WHY THIS IS SO, OTHER THAN TO FALL BACK ON THE OLD ADAGE THAT A WRITER WRITES WHAT HE KNOWS, AND I HAVE KNOWN FEAR ALL MY LIFE.

I DON'T THINK I'M A COWARD — I WOULDN'T BE IN THE POSITION I'M IN NOW IF I WAS A COWARD — BUT I AM THE SORT OF PERSON WHO OVERANALYZES, WORRIES, FRETS. WHEN I HEAR A NOISE SCRATCHING UNDER THE BED — EITHER REAL OR IMAGINED — I STARE AT THE CEILING FOR HOURS AND WONDER WHAT IT MIGHT BE THAT'S TRYING TO CLAW ITS WAY OUT. (I PICTURE IT

5

WITH FANGS, LONG BONY FINGERS, AND BULGING RED EYES.) FOR A PERSON WHO WORRIES LIKE I DO AND HAS A VIVID IMAGINATION TO MATCH, SKELETON CREEK IS THE WRONG SORT OF PLACE TO ENDURE CHILDHOOD.

I KNOW MY WRITING HAS CHANGED IN THE PAST YEAR. THE TWO KINDS OF WRITING — THE MADE-UP SCARY STORIES AND THE DOCUMENTING OF EVENTS IN SKELETON CREEK — HAVE SLOWLY BECOME ONE. I DON'T HAVE TO MAKE UP STORIES ANY LONGER, BECAUSE I'M MORE CERTAIN THAN EVER THAT THE VERY TOWN I LIVE IN IS HAUNTED.

THIS IS THE TRUTH.

AND THE TRUTH, I'VE LEARNED, CAN KILL YOU.

I'M TIRED NOW. SO TIRED.

I HAVE TO PUT THIS DOWN.

EVEN IF I CAN'T STOP THINKING ABOUT IT.

MONDAY, SEPTEMBER 13, 2:00 P.M.

I HAVE TO BE CAREFUL TO KEEP THIS HIDDEN.

I HAVE TO MAKE SURE NOBODY SEES ME WRITING IN IT.

THEY'RE CURIOUS ENOUGH AS IT IS.

THEY'RE WATCHING ME ENOUGH AS IT IS.

I'M A CAPTIVE, REALLY. I'M IMPRISONED IN MY OWN ROOM.

I HAVE NO IDEA HOW MUCH THEY KNOW.

I DON'T EVEN KNOW HOW MUCH _I_ KNOW.

I HAVE SO MANY QUESTIONS, AND NO WAY TO ANSWER THEM.

THERE IS SOMETHING ABOUT HAVING BEEN GONE FOR TWO WEEKS IN A ROW THAT HELPS ME SEE SKELETON CREEK WITH FRESH EYES. I HAVE A NEW IDEA OF WHAT SOMEONE FROM THE OUTSIDE MIGHT THINK IF THEY DROVE INTO MY ISOLATED HOMETOWN WHERE IT SITS ALONE AT THE BOTTOM OF THE MOUNTAINS.

I LIKE TO ACT ON THESE THOUGHTS AND WRITE THEM DOWN AS IF THEY ARE OCCURRING. IT'S A CURIOUS HABIT I CAN'T SEEM TO BREAK. MAYBE THINGS ARE SAFER WHEN I THINK OF THEM AS FICTION.

7

If I imagine myself as a person arriving in Skeleton Creek for the first time it goes something like this:

The sun has barely risen when a car door opens and a man stands at the curb looking out into the forest beyond the edge of town. There is a gray fog that hangs thick and sticky in the trees, unwilling to leave, hiding something diabolical in the woods. He gets back in his car and locks the doors, glancing down side streets through dusty windows. He wonders what has brought this little town to its knees. The place is not dead: it is not even dying for certain. Instead, the driver thinks to himself, this place has been forgotten. And he senses something else. There are secrets buried here that are best left alone.

It is then that the car turns sharply and leaves in the direction from which it came, the driver confident that the growing light of day will not shake the unforeseen dread he feels about the town at the bottom of the mountain.

The driver would not know exactly what it was that scared him off, but I know. Sarah knows, too. We know there's something wrong with this place, and more important, we know we're getting too close to whatever it is.

Someone's coming.

Monday, September 13, 4:30 p.m.

When did our search begin?

If I could get to my old journals, I might be able to figure out the exact date. But they're hidden, and there's no way for me to get to them in my present state. Not without help. And the only person who could help me — Sarah — isn't here anymore.

I guess our searching began with a question she asked me last summer.

"Why Skeleton Creek?"

"You mean the name?"

"Yes, the name. Why call a town Skeleton Creek? Nobody wants to visit a place with a name like that. It's bad for tourism."

"Maybe the people who named it didn't want any visitors."

"Don't you think it's weird no one wants to talk about it? It's like they're hiding something."

"You're just looking for a reason to go snooping around with your camera."

"There's something to it. A name like that has to come from somewhere."

10

I REMEMBER THINKING THERE WAS A STORY HIDDEN WITHIN WHAT SHE'D SAID, AND THAT I WANTED TO BE THE ONE TO WRITE THE STORY. I HAD VISIONS OF EVERYONE IN SKELETON CREEK APPLAUDING MY EFFORTS TO UNCOVER THE PAST. THE FANTASY OF CREATING SOMETHING IMPORTANT APPEALED TO ME.

WE BEGAN OUR QUEST AT THE LOCAL LIBRARY, A GLOOMY TWELVE-BY-TWELVE-FOOT ROOM AT ELM AND MAIN, OPEN ON MONDAYS AND WEDNESDAYS. IT WAS ALSO OPEN ON NEW YEAR'S DAY, CHRISTMAS DAY, AND EASTER SUNDAY, BECAUSE ACCORDING TO GLADYS MORGAN, OUR PREHISTORIC AND VERY UNHAPPY TOWN LIBRARIAN, "NOBODY COMES IN ON THOSE DAYS AND THE LIBRARY IS DEATHLY QUIET, AS A LIBRARY SHOULD BE."

GLADYS MORGAN IS NOT A FRIENDLY WOMAN. SHE STARES AT EACH PERSON SHE ENCOUNTERS IN PRECISELY THE SAME WAY: AS IF EVERYONE IN TOWN HAS JUST KICKED HER CAT ACROSS THE ROOM. SHE HAS SKIN LIKE CRUMPLED NEWSPAPER. HER LOWER LIP HAS LOST ITS SPRING AND HANGS HEAVY OVER HER CHIN. THERE IS AN ALARMING OVERBITE.

I REMEMBER THE DAY WE WALKED INTO

the library, the little bell tinkling at our entry.

The room smelled musty, and I wasn't certain if it came from the old books or from the woman who guarded them. Sarah peppered Gladys with questions as I ran my fingers along the spines of the most boring books I'd ever seen, until at last Miss Morgan put her hand up and spoke.

"This town wasn't called Skeleton Creek until 1959."

She reached beneath her desk, which had sat decaying in the same spot for a hundred years, and pulled out a wooden milk crate. Inside were newspapers, torn and yellowed.

"You're not the first to ask about the past, so I'll advise you like I've done the rest."

She glanced past the dark curtains to the street outside and shoved the box across the desk, leaving a streak where dust had been lifted. She had a peculiar, superstitious look on her face.

"Read them if you want, but let it go after that. Beyond these you'll only stir up trouble."

Gladys took a white cloth from her pocket and removed her wire-rimmed glasses, wiping them with wrinkled hands and casting shadows across the peeling wallpaper behind her.

"I'll make a note you've checked those out. Have them back on Monday or it's a dollar a day."

The town librarian clammed up after that, as if someone had been eavesdropping and she'd said as much as she was allowed to. But Gladys Morgan had given us a beginning, a thread to grab hold of. It would lead us to trouble of a kind we hadn't anticipated.

Monday, September 13, 6:40 p.m.

I stopped there for a while because all of this has made me think of Sarah.

I wonder if she were here whether she'd be telling what happened the same way. Not writing it down — "Not my thing," she always said. But I wonder if she would remember things differently.

I look back, I see warning signs.

Sarah looks back, she sees invitations.

I miss her.

I blame her.

I'm scared for her.

I'm scared of her. Not a lot. But some.

It was wrong of me to write "I blame her."

It's not like she tricked me into anything.

I went along willingly.

I was the one who put my life on the line. Even if I didn't realize I was doing it.

I guess what I'm saying is that none of this would have happened if Sarah hadn't been around.

Now —

I do miss her.

And I do blame her.

14

And I'm sure her story would be different from mine.

But where was I? Oh, yeah — we began reading through the stack of newspapers. From 1947 to 1958, there had been a monthly paper for the 1200 residents. The paper had an uninspiring name — The Linkford Bi-Weekly — but it told us what our town had once been called. Linkford. It had a nice ring to it, or so I thought at the time.

The title of the paper became more interesting in 1959 when it was renamed The Skeleton Creek Irregular. (This was an appropriate name, for we could only find a handful of papers dated between 1959 and 1975, when the publisher fled to Reno, Nevada, and took the printing press with him.)

Linkford sat alone on a long, empty road at the bottom of a forested mountain in the western state of Oregon. It surprised us to discover that an official from the New York Gold and Silver Company had suggested the town name be changed to Skeleton Creek. Actually, we were fairly dumbstruck that anyone from New York would take an interest in our town at all.

"Why in the world would a big city mining company want to change the name of the town?" I remember asking Sarah.

"It's that monstrous machine in the woods," she answered. "The dredge. I bet that has something to do with it. They probably owned it."

The dredge. Already, we were headed toward the dredge. I'll bet Sarah was planning things in her mind even way back then.

Not knowing the consequences.

Just thinking about the mystery.

We pieced together the small bits of information we could gather from those who would talk (hardly anyone) and the newspapers we'd been given (less than thirty in all, none complete editions). We had gone as far as creepy old Gladys Morgan said we should go, and yet we kept pulling on the thread we'd taken hold of.

Of course, I was less enthusiastic than Sarah at first, knowing that if our parents discovered what we were doing, they would demand that we stop prying into other people's business. Privacy has long been the religion of our town.

But Sarah can be persuasive, especially when she finds something she wants to record on film. She could be consumed by filmmaking in the same way that I am with writing. Our creative obsessions seem to draw us together like magnets, and I had a hard time pulling away when she was determined to drag me along.

And so we kept digging.

Of course, I know where all of this is going. I just have to get it down on paper. One last time.

Monday, September 13, 8:30 p.m.

Remember.

I have to try to remember all the details.

They could still be important.

It feels like midnight: it's only 8:30.

How did this happen to me?

Stop, Ryan. Go back.

Remember.

Even if you know how it's going to feel.

Even if you don't have any of the answers.

There were small announcements in four of the newspapers that alluded to something called the Crossbones. They were cryptic ads in nature, containing a series of symbols and brief text that seemed to have no meaning. One such message read as follows: <u>The floor and 7th, four past the nine on door number two. Crossbones.</u> Who in their right mind could decipher such nonsense? Certainly not us.

All of the advertisements came between the years of 1959 and 1963 and all appeared in <u>The Skeleton Creek Irregular.</u> Then, in 1964, they

CEASED ALTOGETHER, AS IF THEY HAD NEVER EXISTED AT ALL. BUT THE SAME SYMBOLS COULD STILL BE FOUND IN VARIOUS PLACES. ONE OF THE SYMBOLS — TWO BONES TANGLED IN BARBED WIRE — COULD BE SEEN ABOVE THE DOOR TO THE LOCAL BAR, ON A SIGNPOST AT THE EDGE OF TOWN, AND AGAIN CARVED INTO A VERY OLD TREE ALONG A PATHWAY INTO THE WOODS. IT MADE US WONDER IF THE MEMBERS OF THE CROSSBONES WERE STILL MEETING. WHO HAD BEEN PART OF THE SOCIETY? WHAT WAS ITS FUNCTION? WERE THERE STILL ACTIVE MEMBERS — AND, IF SO, WHO WERE THEY?

OUR TRAIL DEAD-ENDED WITH THE ADVERTISEMENTS.

WE SEARCHED RELENTLESSLY ONLINE FOR CLUES TO OUR TOWN'S PAST. NEW YORK GOLD AND SILVER WAS BANKRUPTED OVER ENVIRONMENTAL LAWSUITS, AND IT SEEMED TO VANISH INTO THIN AIR AFTER 1985. BUT THIS DIDN'T KEEP US FROM SNEAKING DOWN THE DARK PATH INTO THE WOODS TO EXAMINE WHAT WAS LEFT BEHIND.

DO I WISH WE'D NEVER GONE DOWN THAT PATH?

YES.

NO.

I don't know.

It's too complicated.

Or is it? None of this would have happened if we'd stayed away from the dredge.

The dredge is a crucial part of the town's dreary past. It sits alone and unvisited in the deepest part of the dark woods. The dredge, we discovered, was a terrible machine. Its purpose was to find gold, and its method was grotesque. 24 hours a day, 365 days a year, the dredge sat in a muddy lake of its own making. It dug deep into the earth and hauled gargantuan buckets of stone and debris into itself. Nothing escaped its relentless appetite. <u>Everything</u> went inside the dredge. Trees and boulders and dirt clods the size of my head were sifted and shaken with a near-deafening racket, and then it was all spit out behind in piles of rubble ten feet high. A tail of ruin — miles and miles in length — all so tiny bits of gold could be sifted out.

The trench that was left behind as the dredge marched forward formed the twenty-two-mile

STREAMBED THAT ZIGZAGS WILDLY ALONG THE EDGE OF
TOWN AND UP INTO THE LOW PART OF THE MOUNTAIN.
THE GUTTED EARTH FILLED WITH WATER, AND THE BANKS
WERE STREWN WITH WHITEWASHED LIMBS THAT LOOKED
LIKE BROKEN BONES.

THE NEW WATERWAY TORN FROM EARTH AND
STONE WAS CALLED SKELETON CREEK BY A MAN IN A
SUIT FROM NEW YORK. MAYBE IT HAD BEEN A JOKE,
MAYBE NOT. EITHER WAY THE NAME STUCK. SOON
AFTER, THE TOWN TOOK THE NAME AS WELL. IT WOULD
SEEM THAT NEW YORK GOLD AND SILVER HELD
ENOUGH SWAY OVER LINKFORD TO CHANGE THE TOWN
NAME TO WHATEVER IT WANTED.

THE GREATEST DISCOVERY — OR THE WORST,
DEPENDING ON HOW YOU LOOK AT IT — THAT SARAH
AND I MADE INVOLVED THE UNTIMELY DEATH OF A
WORKMAN ON THE DREDGE. THERE WAS ONLY ONE
MENTION OF THE INCIDENT IN THE NEWSPAPER, AND
NOTHING ANYWHERE ELSE. OLD JOE BUSH IS WHAT
THEY CALLED HIM, SO I CAN ONLY CONCLUDE THAT HE
WAS NOT A YOUNG MAN. OLD JOE BUSH HAD LET HIS
PANT LEG GET CAUGHT IN THE GEARS, AND THE

MACHINERY OF THE DREDGE HAD PULLED HIM THROUGH, CRUSHING HIS LEG BONE INTO GRAVEL. THEN THE DREDGE SPIT HIM OUT INTO THE GRIMY WATER. HIS LEG WAS DEMOLISHED, AND UNDER THE DEAFENING SOUND IN THE DARK NIGHT, NO ONE HEARD HIM SCREAM.

OLD JOE BUSH NEVER EMERGED FROM THE BLACK POND BELOW.

MONDAY, SEPTEMBER 13, 10:00 P.M.

OKAY. I THINK EVERYONE IS ASLEEP NOW.

IT'S AS SAFE AS IT'S GOING TO GET.

LATE LAST NIGHT, ON MY ARRIVAL HOME FROM THE HOSPITAL, I WAS REUNITED WITH MY COMPUTER. THIS MAY SEEM LIKE A STRANGE THING TO WRITE, BUT THE ALREADY WALLOPING POWER OF A COMPUTER IS MAGNIFIED EVEN MORE FOR PEOPLE LIKE ME IN A SMALL, ISOLATED TOWN. IT IS THE LINK TO SOMETHING NOT BORING, NOT DULL, NOT DREARY. IT HAS ALWAYS BEEN ESPECIALLY TRUE IN MY CASE BECAUSE SARAH IS CONSTANTLY MAKING VIDEOS, POSTING THEM, AND ASKING ME TO TAKE NOTICE.

ONE SIMPLE CLICK — THAT'S ALL IT CAN TAKE FOR YOUR LIFE TO CHANGE.

SOMETIMES FOR THE BETTER.

SOMETIMES FOR THE MUCH WORSE.

BUT WE DON'T THINK ABOUT THAT.

NO, WE JUST CLICK.

THERE IS A CERTAIN VIDEO SHE MADE FIFTEEN DAYS AGO, A DAY BEFORE THE ACCIDENT. THIS VIDEO IS LIKE A ROAD SIGN THAT SAYS *YOU'VE GONE TOO*

23

FAR. TURN BACK. I AM AFRAID TO LOOK AT IT
AGAIN, BECAUSE I KNOW THAT AFTER I WATCH IT, I'M
GOING TO HAVE EVEN MORE OF A BEWILDERING
SENSE THAT MY LIFE HAS BEEN BROKEN INTO TWO
PARTS — EVERYTHING THAT CAME BEFORE THIS
VIDEO, AND EVERYTHING THAT WOULD COME AFTER.

As MUCH AS I DON'T WANT TO, I'M GOING TO STOP
WRITING NOW. THERE IS A SAFETY IN WRITING LATE
INTO THE NIGHT, BUT I CAN'T PUT OFF WATCHING IT AGAIN.
I HAVE TO SEE IT ONCE MORE, NOW THAT THINGS HAVE
CHANGED FOR THE WORSE.

IT MIGHT HELP ME.

IT MIGHT NOT.

BUT I HAVE TO DO IT.

I HAVE TO.

I'M AFRAID.

IT'S SO SIMPLE. JUST GO TO SARAH'S NAME
ONLINE. SARAHFINCHER.COM. ENTER THE PASSWORD
HOUSEOFUSHER. THEN CLICK RETURN.

ONE CLICK.

DO IT, RYAN.

DO IT.

SARAHFINCHER.COM
PASSWORD:
HOUSEOFUSHER

MONDAY, SEPTEMBER 13, 11:00 P.M.

SARAH WENT TO THE DREDGE WITHOUT ME THAT NIGHT. WHAT WAS MY EXCUSE? <u>HOMEWORK.</u> SHE KNEW IT WAS A LIE, AND I KNEW IT WAS A LIE, AND INSTEAD OF BEING MAD, SARAH WENT AHEAD WITHOUT ME LIKE SHE ALWAYS DID WHEN I BALKED AT AN OPPORTUNITY FOR ADVENTURE. DID I GET ANY HOMEWORK DONE? NO. I JUST WAITED FOR HER TO GET BACK, FOR HER TO SEND WORD SHE WAS OKAY.

THEN THE PASSWORD APPEARED IN MY INBOX. I WAS GLAD TO KNOW SARAH WAS SAFE, BUT I DIDN'T KNOW WHAT TO MAKE OF THE CREEPY VIDEO SHE'D SENT ME.

I WATCHED IT ABOUT TEN TIMES THAT NIGHT. I SAT AT MY DESK WONDERING IF IT WAS SOMETHING SHE'D CONCOCTED TO SCARE THE WITS OUT OF ME. THAT WOULD HAVE BEEN EXPECTED, SINCE I'D REFUSED TO GO WITH HER INTO THE WOODS. SHE WAS ALWAYS DOING THAT — HOAXING ME INTO FEELING GUILTY.

THE NEXT MORNING, I WALKED DOWN TO HER HOUSE WITH THE INTENT OF CONGRATULATING HER ON GIVING ME A GOOD SCARE. I WANTED TO KNOW HOW SHE'D

GOTTEN THE EFFECT OF THE SCARY FACE IN THE WINDOW. BUT THE CONVERSATION DIDN'T GO AS I'D EXPECTED.

"YOU THINK I MADE IT UP?"

SHE SAID IT LIKE SHE COULDN'T BELIEVE I'D EVEN THINK SUCH A THING. LIKE SHE HADN'T DONE IT TO ME A MILLION TIMES BEFORE.

I THOUGHT IT WAS STILL PART OF THE ACT.

"DON'T GET ME WRONG," I SAID. "IT'S SOME OF YOUR BEST WORK. YOU REALLY SCARED ME WITH THOSE GEAR SOUNDS AND — WHAT WAS THAT — A MAN AT THE WINDOW? YOU MUST HAVE HAD HELP FROM SOMEONE. WHO HELPED YOU?"

SHE SHOOK HER HEAD. I CAN REMEMBER IT SO CLEARLY.

"ALL I DID WAS WALK INTO THE WOODS WITH MY CAMERA. NO ONE HELPED ME DO ANYTHING."

"YOU'RE SERIOUS?"

THERE HAD BEEN A LONG PAUSE, FOLLOWED BY A FAMILIAR LOOK OF DETERMINATION.

"IF YOU DON'T BELIEVE ME, LET'S GO BACK TONIGHT AND YOU CAN SEE FOR YOURSELF."

If this were a video, not a journal, I'd have to stop. I'd have to rewind. I'd have to play that line again.

"If you don't believe me, let's go back tonight and you can see for yourself."

And again.

"If you don't believe me, let's go back tonight and you can see for yourself."

I didn't know what it would lead to. How could I have?

She didn't even ask. It wasn't, "Do you want to go back tonight and see for yourself?"

No, she was smarter than that.

She didn't give me a chance to say no.

"If you don't believe me, let's go back tonight and you can see for yourself."

We watched the video twice more on her laptop, and both times a chill ran up my spine. It seemed real, and usually when I called Sarah's bluff, she admitted it. Besides, I asked myself, how could she have created something so elaborate and so real? Even for someone of Sarah's editing skill, it seemed impossible.

I believed her.

"Tonight at midnight," she said. "Meet me at the trailhead and we'll go together."

"You're sure about this?"

"Are you kidding? This town is mind-numbingly dull. We're going to die of boredom if we're not careful. Finally, something interesting is happening. Imagine what a great story this will make! All this stuff we're digging up, and now this weird — I don't know what to call it — this phantom at the dredge. It's not a question of whether we want to go back or not. We have to go back."

This was Sarah at her most persuasive. She said it with such urgency — no doubt because it involved her filming, the main thing that took the edge off her boredom.

I have a theory about this. I think what I do is safer than what Sarah does. I can write about whatever I want — monsters, ghosts, arms falling off, people buried alive — and it doesn't matter what I write because it all comes from the safety of my own imagination. But filming requires that there be something to film, and that has a way of leading into real danger.

Tuesday, September 14, 1:25 a.m.

. . . but I can't sleep.

It's not the disturbing sound of rusted gears set in motion (though I keep hearing them) or the moving shadows in the upper room of the dredge (I have decided that I <u>hate</u> shadows). What scares me the most is listening to Sarah. I can hear the fear in Sarah's voice. Up until I saw that video I'd never heard her sound like that before.

She just doesn't get scared. When she purchased her first video camera, Sarah interviewed a drifter walking through town. This was a terrible idea. The man was not well-dressed, to say the very least. All of his possessions were tied to his back in black plastic garbage bags and he carried a sign that read <u>Los Angeles</u>, if you please.

Sarah talks to strangers all the time without thinking twice about it. She peers into parked cars, eavesdrops in the café, and occasionally tries to sneak into the bar (for lively conversation, not drinks).

When we were eleven, Sarah convinced me we could climb up a steep ravine to the very top. She was right — we made it — but we couldn't get back down without the help of a park ranger, her father, my father, and half the volunteer fire department (three lumberjacks and a retired police officer). This event preceded my earliest memory of stern fatherly advice: Find some other friends. Try out for football if you want, but stop spending so much time with Sarah. She'll only get you into trouble.

There was the hitchhiking incident, in which Sarah convinced me we needed to visit the metropolis a hundred miles away so that we could "observe city dwellers in their native environment." When night approached and we couldn't find a ride back home, we were forced to call my dad. A second warning was offered on the long ride home. You two had better stop acting like idiots. It's only a matter of time before one of you gets hurt.

There was very little else said.

And then, only a month ago, we were caught trying to break into the library on a Thursday night. It was supposed to be closed and we had hoped to find more old newspapers, but we found Gladys Morgan instead. She was sitting in the dark with a shotgun pointed at the door, reading The Sound and the Fury (one of the dullest books ever written). We were very lucky she recognized us. Otherwise she would have filled us so full of buckshot we'd never set foot in a restaurant again without someone mistaking us for Swiss cheese (her words, not mine). She also told us we were dumber than two bags full of rocks. Then she called our parents.

As you can probably imagine, our two sets of parents have long preferred the idea of us staying as far away from each other as possible. It is this long history of trouble that made them respond so forcefully when something really bad finally did happen.

It's why, if they have their way, Sarah and I will never see each other again.

Tuesday, September 14, 2:00 a.m.

I have just made the mistake of checking my email. This is a bad idea in the middle of the night. I should know better. But there was nothing when I checked for messages earlier, not even a measly welcome home. All day I've been wondering if my parents found something and deleted it. It's hard to tell how closely they're monitoring everything.

But now something's slipped through. And I'll admit — I debated whether or not to open it. Because I knew — the moment Sarah and I were in contact, it would start all over again.

Still, how could I resist? I'd never been able to before.

"Learn from your mistakes," part of me was saying.

"They weren't mistakes," another part of me was saying.

And, of course, curiosity won. Or maybe it was friendship that won.

I opened her email.

Ryan,

I'm so sorry about what happened. At least you're home again — that
makes me feel a little better. I've hardly left my room. I know they've
said we can't see each other because of what happened. I know I'm not
supposed to contact you. But it's important that you see this. Please,
just drop whatever it is you're doing and watch.

Sarah.

I LOVED THAT — JUST DROP WHATEVER IT IS
YOU'RE DOING. SUCH A SARAH THING TO SAY. LIKE I
HADN'T SPENT THE PAST TWO WEEKS GLUED TO A
HOSPITAL MATTRESS, WONDERING WHEN THE PAIN WAS
GOING TO GO AWAY.

THERE WAS A PASSWORD ATTACHED TO THE
BOTTOM OF THE EMAIL. THERAVEN.

I HAVE TO SAY, I DON'T APPRECIATE HER
PASSWORDS. IT'S LIKE SHE'S TRYING TO MAKE THINGS
EVEN SCARIER THAN THEY ALREADY ARE. THINGS ARE
CREEPY ENOUGH WITHOUT BRINGING EDGAR ALLAN
POE BACK FROM THE DEAD. SHE KNEW I'D FIND HER

MESSAGE IN THE MIDDLE OF THE NIGHT WHILE MY
PARENTS WERE ASLEEP AND EVERY SHADOW LOOKED
LIKE SOMETHING OUT TO GET ME.

Once upon a midnight dreary, while I
pondered weak and weary,
Over many a quaint and curious volume
of forgotten lore,
While I nodded, nearly napping, suddenly
there came a tapping,
As of some one gently rapping, rapping
at my chamber door.

Does she even know about this poem or is she
just pulling these passwords out of thin air?
Something happened fifteen nights ago that
has changed everything. I'm sure what Sarah
wants me to watch has something to do with
that night. It's why I'm writing this down, because
my lingering fear has turned to constant
alarm these past weeks. I have a dreadful
feeling someone is watching me all the time, that
someone or something will open the creaking

DOOR TO MY ROOM IN THE COLD NIGHT AND DO AWAY WITH ME. I WANT THERE TO BE SOME KIND OF RECORD.

If I WONDERED WHETHER OR NOT I SHOULD OPEN THE EMAIL, NOW THERE'S NO QUESTION IN MY MIND.

ONCE YOU'RE IN, YOU'RE IN.

ONCE YOU'RE CAUGHT, YOU'RE CAUGHT.

I HAVE TO WATCH WHAT SHE SENT. I HAVE TO WATCH IT RIGHT NOW.

SARAHFINCHER.COM
PASSWORD:
THERAVEN

Tuesday, September 14, 9:00 a.m.

Last night I sort of freaked out. After I watched the video I think I had the second moment of real terror in my life.

The first was having it happen to me.

The second was seeing it.

What was Sarah thinking, sending this to me? I've been scared before — actually, let's be honest, I'm scared most of the time. There's a blind man who sits outside the Rainbow Bar and when I walk by he follows my every move with a clouded white eye — that scares me. At home I hear creaking stairs at night when it should be quiet, and I call out but no one answers. That scares me. The thing living under my bed, Gladys and her shotgun, the woods at night. It all scares me, and it's all like clothes in a dryer that just keep rolling around in my head from one day to the next.

But watching that video last night was different. I couldn't even write. I turned on as many lights as I could reach. I turned on the radio and listened to the church channel until a

MAN STARTED TALKING ABOUT SPIRITUAL WARFARE,
WHICH SHARPENED MY FEAR EVEN MORE.

THE REASON THE VIDEO TERRIFIED ME WAS BECAUSE
IT MADE ME REMEMBER THAT NIGHT. SINCE IT
HAPPENED, I'VE HAD ONLY A FRAGMENTED MEMORY,
LITTLE BITS AND PIECES. BUT NOW I REMEMBER
SOMETHING MORE ABOUT THAT NIGHT. I REMEMBER WHAT
I SAW THAT MADE ME FALL. IT WAS THERE IN THE
CAMERA LENS AT THE END.

IT WAS WATCHING ME.

IT'S ALWAYS WATCHING ME.

Tuesday, September 14, 10:15 a.m.

I remember waking up in the hospital. What it was like.

One moment I was falling. Then I saw Sarah's face hovering in the dim light but couldn't hear what she was trying to say. It felt like the bones in my leg had exploded.

Then I was out. When I opened my eyes I actually expected to see the ceiling of my room and smell my dad's coffee brewing downstairs. My head lolled to one side and there sat my parents, glassy-eyed from sleeplessness.

I remember asking, "What's going on?" and my mom jumping up and saying, "Ryan! Go get the nurse, Paul — go on!"

My dad smiled at me, opened the door, and ran from the room. I heard the muffled sound of him yelling for a nurse outside the door. Mom leaned over the bed rail and held my hand.

"Where are we?" I asked.

"You had an accident, but you're awake now — you're awake and you're going to be just fine."

40

"How long have I been asleep?"

"The nurse — she'll bring the doctor, he'll want to talk to you. Just stay awake. No more sleeping until your dad comes back with the nurse. Okay?"

She squeezed my hand pretty hard, as if it might help keep me from drifting off.

At that point, I didn't have any memory of what had happened to me. There were little bits and pieces, but nothing concrete.

When the doctor came in, I asked if I could use the bathroom and he told me that if I wanted to I could just go ahead and pee. Certain embarrassing arrangements had been made when I was admitted.

"How long have I been asleep?"

"According to your chart you were nonresponsive when they found you at 12:45 a.m. So you've been asleep — or, more accurately, you've been in an unconscious state — for about fifty-five hours."

"So you're saying I've been in a coma?"

"If you want to be dramatic, then, yes, you've been in a coma. You took a pretty good fall. It's amazing you're alive and well enough to tell about it."

"Why can't I move my leg?"

"Because we've surrounded it with a Big Bertha — a really big plaster cast. I'm afraid it will be awhile before you can walk on it again."

I began to fall asleep in the hospital bed. My mom shook my shoulders and yelled at me and the smell of old bicycle tires went away. I tried harder to stay awake after that because my head hurt and having my mom shout in my face made it hurt even more.

Eventually they took most of the tubes out of my body (including the one that let me stay in bed to use the bathroom). I took some rides in a wheelchair, and my parents started to talk to me. Talking with them was nice at first, because they were truly happy I was okay. But then I asked about Sarah and they both took deep breaths and got serious on me.

"We don't want you seeing her anymore," Dad said.

"But she's my best friend," I protested.

Mom took one look at me and I could tell what she was thinking: _What kind of best friend nearly kills you?_

"Then you'll have to find a new friend," Dad said. "We're serious this time, Ryan. If you can't stay away from each other, we'll move. I'll transfer to the city and we'll sell the house. We don't want to, but we will."

"What are you saying?"

"We're saying you can't see Sarah anymore," said my mother. "You're not to contact her — no email, no phone calls — and she won't be coming around when we go home. Her parents agree with us. It's the best thing for a while."

"The best thing for who?"

"You were out in the woods in the middle of the night, breaking into private property," said my dad. He was talking more than usual and for once I wished he'd shut up. "You nearly fell to

YOUR DEATH! I THINK IT'S FAIR TO SAY THAT KEEPING HER AWAY FROM YOU IS BEST FOR EVERYONE, INCLUDING YOU."

"IT WASN'T HER FAULT THIS TIME. IT WAS ME — IT WAS MY IDEA."

"ALL THE MORE REASON TO KEEP YOU TWO APART." MY DAD WAS ON A ROLL. "BOTH YOUR BRAINS GO BATTY WHEN YOU'RE TOGETHER. THERE'S TALK IN SKELETON CREEK OF BURNING THAT DREDGE TO THE GROUND. THE POLICE SPENT A WHOLE DAY DOWN THERE LOCKING IT UP TIGHT SO NO ONE ELSE TRIES TO GET IN. THAT THING IS A DEATH TRAP."

AFTER THAT, MY PARENTS WENT QUIET. NEITHER OF THEM ARE TALKATIVE FOLKS — NO ONE WHO LIVES IN SKELETON CREEK TALKS VERY MUCH. THEY'D LAID DOWN THE LAW ABOUT SARAH, AND THAT WAS THAT. I HAD TO STAY THERE IN THE HOSPITAL FOR ANOTHER TEN DAYS. I COULDN'T GET ONLINE AND MY PARENTS WOULDN'T LET ME USE THE PHONE.

WHAT WOULD THEY DO IF THEY KNEW SARAH WAS CONTACTING ME? THEY'D SELL THE HOUSE, THAT'S WHAT THEY'D DO.

TUESDAY, SEPTEMBER 14, 11:00 A.M.

MOM JUST CHECKED UP ON ME. THE COMPUTER WAS SAFELY OFF.

SHE HAS NO IDEA.

OR MAYBE SHE DOES.

I WONDER IF MY MOM IS SNEAKIER THAN SHE LOOKS.

THE DAY AFTER I WOKE UP IN THE HOSPITAL, THE POLICE CAME TO MY ROOM AND ASKED ME A LOT OF QUESTIONS. THEY WANTED TO KNOW IF I WAS TRYING TO STEAL ANYTHING, WHO ELSE WAS INVOLVED, WHY I'D DONE IT, DID I REMEMBER ANY DETAILS ABOUT WHAT HAPPENED. I DIDN'T TELL THEM ANYTHING THEY DIDN'T ALREADY KNOW OR COULDN'T FIGURE OUT ON THEIR OWN. I WENT TO THE DREDGE, I FELL, I GOT A SERIOUS CONCUSSION AND SHATTERED MY LEG. WHAT ELSE WAS I GOING TO SAY? THAT I WAS LOOKING FOR A PHANTOM AND MIGHT HAVE FOUND ONE? I HAD A STRONG FEELING IF I SAID ANYTHING LIKE THAT THEY'D MOVE ME OUT OF THE HOSPITAL AND INTO THE PSYCH WARD.

AS IT TURNS OUT, MY MENTAL HEALTH WAS THE VERY REASON WHY THEY KEPT ME FOR SO MANY DAYS. I COULD HAVE GONE HOME A WEEK EARLIER, BUT

45

THERE WAS A PSYCHIATRIST WHO KEPT STOPPING BY. MY DAD WAS BACK AT WORK BUT MY MOM WAS STILL HANGING AROUND. SHE LEFT THE ROOM WHENEVER THE PSYCHIATRIST CAME IN. SHE (THE PSYCHIATRIST) WAS PRETTY, IN A BUTTON-DOWN SORT OF WAY. SHE HAD RED HAIR AND GLASSES AND A NOTEPAD. SHE ASKED ME IF I'D BEEN TAKING ANY DRUGS OR DRINKING. SHE ASKED WHAT I DID WITH MY FREE TIME AND ABOUT SARAH. SHE WONDERED IF SHE COULD READ SOME OF MY STORIES, AND I POLITELY DECLINED. I DIDN'T WANT HER DIGGING AROUND IN MY STUFF. I WAS PRETTY SURE IT WOULDN'T LOOK GOOD IF SHE FOUND MY PARANOID RANTINGS ABOUT SKELETON CREEK.

WHEN THEY FINALLY LET ME GO HOME, I HAD THE DISTINCT FEELING I'D BARELY PASSED SOME SORT OF EMOTIONAL EXAM THEY'D RUN ME THROUGH. IT FELT A LITTLE LIKE STANDARDIZED TESTING AT SCHOOL, LIKE I'D SORT OF PASSED BUT NOT REALLY, AND ANYWAY, I'D NEVER KNOW FOR SURE HOW I DID BECAUSE THEY WOULDN'T TELL ME. IT WAS AN EMPTY FEELING.

OKAY, I KNOW I'M AVOIDING SOMETHING. I'M WRITING QUICKLY, BUT I'M ALSO DODGING WHAT I REALLY SHOULD

BE WRITING ABOUT. NOW I'M BACK TO THE PRESENT —
CAN I AVOID IT ANY LONGER? IF I GET IT DOWN ON
PAPER, IT WILL MAKE IT REAL. BUT MAYBE IF I WRITE IT
DOWN, I'LL FEAR IT LESS. THIS STRATEGY OFTEN
WORKS FOR ME WHEN I'M SCARED. WRITING THE THINGS
I'M SCARED OF — ESPECIALLY IF I TURN THEM INTO A
STORY — MAKES THEM FEEL AS IF THEY'VE BEEN
RELEGATED TO THE PAGE AND I CAN ALLOW MYSELF TO
WORRY LESS ABOUT THEM IN REAL LIFE.

So HERE GOES.

THERE WAS A PRESENCE UPSTAIRS WITH ME IN THE
DREDGE BEFORE IT WALKED IN FRONT OF SARAH'S
CAMERA LENS. I WAS EXAMINING THE RUSTED GEARS,
TRYING TO IMAGINE HOW THEY COULD POSSIBLY SPRING
TO LIFE. THE RUST CAME OFF ON MY FINGERS. (DAYS
LATER, MOM WOULD ASK ME ABOUT THE ORANGE MARK
ON MY PANTS WHERE I'D WIPED THE RUST OFF, AND I
WOULDN'T HAVE AN ANSWER FOR HER. I GUESS I HAVE
ONE NOW.)

JUST AS I WIPED MY FINGERS, I TURNED TOWARD
THE DARKENED PATH OF BOARDS THAT LED AWAY
FROM THE GEARS WHERE OLD JOE BUSH HAD WORKED.

There was a long, wide belt that ran into the black.

And sitting on the belt was a hand.

It was attached to an arm,

the arm to a body,

and the body was moving toward me.

There was a faint light all around the body as it moved closer to me.

I can see it now.

I am seeing it.

It was a silhouette. All in black, so I couldn't make out a face. But the body was large. Whoever — whatever — this was, it was big and slow. It stepped forward, steadying itself on the wide belt as it came, and it dragged its other leg behind.

I remember now how I realized three things all at once. The first was that I couldn't speak. I don't know if it was some force of darkness that constricted my throat or if it was simply pure terror, but either way, the best I could do was keep breathing. (Even that, I now recall, came with great effort.) The second thing — and this one was worse than the first — was that I found myself trapped. I was backed up against the wooden rail behind the gears, which was a corner section of the dredge that looked out over the bottom level. This thing that was after me had me cornered. The last realization I had — worse than the first two put together — was that all my terrible nightmares had finally come true. In the back of my mind, there had always been this one important fact: None of the monsters I'd imagined over the years had ever really come to get me. But now I saw that it was true — there really was a monster, and it really was going to scare me to death.

When it was close enough to touch me, I saw the shadow of its lips move. It spoke to me from beneath the wide brim of a workman's hat.

"Number forty-two is mine. Stay away from this place. I'm watching you."

And then, all at once, my own voice returned. I screamed, I backed up, and the old wooden rail fell away. I remember now looking up as I fell and seeing that whatever had stood

OVER ME WAS GONE. IT HAD VANISHED. OR HAD IT BEEN THERE AT ALL?

SARAH'S VIDEO OF THE LEG WALKING PAST, DRAGGING THE OTHER BEHIND IT, MAKES ME SURER THAN EVER THAT WHAT I SAW THAT NIGHT WAS REAL. I CAN'T TELL ANYONE BUT SARAH OR THEY'LL PUT ME IN THE LOONY BIN. I FELT LIKE PEOPLE WERE WATCHING ME BEFORE THE ACCIDENT, BUT NOW IT'S MUCH WORSE. MY PARENTS ARE WATCHING ME. I'M CERTAIN THEY'LL HAVE EVERYONE ELSE IN TOWN WATCHING ME. FRIDAY, HENRY WILL ARRIVE AND HE'LL BE WATCHING. GLADYS WITH HER SHOTGUN IS WATCHING ME. THE RAVEN IS WATCHING AT MY WINDOW.

AND THE THING AT THE DREDGE — IT HAS TO BE WATCHING.

WAITING.

OR MAYBE IT'S COMING TO GET ME.

Tuesday, September 14, nearly PM

My leg feels worse tonight. I think it's the stress. There's a deep pain working its way up my back. Besides going to the bathroom, I haven't gotten out of bed all day. But I've calmed down. Writing everything out helped. It seems more like a story now. It feels better.

I'm finding that dull, lingering pain is ten times worse when it's accompanied by dull, lingering boredom. If not for my laptop I'm pretty sure my parents would have already found me dead from a hopeless case of endless monotony.

I can imagine it:

"Our little Ryan has died of boredom. We should have looked in on him more. Poor thing."

So the laptop rests nicely on Big Bertha. My mom says the psychiatrist gave her some software that secretly tracks my browser history, emails, IMs, everything. It's nice that my mom told me this, because the software isn't very hard to disable. Adults in general take a lot of comfort in these tools, but a fifteen-year-old who can't get around parental controls on a

COMPUTER IS PROBABLY ALSO HAVING TROUBLE TYING HIS SHOES. IT'S JUST NOT THAT HARD.

STILL, TIMING IS IMPORTANT. I CAN'T BE SEARCHING FOR WEIRD STUFF OR SENDING EMAILS TO SARAH WITHOUT HAVING AT LEAST A FEW MINUTES TO COVER MY TRACKS. IT TAKES TIME TO ERASE WHAT I'VE DONE, AND IT'S TOO LATE IF I'VE JUST SENT AN EMAIL AND I HEAR MY MOM WALKING UP THE STAIRS.

NOT THAT I'VE SENT SARAH ANY EMAILS. I STILL DON'T KNOW WHAT TO SAY.

IT'S HARD. MAYBE TOO HARD.

TO KILL THE BOREDOM, I'VE BEEN SEARCHING ONLINE FOR INFORMATION ABOUT THE DREDGE. SARAH AND I HAVE LOOKED BEFORE AND FOUND ALMOST NOTHING OF INTEREST. WE SEARCHED FOR ARCHIVED STORIES, BLOGS BY PEOPLE LIVING IN TOWN, INFORMATION ABOUT THE CROSSBONES, THE SKELETON CREEK IRREGULAR, AND A LOT MORE. IN EVERY CASE WE DISCOVERED WHAT FELT LIKE TINY SHARDS OR FRAGMENTS OF INFORMATION, JUST ENOUGH TO KEEP US GOING BUT NOTHING REALLY EARTH-SHATTERING.

I TRIED ALL THOSE ANGLES AGAIN TODAY WITH THE SAME MEAGER RESULTS. AFTER THREE HOURS OF DEAD

52

ENDS, I LOOKED BACK THROUGH MY NOTES AND MY
EYES LIT ON THE NAME OF THE COMPANY THAT HAD
OWNED THE DREDGE — NEW YORK GOLD AND SILVER.
I'D SEARCHED THAT TERM BEFORE, BUT NOT VERY
AGGRESSIVELY. I WENT LOOKING FOR THEM AGAIN, THIS
TIME WITH MORE TENACITY.

NEW YORK GOLD AND SILVER HAS BEEN OUT OF
BUSINESS FOR OVER TWENTY YEARS, BUT ONE THING ABOUT
BANKRUPTCY I'VE FOUND IS THAT ALL YOUR RECORDS
ARE OPEN FOR VIEWING. I FOUND A PUBLIC FILE OF THE
COMPANY RECORDS IN A SUBSECTION OF THE CITY OF
NEW YORK LEGAL ARCHIVES, AND WITHIN THOSE FILES I
DISCOVERED A FILE MARKED NYGS AM MINS.
80-85. I KNEW NYGS STOOD FOR NEW YORK
GOLD AND SILVER. WHEN I DOUBLE-CLICKED ON THE
FILE, I SAW THAT AM MINS STOOD FOR ANNUAL
MEETING MINUTES AND THAT 80-85 MEANT
1980-1985.

TO CATEGORIZE THIS DOCUMENT AS BORING WOULD
BE WAY TOO KIND. THIS WAS 127 PAGES OF PURE,
UNDISTILLED DRUDGERY. I SKIMMED THE FIRST 30
PAGES OF PE RATIOS, COST-BENEFIT ANALYSES, PLANT
CLOSURES, EQUITY-TO-DEBT RATIOS, SUB-PRIME

HOLDINGS, AND A LOT OF OTHER PAINFULLY TEDIOUS DETAILS OF A ONCE-PROSPEROUS COMPANY. IT WASN'T UNTIL I WAS HALF ASLEEP ON PAGE 31 THAT I REALIZED I COULD SEARCH FOR TERMS I WAS INTERESTED IN RATHER THAN READ EVERY SINGLE WORD.

AND THAT'S WHEN I FOUND SOMETHING ON PAGE 81 AND SOMETHING ELSE ON PAGE 111 THAT MADE ME NERVOUS. I PRINTED THEM OUT, AND I'M GOING TO TAPE THEM IN HERE.

NYGS AM Mins. -- Paragraph 3, page 81.

The #42 asset holding in Skeleton Creek, Oregon, encountered a series of break-ins during the period ending 12-81. Mentioned here due to injuries and subsequent lawsuit brought by local resident Mark Henderson. Claimant asserts he was attacked while searching the #42 dredge on the night of 9-12-81, sustaining injuries to the head and neck, including a major concussion. Lawsuit settled out of court on 11-14-81. Legal department cited private property status in early, low six-figure settlement. No information from local authorities is available on a possible suspect in the attack or if such a suspect exists. #42 asset has been more adequately secured. Consider demolition or removal.

NYGS AM Mins. -- Paragraph 1, page 111.

The #42 asset holding in Skeleton Creek, Oregon, was entered by a private citizen during the period ending 12-84. Three juveniles claim to have visited the dredge repeatedly between 6-84 and 9-84. Court file indicates breaking and entering, destruction of private property, theft of tools, vandalism. One of the three juveniles, Jody Carlisle, claims the three were told not to return by someone they heard but could not see. Legal department strongly advises removal or destruction of asset #42. Approved. Demolition of asset #42 scheduled for 4-11-85.

In the spring of 1985, New York Gold and Silver was served with environmental lawsuits from Oregon, Washington, Alaska, Montana, and Idaho. I guess they were too busy fending off enemies to take action on their agreement to demolish #42. By June of 1985, the company was dissolved in a sea of debt and legal disputes. Things like the dredge in Skeleton Creek were forgotten as lawyers moved on to

HIGHER-PROFILE CASES. THERE WAS NO MONEY TO
BE MADE SUING A DEAD COMPANY.

IT'S ALMOST NINE O'CLOCK NOW. MOM AND DAD
WILL BE IN TO SAY GOOD NIGHT AND CHECK UP ON ME.
THEY'LL WANT TO CHECK MY COMPUTER.
I KNOW WHAT I HAVE TO DO.

Sarah,

This is going to be really quick — I have to cover my tracks before
my mom checks in. I did some digging and found the minutes
from some New York Gold and Silver meetings in the 80s. I'm
copying you on two paragraphs I found (see below). We're not
the first ones to see something weird at the dredge. Every time
someone gets close, they get hurt or scared off. Don't go back
there. Let's just wait until my parents send me back to school so
we can talk without having to be so secretive. That's what —
maybe a month? We can figure things out when they can't stop
us from seeing each other in the halls.

Another thing — New York Gold and Silver called the dredge the
"#42 asset." That night, when you recorded the accident, I heard
something. It was a warning, the same as those other kids must
have gotten.

"Number forty-two is mine. Stay away from this place. I'm watching you."

And I think I saw him — I think I saw Old Joe Bush. Either that or I'm going crazy.

God, I wish I wasn't writing this as the sun goes down. Write me back — let me know you're okay — but don't do it until tomorrow morning. I'll read and delete.

Don't do anything stupid!

Ryan.

P.S. Henry arrives Friday — keep a lookout for him.

I PASTED THE TEXT FROM THE MEETING NOTES UNDER MY NAME AND PRINTED OUT THE EMAIL (WHICH IS WHAT'S INCLUDED ABOVE).

I HOPE SARAH FINDS MY EMAIL BEFORE HER PARENTS DO.

Wednesday, September 15, early am

Mom gave me more painkillers last night — the kind where they warn you not to operate heavy equipment after taking them because you get really drowsy. I fell asleep reading the end of To a God Unknown. Steinbeck could be creepy when he wanted to be, like when Joseph Wayne lives all alone at the black rock and listens to the sounds of the deep night until it drives him crazy. I need to start reading different books. Maybe I'll try a romance novel or a memoir about someone who enjoyed a really happy life.

The big news:

Sarah just sent me an email, which I have read, printed, and deleted.

Ryan,

I'm glad you wrote to me. I was thinking maybe you wouldn't. I would've been okay with that.

It seems like we're doing better detective work apart than we ever did together. You're not the only one making progress. I also found something. I'll send a video and a password tomorrow morning — delete the passwords after you get them. We need to keep all this secure where no one but you and I can access.

You're not writing any of this down, are you? Your parents might read this stuff while you're sleeping — that's exactly the kind of thing parents do when they think their son is up to something. Just try not to write things down all the time, okay?

I listened to the audio track on the video again, and the camera didn't pick up a voice that night. It must have been so quiet only you could hear it. I heard the tapping (makes no sense) but no voice. The #42 reference — maybe it means what we're dealing with is somehow connected to New York Gold and Silver.

It's chilling . . . don't you think? I mean, chilling in a good way. Something really important is going on and we're going to figure it out. Whatever caused you to fall — that spirit or phantom or whatever it is — we have to get to the bottom of it. If it really is a phantom — a real . . . *ghost* — what are we going to do? I have to get more evidence on tape or no one is going to believe us.

That stuff you sent — about the company from New York — I'm not worried about it. Those other people were trying to get money or thrills. What we're doing is different — we're serious, like investigators. I'm being careful and quiet — don't worry about me. I'm fine. Oh, and I asked evil eye outside the bar about Mark Henderson, that guy who sued for money. He's long gone. He left Skeleton Creek right after they gave him the money (figures). The kids weren't named, so I think that's a dead end. I guess we could ask Shotgun Gladys. She makes me nervous.

Check back early tomorrow morning, around 5:30 a.m., before your parents wake up. Make sure to get rid of this stuff — my parents put something on my computer to monitor my activity (I disabled it) — did you check your computer? Some of this new stuff is harder to get around.

How's the leg?

Don't write things down.

XO
— Sarah.

P.S. The fall wilderness ranger arrived last night. He's here from Missoula, probably until everything is snowed in. I might interview him like the ones before. Not sure.

I'D NEVER ASK SARAH TO STOP MAKING MOVIES, SO SHE REALLY SHOULDN'T EXPECT ME TO STOP WRITING. SHE KNOWS I CAN'T STOP. BUT SHE MAKES A GOOD POINT. IF MY PARENTS ARE SNEAKING AROUND IN HERE AFTER I'M ASLEEP, LOOKING FOR MY JOURNALS, I NEED TO MAKE SURE THEY DON'T FIND THEM. I'VE BEEN

PUTTING THIS ONE BETWEEN MY MATTRESS AND THE

HEADBOARD SO I CAN PULL IT OUT AND WRITE IN IT

WHENEVER I WANT TO. I THINK I'D CATCH THEM IF THEY

TRIED TO TAKE IT WHILE I SLEPT. WOULDN'T I?

OH, MAN, THIS REMINDS ME OF <u>THE TELL-TALE</u>

<u>HEART</u>. ONLY SIX PAGES, BUT EVERY ONE OF THEM

SERIOUSLY SPINE-CHILLING. I CAN IMAGINE MY DAD

QUIETLY ENTERING MY ROOM IN THE DARK. HE'S

MOVING SO SLOWLY IT TAKES HIM AN HOUR TO GET TO

MY BED — JUST LIKE THE MADMAN IN THAT STORY. I

HEAR SOMETHING AND SIT UP, BUT IT'S PITCH-BLACK AND

I'M AFRAID TO TURN ON THE LIGHT, SO I DON'T SEE HIM

STANDING THERE. I SIT UPRIGHT FOR A LONG TIME AND I

KNOW SOMEONE IS IN THE ROOM EVEN THOUGH I CAN'T

SEE THEM. I'M TERRIFIED. AND THEN <u>BANG!</u> — HE TAKES

MY JOURNAL AND ESCAPES.

PERFECT. NOW I HAVE ONE MORE THING TO WORRY

ABOUT TONIGHT.

<u>INVESTIGATING</u> IS OFTEN HOW SARAH GETS HERSELF

AND ME INTO TROUBLE, SO I'M WORRIED THAT SHE USED

THE WORD. AND HER EMAIL HAS THAT BLIND

CONFIDENCE SHE GETS SOMETIMES, LIKE SHE'S WEARING

GLASSES THAT ONLY LET HER SEE TWO FEET IN FRONT

OF HER OWN FACE.

THURSDAY, SEPTEMBER 16, EARLY MORNING

LAST NIGHT, AFTER DINNER, MY PARENTS MOVED ME OUT TO THE PORCH SO I COULD GET SOME FRESH AIR. IT'S GETTING CHILLY IN THE EARLY EVENING ALREADY, BUT I LIKE THAT ABOUT LIVING IN THE MOUNTAINS. THE CLEAN AIR IS EVEN CRISPER WHEN IT'S CHILLED. I WAS EXHAUSTED WHEN I FINALLY GOT BACK TO MY ROOM. I FELL RIGHT TO SLEEP (NO DOUBT THE FRESH AIR HELPED). I GOT THE VIDEO AND THE LINK FROM SARAH.

Ryan,

Don't write this down and make sure you delete it and check your tracks. This is SO freaky — we need to talk about it. How? How can we get around your parents?

I'm interviewing the new park ranger with my hidden camera today. Something's not right about him. I saw him at the mart and he wouldn't make eye contact with me. Can't put my finger on it — he's definitely off, like he's trying to hide something. I don't think he knows about what happened at the dredge — or maybe he does. It's on forest service land. Maybe someone told him.

Email me after you watch if you can — my parents are in the house— gotta go.

Sarah.

SARAHFINCHER.COM
PASSWORD:
PITANDPENDULUM

Thursday, September 16, morning

So Sarah thinks my ghost — or whatever it was — was there the first night she went to the dredge. And the dragging leg — that would point to Old Joe Bush, wouldn't it?

It's good that Sarah doesn't think I'm insane.

But that might be because she's insane, too.

Either way, she's good company.

I'm supposed to be the paranoid one. But what is she doing? Driving by my house to make sure I'm okay. Checking the doorway ten times a second to make sure nobody catches her. Asking me not to write anything down.

What's going on?

That might be the worst thing about being trapped in here: I have no idea what's going on outside this room.

I wish I could remember more. I don't think I have amnesia . . . or do I? I remember my name, my age, my address, and my phone number. When my mom comes in my room wearing the

CHILI-PEPPER APRON I GAVE HER WHEN I WAS IN THE EIGHTH GRADE, I RECOGNIZE HER.

I REMEMBER, AT THE AGE OF TEN, HOLDING A COLD MARSHMALLOW MILKSHAKE IN ONE HAND WHILE RIDING MY TEN-SPEED DOWN A HILL. A DOG STARTED CHASING ME AND I SQUEEZED THE FRONT BRAKE. AFTER I FLIPPED OVER THE HANDLEBARS AND LANDED ON MY BACK, I SAT UP AND SAW THAT THE DOG HAD LOST INTEREST IN TRYING TO KILL ME. HE WAS LICKING MY MILKSHAKE OFF THE HOT PAVEMENT.

YOU SEE THERE? I REMEMBER EVERY DETAIL. I REMEMBER EVEN MORE THAN THAT.

I REMEMBER WHEN I LIMPED HOME WITH SKINNED KNEES AND ELBOWS. MY SHIRT WAS ALL DIRTY. MOM WASN'T HOME, SO IT WAS A RARE MOMENT IN WHICH DAD WAS MY LONE HOPE OF SYMPATHY. MOM WOULD HAVE BABIED ME, BUT I RECALL FEELING AS IF I'D BETTER NOT BE CRYING WHEN I REACHED THE PORCH. I KNEW HE WOULDN'T LIKE IT IF I WAS ALL UPSET.

WHEN HE SAW ME, DAD SAT ME ON HIS LAP AND TOUCHED MY STINGING KNEES WITH A COLD DISHRAG FROM THE KITCHEN SINK.

"Mom's not going to like finding blood all over her good rag," I pointed out.

"Don't worry about your mother. I'll cover for you."

That made me smile, even though I was still concerned. "What will you say?"

"Bloody nose. I'll tell her I got in a fight. I'll say someone punched me."

"She's not going to believe you."

"Cutting vegetables?"

"You only cook pancakes."

"You worry too much."

It was a pleasant moment with my dad, like — I don't know — intimate, I guess. It didn't happen very often. He pushed his T-shirt up with a finger and scratched his bare shoulder. I caught sight of a little mark he had.

"What's that?" I asked.

"Tattoo. From a long time ago. You've seen it before."

"Can I see it again?"

He hesitated. I'd only ever seen the tattoo

ABOUT THREE TIMES IN MY WHOLE LIFE. IT WAS SMALL, ABOUT THE SIZE OF A NICKEL. HE CALLED IT HIS LITTLE BIRDIE.

"IT DOESN'T LOOK LIKE A BIRD."

"IT'S NOT A BIRD. I JUST CALL IT THAT."

"WHAT IS IT THEN?"

"IT'S NOTHING."

HE PULLED HIS SLEEVE BACK DOWN AND SET ME ON THE PORCH. THE INTIMATE MOMENT HAD PASSED. I REMEMBER THINKING I'D DONE SOMETHING WRONG.

SO IT SEEMS I REMEMBER A LOT OF THINGS — EVEN LONG STRINGS OF THINGS THAT HAPPENED YEARS AGO. I JUST DON'T RECALL ALL THE DETAILS OF THE NIGHT WHEN I FELL. I GUESS THAT MAKES IT A BLACKOUT, OR IN MY CASE, A GRAY-OUT, SINCE THINGS KEEP CREEPING BACK THAT I DON'T NECESSARILY WANT TO REMEMBER.

I'M NOT SURPRISED BY WHAT SARAH'S SAYING IN THE VIDEO, ABOUT THE SOUND BEING THERE BOTH NIGHTS. IT WAS LIKE I'VE ALREADY SEEN AND HEARD THIS INFORMATION THROUGH A DIRTY WINDOW, AND NOW THE WINDOW HAS BEEN CLEANED. THINGS I ALREADY KNEW HAVE BECOME A LITTLE CLEARER, THAT'S ALL.

Thursday, September 16, 11:00 a.m.

I've watched it now a dozen times. No, more than a dozen. And, yes, I might have discovered something. Not just in the visuals. But the sounds. Especially the sounds — over and over and over again with those sounds. The best way I can describe it is that listening to those sounds again and again is like feeling my memory come unstuck from skipping on an old record. The sound of the leg being dragged — dragged — dragged — and then ping! Something clicked forward in my memory. Something that wasn't there before.

I remember it was dark and I wanted to go home. I was looking at the rusted-over gears, trying to imagine how they could have moved. The flashlight felt clammy in my hand when I pointed it to a thick wooden beam that stood behind the machinery. Leaning over the biggest of the many gears, I peered down onto the hidden floorboards below. There was a little round mark, about the size of a nickel. I'd seen that mark before.

The record started skipping again. It's a birdie, it's a birdie, it's a birdie.

68   What does it all mean?

Sarah,

Your message seems to have nudged my memory. I remember something else from that night that I didn't before. There was a mark or a symbol — I'm not certain what it was — but I saw something carved into one of the wood planks where I stood. It was hidden behind the machinery on the floor. I've drawn a picture and scanned it in so you can see it.

The carving looked like this:

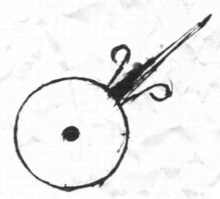

Now, don't get too hysterical, because I have no idea what it means yet, but I'm pretty sure my dad has a tattoo with the same mark. It's the same size and it looks kind of like a bird or an eyeball with some extra junk sticking out.

I'm going to talk with my dad. Don't worry — not about what I saw, not yet at least. I'm just going to ask him about Old Joe Bush and the dredge and see if he tells me anything. My dad could be connected to the dredge somehow — which is really freaking me out — but I don't want to assume anything.

It's also possible I'm imagining what I think I saw. Don't tell anyone this, okay? But sometimes it feels like my mind is playing tricks on me. I was thinking about the birdie, about an old memory I had, then I watched the video like a dozen times in a row and suddenly I remembered seeing the same thing on the dredge that night. Which memory came first? Are they both real or is one of them imagined? I spend a lot of time thinking about things like this. Too much time.

Listen, Sarah, I don't think I'm going to make it unless I turn this into a story. I'm going to crack under all the pressure. I can feel it. So it's a story, right? I'll call it "The Ghost of Old Joe Bush" — that's what it is — a phantom killed by metal and machines on the dredge. I have to give it a name and write it down so it won't scare me so much.

There's a phantom that carries a hammer in one hand and a lantern in the other. Where did the phantom come from? Why is it pounding on the machinery with the hammer? One of its legs is covered in blood and the blood has left a trail. I could follow the trail if I wanted to. It would lead to the bottom of a black lake, to a secret someone is trying to hide.

This could be a very spooky tale if I really put my mind to it. You think?

I'm calling my dad up here to talk with him and then I'm going to write down everything he says. Maybe he'll tell me something because I'm injured. Sometimes he's sympathetic when I'm hurt. I'll have to ask the right questions.

I have a feeling my parents are paying close attention, even more than when I arrived. They keep warning me not to contact you. Don't get in touch with me very often. Only when you have to. Let's just take it slow.

Be careful! — Ryan

P.S. I'm feeling a little better today. I think I'm going to take on the stairs by myself tomorrow and sit outside. The air is starting to catch that chill I like so much in the late afternoon.

I talked to my dad.

I'll try to get it all down here.

This is just like I heard it. I swear.

I can remember what we said because I knew I'd have to remember it. It was almost like I recorded the conversation so I could write it down after.

I started off by asking him, "Do you remember when I crashed my bike and you cleaned me up?"

He looked at me a little strangely — this wasn't what he was expecting me to say. But he went along with it.

"I remember," he said. "Your mother found the dishrag in the laundry. She asked if I'd killed a gopher."

"You never told me that."

He shrugged. "How's the leg?" he asked.

"It's stiff until afternoon. Then it warms up and it's not so bad."

"Henry gets in tomorrow morning. We'll bring you outside and you can get some fresh air on the porch. You can watch me skewer him at cribbage. How'd that be?"

I NODDED SO HE KNEW I THOUGHT IT WAS A FINE IDEA.

THEN I JUST WENT RIGHT OUT AND ASKED, "DID YOU EVER MEET OLD JOE BUSH?"

HE PAUSED, SITTING AT THE FOOT OF THE BED AS HE LOOKED AT MY CAST. HE GOT UP AND LEFT THE ROOM. I WAS SURE I'D COMPLETELY BLOWN IT. BUT WHEN HE RETURNED, THERE WAS A PICTURE IN HIS HAND. HE HANDED IT TO ME.

"THAT'S OLD JOE BUSH RIGHT THERE."

IT WAS A PICTURE OF A MAN STANDING BEFORE THE GEARS ON THE DREDGE, THE SAME GEARS I HAD STOOD IN FRONT OF ON THE NIGHT OF THE ACCIDENT. THE GEARS WEREN'T RUSTED. THEY WERE BLACK AND GREASY. THE MAN WORE WORK GLOVES AND OVERALLS AND GLASSES. HE WAS A BIG MAN, NOT THE SLIGHTEST BIT PHOTOGENIC. HE HAD THE DAZED LOOK OF SOMEONE WHO HAD BEEN BOTHERED AND WANTED TO BE LEFT ALONE. HAD HE BEEN CAUGHT IN THE MIDDLE OF SOMETHING IMPORTANT?

"HE WORKED ON THE DREDGE, RIGHT?" I ASKED.

MY DAD NODDED ALMOST IMPERCEPTIBLY. "HE GOT CARELESS."

"YOU MEAN HE GOT KILLED?"

He pointed to the picture.

"Those gears pulled him right through and spit him down into the water. They say he drowned because every pocket he had was full of stolen gold. Old Joe Bush sank like his feet were in concrete, right to the bottom."

There was a long silence. My dad walked to the window and looked out, then back at me. And then I felt the sting of why he was talking to me.

"Keep that picture. Let it be a warning. Old Joe Bush got pulled into those gears because he wasn't careful. You nearly died doing something careless yourself. Don't let it happen again."

Even though his message was clear, I figured I might as well ask him something he would probably think was stupid. With my father, moments like this — of true conversation — were pretty few and far between.

"Did Joe Bush ever . . . come back?" I asked.

From the look in his eye, I could see I was going to get an answer. My dad likes a good story, though I've never known him to write one down. He can tell one if one is needed. He likes

74

THE IDEA OF MYTHS AND SPIRITS. I THINK IT'S PART OF WHY I WRITE THE THINGS I DO. WE'RE BOTH STORYTELLERS IN OUR OWN WAY AND I DIDN'T FALL TOO FAR FROM THE TREE.

"THERE'S A LEGEND THAT USED TO BE TOLD BY SOME OF THE LAST GUYS WHO WORKED ON THAT DREDGE," HE SAID. "THEY NEVER TALKED ABOUT IT OPENLY, ONLY AMONG THEMSELVES. BUT WORD GETS OUT."

MY DAD ITCHED HIS SHOULDER WHERE THE BIRDIE LAY HIDDEN UNDER HIS SHIRT.

"THEY SAID THEY COULD HEAR OLD JOE BUSH WALKING AROUND AT NIGHT, DRAGGING THAT CURSED LEG OF HIS. THEY COULD HEAR HIM RAPPING ON THE METAL BEAMS WITH THAT BIG WRENCH HE USED TO CARRY AROUND TO WORK ON THE GEARS. BIGGEST WRENCH ANYONE EVER SAW. TAP. TAP. TAP. THEY'D HEAR IT. THEN IT WOULD STOP. SOMETHING WOULD FALL MYSTERIOUSLY INTO THE WATER — SOMETHING IMPORTANT, LIKE A SPECIAL TOOL OR A BOX OF PARTS — BUT NO ONE WAS GOING DOWN INTO THE BLACK TO FIND WHAT WENT MISSING. THEY SAID OLD JOE BUSH HAD WET BOOTS, LIKE HE'D CRAWLED UP

OUT OF THE WATER BENEATH THE DREDGE WHERE HE DROWNED AND CAME BACK TO CLAIM WHAT WAS HIS. ONLY HE COULDN'T FIND IT."

"CLAIM WHAT?"

"WHY, ALL THE MISSING GOLD, OF COURSE. WHAT ELSE WOULD HE BE LOOKING FOR?"

MY DAD LAUGHED AND SAID IT WAS ONLY A TALL TALE. THEN HE HEADED FOR THE DOOR.

"HAVE YOU TALKED TO SARAH?" HE ASKED, AND THIS TIME I WAS SURPRISED BY THE SUDDENNESS OF THE QUESTION.

"NO, SIR," I SAID. TECHNICALLY, THIS WAS TRUE. WE HADN'T ACTUALLY TALKED. BUT STILL I WAS NERVOUS—MY DAD HAD FIGURED ME OUT ON LESSER LIES.

"LET'S KEEP IT THAT WAY," HE SAID.

AND THEN HE WAS GONE.

Thursday, September 16, 9:00 p.m.

Henry arrives tomorrow morning from New York. He hasn't visited since last summer, so I'm very interested to talk with him. When Henry visits, he stays in the guest room downstairs. He and my dad are sort of like best friends, I guess. They fly-fish, hike, play cards, and laugh a lot. My dad doesn't usually laugh that much, so it's very noticeable when Henry is around.

I like Henry because, for starters, he's talkative. It can be difficult to make him shut up, if you want to know the truth. I think it has something to do with the fact that everyone else is pretty quiet around here and he's used to more noise in the city. Maybe the sound of his own voice is like the droning background noise he's accustomed to.

Henry wears rainbow-colored suspenders and a crisp white shirt wherever he goes, so you can see the good time coming from a long way off. He has muttonchops — and I don't mean for dinner — really wide. Like, Elvis in the 70s sideburns.

He has a reputation for throwing the most outrageous poker parties in Skeleton Creek during his visits. Playing cards with Henry is a little different than cards with normal people, because there's always an unknown array of punishments for losing hands. You might be forced to wear oven mitts and keep playing. Or you could end up in a full-body wet suit, snorkel, and an underwater mask. And there are the ridiculous wigs, crank calls to wives and girlfriends, blocks of ice that need sitting on, and helium balloons to be inhaled with preposterous scripts to be read in chipmunk voices. A little bit of money changes hands, but mostly everyone hangs around and laughs really, really hard. Even my dad.

Henry's past in Skeleton Creek is complicated. A long time ago, when the dredge was still tearing up the woods, Henry used to visit more often. That's because he was employed by New York Gold and Silver. He was in charge of what I now know were assets number

42, 43, and 44, all dredges scattered around the western states. That meant constant visits in order to assess progress, hire and fire workers, map the movements of the dredges, package and ship the gold, and basically oversee the operation of not one but three dredges. He was young then, a graduate of Georgetown looking to make his mark in the world. He's changed a lot over the years.

I'm hoping he can help me.

Henry was born and raised in the big city, but I think there was something about Skeleton Creek that affected him from the very beginning. It probably happens to a lot of people from New York. They visit Yellowstone Park or Montana or Sun Valley and when they go back home they realize that skyscrapers are not the same as mountains, a hundred taxis are not the same as a hundred cows, and the subway doesn't ride like a horse.

I also think Henry feels guilty about working for a company that tore up the land,

TOOK ALL THE RICHES, AND LEFT SKELETON CREEK HIGH AND DRY. PEOPLE SEEM TO LIKE HIM AROUND HERE — ESPECIALLY MY DAD — AND THERE DON'T SEEM TO BE ANY HARD FEELINGS. I THINK THAT'S BECAUSE HENRY GENUINELY LOVES SKELETON CREEK AND HATES WHAT HAPPENED TO IT. MAYBE HE'S DOING PENANCE FOR THE WORK HE DID IN HIS TWENTIES, BACK WHEN HE DIDN'T KNOW ANY BETTER. HE KEEPS COMING BACK YEAR AFTER YEAR, BURNING UP ALL HIS VACATION TIME ON A DEAD-END TOWN FULL OF DEAD-END PEOPLE. I GUESS THAT COUNTS FOR SOMETHING.

THIS VISIT WILL BE MUCH MORE INTERESTING THAN HENRY'S PAST VISITS. HE STAYS EVERY FALL FOR TWO OR THREE WEEKS DEPENDING ON HOW MUCH VACATION TIME HE HAS SAVED UP. HE COMES FOR THE SEPTEMBER STEELHEAD RUN, FOR THE POKER, FOR THE FRIENDSHIPS. BUT THIS IS THE FIRST FALL WHEN HIS ARRIVAL COINCIDES WITH MY GREAT INTEREST IN THE DREDGE. IN THE PAST I'VE SPENT ALL MY TIME ASKING HIM EITHER ABOUT NEW YORK OR WHAT PUNISHMENTS HE HAS PLANNED FOR POKER NIGHT. I HAVEN'T ASKED

TOO MANY QUESTIONS ABOUT THE DREDGE, AT LEAST IN PART BECAUSE MY DAD HAS ALWAYS ACTED LIKE IT WAS A BAD IDEA WHENEVER I BROUGHT IT UP.

BUT THIS TIME I'M GOING TO GET HENRY ALONE AND REALLY GRILL HIM.

Thursday, September 16, 10:00 p.m.

Sarah has sent me another video already. Two in one day. She's getting way too careless. I saw the email, but I'm going to wait another hour or two before watching the video so my parents are asleep. The videos are hard enough to watch without the added pressure of wondering whether or not my mom or dad are going to knock on my door. I can't erase my tracks that quickly.

I wonder what she wants.

Thursday, September 16, 11:12 p.m.

That was close. I barely hid my journal in time. If I'd been in the middle of a sentence, I probably would've been caught.

My parents are getting too curious. They're in my room all the time, asking a lot of questions. They keep pestering me about Sarah. Have I talked to her? Have I seen her? Did I know she drove by in the middle of the night?

They came in together right after I finished my last entry.

Dad said, "Don't think just because Henry is coming we're not going to be watching you as closely. We want you out of this bed tomorrow, downstairs or on the porch."

Mom said, "You need to start getting more fresh air. Let's do that tomorrow, okay?"

Then Dad said, "Let's have a look at that computer."

It's just dumb luck Sarah hadn't sent me something in the previous hour, and that I'd already scribbled down the password from her previous email (which I'd already deleted). They'd

HAVE SEEN IT BEFORE I DID, BEFORE I COULD ERASE IT.
MY NERVES ARE SHOT AND I'M REALLY TIRED. I KEEP
HAVING TO STAY UP LATE AND GET UP EARLY SO I CAN
WORK WITH SARAH WITHOUT GETTING CAUGHT. I'M NOT
SURE HOW MUCH LONGER I WANT TO DO THIS.

BUT I CAN'T IGNORE THE LATEST PASSWORD.

A MONTILLADO

FROM THE CASK OF A MONTILLADO — A
TERRIBLE STORY ABOUT DECEPTION AND REVENGE. I'M
CERTAIN SHE'S NEVER READ IT. FORTUNADO TRICKED
AND CHAINED, THE SLOW BUILDING OF A WALL TO TRAP
HIM UNDERGROUND. IT'S A REALLY AWFUL STORY, NOT
ONE OF MY FAVORITES. MAYBE IF I TOLD HER THE
STORY, SHE'D STOP PICKING SUCH GHASTLY PASSWORDS.

TOMORROW MIGHT GET COMPLICATED. I BETTER
WATCH TONIGHT, EVEN THOUGH I CAN BARELY KEEP MY
EYES OPEN.

SARAHFINCHER.COM
PASSWORD:
AMONTILLADO

Thursday, September 16, 11:58 p.m.

What was it that Sarah said?

I'm starting to think everything is connected. The secret society, the dredge, New York Gold and Silver, Old Joe Bush — I think it's all somehow linked together.

But that's not all. It's not just some secret society, New York Gold and Silver, and Old Joe Bush. It's Sarah. And me.

And now this new wilderness ranger.

Why did he ask Sarah if we saw anyone at the dredge?

What does he know?

Which is the same thing as asking:

What don't we know?

I have to try to get some sleep.

If I can.

I HAVE THIS VERY WEIRD FEELING THAT SOMEONE CAME IN MY ROOM LAST NIGHT. I WOKE UP BUT I WAS TOO AFRAID TO LOOK AROUND. PLUS, IT WAS DARK. I COULDN'T SHAKE THE FEELING. AND THEN I STARTED WONDERING IF I'D DELETED THE HISTORY AFTER I WATCHED THE LAST VIDEO. I REACHED UNDER MY PILLOW AND FELT FOR MY JOURNAL. IT WAS THERE. IT DOESN'T SEEM LIKE IT WAS MOVED.

IT'S CRAZY HOW PARANOID I AM.

I'VE BEEN LYING IN BED FOR AN HOUR STARING AT THE PICTURE MY DAD LEFT ME AND REPLAYING THE WARNING IN MY MIND.

OLD JOE BUSH GOT PULLED INTO THOSE GEARS BECAUSE HE WASN'T CAREFUL. YOU NEARLY DIED DOING SOMETHING CARELESS YOURSELF. DON'T LET IT HAPPEN AGAIN.

AFTER SIXTY-ONE MINUTES OF CONTEMPLATION, I'VE DETERMINED THAT WHAT MY FATHER ASKED OF ME WAS STUPID. CARELESSNESS MAY NOT BE A VIRTUE, BUT IT'S UNAVOIDABLE, ESPECIALLY FOR SOMEONE MY AGE. AND BESIDES, SUPER-CAREFUL PEOPLE ARE REALLY BORING. I KNOW A GIRL AT SCHOOL WHO WON'T DRINK

OUT OF THE WATER FOUNTAIN. SHE WON'T EAT FOOD FROM THE CAFETERIA. SHE HAS A NOTE FOR GYM CLASS THAT ALLOWS HER TO SIT OUT WHENEVER WE DO SOMETHING SHE FEELS IS TOO DANGEROUS. SHE BARELY HAS A PULSE.

OLD JOE BUSH DOESN'T LOOK LIKE THE CARELESS TYPE. IF I HAD TO SAY WHAT HE LOOKS LIKE IN HIS PICTURE, I'D SAY . . . WELL, I GUESS I'D SAY HE LOOKS SINGLE-MINDED. PROBABLY HE WAS PUSHED. FOUL PLAY, THAT'S WHAT KILLED OLD JOE BUSH, NOT CARELESSNESS.

IT WAS REALLY LATE WHEN I WATCHED SARAH'S VIDEO LAST NIGHT. I DREAMT ABOUT IT, SO WHEN I WOKE UP I WASN'T SURE IF I'D WATCHED IT AT ALL. IN MY DREAM, DARYL BONNER THE RANGER AND GLADYS THE LIBRARIAN WERE WALKING IN THE WOODS. GLADYS HAD HER SHOTGUN AND THEN OLD JOE BUSH CAME OUT OF THE BUSHES DRAGGING HIS LEG AND SAID, "NUMBER FORTY-TWO IS MINE. STAY AWAY FROM THIS PLACE. I'M WATCHING YOU." GLADYS FIRED BUCKSHOT INTO THE AIR, AND OLD JOE BUSH TRIED TO RUN AWAY, DRAGGING HIS LEG DOWN THE PATH TOWARD THE DREDGE. GLADYS LAUGHED AND LAUGHED, BUT DARYL BONNER

WENT ON AHEAD AND HELPED OLD JOE BUSH STEP
DOWN INTO THE BLACK POND AND DISAPPEAR UNDER
THE WATER. IN MY DREAM, THE POND LOOKED LIKE A
TAR PIT.

THE THING ABOUT DREAMS IS THAT THEY
SOMETIMES MEAN SOMETHING. I HAVE DREAMS ALL
THE TIME, BUT I GET THIS FEELING ABOUT CERTAIN
DREAMS THAT MAKES ME THINK SOMETHING IMPORTANT
IS HIDDEN THERE. THIS WAS ONE OF THOSE DREAMS.
THE STICKY GOO OF THE TAR PIT HIDES THINGS. I
KNOW IT DOES.

I DON'T THINK GLADYS IS IMPORTANT. I THINK SHE'S
JUST IN THERE BECAUSE I'D NEVER GONE THROUGH A
DOOR AND FOUND SOMEONE POINTING A SHOTGUN AT ME.
SHE'S BEEN APPEARING IN A LOT OF DREAMS SINCE. SHE'S
LIKE WALLPAPER. SHE'S JUST THERE.

BUT RANGER BONNER — HE'S NEW — AND HE'S
HELPING JOE INTO THE WATER OR THE TAR. WHY DID
I CONNECT THE TWO IN MY DREAM? MY UNCONSCIOUS
MIND MUST SEE SOMETHING IN THE VIDEO OR THE
PICTURE THAT MY WAKING MIND DOESN'T. AN HOUR OF
LOOKING AT THE PICTURE MY DAD GAVE ME ISN'T
HELPING ME SEE THINGS CLEARER. I'M GOING TO RISK

89

WATCHING SARAH'S VIDEO AGAIN, BUT THIS TIME I'M
GOING TO KEEP THE PICTURE HANDY SO I CAN LOOK AT
IT. IT'S ALMOST 7:30 AND MY MOM USUALLY COMES
IN BETWEEN 7:30 AND 8:00.

I BETTER HURRY.

NO SIGN OF MOM YET, AND I'VE WATCHED THE VIDEO AGAIN. I SCANNED THE PICTURE OF OLD JOE BUSH AND SENT IT TO SARAH. DANGEROUS MOVE. IF HER PARENTS OPEN HER EMAIL BEFORE SHE DOES, THEY'LL SUSPECT I'VE SENT IT. EVEN THOUGH I USED AN ACCOUNT THAT DOESN'T HAVE MY NAME ON IT AND I DIDN'T SAY HARDLY ANYTHING.

This is Joe Bush. Familiar?

I DIDN'T PUT MY NAME AT THE END. I JUST ATTACHED THE PHOTO AND SENT IT.

I THINK I KNOW WHY DARYL BONNER AND JOE BUSH ARE TOGETHER IN MY DREAM. IT'S BECAUSE IN REAL LIFE THEY LOOK SORT OF SIMILAR. THE PHOTO IS GRAINY, BUT THE BONE STRUCTURE, THE NOSE, THE FOREHEAD — THEY'RE SIMILAR. TOO SIMILAR.

WHAT DOES THAT EVEN MEAN?

Friday, September 17, 8:00 a.m.

Mom has been here with my breakfast and gone.
It was a miracle she didn't check my computer,
because I totally forgot to erase my tracks.
It feels like every day I'm a whisper away from
losing everything, including my best friend. I
totally believe my parents when they say
they'll sell the house and move us to the city
if they catch me talking to Sarah. If they knew
how much we were emailing — all the stuff we
were doing — they'd pack the car and have me
out of here tonight.

Like Dad said, I have to be careful. I can't be
careless when it comes to communicating with
Sarah. There's too much at stake.

I've got something weird I want to try — just
to see what will happen. It's not the most
careful thing in the world, but I can't stop
thinking about it.

Here's my plan:

I'll call the ranger station. It's early, so
Ranger Bonner probably won't be on the trail

YET. WHEN HE PICKS UP I'LL ASK FOR JOE BUSH AND SEE WHAT HE SAYS. I WONDER WHAT HE'LL DO? WHAT IF HE HAS CALLER ID? DO RANGER STATIONS HAVE STUFF LIKE THAT?

I'M RISKING IT. IF I GET CAUGHT, I'LL SAY IT WAS A PRANK. I'LL PLAY UP THE FACT THAT I'M CRAZY.

Friday, September 17, 8:10 a.m.

I called Daryl Bonner.

Here's what happened:

Him: "Skeleton Creek Ranger Station."

Me: "Can I speak to Joe Bush?"

Him: "Who is this? Why are you asking for Joe Bush?"

I didn't reply.

Him: "Did Sarah Fincher put you up to this?"

I didn't reply.

Him: "Answer me! Why are you asking about Joe Bush?"

I hung up.

And now I wonder:

Why was he so freaked out?

I have just endured an eventful hour and five minutes. About two minutes after I hung up, the phone rang. I tried to intercept the call myself, but I picked up at the same moment my dad did. He's a notoriously quick grabber of the phone. He hates hearing it ring and ring. I thought he'd already be halfway out the door for work, but I guess he stayed late this morning.

Just my luck.

Dad: "Hello."

Bonner: "This is Daryl Bonner at the ranger station. Did you just call this number?"

Dad: "I did not. My son might have."

Bonner: "Is this the home of the boy who had the accident at the dredge?"

Dad: "Might be."

Bonner: "I think he might be getting bored. He just called here with — I don't know — I guess you'd call it a prank call. He asked for Joe Bush, whoever that is. And the girl involved in that accident — Sarah Fincher — she seems

95

INTERESTED IN THE DREDGE AS WELL. IT MIGHT BE A GOOD TIME TO KEEP AN ESPECIALLY CLOSE EYE ON THEM BOTH. THE DREDGE ISN'T SAFE — AT LEAST THAT'S WHAT THE STATE SUPERVISOR TOLD ME. NO ONE SHOULD BE GOING OUT THERE."

DAD: "I'LL HAVE A TALK WITH MY SON."

BONNER: "THANK YOU."

I HUNG UP RIGHT AFTER THEY DID, THEN LISTENED TO MY DAD COMING UP THE STAIRS AND WONDERED IF MY ACTIONS QUALIFIED AS MORE THAN CARELESS. I HAD THE FEELING THEY DID. SARAH'S INTERVIEW RAN THROUGH MY HEAD, THEN MY CALL. I FELT STUPID FOR HAVING DONE IT. THERE WERE DOTS THAT COULD BE CONNECTED. SARAH, BONNER, ME. THERE WAS A FLURRY OF ACTIVITY. MAYBE IT WAS ENOUGH TO GET THE HOUSE ON THE MARKET.

I ALREADY HAD A FONDNESS FOR HENRY, BUT WHEN THE DOORBELL RANG AND MY DAD WENT BACK DOWNSTAIRS I LIKED HENRY TEN TIMES MORE. OUR FALL VISITOR HAD ARRIVED, AND I WAS SPARED MY DAD'S WRATH. HIS ANGER USUALLY BOILED OVER PRETTY FAST. IF I COULD STAY OUT OF HIS CROSSHAIRS WHILE HE

CALMED DOWN, THE CONSEQUENCES WERE ALWAYS LESS

SEVERE. UNTIL HE SHOWED UP IN MY ROOM WITH

HENRY IN TOW, I EVEN HAD A GLIMMER OF HOPE THAT

MY DAD HAD FORGOTTEN ALL ABOUT THE PHONE CALL.

"THAT'S ONE HECKUVA CAST!"

THOSE WERE THE FIRST WORDS OUT OF HENRY'S

MOUTH WHEN HE CAME INTO MY ROOM WITH MY DAD.

THEY WERE BOTH SMILING AND I BREATHED A SIGH OF

RELIEF.

HENRY WENT ON, "ANY CHANCE I COULD HAVE IT

WHEN YOU'RE DONE? THAT THING COULD BE A REAL

HIT AT THE CARD TABLE."

"THEY'LL HAVE TO CUT IT OFF. I COULD ONLY GIVE

YOU THE PIECES."

"I'VE GOT DUCT TAPE. IT'LL BE PERFECT."

HENRY HAD HIS FISHING HAT ON, RIMMED WITH FLIES,

AND HIS RAINBOW SUSPENDERS.

"YOUR DAD TELLS ME HE NEEDS TO RUN ACROSS

TOWN AND SEE THE RANGER. MIND IF I KEEP YOU

COMPANY WHILE HE'S GONE?"

"I'D LIKE THAT."

MY DAD ASKED FOR HIS PICTURE OF OLD JOE

BUSH, AND I GAVE IT TO HIM. HE LOOKED AT ME AS IF

to say, We're not quite through here yet, I'll be back, and then he left me and Henry alone in my room. I so wish I'd never made that phone call. It feels like I've opened a can of worms and they're squirming out all over the place.

Henry chimed in when the sound of our front door closing reached my room.

"Can you get down those stairs?" he asked.

"I think I can. But I always feel better in the afternoon. I think I'll wait a little bit."

"Fair enough. How bored are you?"

"Very."

"I suspected."

"How long are you staying?"

"Seventeen days of bliss! Two poker nights, fishing on the river, and your mom's home cooking. You don't appreciate it now, but Cynthia is the queen of comfort food. Old bachelors love comfort food, especially when we're from the city. She's making that baked noodle dish with the crunchy cheese on top tonight. I've been thinking about it for three days."

"You should get married," I joked.

"And give up Yankee games, dirty laundry, and my twelve girlfriends? I don't think I'm ready for that kind of sacrifice."

"You don't have twelve girlfriends."

"Do so."

"Liar."

"Well, I've <u>had</u> twelve girlfriends. It's the same thing."

"I bet all twelve are now married with kids and have long since forgotten the Yankee-loving slob they dated ten years ago."

"You shouldn't talk like that with a cast on your leg. You won't be able to run away when I dump a bucket of cold water on your head."

"You're all talk."

"I'm making your lunch."

Henry smiled and I knew I was in big trouble. I hated not knowing what disgusting thing he might add to a Hot Pocket or swirl into peanut butter before spreading it around. He probably wouldn't do anything, but I'd never know for sure, and it would drive me crazy.

We talked about the accident and about how I

couldn't see Sarah anymore. The news about Sarah bothered him and he said he would talk to my parents. He liked Sarah and I appreciated it, but I knew somewhere deep down that it didn't matter what Henry said. My parents had already made up their minds.

I had no idea how many more times I'd have Henry to myself. I decided it was time to begin my inquisition, especially since he was in such a friendly mood.

"Hey," I said. "How come you never talk about when you used to work for New York Gold and Silver?"

"It's not my best chapter."

"Why not?"

Henry took off his hat and laughed nervously. Then his smile went away and I felt terrible for asking him.

"Since you're all busted up, I suppose I'll tell you. I made a lot of mistakes back then because I was young and ambitious. I could lie and say I didn't really know what I was doing, but I knew.

Skeleton Creek got into my bones, though. It saved me."

"Did you ever meet Joe Bush?"

Henry looked at me a little curiously then, but he still answered. "Why sure I did — lots of times. He was a hard worker. You know he died on the dredge?"

"I do."

"That accident was the beginning of the end. I quit not too long after that. There were a lot of lawsuits flying around. They were asking me to do things I couldn't do."

"Like what?"

"You sure are curious when you're laid up."

"Like what, Henry?"

"They wanted me to lie about things, and that's when I knew for sure I'd been doing something wrong all along."

"Did you ever hear of Old Joe Bush coming back?"

"You mean like a ghost?"

"I guess so."

"Let's just say there are stories floating around — none of them true, mind you — about the ghost of Old Joe Bush. It's all hogwash."

"Can I ask you one more thing?"

"Sure you can."

"Have you ever heard of the Crossbones?"

"Now there's an interesting question!"

"Really?"

"It's especially interesting for an outsider like me. Did you know membership is only allowed if you can prove you were either born here or have a relative that was born here?"

"No. I didn't know that."

"That's the truth — or at least I think it is. I'm pretty sure the Crossbones came into existence back when the dredge was still working."

"Why do you say that?"

"There was talk of a secret group forming. You hear things."

"What did they do?"

"If I knew that, I'd be a member. But as I said, I'm from the outside. A New Yorker, no less! No

MATTER HOW MUCH I LOVE THIS PLACE OR HOW MANY TIMES I COME BACK, I'LL NEVER KNOW MORE THAN I DO RIGHT NOW ABOUT THE CROSSBONES. WHICH ISN'T MUCH."

I WAS AFRAID TO ASK ONE LAST QUESTION, BUT I ASKED ANYWAY.

"IS MY DAD A MEMBER?"

"IF I WERE A BETTING MAN, I'D PUT GOOD MONEY ON IT. BUT THE TRUTH IS, I HAVE NO IDEA. WE TALK ABOUT A LOT, BUT NOT ABOUT THOSE KINDS OF THINGS."

THEN HE LEFT TO UNPACK HIS THINGS, AND I WROTE ALL OF THIS DOWN.

I CAN'T WAIT TO TELL SARAH.

BUT HOW?

IT'S RISKIER WITH SOMEONE ELSE AROUND. I DON'T THINK HENRY WOULD TELL MY PARENTS IF HE CAUGHT ME EMAILING — BUT I CAN'T BE SURE.

Friday, September 17, 11:00am

When Dad came back, the steam had gone out of his anger and he didn't say a lot about the call I'd made. He didn't give me back the picture of Joe Bush and I didn't ask for it.

"I know you're bored," he said, "but leave that poor man alone. He's new in town and he's got work to do like the rest of us. Find something productive to do."

Like the <u>rest</u> of us? I don't know what he's talking about. My dad is on vacation for the next two weeks while my mom keeps working at the post office like she always does. Henry and my dad will sleep late, make pancakes and strong coffee, then fish and play cards.

I keep wondering how my dad would feel if someone told him he couldn't see Henry ever again. I'm pretty sure he'd go down fighting.

The two of them are downstairs going through their fly boxes, comparing gear, getting ready to go fishing on the river for the afternoon. Skeleton Creek drains into a bigger creek, and that bigger creek drains into the

RIVER, WHERE THEY'LL SEARCH OUT WINTER—RUN
STEELHEAD (BASICALLY A GIANT TROUT). THE PLACE
THEY'RE GOING TO IS AN HOUR OUTSIDE OF TOWN IF MY
DAD IS DRIVING THE OLD PICKUP. HE HAS TO BABY IT OR
THEY'D BE THERE IN HALF THE TIME.

WHEN DAD AND HENRY GET BACK THEY'LL
THROW TOGETHER A LATE LUNCH AND HELP ME DOWN
TO THE PORCH AND WE CAN PLAY CARDS BEFORE
MOM GETS HOME.

WHAT DID MY DAD SAY TO RANGER BONNER?
HE MIGHT NOT HAVE EVEN SEEN THE RANGER.
MAYBE HE ONLY SAID HE WAS GOING TO SEE RANGER
BONNER AND ACTUALLY WENT TO TALK WITH SARAH'S
PARENTS OR, WORSE, A REAL ESTATE AGENT. THERE
COULD BE A SIGN GOING UP IN THE FRONT YARD ALREADY.

I DESPISE ALL REAL ESTATE AGENTS.

THEY LEFT HERE FIFTEEN MINUTES AGO AND I DRIFTED OFF TO SLEEP. AT FIRST I THOUGHT THERE WAS A PHONE RINGING IN MY DREAM, BUT IT KEPT RINGING, AND ON THE FOURTH RING I REACHED OUT MY ARM AND FUMBLED FOR THE CORDLESS. I EXPECTED IT TO BE MOM CHECKING ON ME. SHE HAS A WAY OF KNOWING WHEN I'M HOME ALONE. SHE TELLS ME TO REST, EAT, AND STAY OFF THE INTERNET.

I CLICKED ON THE RECEIVER AND ANSWERED GROGGILY, HOPING SHE'D HEAR THE FATIGUE IN MY VOICE AND GO EASY ON ME WITH THE LECTURING. WHEN I ANSWERED, THERE WAS THE FAINTEST SOUND OF — WHAT WAS IT? — LEAVES MOVING IN THE TREES? OR WAS IT WATER MOVING? IT HAD THE DISTINCT BUT INDEFINABLE SOUND OF NATURE. AT LEAST THAT'S WHAT I THOUGHT BEFORE WHOEVER IT WAS HUNG UP ON ME.

MY FIRST THOUGHT WAS THAT MY DAD WAS CALLING FROM THE STREAM TO MAKE SURE I WAS STAYING PUT. BUT WHY DID HE HANG UP? I LOOKED AT THE CALLER ID AND DIDN'T RECOGNIZE THE NUMBER. IT WAS A 406 AREA CODE. NOT LOCAL.

I dialed the number and waited. One ring. Two rings. Three rings. Voice mail.

"This is Daryl Bonner with the Montana Department of Fish and Wildlife. I'm currently stationed in Skeleton Creek, Oregon, returning to the Wind River Station on November third. Please leave a message."

Why is Ranger Bonner calling my house and then hanging up? Was he looking for my dad and got me instead?

I shouldn't have called him and asked if Old Joe Bush was there.

What if he thinks I know something I'm not supposed to?

Friday, September 17, 1:20 p.m.

I've spent the last couple of hours scouring the web for anything about Skeleton Creek, the dredge, Old Joe Bush. I'm so frustrated. It's like I've dug up all the bones I'm going to find and they make up only about a tenth of what I'm searching for. The deeper I go, the harder the ground feels. I feel like I've hit a layer of solid rock.

I need to send a warning to Sarah, but I'm afraid to. What if my dad went to her parents and they've taken her computer? I can see them sitting at the kitchen table hitting refresh every fifteen minutes waiting for my email to come through. The death email. The email that sends me packing.

I can't risk it.

Obviously Sarah doesn't feel as concerned as I do, because I just got an email from her. I guess that puts to rest my concern about her parents confiscating her laptop. Unless — and this is entirely possible — they're baiting me. What if they sent the email? Or, worse, what if my dad is on Sarah's laptop at her house with her parents sending me emails? It's an underhanded move, but it could happen.

I'd like to think Henry would tip me off. But how could he?

I'm hungry and tired, which sometimes makes me nervous. But seriously — I am so paranoid. It's ridiculous. Maybe I need group therapy. Me, Sarah, and Old Joe Bush.

Actually, to be fair, what I got from Sarah wasn't really an email if you consider there were no words in the message, only a string of letters in the subject line and nothing else.

drjekyllandmrhyde

So now she's diverging from Poe into Stevenson. Fair enough. I sometimes think she's trying to tell me something with these passwords. Like in this case, is she saying that Daryl Bonner is Dr. Jekyll, and the ghost of Joe Bush is Mr. Hyde? Or is Daryl Bonner both?

Or is my dad both?

I can't believe I just wrote that. I might as well be Jekyll and Hyde, I keep going back and forth.

I have to get out of this house.

Dad and Henry could come back early. I haven't covered the tracks of my two hours of searching online. I haven't deleted Sarah's email or watched the video. There's a lot to do while I have the house to myself.

I'm getting rid of everything first. Then, if I'm still safe, I'll watch the video.

SARAHFINCHER.COM
PASSWORD:
DRJEKYLLANDMRHYDE

Friday, September 17, 1:52 p.m.

I should have watched the video first! Why am I
even writing this? Because it calms me down.
That's why I'm writing. It calms me down. I think
better when I write.

I can figure this out if I settle down.

Recap:

Sarah went to the dredge.

Ranger Bonner was there. Sarah thinks he
was waiting for her. But she could just be
overreacting.

She borrowed his phone. She dialed the last
number in his incoming calls list.

It was my house. And it was after Dad had
already gone over to talk to Bonner.
Supposedly. And when I called back? He must
have had the ringer silenced in case it went off
while he was tailing Sarah through the woods. For
once I'm glad there are cell towers scattered
out there — at least she could get a signal and
call me, even if she couldn't say anything.

Sarah thinks Dad tipped Bonner off. But how
could he know she'd be there?

WAS HE IN MY ROOM LAST NIGHT? HAS HE READ THIS? HE COULD HAVE SNUCK IN HERE JUST LIKE THAT CRAZY NUT JOB IN THE TELL-TALE HEART. I WOKE UP — IT FELT LIKE SOMEONE WAS IN THE ROOM, BUT THERE WAS NO ONE. OR AT LEAST NO ONE ANSWERED IN THE DARK.

IF MY DAD KNOWS, THEN WHY ISN'T HE CONFRONTING ME? WHY ISN'T THE HOUSE UP FOR SALE? WHY ISN'T MY MOM FREAKING OUT? SHE'S NOT, SO THAT MEANS HE HASN'T TOLD HER.

HOW MANY QUESTIONS IS THAT — FIFTY? I CAN'T ANSWER ANY OF THEM FOR SURE. I NEED MORE INFORMATION. I NEED TO NARROW THIS DOWN.

WHAT'S THE MOST IMPORTANT QUESTION RIGHT NOW? DAD. WHAT'S GOING ON WITH DAD?

TWENTY MINUTES TOPS, MAYBE FIFTEEN. I CAN'T RISK SNEAKING AROUND BEYOND THAT. THEY'LL STOP FISHING WHEN HENRY GETS HUNGRY. HENRY LIKES TO EAT. HE'LL WANT TO KNOCK OFF EARLY. I BET THEY'LL BE HERE BY 2:30, MAYBE EVEN EARLIER.

I'M JUST GOING TO TAKE MY JOURNAL WITH ME — THAT'S WHAT I'M GOING TO DO. I'LL KEEP WRITING. I'LL HOBBLE TO MY PARENTS' ROOM, RIGHT DOWN THE HALL.

113

I can make that work. I'll go in there. I know where my dad's dresser is. I know he keeps his personal stuff in the top drawer because Mom told me when I was little. She caught me in there and slapped my hand really hard and said I should never search through other people's things without asking. She said it was the same as stealing, which I never really understood.

I'm in the door. My watch says 2:03 but I'm leaving the door open so I can hear it if they come in. Henry will be loud — he'll be talking. I'll be able to get out.

My parents' closet smells like my mom, not like my dad. I'm having some trouble breathing. I just can't seem to calm down. I remember when she slapped my hand and how it stung. The blood is rushing through my leg and I can feel every part that's broken. It feels like my mom took a broomstick and started beating me with it. Whack! Whack! Whack!

I've got this journal open on the top of the dresser. The lightbulb doesn't make it very bright in here. It's sort of a yellow light. Oh,

MAN, I CAN'T BREATHE VERY WELL. DO I HAVE ASTHMA? I MIGHT HAVE ASTHMA, THE MORE I THINK ABOUT IT. I'VE KICKED UP SOME DUST IN HERE. MY LEG IS KILLING ME. IT DOESN'T LIKE BEING STOOD UP FOR TOO LONG ALL AT ONCE.

I KNOW IT'S CRAZY FOR ME TO BE WRITING AS I DO THIS. BUT I HAVE TO.

I MIGHT NOT GET ANOTHER CHANCE TO DO THIS. AND I CAN'T RELY ON MY MEMORY. I HAVE TO GET EVERYTHING DOWN.

THE DRAWER IS OPEN. THERE'S LOTS OF STUFF IN HERE. MY GRANDFATHER'S BELT BUCKLE — HE'S DEAD NOW. IT'S GOT RHINESTONES IN IT. A STACK OF DOCUMENTS — LEGAL STUFF, I THINK. A CIGAR BOX WITH A LITTLE LATCH ON IT. SOME RINGS AND PENS AND OLD WATCHES.

I'VE OPENED THE CIGAR BOX. IT'S GOT A ROW OF TEN OR TWELVE MATCHING CUFF LINKS PUSHED INTO A SHEET OF CARDBOARD. MY DAD NEVER WEARS CUFF LINKS. THERE'S A CAMPAIGN BUTTON, A STACK OF EXPIRED CREDIT CARDS AND LICENSES. THERE'S NOTHING OMINOUS HERE. THERE'S NO SIGN OF A SECRET SOCIETY.

2:12. I HAVE TO GET OUT OF HERE.

WHY CUFF LINKS? I BET THEY'RE FROM THEIR
WEDDING DAY — MAYBE IT'S ALL THE CUFF LINKS FROM
ALL THE MEN IN THE WEDDING PARTY. THEY ALL LOOK
ALIKE, AS IF THEY WERE WORN ONCE AND NEVER AGAIN.

2:13.

I TRIED TO PICK UP ONE OF THE CUFF LINKS, AND
THE WHOLE PIECE OF CARDBOARD LIFTED UP OUT OF THE
CIGAR BOX. WHEN I FLIPPED IT OVER, I FOUND A PIECE
OF PAPER TAPED TO THE BACK. I UNFOLDED IT AND
FOUND SOMETHING THERE. I CAN'T BREATHE. I REALLY
HAVE TO GET OUT OF HERE.

2:15.

THEY'RE GOING TO BE BACK ANY SECOND NOW. I
CAN FEEL IT. I'VE SHUFFLED BACK DOWN THE HALL TO
MY ROOM, DRAGGING MY LEG BEHIND ME. MY
COMPUTER IS SCANNING THE PIECE OF PAPER WHILE I
WRITE. COME ON — FINISH!

2:18.

THE SCAN IS DONE. TIME TO RETURN THE
ORIGINAL.

2:20.

THEY'RE HOME! HENRY JUST YELLED UP THE
STAIRS.

116

"I'M MAKING LUNCH, CHAMP! I HOPE YOU'RE READY FOR A SURPRISE!"

I'M STANDING IN FRONT OF MY DAD'S DRESSER WITH THE LITTLE YELLOW LIGHT ON. I CAN'T MOVE. HE'LL COME UP HERE ANY SECOND, I KNOW HE WILL. THEN WHAT WILL I DO? I SHOULD RUN. I SHOULD GET OUT OF HERE. I'VE CLOSED THE DRAWER BUT I CAN'T MOVE.

WHAT AM I GOING TO DO?

HE'S COMING.

Friday, September 17, 2:41 p.m.

I've calmed down now. I'm not shaking so much anymore. I can breathe again. My dad went straight to the hallway bathroom on his way to my room. I heard him yell.

"Just going to use the head and I'll stop in and see you. Fishing was good! Better than last year."

I made it out of his room, into the hallway outside the bathroom door. I tucked this journal in the top of my cast and sucked in my breath. The door opened with a whoosh of air.

"Look at you! Up and walking around. You must really want to play some cards."

He looked happy to see me. I felt guilty about that. What was I doing?

"Count me in," I told him. "I'm tired of lying down."

"Looks like you just ran a marathon. How about lunch in bed, then we'll help you to the porch? Deal?"

"Deal."

AND SO DAD DELIVERED ME BACK TO MY ROOM, AND THEN HENRY BROUGHT IN A GRILLED-CHEESE-AND-BACON SANDWICH WITH TOMATO SOUP. IT WOULD BE EASY TO HIDE ALL SORTS OF GROSS THINGS IN CREAMY RED SOUP OR MELTED ORANGE CHEESE. BUT IT WAS LATE AND I WAS STARVING. HE WOULDN'T DARE TRICK A KID WITH A CAST. WOULD HE?

FRIDAY, SEPTEMBER 17, 2:41 P.M.

DAD AND HENRY WILL BE UP TO GET ME ANY MINUTE. I PRINTED OUT THE SCAN OF WHAT I FOUND. I'M STICKING IT TO THIS PAGE. IT SCARES ME.

THE ALCHEMIST DIAGRAM of 79 for PAUL McCRAY

NUMBER One IS WEARY WHEN THREE GOES PAST THE TWO
1st day \ next month \ 2:50am

TWICE ROUND THE MOON WITH SEVEN FINGERED SAM
7th day \ current month \ 1:00 am

TWELVE TIMES THE TORTOISE WHEN THREE TURNS THE HARE
15th day \ current month \ 3:00 am

FIVE MY SING ING MISTRESS, TWELVE TAKES THREE TO DINNER
8th day \ next month \ 12:30 am

SLeeP You COWARD FooL, WAKE WHEN BiRDiE tURNS
people are watching \ keep quiet for a time

EIGHT BALL CORNERED, BISHOP TAKES QUEEN
16th day \ current month \ 4:00 am

A STRaiGHT SHOT TO MARTHA'S AT TEN PAST THE KNOB
emergency meeting \ tonight \ 10 past midnight

THE FLOOR AND 7%. FOUR PAST THE NINE On DooR NUMBER TWO!
LIBRARY ATTIC. ENTER THROUGH THE ALLEY DOOR MARKED 221.

MAN PLAYS FIDDLE AT NINE IN THE MIDDLE UNDER STAIRS ON SIX
OPEN THE FLOOR MARKED 9 IN LIBRARIES BLACK STAGE THE SIXTH STAIR DOWN

FRIDAY, SEPTEMBER 17, 7:30 P.M.

There's no two ways about it: Navigating stairs is complicated with a full-leg cast and crutches. Our stairwell is narrow and there are family pictures hanging like clumps of grapes all the way down both sides. I think I would have been fine if I hadn't insisted I could do it alone. Henry and Dad were watching from the bottom of the stairs when I pitched forward somewhere near the middle and lost my balance.

Dad met me with outstretched arms, and my face smashed into his gray T-shirt. He smelled like a fisherman.

My hands fanned over about a dozen family pictures in frames on the way down but by some miracle of gravity none of them fell to their deaths. They wobbled back and forth and knocked into one another, but they held. It looked like a big gust of wind had rushed through.

In my defense, the cast is really heavy and . . . let's see . . . what's the word I'm searching for? . . . Unbending. A cast like big

BERTHA MAKES A PERSON WANT TO BEND LIKE NEVER BEFORE. I'M <u>DYING</u> TO BEND MY LEG. IT'S LIKE A FEROCIOUS ITCH I CAN'T SCRATCH. (WHICH REMINDS ME: THIS THING ITCHES LIKE MAD, SO ADD THAT TO MY LIST OF COMPLAINTS.)

WHEN I FINALLY MADE IT TO THE FRONT PORCH, THE FLOORBOARDS CREAKED UNDER THE WEIGHT OF MY CAST. I SETTLED DOWN ON A GOLD, TATTERED COUCH WITH MY LEG PROPPED UP ON A WOODEN STOOL AND BREATHED IN THE CRISP FALL AIR.

OUR PORCH IS A LOT LIKE AN OUTDOOR LIVING ROOM. WHEN A PIECE OF FURNITURE IS REPLACED INSIDE THE HOUSE, THE OLD ITEM FINDS A HOME ON THE PORCH. AFTER A WHILE — A YEAR, MAYBE TWO — THE SAME ITEM MOVES TEN MORE FEET AND BECOMES AN ITEM IN ONE OF MOM'S MANY YARD SALES. IT'S A NATURAL PROGRESSION, A SLOW BUT STEADY MARCH OFF THE PROPERTY.

I SEARCHED THE SKIES FOR FLYING DR PEPPER CANS OR OTHER SIGNS OF SARAH, BUT THERE WAS NOTHING. HENRY ASKED IF I WANTED TO PLAY THREE-HANDED CRIBBAGE. NOT A GREAT GAME IF YOU ASK ME. I'M NOT SURE WHO CAME UP WITH IT, BUT PROBABLY IT WAS THREE PEOPLE SITTING IN A ROOM WITH ONE

CRIBBAGE BOARD AND THE PERSON SITTING OUT WANTED

TO JOIN IN. I PLAYED ANYWAY. IT WAS NICE TO THINK

ABOUT SOMETHING OTHER THAN HAUNTED DREDGES AND

SECRET SOCIETIES.

"HOW MUCH LONGER?" HENRY ASKED AFTER A

LITTLE WHILE. HE WAS HOLDING HIS CARDS WITH ONE

HAND AND TUGGING SLOWLY ON ONE RAINBOW

SUSPENDER WITH THE OTHER.

"BEFORE WHAT?"

"BEFORE YOU CAN WALK AROUND WITHOUT

SOMETHING ON YOUR LEG?"

"HOW LONG, DAD?"

.- .-. . | -.-- --- ..- | - .... . | .- -... --.- .... . -- .. ... - |

HENRY COULDN'T BELIEVE IT. "SEVEN WEEKS!

YOU'LL HAVE TO SHIP THE CAST TO ME. I'LL LEAVE

A BOX."

"YOU'RE NUTS," I TOLD HIM.

"I BET IT ITCHES LIKE TERMITES."

"IT DOES."

"YOU COULD JAM A COAT HANGER DOWN IN

THERE."

HENRY IS A GREAT CARD PLAYER. HE HAS THIS

MADDENING WAY OF DISTRACTING EVERYONE WITH ALL

SORTS OF MINDLESS SMALL TALK. HE'D NEVER ADMIT IT,

BUT I'M SURE THIS IS PART OF HIS STRATEGY. IT'S HARD TO CONCENTRATE WHEN SOMEONE'S TALKING ABOUT HAVING AN EMPTY CAST SHIPPED TO NEW YORK. I STARTED THINKING ABOUT WHAT THE BOX WOULD LOOK LIKE. I WONDERED WHAT HIS TWELVE GIRLFRIENDS WOULD SAY WHEN THEY SAW THE CAST PROPPED UP AGAINST THE WALL IN HIS APARTMENT. I STARTED FEELING ALMOST POSITIVE THERE WERE BUGS CRAWLING AROUND INSIDE MY CAST. I BEGGED MY DAD TO GO GET ME A COAT HANGER. AND ALL THE WHILE I MADE STUPID PLAYS ALL OVER THE CRIBBAGE BOARD.

EVENTUALLY I GOT MY COAT HANGER STRAIGHTENED OUT AND JAMMED IT ALL THE WAY DOWN TO MY KNEECAP. THAT WAS AN IMPROVEMENT. WE BASICALLY SAT THERE PLAYING CARDS FOR ABOUT AN HOUR, TALKING ABOUT NOTHING IN PARTICULAR — MOSTLY, HENRY WAS TRYING TO THROW US OFF, AND WAS DOING A HIT-OR-MISS JOB. EVENTUALLY MOM CAME HOME, AND AFTER CALLING HELLOS, WE HEARD HER POUNDING AWAY ON THE PIPES IN THE KITCHEN.

"YOU SHOULD GO HELP HER," HENRY SAID.

Henry has a lot of sympathy for my mom. He knows my dad isn't very good about taking on home projects. My dad is plenty capable, but he lacks motivation for certain kinds of tasks.

"You go help her," Dad said.

"What's she doing in there?" Henry asked.

"Trying to unclog the garbage disposal," my dad said. "She's under the sink, hitting the pipe with a rolling pin. Believe it or not, it usually works."

"Sounds a little like the old dredge when it was really cranking."

My mom started yelling at the sink, which prompted my dad to set his cards down, sigh deeply, and walk indifferently to her rescue.

There was something about that noise — the sound of banging on metal — that made me think again of the night I'd fallen and smashed my leg. There had been a clanging sound, barely audible, as if someone was hitting metal on metal.

I decided to ask Henry about his comment.

"What sound do you mean?"

Henry leaned back in his chair until it was only on two legs.

"The dredge was incredibly loud. Tons of rocks were scooped from the ground and dumped inside. The conveyor belts were rimmed with thick planks of wood that kept everything from falling out. It was like a long water slide — you've seen those? — but instead of water shooting through, it was boulders. It echoed like mad, which seemed to quadruple the rumbling. Such a horrible sound. A crew of four was required to run the dredge, and they were separated by quite a distance. One was stationed at the gears in front where they watched everything come in. That person greased the machines and pulled the stop-chain if things got jammed up. Another was at the far end, watching the tailings dump out. There was a man at the control booth and one more we called a roamer — a guy who fixed things on the fly from a running list of problems."

"But the sound — the banging — what sound was that?"

125

"The workers couldn't hear one another. They couldn't yell that loud. So they used signals. They banged metal wrenches or hammers against the iron girders of the dredge to tell each other things. It was like Morse code, simple but effective in those days."

When Dad returned, the conversation veered quickly away from the dredge. I didn't want him to hear us talking about it, and maybe Henry didn't, either. Instead, we all played cards and talked about the Yankees and the Mariners. After a while, Mom brought the casserole with the crispy cheese top and the last of the late summer bees started swarming around the porch.

Friday, September 17, 9:00 p.m.

I've spent a lot of time away from my bedroom today, which makes me feel anxious. I feel like the FBI has scoured my mattress and squeaky box spring, taken pictures, dusted for fingerprints — all the while with two-way radios wired to the kitchen so Mom could tell them if I was on my way and they could jump out the second-story window. I know this sounds stupid, but it's how I feel all the same.

The room appears untouched. Before I left I took Sarah's advice and found a better hiding place for this journal. I slid it inside my ninth-grade annual from last year and put the annual between a whole bunch of other books. I also taped it shut. It doesn't look to me like they found it. The seal hasn't been broken.

They'll leave me alone for a while — Henry's got all their attention — so it's a good time to email Sarah and tell her about what I found in my dad's dresser.

Friday, September 17, 9:20 p.m.

Too late, she already emailed me. It was a short, bad email. The worst kind.

I'm going back tonight. I have to. Don't worry — I'm fine. I'll contact you tomorrow. Delete this!   S

So I emailed her back.

Sarah,
Have you lost your mind? Don't get anywhere near the dredge right now!
People are probably watching. And besides that, I'm digging up all sorts
of reasons to stay clear of that thing (as if a phantom isn't reason enough!).
I found something in my dad's room. You're amazed I went in there, right?
Me too. Trust me, it was insane. I attached a scan of what I found. It feels
like dangerous information to have. It will ring a bell from the ads we found
in the old newspapers about the Crossbones. I think they're still meeting.
I think my dad is one of them. Did I mention that I'm shaking right now?
I'm telling you, Sarah, stay away from the dredge. Don't go back there
tonight. We're getting too close.

I found out something else about the sounds I heard that night — I have
to get off-line but I'll send it later. I'm still figuring it out.

Stay put!!

Ryan

FRIDAY, SEPTEMBER 17, 9:40 P.M.

IS IT NORMAL TO GET IN THE HABIT OF ERASING EVERYTHING? I GET THE DISTINCT FEELING I'LL BE DOING IT FOR THE REST OF MY LIFE. I'LL GROW UP TO BE A CONSPIRACY THEORIST. THE GOVERNMENT WILL BE OUT TO GET ME. I'LL ERASE MY IDENTITY AND MOVE TO A SOUTH AMERICAN FISHING VILLAGE BUT THEY'LL TRACK ME DOWN AND DRAG ME BACK AND MY PARENTS WILL PUT ME IN A GROUP HOME.

I HATE TECHNOLOGY.

IT'S A GOOD THING I'M WRITING EVERYTHING ON GOOD OLD-FASHIONED PAPER. SOMEONE IS GOING TO FIND THIS AFTER I'M GONE. WHEN YOU GET TO THIS PART AND I'VE DISAPPEARED, GO BACK AND WATCH THE VIDEO OF WHEN I FELL. THE ONE WITH <u>THERAVEN</u> FOR A PASSWORD. LISTEN TO THOSE DISTANT SOUNDS OF METAL ON METAL. I DID. I LISTENED TO THE SOUNDS OVER AND OVER AGAIN, AND NOW I'LL NEVER FORGET THEM EVEN IF I TRY.

GO ON. GO BACK AND LISTEN.

I'M FEELING LESS GLOOMY AND MORE EDGY IN THE
LAST HALF HOUR. SURFING ONLINE ALWAYS HAS THAT
EFFECT ON ME. IT TENDS TO FRY MY NERVES. I FOUND
AN IMAGE WITH ALL THE MORSE CODE LETTERS AND I
READ ALL ABOUT HOW THE TAPS AND THE GAPS IN
SOUND ARE SUPPOSED TO WORK.

I FIGURED OUT THAT WHAT I HEARD ON THE DREDGE
WAS LIKE MORSE CODE, BUT NOT ENTIRELY THE SAME.
THE LONGER SOUND — THE ONE MADE BY THE DASH —
THAT ONE DOESN'T MATCH UP. THAT'S BEEN REPLACED
INSTEAD BY A DIFFERENT TONE. THERE ARE TWO
TONES ON THE DREDGE THAT REPRESENT THE DOTS
AND THE DASHES. I IMAGINE THE DOTS BEING A
HAMMER HITTING IRON, AND THE DASHES BEING A WRENCH
HITTING THE SAME SPOT. THE TWO SOUNDS ARE
DIFFERENT IN TONE INSTEAD OF LENGTH, SO IT STILL
WORKS.

THIS IS THE MESSAGE THAT PLAYED ON THE DREDGE
THE NIGHT I FELL:

.- .-. . | -.-- --- ..- | - .... . | .- .-.. -.-. .... . -- .. ... - |

THE DOTS ARE THE HAMMER, AND THE BARS ARE
THE WRENCH. THE MESSAGE ASKS A QUESTION.

Are you the alchemist?

Eerie, right? I'll admit — I'm freaking out. Because when I was measuring it all out, I didn't think it would add up to anything. I thought it would be nonsense.

But no.

It's a question.

Whatever asked the question was expecting an answer it didn't get. Sarah won't know the answer tonight any better than she did the night of the accident. Maybe the ghost of Old Joe Bush has a message for someone — the alchemist. It would be useful if I knew what an alchemist was.

And there's the piece of paper I found.

The Alchemist Diagram of 79 for Paul McCray

Paul McCray. That's my dad. So there's no doubt anymore. My dad is somehow entangled in this mess, and so is the Crossbones. Was my dad making the sounds? If so, maybe the ghost of Old Joe Bush is trying to make contact, trying to find something or someone.

Are you the alchemist?

What about Daryl Bonner? He looks like Old Joe Bush. He could be the alchemist.

What would happen if I knew the answer and I gave it to Old Joe Bush on the dredge? What would he tell me? What would he do to me?

Whatever it was that made the sounds that night saw Sarah and me as intruders in its secret domain. We didn't understand the question, so we didn't reply. And because of that, it got angry and came for me.

I need to make sure Sarah doesn't go back there again.

She can't go back.

Not ever.

Friday, September 17, 10:41 p.m.

My parents have turned in and Henry is in the guest room downstairs. It's been a long day of fishing, cards, and comfort food. They'll all be tired. I can't just sit here. Sarah could already be at the dredge or about to leave. I have to get out of here. The walk to her house isn't that far, half a mile. I could do it with my crutches. Maybe. I could tap on her window like the raven and she'd be safe because she wouldn't go. She's not the alchemist. She can't go in there if she's not the alchemist or she might never come out. I could wake up tomorrow morning and she'd be gone. No one would know where she went.

FRIDAY, SEPTEMBER 17, 11:46 P.M.

I MADE IT TO THE BOTTOM OF THE STAIRS THIS
TIME. IT WAS DARK, SO IT WAS SLOW GOING, BUT
I MADE IT WITHOUT KNOCKING ANYTHING OVER. I
BUMPED THE COFFEE TABLE WITH MY CAST AND
IT MADE A SOUND, BUT NO ONE STIRRED.

I OPENED THE FRONT DOOR TO THE PORCH
AS QUIETLY AS I COULD. THE SCREEN DOOR
REMAINED CLOSED IN FRONT OF ME, AND THIS I
KNEW WAS A MORE COMPLICATED MATTER. IT'S
OLD AND SQUEAKY. ANOTHER OF THOSE HOME
PROJECTS MY DAD NEVER GOT AROUND TO
FIXING. SO I WENT ABOUT OPENING THE SCREEN
DOOR VERY SLOWLY, UNTIL THERE WAS A GAP
BIG ENOUGH FOR ME AND MY LUMBERING CAST
TO FIT THROUGH.

IT GETS REALLY COLD AT THE BASE OF THE
MOUNTAIN AT NIGHT IN THE FALL — WE'RE AT

5,200 FEET. I WAS THINKING ABOUT HOW COLD IT MUST BE — WAS IT 30 OR 35 DEGREES OUTSIDE? SOMETHING LIKE THAT. 70 DURING THE DAY AND BITTER COLD AT NIGHT — THAT'S FALL IN SKELETON CREEK.

When I passed through the gap my cast touched the floorboards and they creaked. That's when I heard the voice.

"Hey, partner! Must be hot upstairs. Your mom's got the heat blasting in there."

It was Henry with a bottle in one hand, lying on the old couch, covered in an even older blanket.

"There's no air like this in New York. Not even one breath full."

"I never thought of it that way."

"Well, it's true. When I retire, I'm going to permanently plant my butt on this couch."

"Better talk to my mom. She might sell it."

"She wouldn't. Would she?"

We small-talked a little bit more and then I said I was going back to bed.

"Let me help you up those stairs."

"It's okay — really — I want to do it alone. If you hear a crash, come running. Otherwise, I'll be fine."

"Suit yourself."

I WENT BACK INSIDE, PAST THE LIVING ROOM AND THE DINING ROOM AND INTO THE KITCHEN AT THE BACK OF THE HOUSE. WE HAVE A YELLOW PHONE IN THERE THAT HANGS ON THE WALL, AND I DIALED SARAH'S NUMBER. I KNOW — STUPID — BUT I WAS OUT OF OPTIONS. IT WAS A TERRIBLE RISK, BUT I TRULY FELT SHE WAS IN TROUBLE. IF KEEPING HER SAFE MEANT GIVING HER UP, THEN I WAS READY TO PAY THAT PRICE.

IT RANG FOUR TIMES AND I ALMOST HUNG UP. SARAH'S MOM ANSWERED. SHE SOUNDED LIKE I WOKE HER.

"HELLO?"

ALREADY IT FELT LIKE A MISTAKE. BUT I HAD TO KEEP GOING.

"HI, MRS. FINCHER. IT'S ME, RYAN."

"ARE YOU OKAY? WHAT'S WRONG?"

"I WOKE UP WORRIED ABOUT SARAH. I DON'T KNOW WHY. COULD YOU DO ME A FAVOR AND MAKE SURE SHE'S OKAY?"

"HANG ON."

THERE WAS A LONG PAUSE IN WHICH I THOUGHT I

WOULD CRAWL OUT OF MY OWN SKIN. MY PARENTS
COULD COME DOWN ANY SECOND. SARAH COULD BE
GONE. HENRY COULD WALK IN. . . .

AFTER ABOUT TEN YEARS, SARAH'S MOM CAME
BACK ON THE LINE.

"SHE'S ASLEEP."

"OH, THAT'S GREAT. OKAY, I'M FINE NOW — SORRY
TO BOTHER YOU. REALLY SORRY."

"RYAN, YOU CAN'T BE CALLING HERE. YOU
KNOW THAT."

"PLEASE DON'T TELL MY PARENTS — I WAS JUST
WORRIED — I HAVEN'T TALKED TO HER IN A WHILE."

"HOW ARE YOU HOLDING UP?"

"GREAT! I'M JUST GREAT, MRS. FINCHER. THE LEG
FEELS MUCH BETTER. THANKS FOR ASKING."

"GOOD NIGHT, RYAN."

"NIGHT."

I DON'T THINK SHE'S GOING TO TELL THEM. OR
MAYBE THAT'S JUST MY HOPE TALKING.

I WENT BACK TO MY ROOM AS QUIETLY AS I COULD,
WHICH TOOK A LONG TIME. WHEN I GOT BACK IN BED, I
FELT A WAVE OF RELIEF.

Now, reading this over, I'm not sure. I think I did the right thing.

All the other troubles in my life don't matter as long as I know Sarah is safe.

The truth about Skeleton Creek is not worth dying for.

Saturday, September 18, 7:21 p.m.

I don't remember falling asleep. I woke to find this journal sitting at the foot of my bed with the pen tucked inside. Did I do that? I don't think I did. Someone came in here and read it.

There's no other explanation.

I know this because I don't put the pen in like that and because I would never set it on the edge of my bed. It was Dad or Mom. Either way, I'm doomed. It's so much harder to be careful when I'm too tired to keep my eyes open.

SATURDAY, SEPTEMBER 18, 7:35 A.M.

I JUST CHECKED MY EMAIL, AND SARAH'S SENT ME
ANOTHER VIDEO.

SARAHFINCHER.COM
PASSWORD:
PETERQUINT

141

Saturday, September 18, 7:38 a.m.

She's driving me crazy! Someone needs to get her under control. I can't believe she actually went to the dredge — and that she's planning on going back.

Doesn't she understand why I called last night?

Doesn't she realize she could get hurt? Or worse?

And I can't believe she's going to make me wait to see what she found out yesterday. That's such a Sarah thing to do — make me feel even more stuck than I felt before. It makes me furious when she holds out on me. She knows that. What I want to do is get my crutches and walk to her house. I'd tell her face-to-face to stop feeding me information with a spoon. What am I, a two-year-old? And while I was at it, I'd tell her to stop being so reckless. It's the same thing all over again, only this time it will be her that gets hurt.

(Is it me, or am I starting to sound a lot like my dad?)

142

SOMETIMES I FEEL LIKE SARAH IS A LIT MATCH AND I'M A STICK OF DYNAMITE. WHATEVER IT IS THAT'S DRAWING US TOGETHER WILL EVENTUALLY LEAD TO AN EXPLOSION.

No, WAIT — THAT'S NOT IT — IT'S DIFFERENT. IT'S MORE LIKE SARAH AND I ARE POLAR OPPOSITES BEING PULLED TOWARD THE SAME DANGEROUS MIDDLE. WHY CAN'T WE BE DRAWN TOGETHER BY SOMETHING SAFE — LIKE RAISING A COW FOR THE STATE FAIR?

WHY DOES EVERYTHING HAVE TO BE SO DANGEROUS?

143

Saturday, September 18, 8:15 a.m.

Because a cow is a dull animal and raising one would be a dull undertaking.

Dangerous is more exciting.

SATURDAY, SEPTEMBER 18, 8:35 A.M.

THE TRUTH IS I'M JUST MAD BECAUSE I CAN'T STAND IT THAT SHE'S HAVING ALL THE ADVENTURE AND I'M STUCK AT HOME WITH THIS STUPID CAST AND MY MEDDLING PARENTS. SHE'S MY BEST FRIEND AND IT'S HARD TO BE APART AND TO WORRY ABOUT HER. AND PLUS I MISS HER AND I GUESS I'M LONELY.

I'M GOING ONLINE TO FIGURE OUT WHAT AN ALCHEMIST IS.

Saturday, September 18, 8:55 a.m.

I've got a lot of studying to do. Alchemy is . . . deep and wide. Precious metals like gold and silver play an important part. Very interesting.

Today I have to drive all the way into the city with my mom to see the doctor. He's on call on Saturday mornings, so it worked out to have Mom drive me when she didn't have to work. We're leaving in half an hour, so I've only had time to print out a chart I found. I'm sticking it in here. I need to send an email to Sarah, too, so she can see this.

He's going to let me get out more — the doctor, I mean. I'm sure of it. Then I'll feel better. Then I can do more. I could be useful. I could look around town for the alchemist or the secret society. I could even go to the dredge if I wanted to.

I've felt this way before. I know what's going on here.

Sarah's dragging me back in again.

This is what I just wrote to her.

~~Sarah,~~

I'm out all day visiting the doctor but I'll be back by six and I'll go straight ~~to my room so I can see what you've found. I wish you'd just told me. When~~ I find things, I tell you right away — why can't you do the same? I understand you want to show me, not tell me, when you discover things, but it's ~~frustrating from over here!~~

I can get around better. I'm getting used to walking. I'm slow, and stairs are a problem, but I can definitely get out of the house. If you go to the dredge again, I want in. I'm not letting you go out there all by yourself anymore. We have to stick together, even if it feels like the whole world is trying to keep us apart.

Someone was sending us a message that night, but we didn't understand it. Do you remember the clanging sounds? Henry told me the workers used to bang on metal to tell each other things because the machinery ~~was so loud. Those sounds that night — they were a question.~~

Are you the alchemist?

I found the attached file this morning at an alchemy site. I'm not sure what to make of it.

Do you see it? Do you see the birdie?

Let's stay together on this, okay? No more running around at night alone in the woods.

Ryan.

AND THEN I SHOWED HER THE SYMBOLS.

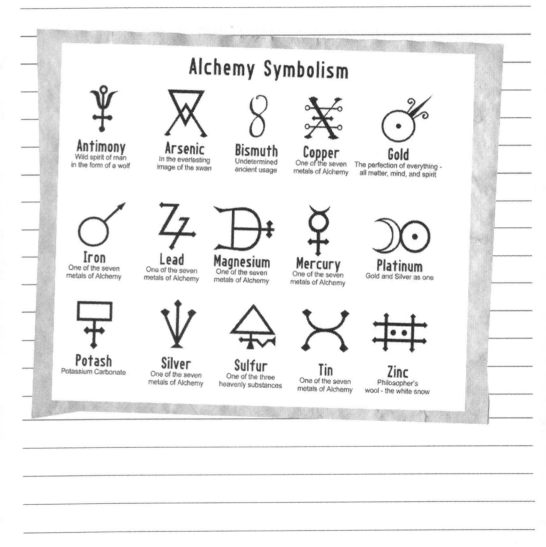

Alchemy Symbolism

Antimony
Wild spirit of man
in the form of a wolf

Arsenic
In the everlasting
image of the swan

Bismuth
Undetermined
ancient usage

Copper
One of the seven
metals of Alchemy

Gold
The perfection of everything -
all matter, mind, and spirit

Iron
One of the seven
metals of Alchemy

Lead
One of the seven
metals of Alchemy

Magnesium
One of the seven
metals of Alchemy

Mercury
One of the seven
metals of Alchemy

Platinum
Gold and Silver as one

Potash
Potassium Carbonate

Silver
One of the seven
metals of Alchemy

Sulfur
One of the three
heavenly substances

Tin
One of the seven
metals of Alchemy

Zinc
Philosopher's
wool - the white snow

We have a minivan, which my dad hates and will not drive. I personally like minivans. If you ask me, they get a bad rap. I like that both rows of seats come out and, with the doors shut, a whole sofa fits in there. I can see where that would be handy. And when we go on a long drive, there's room to roam. I don't have to sit in one place all the time. I'm restless, so I appreciate the options.

Having a really long cast on my leg has given me a whole new reason to appreciate the spaciousness of this vehicle. Henry and my dad took the middle seats out and I'm sitting all the way in the back. Plenty of room to rest my leg, and I can write in peace back here. The suspension on this van is really pretty good. A writer can tell.

Saturday, September 18, 1:15 p.m.

Okay I'm alone in the examining room, or whatever they call it. Since I didn't want to risk anyone seeing the journal, I'm writing this in a regular notebook. I'll paste these pages (and the page from the van) into the journal later.

This was definitely a good idea. Because when I took the notebook out to write about the minivan — not exactly the most controversial of subjects — Mom kept looking in the rearview mirror. I could tell she wanted to know what I was writing. Maybe she was extra curious because she was the one who sneaked in and looked at my journal before. Maybe she was thinking she'd have to take a look at this new one soon.

It's the pits not being able to trust your own parents.

Finally, while I was writing about the van's suspension, she came right out and asked, "What're you writing there, Ryan?"

"Just stories," I said. "Maybe I'll show them to you one day."

"So you keep telling me."

I pretended to joke with her. "Then you haven't read them?" I said lightly.

Her tone was just as jokey. "Nope. Too busy feeding Henry and sorting mail."

"So I can trust you?"

Then she got all serious.

"It's like faith," she said. "You just have to believe. I can't prove it to you."

This was, I think, a good answer.

"Do you think dad has read my stories?" I ventured.

She met my eye briefly in the rearview mirror, then looked back to the road. "If he has, he's the biggest hypocrite in three counties. You know how he respects privacy. Worth its weight in gold, right?"

"Right."

We drove a little bit more in silence. I wondered what she was thinking, because the next thing she asked was, "Have you emailed Sarah?"

I lied and told her I hadn't.

"Trust goes both ways, you know," she said.

I told her I knew.

Being friends with Sarah makes me a liar.

There's no way around it.

Why does everything have to be so complicated?

Saturday, September 18, 5:20 p.m.

Driving home now.

Mom is watching. But I'm too far back for her to be able to read anything.

Everything went fine at the hospital. The doctor cut the hard cast off my leg and replaced it with one that straps on even tighter than plaster. He made me promise to keep it on unless I'm in the shower (and even there I have to sit down on a chair). I asked the doctor if I could keep the cast and he said I could. I'm very excited to get home and surprise Henry with it.

The doctor wants me to start walking around more, which is both good and bad since I'll probably be going to the dredge tonight. Good because I'll have a little more mobility with the lighter leg brace, bad because I'm more likely to reinjure myself if I have a reason to run away.

It's been a quiet drive home and I've been thinking about everything. So much has piled up in the past couple of days, I haven't taken the time to try and piece it all together. I'm afraid of going back, especially at night. I don't want to

SEE OLD JOE BUSH COME OUT OF THE BLACK POND. WHAT IF HE GRABS ME THIS TIME? EVER SINCE I TOLD SARAH I'D GO WITH HER, I'VE BEEN THINKING THAT HE'LL GET ME AND DRAG ME DOWN INTO THE WATER WITH HIM. WHAT A NIGHTMARE.

I FEEL CERTAIN EVERYTHING IS CONNECTED, LIKE SARAH SAID. THE DREDGE, MY DAD, THE CROSSBONES, THE ALCHEMIST, THE GHOST OF OLD JOE BUSH, EVEN RANGER BONNER. I'M STARTING TO WORK ON A THEORY I'LL TELL SARAH TONIGHT.

THE WORST THING I HAVE TO FACE IS THAT THE DREDGE REALLY IS HAUNTED, AND THAT I PROBABLY HAVE TO GO BACK THERE. I WONDER IF I'LL DRAG MY LEG, AND OLD JOE BUSH WILL THINK I'M MAKING FUN OF HIM. HE WON'T LIKE THAT.

SATURDAY, SEPTEMBER 18, 7:10 P.M.

THERE ARE TOO MANY PEOPLE AROUND. I CAN'T RISK CHECKING THE COMPUTER. I BARELY MADE IT OFF THE PORCH!

OKAY — I'LL ADMIT IT.
I'M HIDING IN THE BATHROOM, SO I CAN AT LEAST HAVE TIME TO WRITE A FEW THINGS DOWN.
I AM DYING TO GET TO MY ROOM AND HEAR FROM SARAH. I CAN ONLY HOPE MY MOM AND DAD DON'T GO UP THERE, CHECK MY EMAIL, AND SEE THAT SARAH HAS SENT ME A VIDEO TO WATCH. THAT WOULD BE A CATASTROPHE.
BUT THEY'RE PRETTY BUSY RIGHT NOW, SO I THINK I'M OKAY.
HENRY AND DAD CAUGHT TWO MONSTER STEELHEAD TODAY AND DECIDED TO HAVE A FISH FEED ON THE FRONT PORCH. I HATE FISH FEEDS. ABOUT A MILLION NEIGHBORS HAVE COME OVERR WITH POTATO SALAD, COLESLAW, BAKED BEANS, AND POTATO CHIPS.

I'VE BEEN SITTING ON THE GOLD COUCH FOR OVER AN

HOUR SUFFERING QUESTION AFTER QUESTION ABOUT MY

ACCIDENT. NOBODY WANTS TO COME RIGHT OUT AND

ASK WHAT I WAS DOING AT THE DREDGE, BUT I CAN TELL

THEY WANT TO KNOW. I CAN TELL THEY HAVE

THEORIES.

NOBODY MENTIONS SARAH'S NAME. ALL THESE

NEIGHBORS WHO'VE SEEN US GROW UP TOGETHER.

NOT A SINGLE ONE.

I KNOW I CAN'T STAY IN HERE FOREVER, BUT IT'S

THE ONLY PLACE PEOPLE WILL LEAVE ME ALONE. IT'S

COOLING DOWN OUTSIDE, BUT A FISH FEED IS A BIG DEAL

IN A TOWN AS DULL AS SKELETON CREEK. NO ONE'S

LIKELY TO LEAVE UNTIL THEIR TEETH START

CHATTERING. THERE'S AN OPPRESSIVE FEELING OF

SECRECY IN THE AIR, AND IT'S INTENSIFIED BY THE SIZE

OF THE CROWD.

WHEN I WAS FIVE, DAD TOOK ME FISHING ON THE

CREEK. HE HOOKED A NICE TROUT AND HANDED ME THE

ROD. WE DRAGGGED IT IN TOGETHER, HIS BIG HAND OVER MINE ON THE REEL. THEN HE TOOK THE FISH OFF THE HOOK AND BASHED ITS HEAD AGAINST A ROCK UNTIL IT WAS DEAD. I CRIED ALL THE WAY HOME.

I ALWAYS THROW ALL MY FISH BACK. AFTER I CATCH THEM, I MEAN — I THROW THEM BACK.

I'D RATHER HOLD A FISH UNDERWATER AFTER I CATCH IT AND LET IT PUMP ITS GILLS IN MY HAND UNTIL IT'S READY TO SWIM OFF. I TALK TO THE FISH I CATCH: BE CAREFUL NOW. I'M A NICE FISHERMAN, BUT THE NEXT GUY MIGHT TAKE YOU HOME AND COOK YOU. TELL YOUR BUDDIES.

IT MAKES ME SAD THE WAY WE KILL THINGS WITHOUT ANY REASON. WHY BEAT THE LIFE OUT OF A WILD TROUT WHEN THERE'S PERFECTLY GOOD CANNED TUNA DOWN AT THE STORE?

HENRY IS HAVING A POKER PARTY TONIGHT. HE WAS THRILLED TO HAVE MY OLD CAST AT HIS DISPOSAL AND THANKED ME ENDLESSLY. CARDS WILL PROBABLY GO UNITL ABOUT MIDNIGHT, WHICH MEANS IT WON'T BE SAFE FOR ME

TO LEAVE THE HOUSE FOR A LONG TIME.

I NEED TO TELL SARAH.

GLADYS THE LIBRARIAN SHOWED UP AT THE FISH FEED WITH A BAG OF CARROTS. SHE CAME OVER A HALF HOUR AGO AND HELD ONE OUT TO ME.

"EAT ONE OF THESE. IT'LL HELP YOU SEE TROUBLE COMING," SHE SAID.

ALL I COULD SPUTTER OUT WAS, "YES MA'AM."

I GOT THE CHILLS WHEN SHE TURNED TO GO. I WAS THINKING IN TERMS OF THE ALCHEMIST DIAGRAM OF 79.

THE FLOOR AND 7TH, FOUR PAST THE NINE ON DOOR NUMBER TWO = LIBRARY ATTIC, ENTER THROUGH THE ALLEY DOOR MARKED 213.

I FEEL LIKE SHE'S INVOLVED. BUT HOW?

OUR PARK RANGER, DARYL BONNER, ALSO SHOWED UP. IT WAS STRANGE TO SEE HIM, BECAUSE I HAD TO PRETEND I DIDN'T KNOW WHAT HE LOOKED LIKE. I ACTUALLY WENT OUT OF MY WAY TO ASK MY DAD WHO HE WAS. LUCKILY, HE WASN'T WEARING A PARK RANGER OUTFIT OR ANYTHING, SO I didn't sound too out of it. He brought a frozen Gardenburger with him, and my dad dropped it on the grill like a hockey puck. The two of them talked quietly until Henry came over and gave Bonner a hard time.

"Those are made of dog food," Henry said. "Did you know that?"

"I hadn't heard."

All three of them swigged their drinks and stared at the hockey puck on the grill.

"We just had our fourth player drop out. Care to play cards tonight?"

"I'd be delighted."

"Bring one of those frozen Frisbees. I have an idea I could use one."

Being new in town, Daryl has no idea that Henry might be duct-taping the frozen Gardenburger to his forehead before the night is over. I feel a little sorry for him.

And I also feel really strange that we're under the same roof.

I think I'm going to tell my mom I'm tired.

Maybe she'll let me go upstairs and lie down.

There's enough noise that it'll make sense for my door to be closed.

I just hope they won't realize it's also locked.

Saturday, September 18, 7:30 p.m.

My clothes smell like fried fish, which makes me mad at Henry and Dad for going on a killing spree on the river today. You'd think grown men would know better.

It doesn't seem like anyone's been in here. I mean, Dad's been with Henry and I've been with Mom. I should be safe. Plus, they assume there's no activity because I haven't been here. But Sarah's sent me a new password. Finally I'll get to see what she hinted at this morning.

Ryan,

Nice detective work on the alchemist chart. Did you know 79 is the chemical element number for gold? I looked it up. I guess it should stand to reason that everything secret in this town would revolve around gold. Do you think there's a hidden stash of it somewhere?

Sorry I've been mysterious about showing you this, but you're right - it has to be shown, not told.

More talk in the video, especially about visiting the dredge. Password: lucywestenra

Sarah.

I've heard that name – Lucy Westenra – but I can't place it. Who is that? Peter Quint, I knew – but Lucy . . . I know I've heard that name before. I'll have to look it up later.

Now, I have to go watch a video.

SARAHFINCHER.COM
PASSWORD:
LUCYWESTENRA

Saturday, September 18, 7:55 p.m.

This is too much.

Sarah thinks Joe Bush was killed by the Alchemist.

But we don't know who the alchemist is, or even if there's only one of them.

And she thinks Joe Bush's ghost is guarding something. Well, not exactly guarding. He's haunting the place where the alchemist keeps his secrets. Waiting to take revenge.

But what about the dredge? Waht about that secret handle she seems to have found, which appears to have vanished between then and now, in a place that was supposedly untouched?

What about what I saw?

She can't go back there.

It's too dangerous.

Especially if she's alone.

I can't believe I'm even thinking about going back.

IN MY CONDITION.

BUT THERE WON'T BE ANY WAY TO STOP HER, SHORT OF CALLING IN OUR PARENTS. AND I CAN'T DO THAT. THAT WOULD BE THE END OF EVERYTHING. I HAVE TO GET THERE MYSELF.

IT'S ALREADY DARK. PRETTY SOON SOMEONE WILL BE WEARING MY CAST AT THE POKER TABLE, HOLDING THEIR CARDS WITH OVEN MITTS. I CAN GO DOWN THERE AND WATCH FOR AN HOUR AND SEE IF I CAN GUESS HOW LATE THEY'LL GO. SOME OF THE PLAYERS ARE PRETTY OLD, SO HOPEFULLY THINGS WILL BREAK UP BY MIDNIGHT. WHICH WILL GIVE ME OVER AN HOUR.

OKAY, I JUST EMAILED SARAH. THIS IS WHAT I SAID.

Sarah,

I'm going with you and that's final. Pick me up in the alley behind the house at 1:45AM. I'll be the the one with the brace on his leg.

Can't wait to see you.

Ryan

Saturday, September 18, 10:00 p.m.

I just went downstairs without telling anyone so I could see how fast I'd get to the bottom without making any noise or falling on my face. No one saw me, so I did it twice. The second time was slower and more painful than the first, but that was mostly because I'd just come back up and I was winded. The brace is still big and heavy but I can move a little better. I think I can do this. If I take one of the crutches with me I'll be fine.

When I arrived on the porch, the poker game was in full swing. The burn barrel had been moved up next to the card table where it blazed with warmth and orange light. Ranger Bonner was wearing a football helmet, and when he nodded in my direction it wobbled up and down over his brow. I felt like everyone was taking turns staring at me, like they were trying to have a good time but my being there made them suspicious. Ranger Bonner and my dad especially.

They kept glancing at each other, then at me. It was very unnerving.

I felt like I was ruining Henry's card game, so I lied and said I was turning in for the night. No one tried to stop me.

I give it another hour — two at the most — and my mom will tell everyone to clear out.

No word yet from Sarah. Where is she?

Saturday, September 18, 11:00 p.m.

The card game broke up early and I'm getting a bad case of the shakes. It's dark outside. My window is a sheet of black in which I keep imagining Old Joe Bush's face peering in, watching me, water dripping off his nose. Or is it blood? I can't tell. It's too dark out there.

That's one thing about a very small town: it's extremely dark at night. Ther are only three streetlights and none of them are near my front door. The moon is also absent tonight, so I'm sure the woods will be especially dark.

That is, if I make it to the woods. Getting out of the house is going to be a trick. Our house was built about a million years ago and it makes old house sounds, the kind that wake parents up. There are seven squeaky steps on the staircase alone.

My hands are so clammy I keep having to stop writing and wipe them on my sheet.

I'M NOT SURE I CAN DO THIS.

FINALLY, AN EMAIL.

Ryan,

Come and see. Password: miltonarbogast

Sarah.

SARAHFINCHER.COM
PASSWORD:
MILTONARBOGAST

Saturday, September 18, 12:22 p.m.

It appears that I'll be sneaking out of the house tonight to see the one person my parents have forbidden me to associate with. The two of us will wander off into the woods at 1:00 in the morning and cut through a chain so we can break into a condemned structure before they burn it down. And, meanwhile, her camera will be feeding the footage back to her web site so that if we don't come back, the authorities can — what was her phrase? — oh, yeah — find our bodies.

Has Sarah lost it?

What am I doing?

If I get caught, my parents won't just move me to a new town, they'll ground me for a hundred years and feed me boiled beans for breakfast, lunch, and dinner for the rest of my life.

Even still, I almost wish I'd get caught. The alternative is definitely worse.

The dredge at night. I'm not even there yet

AND I CAN ALREADY FEEL THE HAUNTED PRESENCE OF A

GHOST DRAGGING ITS LEG IN MY DIRECTION, ASKING ME

QUESTIONS I CAN'T ANSWER. AND THIS TIME, WHEN THE

GHOST OF OLD JOE BUSH COMES FOR ME, I WON'T BE

ABLE TO RUN AWAY.

Ryan,

We're on - meet me where I said at one, then we'll go straight to the dredge.
Check the webcam from your computer (I'll send you the password in a seperate
email). and email me back. You should see me waving.

Delete!! - Sarah

Sunday, September 19, 12:33 A.M.

I checked the site and saw her waving and now I have to go. I'm confused by this turn of events.

My hands are shaking and I can hardly hold my pen. I know why I'm shaking so badly. It's the same reason why I have to go to the dredge tonight. I think Old Joe Bush has snuck into my brain, because there's a nightmare I keep having. Every night I have the nightmare, only I don't tell anyone — I don't even write it down — because it's a really bad one. It's the kind that if someone reads it, they think you're crazy.

Sarah is in the nightmare. We're together on the dredge, going up the decayed stairs. When we reach the top she turns to me and leans in like she's going to kiss me. I'm so surprised by this I lean back and lose my balance and I grab for her arm. The rotted railing breaks free behind me and I can't let her go, even though I try. It's like electricity is holding us together. We're two magnets falling. We roll through the air and she lands beneath me. There is the sound of

smashing bones and then I wake up.

Sunday, September 19, 12:39 a.m.

I just had to stop and think for a second.

I remember struggling over the beginning of this story, rewriting it a dozen times.

There was a moment not long ago when I thought: This is it. I'm dead.

I remember how that opening set just the right tone. The reader would know that something bad had happened, but they wouldn't know what it was. Things came easy after that, but were confusing, too. The Sarah nightmare bothered me.

Now I feel as if I'm driving around at night in the middle of nowhere. I've lost my sense of direction. Did I have all the videos before? Have I been retracing my steps and she's already gone? Maybe tonight is the last chapter of a story I've already lived through.

I'm going to assume for the moment that the nightmare of Sarah crushed beneath me is just that — a nightmare — and that all of what I've been writing is

175

REAL. I'M GOING TO MAKE THIS GUESS BECAUSE IF WHAT I'VE

BEEN WRITING IS NOT THE TRUTH, THEN MY MIND IS TRYING TO

HIDE SOMETHING FROM ME. IF I'VE BEEN MAKING ALL THIS UP

AND SOMETHING HAPPENED TO SARAH AND IT'S MY FAULT, THEN

I WON'T BE ABLE TO LIVE WITH MYSELF.

I'M GOING TO STAND UP AND PUT ALL MY WEIGHT ON MY

ONE GOOD LEG AND START DOWN THE DARKENED HALL TOWARD

THE STAIRS. WHEN I LOOK OVER MY SHOULDER, OLD JOE

BUSH WILL BE OUTSIDE, STARING THROUGH MY BEDROOM

WINDOW WITH THE RAVEN ON HIS SHOULDER. HE'LL BE

WATCHING ME LEAVE SO THAT HE CAN GO TO THE DREDGE

AHEAD OF ME AND WAIT FOR MY ARRIVAL. HE'S FASTER ON ONE

GOOD LEG THAN I AM.

WHEN I REACH THE OPENING TO THE STAIRCASE, MY

HEART WILL BE POUNDING AND I'LL LOOK DOWN AND SEE THAT

THERE IS NO LIGHT. IT WILL BE A LONG FALL IF I MISS A STEP.

MY HAND WILL BE SWEATY AND IT WILL SLIDE WHEN I HOLD

THE BANISTER. I FEEL LIKE I KNOW THIS ALREADY, LIKE I'VE

DONE IT ALL BEFORE.

WORDS AND SOUNDS WILL TUMBLE IN MY TROUBLED

MIND.

THE CROSSBONES. ARE YOU THE ALCHEMIST? DARYL BONNER. GLADYS WITH HER SHOTGUN. OLD JOE BUSH. IS THAT MY DAD'S NAME ON THE PAPER? A KISS. THE SOUND OF SMASHING BONES.

AND HANGING OVER IT ALL WILL BE THE ONE WORD — GOLD. IT'S ALL ABOUT THE GOLD, I KNOW IT IS. SOMEONE KILLED JOE BUSH FOR THE GOLD AND NOW JOE WANTS REVENGE. HE WON'T REST UNTIL HE GETS WHAT HE WANTS.

IT WILL BE A SLOW JOURNEY THROUGH A QUIET HOUSE AND I HAVE NO CHOICE BUT TO LEAVE. I HAVE TWENTY MINUTES AND IT WILL TAKE EVERY BIT TO SNEAK OUT OF HEAR. I WANT TO TAKE THIS JOURNAL WITH ME BUT I CAN'T. IT WILL MEAN I'VE LEFT THE STORY BEHIND FOR SURE AND RETURNED TO THE REAL WORLD. I'M LEAVING IT FOLDED INTO MY SHEETS SO THEY'LL FIND IT IN THE MORNING IF I'M NOT HERE.

PLEASE — IF YOU FIND THIS — GO TO SARAHFINCHER.COM. USE THE PASSWORD TANGINABARRONS.

THERE YOU'LL SEE WHAT HAPPENS NEXT TO ME AND SARAH.

I'VE GOT TO GO NOW.

SARAHFINCHER.COM
PASSWORD:
TANGINABARRONS

PATRICK CARMAN's
GHOST IN THE MACHINE

PC STUDIO

WATCH THIS FIRST!

SARAHFINCHER.COM
PASSWORD:
LEONARDSHELBY

Sunday, September 19, after midnight

Am I really doing this?

What's taking her so long?

It's cold in here.

I can't go down there again.

Birdie carved in wood under the gears. Why?

Careful now.

You have been warned.

Remove this Cryptix and suffer the consequence.

When curiosity meets deadly explosive force.

That sound again — not the steps — something else.

Sarah's eyes are big. She's terrified.

I couldn't see it.

I only felt it.

Don't make me come looking for you.

Francis Palmer. Jordan Hooke. Wilson Boyle.

Hector Newton. Joseph Bush. Dad.

Gladys. The Apostle. Dr. Watts.

Sunday, September 19, 7:20 a.m.

How did I get back in my room?

The last thing I remember really clearly is standing at the top of the stairs in the dredge and looking down. After that, everything is fuzzy around the edges. Something about seeing my own bloodstain on those old floorboards sort of did me in.

So it was shock. That's it — I was in shock. My brain was smart enough to shut down. I was a zombie, more or less.

I sure looked like one on that video.

I can piece this together. Between the video and my notes from the dredge, I'm sure I can do this. Brand-new journal, brand-new memories. I'm glad I started with a blank slate. It's like a new lease on life. This is totally going to work.

I remember walking up the alley and there she was, standing in the headlights with her camera on. I didn't realize how much I missed seeing her until I shuffled up on my crutches like an idiot and gave her the lamest hug ever.

I REMEMBER GETTING IN HER CAR AND FEELING VERY NERVOUS AS WE LEFT THE ALLEY, LIKE I WAS GOING TO THROW UP. SARAH DIDN'T WANT BONNER DRIVING AROUND AND SEEING HER CAR AND MAYBE COMING AFTER US IN THE MIDDLE OF THE NIGHT, SO WE PARKED A LONG WAY FROM THE TRAILHEAD. THIS MADE THE ENDLESS WALK THROUGH THE WOODS SEEM EVEN LONGER. LET ME TELL YOU, DRAGGING A WRAPPED-UP LEG THROUGH THE WOODS IS NO PICNIC. IT'S A LONG HOOF OUT THERE — I MEAN REALLY LONG. BY THE TIME WE GOT THERE I WAS THINKING WE'D MADE A BIG MISTAKE.

I'M SURE THAT'S WHY I SCRIBBLED AM I REALLY DOING THIS? AT THE TOP OF THE FIRST PAGE OF THIS NEW JOURNAL. (FOR OBVIOUS REASONS, I DIDN'T WANT TO TAKE THE OLD ONE WITH ME AND RISK IT BEING LOST OR, I DON'T KNOW, CAPTURED.) AND THOSE NEXT WORDS — WHAT'S TAKING HER SO LONG? — I REMEMBER THOSE WORDS, TOO. WE'D FINALLY ARRIVED AT THE DREDGE, AND SARAH LEFT ME ALONE WITH THE CAMERA. I PANNED IT OVER EACH OF THE WINDOWS IN THE DREDGE WHILE I WAITED FOR HER TO COME BACK AND TELL ME SHE'D CUT THE LOCK ON THE DOOR. I

DIDN'T WANT TO SEE A GHOST IN ONE OF THOSE WINDOWS, BUT I COULDN'T STOP LOOKING FOR ONE. WHEN SARAH CAME BACK, I FOLLOWED HER DOWN THE LAST PART OF THE PATH.

BEFORE I KNEW IT, WE WERE INSIDE.

<u>IT'S COLD IN HERE.</u>

I REMEMBER THINKING IT WAS CHILLY. SEPTEMBER IN SKELETON CREEK IS PRECEDED BY A LONG WARM SUMMER THAT LULLS YOU TO SLEEP. THEN <u>BANG</u>, THE COLD NIGHTS SHOW UP OUT OF NOWHERE LIKE A SCREEN DOOR IN YOUR FACE.

SO IT WAS COLD IN THE DREDGE, AND THAT'S WHY SARAH WAS TALKING WITH A TINY PATTERN OF STARTS AND STOPS IN HER VOICE. IT WASN'T BECAUSE SHE WAS AFRAID. SHE WAS COLD.

<u>I CAN'T GO DOWN THERE AGAIN.</u>

THIS IS WHERE THE SHOCK SET IN, I'M PRETTY SURE. I DIDN'T SAY I COULDN'T GO DOWN THE STAIRS AGAIN, BUT WHEN WE REACHED THE TOP, I KNEW I COULDN'T DO IT. STAIRS WERE A BAD OMEN IN EVERY ALFRED HITCHCOCK MOVIE I'D EVER SEEN, A PRELUDE TO SOMETHING SINISTER ABOUT TO HAPPEN. AND WHAT WAS MUCH WORSE, THIS WAS THE PLACE I'D HAD THE

184

ACCIDENT AND ALMOST DIED. THAT WAS IT FOR ME. IT WAS EITHER GET OUT BY ANOTHER WAY OR DIE TRYING. I REMEMBER HOW IT FELT TO BE BACK THERE, SORT OF LIKE SOMEONE HAD CUT OFF THE OXYGEN TO MY LUNGS AND LEFT ME FOR DEAD. I FLOATED THROUGH THE REST AND THEN I WOKE UP IN MY BED.

I STILL CAN'T BELIEVE EVERYTHING ON THAT VIDEO. SOMEHOW MY ZOMBIE FORM ARRIVED INSIDE THE SECRET ROOM. SEEING THAT VIDEO REMINDED ME OF SOMETHING. I SAW THE BIRDIE CARVED IN WOOD. I REMEMBER LEANING OVER INTO THE GEARS INSTINCTIVELY AND GLANCING DOWN INTO THE OPENING. THERE'S A MEMORY PACKED IN FROZEN STORAGE SOMEWHERE IN WHICH I'VE DONE THIS BEFORE. I CAN'T CRACK THE ICE, BUT IT'S THERE.

WHAT JOLTED ME BACK TO REALITY? IT MUST HAVE BEEN SEEING SARAH TURNING THE DIALS AT THE SAME TIME I WAS READING THE WARNING ABOUT THE WHOLE PLACE EXPLODING. IT WAS LIKE SHE HAD A STICK OF LIT DYNAMITE IN HER HAND.

STOP TOUCHING IT!

I SCREAMED THESE WORDS, OR AT LEAST I THOUGHT I DID. BUT WATCHING THE VIDEO, I SEE THAT I ONLY

SCREAMED IN MY HEAD. I HATE THAT I CAN'T TRUST WHAT I SAW AND WHAT I FELT. IT'S LIKE A REPEAT OF THE NIGHT I FELL, WITH EVERYTHING GRAYED OUT. I STILL CAN'T REMEMBER THE RIGHT ORDER OR WHETHER CERTAIN THINGS HAPPENED OR NOT. THE SCARIEST THING ABOUT WATCHING SARAH'S VIDEOS IS THAT I DON'T ALWAYS KNOW WHAT'S COMING NEXT.

THAT SOUND AGAIN.

OKAY, THIS I RECALL PERFECTLY. I'VE READ THOSE THREE WORDS ON THE FIRST PAGE OF THIS JOURNAL FOUR OR FIVE TIMES ALREADY, AND EVERY TIME I HEAR THE SAME SOUNDS. IT'S LIKE A SOUNDTRACK. THAT SOUND AGAIN, THAT SOUND AGAIN, THAT SOUND AGAIN. I CAN'T DESCRIBE IT, BUT I HEARD IT AT LEAST TWICE IN THE VIDEO. ONCE WHEN WE WERE IN THE ALLEY AND ONCE WHEN I SAW THE BIRDIE. I NEED TO WATCH THAT VIDEO AGAIN BECAUSE I CAN'T SAY FOR SURE IF THE SOUND IS REALLY THERE OR NOT. IT'S LIKE I SEE THINGS — THE GHOST OR THE BIRDIE — AND I HEAR THE SOUND. AM I HEARING IT IN MY HEAD? IS THERE SOME SORT OF VISUAL CUE THAT'S MAKING MY BRAIN CREATE THE SOUND? OR IS THE SOUND REALLY THERE?

I SCRIBBLED THE NAMES. ALL OF THEM. BUT HERE'S THE STRANGE PART: I DON'T REMEMBER WHEN I WROTE THE NAMES DOWN. IT'S AN AWFUL LOT TO REMEMBER, ALL THOSE NAMES, BUT I DON'T THINK I WROTE THEM UNTIL LATER. BELIEVE IT OR NOT, I THINK I WOKE UP IN THE DARK IN MY OWN BED AND DID IT. I'VE ACTUALLY DONE THIS BEFORE, WHEN I WAS SMALL. I USED TO DO IT ALL THE TIME. I'D WAKE UP WHEN I WAS FIVE OR SIX YEARS OLD AND FIND THAT I'D DRAWN THE WORDS GREEN EGZ HAM IN CRAYON ON THE WALL IN THE MIDDLE OF THE NIGHT.

"WHY DID YOU DO THAT?" MY DAD WOULD ASK IN THE MORNING.

"I WAS ASLEEP. SOMEONE ELSE DID IT."

"WE'VE TOLD YOU NOT TO WRITE ON YOUR WALLS," DAD WOULD SAY, ALL STERN LIKE HE WAS GOING TO PUNISH ME.

"I DIDN'T DO IT," I'D INSIST.

"IS THAT SO? THEN WHO DID?"

"DID YOU LOCK THE DOORS LAST NIGHT?"

MY DAD (AND MY MOM, FOR THAT MATTER) KNEW THEN WHAT THEY KNOW NOW: I COULD TALK THEM INTO

THEIR GRAVES IF THEY LET ME. I COULD GO ON AND ON

ABOUT WHETHER THEY LOCKED THE WINDOWS AND

CHECKED EVERY ROOM AND FLUSHED THE TOILETS AND

A HUNDRED OTHER THINGS THAT MIGHT OR MIGHT NOT

HAVE TO DO WITH HOW MY WALLS GOT COVERED IN

PURPLE CRAYON.

"STOP WRITING ON YOUR WALLS."

THAT'S ALL MY DAD HAD THE ENERGY TO SAY

ONCE HE COULD SEE I WAS HEADING DOWN A PATH THAT

MIGHT TAKE TWENTY MINUTES AND WOULD LEAD

ABSOLUTELY NOWHERE.

MOST OF THE TIME, OR SO IT SEEMS TO ME, IF

DAD SAYS ANYTHING IN MY GENERAL DIRECTION, IT'S

EITHER A WARNING OR A REPRIMAND. I HAVE COME TO

ACCEPT THIS FACT, WHICH TECHNICALLY SPEAKING IS

PRETTY SAD.

AT LEAST HE NEVER YELLS AT ME.

SO ANYWAY, THIS IDEA OF SLEEPWRITING LIKE

SOMEONE MIGHT SLEEPWALK, I THINK IT MIGHT HAVE

REVISITED ME LAST NIGHT. BECAUSE I'M JUST ABOUT

SURE I DIDN'T CONSCIOUSLY WRITE THOSE NAMES ON THE

FRONT PAGE. LOOKING AT THE SCRAWLED NAMES, I'M

ASKING MYSELF, JUST LIKE MY DAD USED TO ASK: WHY DID YOU DO THAT?

FRANCIS PALMER. JORDAN HOOKE. WILSON BOYLE. DR. WATTS. WHO ARE THESE PEOPLE? AND WHAT ABOUT HECTOR NEWTON AND THE APOSTLE — WHO ARE THEY? I'VE NEVER HEARD OF A SINGLE ONE OF THEM, SO WHY ARE THEIR NAMES CARVED IN STONE INSIDE A SECRET ROOM ON THE DREDGE?

AND WHILE WE'RE AT IT, WHY IS MY DAD'S NAME HIDDEN IN THAT ROOM RIGHT UNDER JOE BUSH'S NAME? AND THE LOCAL LIBRARIAN?

SARAH'S EYES ARE BIG. SHE'S TERRIFIED.

I COULDN'T SEE IT.

I ONLY FELT IT.

I'M GLAD I DIDN'T SEE OLD JOE BUSH FOR MYSELF WHEN WE WERE TRAPPED IN THE SECRET ROOM. I'M GLAD I WAS WEDGED IN THERE, FACING THE WALL SO I COULDN'T TURN AROUND. SEEING A GHOST ON VIDEO IS BAD ENOUGH; I DON'T NEED TO SEE IT IN PERSON.

LATER IN THE CAR — I SORT OF REMEMBER THIS CONVERSATION NOW — SARAH SAID IT WAS THE SCARIEST THING SHE'D EVER SEEN, LIKE WHATEVER

TERRIBLE THING WAS OUT THERE HAD HER TRAPPED AND WANTED HER DEAD. SHE SAID THE GHOST OF OLD JOE BUSH SNIFFED THE AIR, WHICH I DIDN'T REALLY GET FROM WATCHING THE VIDEO, BUT THAT'S HOW SHE FELT ABOUT IT. WHEN HE LEANED IN, SHE SAW HIS FACE AND ALMOST SCREAMED. SHE'D WANTED TO SCREAM, BUT OLD JOE BUSH WAS ALMOST TOUCHING THE BACK OF MY HEAD AND SHE WAS COMPLETELY PARALYZED WITH FEAR.

I REMEMBER SOMETHING ELSE NOW, SOMETHING HORRIBLE. I REMEMBER AT THAT MOMENT IT FELT EXTRA COLD, LIKE A GIANT BLOCK OF ICE WAS ABOUT TO TOUCH THE BACK OF MY NECK.

BUT I DIDN'T TURN AROUND. I DIDN'T GET TO SEE IT UNTIL I WATCHED THE VIDEO A FEW MINUTES AGO. THE MORE I REMEMBER, THE MORE I WISH SARAH HAD NEVER SHOWN IT TO ME.

THERE'S A BIG GAP NOW, A WHOLE SECTION I JUST DON'T REMEMBER AT ALL. I DON'T REMEMBER GETTING OUT OF THE SECRET ROOM OR COMING TO THE STAIRS AND INSISTING ONCE AGAIN THAT I COULDN'T GO DOWN. I DON'T REMEMBER RACING THROUGH PARTS OF THE

DREDGE I'D NEVER SEEN BEFORE OR COWERING IN THE CORNER. I ABSOLUTELY DON'T RECALL GETTING BACK UP AND MAKING MYSELF HOBBLE FORWARD UNTIL WE CAME TO THE WAY OUT.

Don't make me come looking for you.

A MESSAGE SMEARED ON THE DOOR. THE KIND OF WORDS THAT SAY DON'T YOU DARE TELL THE COPS, DON'T TELL YOUR PARENTS, DON'T TRUST ANYONE IN THIS TOWN, AND, MOST OF ALL, DON'T EVER COME BACK INTO THE DREDGE AGAIN.

THAT I REMEMBER. I REMEMBER IT MORE THAN ANYTHING ELSE FROM LAST NIGHT, FOR THE WORST POSSIBLE REASON. I REMEMBER IT BECAUSE WHEN I WOKE UP THIS MORNING, I GOT OUT OF BED AND SHUFFLED OVER TO MY DESK. WHEN I TURNED AROUND, I SAW THAT I'D SCRAWLED THOSE VERY WORDS ON THE WALL OVER MY BED.

IT'S VERY DISTURBING WHEN YOU COME TO THE REALIZATION THAT YOU'VE BEEN AWAKE WITHOUT KNOWING IT, DOING BIZARRE THINGS YOU CAN'T RECALL.

THEN AGAIN, MAYBE I DIDN'T WRITE THE MESSAGE ON THE WALL OVER MY BED.

It could be someone else's writing.

I guess it could be my dad's or Ranger Bonner's.

Or, more likely, the ghost of Old Joe Bush followed me home so he could make sure I understood him the first time.

SUNDAY, SEPTEMBER 19, 8:15 A.M.

I JUST SPENT THE LAST TWENTY MINUTES STANDING ON MY BED WITH A WET RAG, SCRUBBING WORDS OFF THE WALL. INK IS A LOT HARDER TO WASH OFF THAN A PURPLE CRAYON. IT'S ESPECIALLY DIFFICULT BECAUSE MY LEG IS STILL KILLING ME AND STANDING ON MY BED WITHOUT FALLING OFF IS A REAL TRICK.

FOR SOME REASON THE WORD <u>DON'T</u> WAS DARKER THAN ALL THE OTHER WORDS, SO IT READS MORE LIKE <u>DON'T</u> MAKE ME COME LOOKING FOR YOU. BUT IT DIDN'T REALLY MATTER, BECAUSE TWENTY MINUTES OF SCRUBBING DID ALMOST NOTHING TO REMOVE THE WORDS. WHAT I REALLY NEED IS SOME SANDPAPER AND A CAN OF PAINT.

I MOVED MY <u>DARK SIDE OF THE MOON</u> POSTER TO COVER THE MESSAGE. I HAVEN'T EVEN NOTICED THAT POSTER FOR MONTHS AND MONTHS — I THINK I ONLY EVER LISTENED TO PINK FLOYD FOR ABOUT A WEEK IN THE EIGHTH GRADE TO BEGIN WITH. I HAVE NO IDEA WHY I STILL HAVE IT HANGING IN MY ROOM.

MY MOM CAME IN A FEW MINUTES LATER AND STOOD OVER MY BED, STARING AT THE POSTER I'D MOVED.

"I used to listen to that music when I was your age," she said. "Did I ever tell you that?"

She'd told me about a thousand times, so I nodded.

"Why did you move it?"

I shrugged and changed subjects, hoping she wouldn't notice I'd pinned it up slightly crooked and try to fix it.

"I think I'll stay in bed a little longer. I didn't sleep so well last night."

Mom was still staring at the poster, like it brought back some memory she hadn't had in a while. Then she looked down at me.

"Your dad wants you out of this room and doing something with your life. Back to school in only a week, remember? You've really got to get used to walking on that leg."

If only she'd known how far out of my room I'd been the night before. I gave her my tired look, which wasn't hard because I was exhausted.

She sighed. "I can hold him off another half hour with bacon and eggs." Then she went to the

DOOR AND TURNED BACK FOR ONE MORE LOOK AT THE POSTER. "YOU KNOW IT'S CROOKED, RIGHT?"

I CLOSED MY EYES LIKE I WAS DOZING OFF AND NEARLY FELL ASLEEP BY ACCIDENT.

WHEN THE DOOR WAS SHUT AND I WAS SURE SHE WAS GONE, I PULLED MY PHONE OUT FROM UNDER MY PILLOW. SARAH HAD SAID 8:30 A.M. AND IT WAS 8:30 A.M. THERE WAS A ONE-WORD TEXT MESSAGE ON MY SCREEN, WHICH I RECOGNIZED FROM ONE OF MY FAVORITE BOOKS. DOES SARAH THINK I'M LOSING MY GRIP ON REALITY, JUST LIKE JACK TORRANCE DID? I WISH I COULD REMEMBER EVERYTHING FROM LAST NIGHT, BUT I CAN'T. MAYBE I <u>AM</u> GOING CRAZY AND I JUST DON'T KNOW IT. I SUPPOSE IF I WERE LOSING MY MARBLES, I'D BE THE LAST ONE TO KNOW.

I DELETED THE PASSWORD, WENT TO MY DESK, AND LOGGED ON TO SARAH'S SITE.

SUNDAY, SEPTEMBER 19, 11:00 A.M.

I COULDN'T GO BACK TO SLEEP AFTER WATCHING SARAH'S NEWEST VIDEO . . . AND I WAS HUNGRY BESIDES. THE BREAKFAST SMELL WORKING ITS WAY UP THE STAIRS AND UNDER MY DOOR IS TOUGH TO IGNORE, ESPECIALLY ON SUNDAY MORNING WHEN WE ACTUALLY GET A WEEKLY PAPER AND MOM DOESN'T GIVE ME A HARD TIME ABOUT DRINKING COFFEE. ANY OTHER MORNING SHE'S ON MY CASE, BUT SUNDAY IS A FREE PASS FOR REASONS I DON'T ENTIRELY UNDERSTAND.

HAVE YOU EVER LOOKED ACROSS THE TABLE, PAST A PLATE OF SCRAMBLED EGGS, BACON, AND TOAST, AND WONDERED IF YOU COULD TRUST YOUR OWN PARENTS?

I JUST DID.

"WHERE'S HENRY?" I SAID, AND THEN I SHOVED MOST OF A PIECE OF TOAST IN MY MOUTH AND WASHED IT DOWN WITH COFFEE. HENRY IS MY DAD'S BEST FRIEND, WHO VISITS FROM NEW YORK FOR A COUPLE OF WEEKS EVERY YEAR. HE'S GOT A COMPLICATED PAST WHEN IT COMES TO THE DREDGE.

"FISHING," DAD SAID. HE WAS STARING AT THE PAPER, WHICH WAS ON THE TABLE NEXT TO HIS PLATE. HE GLANCED UP AT ME, THEN BACK AT THE EDITORIAL

PAGE. "YOU'RE GOING TO SCHOOL NEXT WEEK," HE

WENT ON.

"I KNOW."

"THAT'S NOT A LICENSE TO TALK WITH SARAH

FINCHER. YOU KNOW THAT, RIGHT?"

I DIDN'T ANSWER HIM. INSIDE I WAS SEETHING, BUT

THERE WAS NO POINT SAYING ANYTHING. I WAS

ALREADY TALKING WITH SARAH PRACTICALLY EVERY

DAY WITHOUT EITHER OF MY PARENTS KNOWING ABOUT

IT. GETTING THEIR PERMISSION HAD FOUND ITS WAY TO

THE BOTTOM OF MY PRIORITY LIST.

MOM PIPED IN. "HE KNOWS, PAUL. JUST READ

YOUR PAPER AND LET THE BOY EAT IN PEACE."

"ALL RIGHT, ALL RIGHT. BUT WE AGREED. SCHOOL

NEXT WEEK, NO EXCUSES. AND NO SARAH FINCHER."

THEY BLAMED SARAH FOR MY ACCIDENT. THEY

SAID SHE WAS TROUBLE.

THEY WERE TOTALLY WRONG ABOUT THE

FIRST PART.

THE SECOND PART REMAINED TO BE SEEN.

I FINISHED MY BREAKFAST AND CAME BACK TO MY

ROOM. I COULD TELL DAD WANTED TO INSIST I GO

OUTSIDE, BUT MOM WAS PRETTY MAD ABOUT HOW HE

WAS BADGERING ME, SO HE LEFT ME ALONE. I THINK I'VE
GOT A FEW HOURS OF PEACE AND QUIET UP HERE, AT
LEAST UNTIL HENRY GETS BACK. AFTER THAT, ALL
BETS ARE OFF. HE'LL WANT TO PLAY CARDS OR TALK.

WHAT'S MY DAD HIDING? HIS NAME IS ON A SLAB IN
THE DREDGE THAT TIES HIM TO A WHOLE BUNCH OF
OTHER NAMES. HE'S PART OF A SECRET SOCIETY. HE'S
GOT THE ALCHEMY SYMBOL FOR GOLD TATTOOED ON
HIS SHOULDER AND THAT ALCHEMIST DIAGRAM IN HIS
DRAWER.

IT HAS TO ADD UP TO SOMETHING. BUT WHAT?

I'LL START WITH THE NAMES FROM THE SECRET
ROOM — THAT'S MY BEST CLUE. I'LL WORK MY
WAY DOWN THE LIST AND FIGURE OUT WHO THESE
PEOPLE ARE.

MAYBE SOME OF THEM ARE STILL ALIVE.

LIKE THE LIBRARIAN.

LIKE MY FATHER.

Sunday, September 19, 2:00 p.m.

Other than my mom stopping by an hour ago with lunch, I've had three hours of uninterrupted research time on my laptop. I keep it very quiet in my room — no music or anything like that — so I could hear the ting of a butter knife on the edge of a glass mayonnaise jar as she made my sandwich. This was my signal to erase everything I was working on. I've gotten to where I can do this and re-enable the software my parents think is keeping tabs on me in less than thirty seconds. Unless they're watching with a camera, there's no way they're keeping track of what I'm doing up here.

I almost spilled the beans to my mom when she was in here. It's like I want to trust her, but she's married to my dad and he's tangled up in this secret stuff. She'd tell him. I know she would. And she was just as mad at me after the accident. Maybe madder.

After Mom set the Coke and the sandwich on my desk, she stared out the window.

"You coming down anytime soon?"

I shrugged and popped the top on the Coke can.

"Is Henry back yet?" I asked.

My mom shook her head. "Your dad went after him. Fishing must be good."

I hesitated a second, then said, "Have you ever been in the old dredge, Mom?"

She looked at me like I was slipping through her fingers and falling down a steep hill. You know the look. The one where your mom thinks you're in trouble but can't help you.

"I haven't been out to the dredge in years. Why do you ask?"

I could see she was nervous, like I was dancing around the edge of something she was afraid to hear. So I totally backed off.

"No reason. It's been out there a long time. I figured you'd been inside."

She looked relieved, which made me glad I hadn't told her I was seeing ghosts, hanging out with Sarah, and wandering around the dredge in the middle of the night getting trapped in secret rooms. My mom wanted a normal son, who was in school and didn't get into strange kinds of trouble all the time. I can't really say that I blame her.

"Eat your sandwich," she said, and then we talked about something else. (It'll make more sense if I explain it later. But we did talk some more.)

Then she left and I was all alone.

That was the only interruption I had in a very successful three hours online, as detective work goes.

Here's what I did:

First I made a list of all the names that were on the slab in the secret room. I added Daryl Bonner's name to the list because I don't trust him at all. Neither does Sarah. The names became, I guess, my suspect list. Suspects of what crime, I don't know — YET.

But I'm closer to finding some answers now than I was last night.

This was the list I began with, in the order I wanted to investigate them:

Joseph Bush

Francis Palmer

Paul McCray

Gladys Morgan

The Apostle

Dr. Watts

Jordan Hooke

Wilson Boyle

Hector Newton

Daryl Bonner

First things first: Scratch Joseph Bush from the list.

That guy is already dead.

I went back to my old journal and read my entry from September 13th. I've torn it out and moved it here as evidence:

The greatest discovery — or the worst, depending on how you look at it — that Sarah and I made involved the untimely death of a workman on the dredge. There was only one mention of the incident in the newspaper, and nothing anywhere else. Old Joe Bush is what they called him, so I can only conclude that he was not a young man. Old Joe Bush had let his pant leg get caught in the gears, and the

203

MACHINERY OF THE DREDGE HAD PULLED HIM THROUGH, CRUSHING HIS LEG BONE INTO GRAVEL. THEN THE DREDGE SPIT HIM OUT INTO THE GRIMY WATER. HIS LEG WAS DEMOLISHED, AND UNDER THE DEAFENING SOUND IN THE DARK NIGHT, NO ONE HEARD HIM SCREAM.

OLD JOE BUSH NEVER EMERGED FROM THE BLACK POND BELOW.

WHENEVER I SEE OR HEAR THAT NAME, MY LEG STARTS TO ACHE AND I THINK OF ALL THE TIMES I'VE SEEN AND HEARD WHAT REMAINS OF OLD JOE BUSH. I'VE HEARD HIM WITH MY OWN EARS, DRAGGING THAT CRUSHED LEG ACROSS THE OLD FLOOR OF THE DREDGE. I'VE SEEN FOOTAGE OF HIM — AM I REALLY SAYING THIS? — SEEN HIM THROUGH THE BROKEN WINDOW AND LEANING DOWN INTO THE SECRET ROOM AND MOVING ACROSS A CAMERA THAT'S BEEN DROPPED. I'VE FELT HIM PUSH ME OVER A RAIL, HIGH ENOUGH OFF THE GROUND TO KILL ME.

THE IMPORTANT THING RIGHT NOW IS THAT JOSEPH BUSH IS OFF THE LIST. AND HE'S NOT THE ONLY

WORKER WHO DIED ON THE DREDGE. I SEARCHED AND
SEARCHED FOR FRANCIS PALMER AND DIDN'T HAVE ANY
LUCK AT ALL UNTIL I REMEMBERED ALL THOSE MINUTES
AND REPORTS FROM THE NEW YORK GOLD AND
SILVER COMPANY. THOSE WERE BIG FILES AND THERE
WERE LOTS OF THEM, PLUS I HAD GONE IN AND STARTED
HIGHLIGHTING DIFFERENT AREAS OF INTEREST. I COULDN'T
KEEP THOSE FILES ON MY COMPUTER, SO I'D
TRANSFERRED THEM TO A FLASH DRIVE AND TAPED IT
UNDER ONE OF THE DRAWERS TO MY DESK.

AND YOU KNOW WHAT? IT'S A GOOD THING I DID
THAT. BECAUSE WHEN I WENT LOOKING FOR THOSE FILES
ONLINE A COUPLE OF HOURS AGO, A BIG CHUNK OF THEM
WERE GONE. SOMEONE, SOMEWHERE, WAS ABLE TO
CLASSIFY THOSE OLD FILES OR KNEW SOMEONE WAS
LOOKING AT THEM. MAYBE THEY TRACKED MY IP
ADDRESS TO SKELETON CREEK AND DIDN'T LIKE
SOMEONE SNOOPING AROUND. IT'S NOT A GOOD SIGN
THAT THINGS FROM THE PAST ARE BEING HIDDEN AWAY.
PEOPLE ONLY HIDE REPORTS IF THEY THINK SOMEONE
WILL FIND SOMETHING BAD IN THEM.

WHICH IS EXACTLY WHAT I FOUND.

I PULLED UP THE FILES FROM THAT FLASH DRIVE AND
RAN A PROGRAM I HAVE THAT WILL SIFT THROUGH
MULTIPLE DOCUMENTS FOR KEY WORDS ALL AT ONE
TIME. I PUT IN THE KEY WORDS FRANCIS PALMER. I
GOT A RETURN ON A DOCUMENT DATED WITHIN MONTHS
OF THE DEATH OF JOSEPH BUSH. WHEN I HIGHLIGHTED
THE ENTRY FROM A BOARD OF DIRECTORS MEETING, I
REALIZED THE DEATH OF FRANCIS PALMER TOOK
PLACE ONLY TWENTY-SEVEN DAYS AFTER THE DEATH
OF JOSEPH BUSH.

NYGS PM Mins. -- Paragraph 9, page 25.

The #42 asset holding in Skeleton Creek, Oregon,
was the location of a fatal accident on 8-12-63. The
second fatality in less than a month has led to an
internal safety and structural investigation of
assets #31-#47. The victim, Francis Palmer, was a
long-term night shift control room operator. He was
found dead in the water below asset #42, an apparent

accidental drowning. Legal department advises adding safety precautions to asset #42 in the form of railings and window bars. Approved. Cost analysis for modifications to asset #42 scheduled for 9-15. Insurance claims pending with Palmer family.

SCRATCH FRANCIS PALMER OFF THE LIST.

DEAD.

HE AND JOE BUSH WERE BOTH IN THE CROSSBONES AND BOTH OF THEM DIED ON THE DREDGE WITHIN A MONTH OF EACH OTHER. I HAD A BRIEF MOMENT OF CONCERN AS MY DAD'S FACE FLASHED BEFORE MY EYES. TWENTY PERCENT OF THE PEOPLE ON THE LIST HAD ALREADY BEEN KILLED OFF, AND I HADN'T EVEN BEEN INVESTIGATING FOR AN HOUR.

THE NEXT TWO PEOPLE ON THE LIST WERE DAD AND GLADYS MORGAN, THE LIBRARIAN. I AT LEAST KNOW THESE TWO ARE STILL ALIVE. FOR SOME REASON

I just couldn't go searching around online for my dad. It was too weird. Who knew what kind of junk I might dig up about Paul McCray? He was involved, he was alive, he was secretive like everyone else in town, he'd lived here his whole life, he had a diagram with symbols and strange statements on it, he had a secret tattoo, and he was living in the same house as me.

So I moved on to Gladys Morgan, expecting to find out she was a dreary old windbag with a long, eventless life full of long, eventless days, weeks, and months.

Boy, was I wrong.

The first thing I found? Gladys Morgan hasn't always stayed in Skeleton Creek, contrary to what she tells everyone. She also spent some time in New York City, if you can believe that. How do I know Gladys Morgan was in New York City? Because the <u>New York Times</u> is archived online, and Gladys Morgan once made the news. That's right — <u>our</u> Gladys Morgan — in the <u>New York Times</u>! And here's

THE MOST INTERESTING PART: SHE WAS IN THE NEWS RIGHT AFTER THE ACCIDENTS ON THE DREDGE OCCURRED.

HERE'S A SMALL PART OF THE ARTICLE I FOUND:

PROTEST ERUPTS OVER ENVIRONMENTAL ALLEGATIONS

New York Gold and Silver board members arrived on Park Avenue this morning and found more than fifty protesters from all across America. The company, which operates dozens of gold dredges in remote parts of Alaska, Oregon, and Montana, has come under fire in recent months for what many are calling a disregard for environmental concerns in small towns across the West.

One of those in attendance, Gladys Morgan, came all the way from rural Oregon to join in the protest.

"They've got some explaining to do, simple as that," Morgan said. She, like many of those in attendance, lives in a small town where a New York Gold and Silver dredge grinds along the outskirts of town twenty-four hours a day, seven days a week. "They haven't kept up their end of the bargain. I'm here to tell them they're gonna, whether they like it or not."

Jim Pearson, a lumber mill worker from Billings, Montana, who drove the entire 3,000-mile journey with his dog, Skipper, had similar complaints.

What was she doing there? I get that she was angry, but going all the way to New York to complain with a bunch of other small-town folks? I think there was more to it than that. What if she was there as a member of the Crossbones? Two of them were dead in the span of a month. Or maybe the whole thing was a cover, especially her participation in this rally, and she worked for New York Gold and Silver all along. She could have killed them both. It's possible. She sure has the temper for it.

In detective terms, I think the evidence clearly points to Gladys Morgan as a person of interest.

The next name on my list, The Apostle, led nowhere. I couldn't find anything online that made any sense or connected anyone with that title to Skeleton Creek or the dredge. The only thing I can think of now is to check with one of the old churches in town. Maybe they know something. With a name like The Apostle, a house of worship seems like the most obvious place to look.

DR. WATTS — NOW THAT ONE'S INTERESTING. HE WAS SURPRISINGLY EASY TO FIND IN THE SKELETON CREEK HISTORICAL ARCHIVES. I WAS RIGHT IN THE MIDDLE OF WORKING ON THIS LEAD WHEN I HEARD MY MOM MAKING THE SANDWICH DOWNSTAIRS. THAT'S WHY, WHEN I WENT DOWN THERE, I STEERED THE CONVERSATION TO DR. WATTS, BECAUSE I FIGURED SHE WOULD HAVE HEARD OF HIM. WHEN I MENTIONED HIS NAME, SHE CRINGED.

"THAT OLD GEEZER?" SHE SAID. "HE HAD THE WORST BEDSIDE MANNER OF ANY DOCTOR I'VE EVER MET. AND HE HATED KIDS. I KNOW, BECAUSE I WAS ONE OF HIS PATIENTS."

"IS HE STILL ALIVE?" I ASKED.

"FAR AS I KNOW. I GUESS HE RETIRED ABOUT TWENTY YEARS AGO, BEFORE YOU WERE BORN. HE'D BE ABOUT EIGHTY BY NOW. HE'S RECLUSIVE. BUT HE LIVES RIGHT OFF MAIN STREET."

"YOU MEAN HE DOESN'T GET OUT MUCH?"

"I MEAN HE NEVER GETS OUT. AT LEAST I HAVEN'T SEEN HIM. MARY OVER AT THE STORE DELIVERS HIS GROCERIES AND CLEANS UP AFTER HIM. SHE SAYS HE'S OBSESSED WITH ALCHEMY. YOU KNOW WHAT THAT IS?"

I shook my head, not wanting her to know how much or how little I knew. The fact that Dr. Watts was into alchemy was a big deal.

"Well, it's sure not good medicine. Something about mixing metals or chemicals. I think it's making him soft in the head, whatever it is."

Very interesting. Dr. Watts is alive, so that makes three. And, just as important, he's messing around with alchemy, which has to be connected to the alchemy chart I found in my dad's dresser.

And speaking of threes — the last three names on the list inside the dredge were connected. Here's how I figured it out:

First I searched each of the names separately: Jordan Hooke, Wilson Boyle, Hector Newton. The searches for those names didn't lead anywhere interesting. Then I put all three names in at one time and searched them together. To my surprise, things started adding up. It was only the last names that mattered, and it quickly became clear that the first names were bogus, placed there to throw an outside observer off the track. Jordan, Wilson, and

Hector were there for show, but Hooke, Boyle, and Newton? Those were incredibly interesting last names when taken together.

Sir Isaac Newton — obviously I'd heard of him. Gravity and all. But the other two — both with the first name Robert — were even more interesting. Robert Hooke and Robert Boyle were contemporaries of Newton's and often worked right alongside him (if not in his enormous shadow). All three scientists were fiercely competitive and laid claim to similar finds.

Here's where the dots start to connect: Boyle in particular was a great enthusiast of alchemy. It was a secret fascination. As I read more about it, I began to understand that alchemy is, at least in part, the science of trying to turn one kind of metal into another. Boyle — I almost fell out of my chair when I read this — was totally obsessed with the properties of one thing in particular: gold.

Alchemy, gold, the dredge, the Crossbones, Dr. Watts — these things are all connected somehow. And that chart in my dad's dresser drawer, The Alchemist Diagram of 79 for Paul McCray.

Henry and my dad are going to be home soon. I should go downstairs and sit on the porch so they don't wonder what I'm doing up here. No sense getting them suspicious when I don't have to.

This is what I have so far:

~~Joseph Bush~~ — dead

~~Francis Palmer~~ — dead

Paul McCray — my dad, alchemy chart

Gladys Morgan — New York visit

The Apostle — send Sarah to check the churches

Dr. Watts — alive, alchemy, reclusive

~~Jordan Hooke~~ — fabricated

~~Wilson Boyle~~ — fabricated

~~Hector Newton~~ — fabricated

Daryl Bonner — shows up mysteriously, can't be trusted

A few hours' work and I've cut the list in half.

Not bad.

Sunday, September 19, 10:00 p.m.

It's clear my parents are serious about keeping me out of my room. And they've enlisted Henry to help them.

Is it really ten?

I'm tired.

As soon as I got out on the porch, Henry and my dad came back home. They'd caught a slew of fish (September is always good up here on the creek) and they didn't let up for almost an hour talking about this fly pattern and that rising fish and the one that got away. This is a little bit like watching a golf tournament on television, more background noise than anything that requires serious concentration.

About a half hour into this endless stream of fish talk, my mom informed me that Randy and Dennis were coming over for HBs with their parents. This was not good news. Randy and Dennis are brothers who live in town. My mom keeps trying to set us up, sort of like a playdate for teenagers.

215

THESE GUYS ARE ABOUT AS INTERESTING AS DIRT.
WE HAVE EXACTLY ZERO THINGS IN COMMON, PLUS
THEY'RE LOUD AND THEY LIKE TO BEAT UP ON EACH
OTHER. I'M NOT EVEN SAYING THEY'RE BAD PEOPLE,
EXACTLY — JUST THAT I CAN'T THINK OF A SINGLE
REASON WHY I WOULD WANT TO SPEND MY SUNDAY
EVENING LISTENING TO THEM TALK ABOUT VIDEO GAMES,
DIRT BIKES, AND FARTS.

BUT THEY SHOWED UP ANYWAY BECAUSE I COULDN'T
BRING MYSELF TO TELL MOM TO CANCEL AND,
TRUTHFULLY, IT WAS ALMOST WORTH IT FOR THE HB.

AN HB, IN CASE I DIE AND THIS JOURNAL IS FOUND
IN A DITCH SOMEWHERE A HUNDRED YEARS FROM NOW, IS
A HENRY BOMB. THIS IS A BURGER THAT IS HUGE
BEYOND ALL REASON. PART OF THE FUN OF HAVING AN
HB IS TO SEE HOW MUCH OF IT YOU CAN EAT. NO ONE,
TO MY KNOWLEDGE, HAS EVER FINISHED A HENRY
BOMB. MY MOM AND RANDY AND DENNIS'S MOM SPLIT
HALF OF ONE HB, IF THAT TELLS YOU ANYTHING. AND
MY MOM IS NO SLOUCH. SHE CAN PUT AWAY A
WHOPPER NO PROBLEM. BUT THIS THING? HALF AN
HB IS LIKE A WHOLE MEAT LOAF.

Our grill is pretty good size, but Henry only cooks one Henry Bomb at a time because they're extraordinarily "made to order." Tomatoes, lettuce, onions, special sauce (it's a secret, it's orange, and it's awesome), every kind of pepper, about a dozen ziplock bags filled with seasoning salt of varying degrees of heat (total wimp all the way up to blow your head off). Don't even get me started on the HB buns, which Henry makes himself from frozen bread dough (think Frisbee and you're in the ballpark).

I tried and failed to eat an entire HB.

It took a long time.

Just checked my phone and Sarah texted me:

9 EMV at 630am. MU EL

Delete.

Nine means her parents are watching. They must be paying closer attention than usual. Emailing Video at 6:30 a.m., she misses me, ends with Evil Laugh.

Actually, I'm sort of glad she's not sending me a video until tomorrow morning. Half the

TIME I GET THESE THINGS AT NIGHT AND THEN I CAN'T

SLEEP.

I'M TAKING FIVE MINUTES TO WRITE HER AN UPDATE

ON ALCHEMY AND THE APOSTLE AND EVERYTHING

ELSE I FIGURED OUT, AND THEN IT'S LIGHTS OUT.

Monday, September 20, 6:30 a.m.

Monday morning. Exactly one week from now I'll be getting ready for school. Maybe classes and homework will make my life feel normal again.

The second I woke up, I sat up and looked at all the walls in my room. There was no new writing. Either I couldn't find a pen in my sleep last night (this is possible since I made a point of putting every pen I have at the back of a drawer and shutting it tight) or whoever wrote the first message doesn't feel like he needed to tell me twice.

And then there was this other, worse feeling as I woke up and looked at the poster I moved. If I lifted it and looked underneath, would the words even be there?

Don't Make Me Come Looking For You.

This is how messed up my memory is becoming.

Can I even tell the difference between truth and fiction?

I checked my phone — no password. I checked my email — no password. Then I looked out the

WINDOW AND SAW A PIECE OF PAPER WAS TAPED TO THE OUTSIDE.

This can't be good.

I pulled the window up just far enough to reach my hand under and take the note.

I could hear my parents talking down the hall, getting ready to leave for work. Henry would sleep in late and probably go fishing. Pretty soon I'd have the house to myself.

Here's what the note said:

No more email or text messaging for a couple days! My parents are really cracking down. Bonner stopped by here yesterday — Sunday, can you believe that? He told my parents someone had cut the lock on the dredge and gone back in. He came right out and said he suspected it was me. Unbelievable. He kept giving me the evil eye, like when I was in his office the other day. It's a good thing I grabbed those bolt cutters on the way out or we'd be finished. Don't be surprised if he shows up at your front door.

I got your message about the alchemy — veeeeery interesting. I wish we could sit down and talk! It's killing me. I'll do some digging at the church on the edge of town after school. For now, I've got some big news of my own — just go to the site and use <u>castleofotranto</u> as the password. I have to get back to my house before it gets light out.

I can't wait to see you! But don't send any more emails or texts — at least for today — it's too risky. Leave me messages at the blue rock like we used to when we were kids and I'll do the same.

Sarah

P.S. I heard you had Henry Bombs last night. <u>Everyone</u> heard. I'm so mad I couldn't be there. I bet you tried to eat a whole one since we couldn't split it, didn't you?

THAT MIGHT BE THE BEST PASSWORD YET. VERY IMPRESSIVE.

AND SHE'S RIGHT. I DID MISS HAVING HER THERE TO EAT HALF MY DINNER. BEING A GLUTTON ABOUT IT

DIDN'T MAKE ME ANY LESS LONELY. PLUS I GOT A
STOMACHACHE.

THE BLUE ROCK. A HASSLE, BUT AT LEAST IT'LL BE
SAFER WITH DARYL BONNER SNOOPING AROUND. EVER
SINCE THAT GUY CAME TO TOWN A FEW WEEKS AGO,
THERE'S BEEN NOTHING BUT TROUBLE. WHAT'S HIS REAL
REASON FOR TRANSFERRING HERE?

I CAN HEAR PEOPLE IN THE HOUSE.

DAD'S SHAVING, MOM IS MAKING COFFEE.

I BETTER MAKE A SHOWING. THEN I'LL COME BACK
AND CHECK THE VIDEO.

MONDAY, SEPTEMBER 20, 7:45 A.M.

PARENTS ARE GONE AND HENRY IS STILL ASLEEP
DOWNSTAIRS.

TIME TO CHECK THAT VIDEO.

SARAHFINCHER.COM
PASSWORD:
CASTLEOFOTRANTO

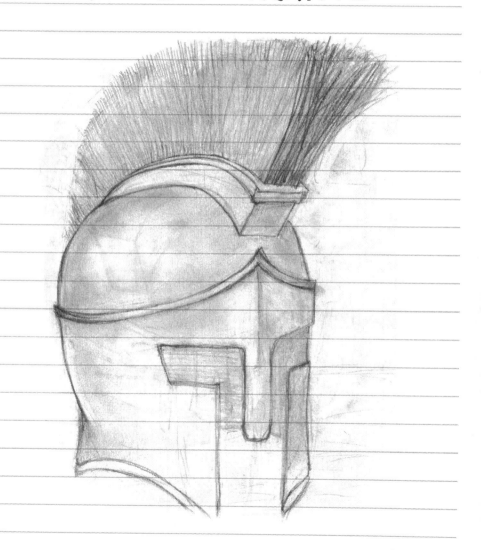

MONDAY, SEPTEMBER 20, 8:15 A.M.

I REALLY HOPE THAT ALL LIBRARIANS AREN'T LIKE GLADYS MORGAN. BECAUSE I'D REALLY LIKE, AT SOME POINT, TO WALK INTO A LIBRARY AND NOT BE AFRAID FOR MY LIFE.

IT DEFINITELY LOOKED LIKE SHE WAS TRYING TO HIDE THAT WOODEN CROW. BUT WHY BOTHER? I'VE SEEN IT DOZENS OF TIMES OVER THE YEARS AND NEVER THOUGHT TWICE ABOUT IT. I EVEN REMEMBER THINKING IT WAS CROOKED ONCE AND THINKING SOMEONE SHOULD NAIL IT UP THERE TIGHTER SO IT WOULDN'T FALL OFF IF THE WIND BLEW DOWN MAIN STREET.

IT'S FUNNY HOW YOU CAN LOOK AT SOMETHING AND ASCRIBE NO MEANING TO IT FOREVER AND EVER. THEN ONE DAY YOU SEE IT IN A COMPLETELY DIFFERENT WAY. THAT WOODEN CROW HAS SAT QUIETLY TURNING FOR YEARS WHILE NO ONE PAID ANY ATTENTION.

ALMOST NO ONE.

MY DAD WAS PAYING ATTENTION. SO WAS GLADYS. OLD JOE BUSH AND FRANCIS PALMER USED TO PAY ATTENTION, BEFORE THEY DIED.

224

HENRY WANDERED UP HERE WITH A CUP OF COFFEE. HE DIDN'T EXACTLY STARTLE ME WHEN HE CAME IN, BUT HENRY DOESN'T REALLY KNOCK SO MUCH AS BARGE. HE WAS STANDING IN THE DOORWAY WHEN I REALIZED I HAD A BUNCH OF NAMES FROM THE SECRET ROOM WRITTEN ON A PIECE OF PAPER NEXT TO MY LAPTOP. SOME OF THE NAMES WERE SCRATCHED OUT BECAUSE I'D DISCOVERED THEY WERE DEAD.

I SET MY ELBOW ON THE LIST.

HENRY ALREADY HAD HIS FISHING BOOTS ON, WHICH MY MOM HATES BECAUSE THEY SMELL LIKE A MOLDY LOAF OF BREAD. HE'S NOT SUPPOSED TO WEAR THEM IN THE HOUSE. IT MADE ME WONDER IF HE'D WORN THEM TO BED.

HE STARTED TALKING TO ME THE SECOND HE ENTERED THE ROOM.

"I SLEEP LIKE THE DEAD UP HERE IN THE MOUNTAINS. YOU?"

I NODDED AND HENRY LOOKED AROUND THE ROOM. HIS EYES LOCKED ON THE DARK SIDE OF THE MOON POSTER.

"HOW COME YOU MOVED THAT?"

"Trying to change things up, I guess."

"I remember one of those songs. Used to get stuck in my head a lot."

And then he sang a verse off-key, which sort of freaked me out. It was the one about the rabbit running and digging holes and never getting to stop. I think Henry was half amazed he could remember the words.

"I can hear that song in my head like it was yesterday," he said. Then he was a little sad — an emotion I'd almost never seen him display.

"Two more days and it's back to the city for old Henry," he went on. "Time to dig another hole, I guess, like the good song says."

"Why don't you just quit and come live here with us?" I asked. "I think my dad would like that."

"For starters, your mother would kill me. Me and my boots and poker and dragging your dad out to the river. Two weeks a year is pushing things as it is."

"My mom loves you," I said. And I meant it.

"I'm easy to love for a couple of weeks. It gets a little harder after that."

He laughed this comment off, but I think deep down he was serious.

I'd never really thought of it that way, but I could see he might have a point. The charm of an old bachelor like Henry probably wears thin after a while. I don't mind him hogging all the time with Dad, but if he were here all the time? I'd mind. I like Henry's loud voice and his energy and the way he can get everyone to play cards. But there's a twitch that sets in after a couple of weeks when it starts to feel like he's almost annoying.

Henry's smarter than he knows, to leave us wanting more and never overstay his welcome.

I decided to ask him a question.

"You ever talk to Gladys, the librarian?"

Henry was leaning against the doorjamb. It appeared he was trying to remember the next verse to the song he'd sung.

Finally, he refocused. "I haven't said a word to Gladys Morgan in ten years. Me and her had a run-in. If I see her coming, I head for the other side of the street."

I THOUGHT THIS SOUNDED LIKE THERE MIGHT BE A GOOD STORY, SO I PRODDED HIM.

"WHAT HAPPENED? WHAT DID SHE DO?"

"LET'S JUST SAY SHE'S NOT AS PATIENT AS YOUR MOM. I STEPPED INTO HER PRECIOUS LIBRARY WITH MY WET BOOTS ON, JUST OFF THE STREAM. SLOSHED RIGHT UP TO HER DESK AND ASKED IF SHE HAD ANYTHING ON BARBECUING A PIG."

"YOU'RE KIDDING."

"NOPE. SHE LOOKED ME UP AND DOWN LIKE I'D PICKED UP HER CAT AND THROWN IT IN FRONT OF A MOVING TRUCK. THAT WOMAN CAN GLARE BETTER THAN ALL THE NEW YORK LADIES THAT'VE TURNED ME DOWN FOR A DATE. SO SHE GLARED, THEN — GET THIS — SHE GOT OUT OF HER CHAIR, CAME AROUND THE DESK, AND KICKED ME."

"SHE DIDN'T."

"NOT ONLY THAT, BUT SHE TOLD ME I BETTER TAKE MY STUPID PIG AND MY WET BOOTS AND GO OUTSIDE AND NEVER COME BACK. I TOLD HER I DIDN'T EXACTLY HAVE THE PIG WITH ME, IT WAS JUST SOMETHING I WAS THINKING ABOUT. THAT DIDN'T GO OVER TOO WELL."

228

The scary thing was, I can totally picture all this happening. "What'd she say when you told her you didn't have the pig?" I asked.

"She said if it was between me and a chicken and she could only save one of us, she'd definitely save the chicken."

Henry laughed his big laugh again, and I laughed, too.

That Gladys Morgan, what a kook.

I was feeling bold, so I kept going.

"You ever see Dr. Watts?" I asked.

"He's dead," said Henry.

"No, he's not. Mom said so."

Henry scratched his stubbly face.

"I thought he was dead. I haven't seen him in forever. You sure he's alive?"

"That's what Mom said."

Henry seemed a little perplexed.

"Well, if she says so."

Henry looked at the Pink Floyd poster again, and I was sure he'd see it was crooked and want to move it.

229

"You see that story in the paper about the dredge?" he said.

Henry had been sensitive to my accident there and didn't mention it much.

"Yeah," I said. "They're burning it down."

"It's a shame I'm leaving so soon. Hate to miss the biggest bonfire in three counties. But you know how some people feel about me around here. Probably best if I'm gone when the old relic finally gets what's coming to it."

I know I've mentioned this before, but Henry used to work for New York Gold and Silver. He'd come out when the dredge was running, way back in the day, to keep an eye on #42. He hated what the dredge did to the land, but he was young and ambitious back then. He told me as much. He wanted a big career at a big company in a big city, just like a lot of people.

Skeleton Creek stayed in his bones long after New York Gold and Silver went bankrupt. Some say Henry keeps spending all his vacation time here because he feels bad about

WORKING FOR A COMPANY THAT ALMOST DESTROYED THE TOWN. I THINK HE COMES HERE BECAUSE HIS BEST FRIEND IS HERE — MY DAD — AND BECAUSE HE LOVES THE MOUNTAINS.

I FELT A LITTLE SORRY FOR HENRY WHEN HE PEELED HIMSELF FROM MY ROOM AND WENT DOWNSTAIRS. I HEARD THE SCREEN DOOR FLAP AGAINST THE WALL AND KNEW HE'D GONE TO THE CREEK.

SO NOW I'M ALONE IN THE HOUSE AGAIN, AND I CAN'T HELP THINKING ABOUT WHAT IT FEELS LIKE TO LIVE IN SKELETON CREEK. I'VE BEEN TRYING TO PUT MY FINGER ON IT FOR A LONG TIME. NO ONE NEW EVER MOVES HERE. IT'S THE SAME OLD PEOPLE KEEPING MOSTLY TO THEMSELVES. THERE'S A KIND OF GOTHIC LONELINESS ABOUT EVERYTHING.

YOU KNOW WHAT IT FEELS LIKE?

IT FEELS LIKE THE DREDGE DUG THE HEART OUT OF MY TOWN AND CHUCKED IT INTO THE WOODS. ALL THAT'S LEFT ARE THE GHOSTS WALKING AROUND.

MONDAY, SEPTEMBER 20, 4:10 P.M.

WELL, MY PARENTS CAN'T COMPLAIN ABOUT ME SITTING IN MY ROOM ALL DAY. HENRY CAME BACK AND TALKED ME INTO GOING DOWN TO THE CREEK WITH MY FLY ROD. I HAVEN'T BEEN UP TO FISHING SINCE BEFORE THE ACCIDENT AND I PROBABLY HAD NO BUSINESS STANDING ANYWHERE NEAR FAST-MOVING WATER WITH A SHATTERED LEG BARELY OUT OF A FULL LEG CAST.

HENRY DID MOST OF THE CASTING, CATCHING, HOOTING, AND HOLLERING. I MOSTLY SAT IN THE SHADE AND WATCHED HIM WORK HIS WAY UP AND DOWN THE BEST STRETCHES OF SKELETON CREEK, HOOKING FISH AFTER FISH. I HAVE TO GIVE HIM CREDIT: HE'D LEARNED THE WATER AND KNEW WHAT TO THROW. I'VE BEEN FISHING NOTHING BUT SKELETON CREEK ALL SUMMER FOR YEARS AND I'VE NEVER CAUGHT AS MANY BIG FISH AS I SAW HENRY CATCH TODAY. THE GUY IS A MACHINE.

BEING OUT NEAR THE WATER TODAY MADE ME VALUE IT MORE THAN EVER. THE CREEK IS LINED WITH THESE GREAT BIG COTTONWOOD TREES THAT FILL THE AIR WITH WHAT LOOKS LIKE SNOW EVERY TIME THE WIND BLOWS. AND THERE ARE GROVES OF ASPEN —

THIN TREES WITH WHITE BARK AND GOLD LEAVES —
HUDDLED CLOSE ALONG THE BANKS OF SOME OF THE
BEST WATER. THOSE ASPEN GROVES WILL TAKE YOUR
BREATH AWAY. AND THERE'S ONE OTHER THING, A PART
OF THIS PLACE THAT MAKES IT UNLIKE ANY OTHER. ALL
THOSE BIG PILES OF ROCK AND EARTH THE DREDGE DUG
UP FORMED AN ENDLESS LINE OF ROLLING HILLS ALONG
THE BANKS OF THE CREEK. OVER THE YEARS THE
SURFACE FILLED WITH GRASS AND TREES AND FLOWERING
PLANTS. THE CREEK IS LIKE A SECRET PARADISE NO
ONE HAS DISCOVERED WAY UP HERE, TUCKED AWAY IN
THE WOODS NEXT TO A RAMSHACKLE TOWN THE SIZE OF
A POSTAGE STAMP. THERE ARE BIRDS EVERYWHERE,
LITTLE CREATURES SCAMPERING AND CHIRPING OVER
THE HILLS, AND LARGER ANIMALS RUSTLING IN HIDDEN
PLACES NEARBY.

ALL THESE SIGHTS AND SOUNDS TODAY MADE ME
REALIZE HOW MUCH I MISSED VISITING THE CREEK. IT
GAVE ME A VIEW OF THINGS I HADN'T THOUGHT OF
BEFORE. I'D ONLY EVER HATED THE DREDGE LIKE
EVERYONE ELSE. BUT RIGHT HERE, RIGHT UNDER MY
NOSE, IS THIS SPECTACULAR THING THE DREDGE LEFT
BEHIND. IT MAKES ME WONDER IF THIS IS A PRINCIPLE

THAT CAN BE COUNTED ON: Good THINGS CAN BE

CREATED FROM BAD.

   I CAN'T STOP THINKING ABOUT HOW THIS OLD TOWN

OF MINE JUST NEEDS A LUCKY BREAK TO START HEADING

IN THE RIGHT DIRECTION AGAIN.

MONDAY, SEPTEMBER 20, 7:25 P.M.

SOMETIMES, AFTER ONE OF HENRY'S BARBECUES OR A
MORNING AT THE CAFÉ EATING CHICKEN-FRIED STEAK
AND EGGS, MY MOM DECIDES THE McCRAYS NEED TO
EAT A HEALTHY DINNER. THIS IS A TERRIBLE IDEA AND
ALWAYS PUTS MY DAD IN A BAD MOOD.

"JUST EAT. IT'S NOT GOING TO KILL ANY OF YOU."

THESE WERE MY MOM'S WORDS AS MY DAD,
HENRY, AND I SAT STARING AT THE FOOD SHE'D PLACED
BEFORE US.

"WHAT IS IT?" HENRY WAS BRAVE ENOUGH TO
ASK. HE WAS ABOUT HALF SERIOUS AND HALF HONESTLY
CURIOUS AS HE STARED AT THE THREE BOWLS
CLUSTERED TOGETHER IN THE MIDDLE OF THE TABLE.

"THAT RIGHT THERE IS RICE," I SAID, POINTING TO
THE ROUND BOWL IN THE MIDDLE.

"IT'S BROWN RICE," MY MOM CORRECTED, STARING
AT HENRY. "ARE YOU GOING TO TELL ME YOU'VE
NEVER SEEN RICE BEFORE?"

HENRY HAD SEEN RICE. IT WAS THE MAIN DISH HE
WAS WORRIED ABOUT.

"WHAT ABOUT THAT STUFF?" HE ASKED.

He pointed to a bowl filled with something that looked like green logs floating in a purple lake.

"You really want to know?" asked my mom. "Because you're eating it whether I tell you or not."

Henry pondered his options, swallowed hard, and nodded. "Tell me."

My mom scooped up a big spoonful of brown rice and slapped it onto Henry's plate, then she ladled a glob of purple lake water and green sticks over the top.

"Low-fat yogurt with whole beets, pulverized in a blender and poured over a can of green beans. Eat up."

Henry looked like he was about to barf.

The last item was a flat pan of green Jell-O with sad little mandarin oranges trapped all through the middle. My dad put about half the pan of Jell-O on his plate so there was no room for anything else, and then he sat there, slurping miserably with a spoon.

"Stop that," my mom said. She can't stand it when people slurp their Jell-O.

The best part was when Mom took a bite of this crazy concoction and chewed and chewed but couldn't swallow without washing it down with a Diet Coke. She tried really hard to keep a straight face, but once Henry took a bite himself, just to be a good sport, his eyes started bulging and Mom came completely unglued.

We all had a pretty good laugh and then she let Henry and my dad go to the kitchen and make pancakes for dinner.

We sat there — me and my mom — eating Jell-O without slurping.

"You doing okay?" she asked.

"Yeah. It was nice going to the creek today. I haven't done that for a while."

"I'm glad you went outside. The fresh air is good for you."

I nodded and took another bite of green Jell-O.

"I checked your computer last night," she said. "It looked clean — a little too clean, if you get my drift."

Uh-oh. Maybe my mom knows more about computers than I thought. Was I erasing everything? Was I making it look too perfect?

I pretty much expected what came next.

"Have you been talking to Sarah?"

The big question I was asked in one form or another every day. It should have gotten easier to lie, but the guilt was starting to pile up, so it only got harder.

"I'm not talking to anyone. I just like my computer clean. It runs faster that way."

Mom looked at me sideways.

"Now we're talking!" Henry yelled. He was balancing some king-size pancakes on a spatula in one hand and carrying a handful of paper plates in the other. My mom kept looking at me, but Henry had saved me from any more cross-examination at the dinner table. She left me alone after that, but I had the feeling she didn't

TRUST ME. I COULDN'T BLAME HER, AND WAS WORRIED IT WOULD MEAN SHE'D BE WATCHING EVEN CLOSER THAN BEFORE. WITH SCHOOL STARTING IN ONLY A WEEK, HER RADAR WAS DIALED IN AND SEARCHING FOR CLUES.

IN ANOTHER HALF HOUR, IT'LL BE DARK. I CAN'T GET OUT OF HERE. IF I GO FOR A WALK ALONE, THEY'LL ASSUME I'M TRYING TO SEE SARAH.

I HAVEN'T HEARD FROM HER ALL DAY.

I BET SHE'S SENT ME SOMETHING.

THE BLUE ROCK IN THE MORNING — THAT'S THE SOONEST I CAN TRY TO CONTACT HER.

239

As soon as my parents left for work, I crept out the screen door and down the front porch. (Henry snored in the guest room, so getting by him wasn't a problem.) I walked through town, down the main artery of Main Street, passing the twenty side streets that shoot off like veins. It still amazes me that this is our whole town. My house more or less on one end, and Sarah's on the other end, down a street that doesn't look a whole lot different from mine.

I remember when we were seven or eight years old and we spent an entire day trying to figure out the exact halfway point between our houses. We did it because neither of us liked to walk any farther than we had to, and we thought it was only fair to split the distance as precisely as possible. After hours of pacing and figuring and drawing a map of the town, we came to the conclusion that the old station house for the train conductor was exactly halfway between our houses. We would sometimes call each other on the phone and then race there.

She won every single time. After a while I figured out that she'd tricked me by putting the middle on her side of Main Street, not mine, thereby making it possible for her to use a shortcut we hadn't used when calculating the distance.

I think girls are much craftier than boys when they're little.

In any case, by the time I figured out the whole distance problem, it was too late. We'd decided we needed a marker at our spot.

First we found the rock. It took both of us to move it under the station house and center it just right.

"Let's paint it," said Sarah.

"Why?" I said.

"Because I want to paint it. Don't you want to paint it?"

"Sure. Let's paint the rock. Why not?"

This very short conversation says a lot about my relationship with Sarah. She wants to do something, I don't necessarily care one way or the other, and so we do it. Eight years later,

I HAVE COME TO DISCOVER THIS IS NO WAY TO LEAD

A LIFE.

IT CAN GET YOU INTO A LOT OF TROUBLE.

IT MIGHT EVEN GET YOU KILLED.

IT WAS MORE OUT OF OPPORTUNITY THAN ANYTHING

ELSE THAT THE ROCK BECAME BLUE. IT IS THE COLOR

OF SARAH'S HOUSE BECAUSE SHE STOLE AN OLD CAN OF

PAINT FROM HER GARAGE. WE DIDN'T HAVE A BRUSH, SO

SHE JUST POURED THE PAINT OVER THE TOP LIKE HOT

FUDGE ON ICE CREAM.

AND YOU KNOW WHAT'S FUNNY ABOUT THIS? THE

PAINT CAN IS STILL UNDER THERE, TOO.

WE DIDN'T KNOW WHAT ELSE TO DO WITH IT.

WHAT IF WE TOSSED IT IN A DITCH AND SOMEONE FOUND

IT? IT WAS SARAH'S HOUSE BLUE, AND SOMEONE

WOULD TELL.

THE BLUE ROCK BECAME THE PLACE WE MET,

WHERE WE PUT SECRET NOTES AND TREASURES WE'D

FOUND AND CANDY WE WANTED TO SHARE.

WE WERE SECRETIVE LIKE EVERYONE ELSE IN

TOWN, EVEN BACK THEN. WE DIDN'T WANT ANYONE

HEARING US TALK ABOUT THE BLUE ROCK. IT WAS OURS.

AND IT WASN'T EASY TO FIND.

The train still comes through town in the early morning, but it never stops here anymore. It used to, a long time ago, when the dredge was pounding away 24/7, digging up something worth stopping for. But the old station house was already abandoned when we were kids, so we set about exploring it. It wasn't too intimidating, only about the size of a backyard storage shed on the edge of the tracks. It was locked up tight, but the cool thing was you could climb underneath it. The station house was up off the ground for some reason — I think so it was the same height as the train conductor when he came by — and the cheapest way to accomplish the extra height was to put this little shack on a bunch of cinder blocks. Weeds had grown up all around the edges, sort of like a curtain you could pull back. It was cold gravel underneath, and when we crawled inside, it crunched under our knees.

As we grew older, there wasn't much point in meeting at the blue rock or leaving secret notes there. I hadn't been back there in years. My leg

WAS ALREADY TIRED AND SORE FROM THE LONG WALK,
AND THE SPACE UNDER THE STATION HOUSE SEEMED A
LOT SMALLER THAN WHEN I WAS SEVEN. I'D BE LUCKY IF
I FIT AT ALL.

DID I MENTION THAT I DON'T LIKE CONFINED
SPACES?

I SQUEEZED IN ON MY BACK AND SLID UNDER,
THROUGH THE WEEDS, UNTIL I HIT MY HEAD ON THE
BLUE ROCK.

IT WAS A BIG ROCK, AND I HIT IT HARD ENOUGH THAT
I YELLED.

ONCE I RECOVERED, I CRANED MY NECK AROUND
AND SAW A PIECE OF PAPER TAPED TO THE ROCK. I
TOOK IT, CAREFULLY REMOVED THE TAPE, AND TAPED
MY OWN NOTE TO THE SLICK, BLUE SURFACE.

THE NOTE I HAD WRITTEN WAS SHORT.

YOUR PARENTS AREN'T THE ONLY ONES
WATCHING CLOSELY. MY MOM IS ON MY
CASE, TOO. I THINK BONNER MIGHT HAVE SAID

SOMETHING TO HER BUT I CAN'T TELL FOR SURE. SHE AND MY DAD ARE VERY WORRIED ABOUT ME GOING BACK TO SCHOOL — I CAN TELL. I BET THEY'VE TOLD ALL OUR TEACHERS TO KEEP AN EYE ON US SO WE DON'T TALK TO EACH OTHER. I HATE THIS!

I'M NOT SURE I EVEN WANT TO GO BACK TO SCHOOL.

<u>EVER.</u>

TOO MANY PEOPLE IN THAT PLACE.

BEING AWAY FROM YOU MAKES EVERYTHING FEEL LIKE IT'S FADING AWAY.

I SHOULD BE MORE AFRAID, RIGHT?

I HOPE YOU SENT A VIDEO.

I NEED TO SEE YOU.

RYAN

I READ SARAH'S NOTE ON THE WALK HOME. IT WAS EASY, SINCE IT WAS SO SHORT. IT WASN'T EVEN A LETTER AT ALL. I WISH SHE'D WRITE ME A LETTER, BUT SARAH DOESN'T WRITE IF SHE CAN SAY IT IN A VIDEO.

Hey, Ryan — Miss you / wish I could see you
Password carlkolchak
xoxoxo Sarah

TECHNICALLY THAT'S NOT EVEN A NOTE; IT'S JUST A HANDOFF OF SOME VITAL INFORMATION.

No PUNCTUATION, UNLESS YOU COUNT DASHES AND SLASHES.

AND WHO'S CARL KOLCHAK?

THIS IS THE FIRST TIME SHE'S USED A PASSWORD I'VE NEVER HEARD OF.

ANYWAY, WHEN I GOT HOME, I FOUND HENRY ON THE PORCH EATING LEFTOVER PANCAKES WITH PEANUT BUTTER.

"YOU DIDN'T GO DOWN THERE AND THROW ROCKS IN MY FAVORITE FISHING HOLE, DID YOU?" HE ASKED.

246

He seemed genuinely nervous that I'd gotten up early and scared all the fish out of his number one spot on the creek.

"Just out for a walk is all," I said. "The fish are fine."

He stuffed a big slab of pancake in his mouth and gave me his best comic evil eye as I walked past.

Finally, I got back here to my room, so I could write down these words.

Sarah's at school and I'm stuck here at home.

I already checked out that password online. I'm sort of surprised I didn't catch it, but then again, that show aired before I was born. I can't be expected to know every scary pop culture reference, right?

Still, I had to laugh at that Carl Kolchak. Classic.

I wonder what Sarah found?

248

She got me.

I mean she REALLY got me.

I just about had my nose on the screen when that thing went off.

I screamed so loud I think it woke Henry downstairs.

I can hear him moving around in the kitchen.

But it was good — it was okay.

Seeing Sarah laugh was worth it.

That's the part I replayed seven or eight times. Watching her smile like that makes me believe we could get back to where we once were. Before Old Joe Bush and Daryl Bonner. Before I couldn't trust my dad or see my best friend.

I just watched it again.

She's got a great laugh.

Sarah must have sent that video really early this morning while I was sleeping.

Only forty-five minutes and she'll be in the computer lab at school.

I'm getting breakfast.

SARAH SENT ME SOMETHING SORT OF SCARY FROM
SCHOOL, WHICH I HAVE ALREADY WATCHED.

HERE'S WHAT HAPPENED, STARTING WHEN I LEFT MY
ROOM AN HOUR AGO:

I TOOK MY PHONE DOWNSTAIRS WITH ME AND LEFT
IT IN THE FRONT POCKET OF THE SAME HOODIE I WORE
TO BED LAST NIGHT. I ALWAYS LEAVE IT SET ON
VIBRATE INSTEAD OF SOUND, AND IT WENT OFF WHILE I
WAS DRINKING COFFEE WITH HENRY (UNLIKE MY MOM,
HENRY COULDN'T CARE LESS WHAT I DRINK FOR
BREAKFAST). I COULDN'T CHECK MY PHONE UNTIL I WAS
ALONE . . . AND I COULDN'T BE ALONE BECAUSE HENRY
WANTED TO PLAY A GAME OF CRIBBAGE AT THE
KITCHEN TABLE.

I WAS WHIPPING HIM GOOD, WHICH IS HARD TO DO
BECAUSE HE'S PLAYED A LOT OF CRIBBAGE. I COULDN'T
JUST FOLD UP AND LEAVE, SO I STAYED AND FINISHED
THE GAME. HE CAME BACK FROM THIRTY PEGS BEHIND
AND BEAT ME IN THE FINAL HAND.

"YOU LOST YOUR CONCENTRATION RIGHT
THERE," SAID HENRY, POINTING HIS FINGER TO THE
GENERAL AREA WHERE MY PEGS WERE SITTING

250

WHEN THE POCKET OF MY HOODIE HAD STARTED TO VIBRATE.

He didn't know how right he was.

If Sarah had sent me a message, I didn't care about winning, I just wanted the game to be over.

"Better luck next time, champ," said Henry.

I wasn't sure what to make of Sarah's message, which I snuck a look at once I was free of the kitchen and had started up the stairs.

"Be careful checking that thing," said Henry. "Stairs require the full attention of a one-legged man."

I was startled to hear Henry's voice. He'd obviously followed me out of the kitchen and somehow knew what I was doing. I pocketed my phone and turned all in one motion and saw that Henry had already gone into the guest room. He peeked around the corner and looked up at me where I stood on the second stair.

"I don't care if you talk to her. I think

KEEPING YOU TWO APART IS ABOUT THE STUPIDEST THING
I'VE EVER HEARD. I TOLD YOUR DAD THAT."

I WAS SHOCKED. DID HE REALLY KNOW I'D GOTTEN
A MESSAGE FROM SARAH?

"WHAT DID HE SAY?"

"SORRY, PAL, HE'S FIRM AS CONCRETE ON THIS. HE
WON'T BUDGE. BUT I WON'T SPY FOR HIM. IF YOU WANT
TO CALL SARAH, I WON'T SAY A WORD. I'VE ALWAYS
LIKED HER."

"THANKS, HENRY."

"YOU OWE ME ONE. I'M SURE I'LL FIGURE OUT A
WAY TO COLLECT BEFORE I GO."

HE WENT BACK INTO HIS ROOM AND STARTED
PACKING SOME OF HIS THINGS. HE'D BE GONE IN A DAY,
AND I WAS SURE GOING TO MISS HIM.

I WENT TO MY ROOM AS FAST AS I COULD AND SHUT
THE DOOR.

SHE MUST HAVE SEEN SOMETHING TO TAKE
THIS KIND OF RISK. NO MESSAGE, NO NOTE, NOTHING —
JUST THREE WORDS RUN TOGETHER ON MY
PHONE. IMATSCHOOL

I figured that must be the password —
imatschool — so I jumped online and went
straight to Sarah's site.

What I saw there made me realize something
important.

Something big was about to happen.

SARAHFINCHER.COM
PASSWORD:
IMATSCHOOL

TUESDAY, SEPTEMBER 21, 11:00 A.M.

I KNEW IT! MR. BRAMSON NEVER WATCHES US IN COMPUTER LAB. <u>NEVER</u>. HE'S PRACTICALLY NONEXISTENT BECAUSE WE RUN THESE TUTORIALS THAT TELL US HOW TO USE MICROSOFT EXCEL OR WORD OR SOME OTHER EVIL EMPIRE PROGRAM. MR. BRAMSON TYPES AWAY ON HIS OWN COMPUTER, WHICH SITS ON THE CORNER OF HIS DESK. HE'S PROBABLY SENDING EMAILS OR READING NEWS HEADLINES. HE DOESN'T EVEN LOOK UP UNLESS SOMEONE ASKS HIM A QUESTION, WHICH IS BASICALLY NEVER.

So WHY IS MR. BRAMSON WATCHING SARAH? I'LL TELL YOU WHY — BECAUSE MY PARENTS HAVE TOLD HIM TO. MR. BRAMSON IS SPYING ON US!

I KNEW THEY WERE RUTHLESS, BUT SERIOUSLY — MY PARENTS TELLING OUR TEACHERS TO MAKE SURE WE'RE NOT TALKING TO EACH OTHER? THEY'VE GONE EVEN FURTHER THAN I THOUGHT THEY WOULD. DO THEY REALLY THINK SARAH AND I ARE THAT DANGEROUS TOGETHER? I MEAN, WHAT DO THEY <u>REALLY</u> THINK? WE'RE GOING TO GET INTO DEADLY TROUBLE OR SOMETHING?

FINE.

If it's deadly trouble they want, then deadly trouble they're going to get.

Breaking and entering? Check.

Planting secret cameras at a meeting for a society that appears to be killing people left and right? Check.

Seeing Sarah as much as I want? Check! Check! Check!

I don't even care anymore.

Tuesday, September 21, 2:00 p.m.

I've calmed down a little bit, but I'm still mad.

I went for a long walk.

I don't feel like writing.

TUESDAY, SEPTEMBER 21, 10:00 P.M.

I SAT THROUGH DINNER AND SAID ALMOST NOTHING.

HENRY LEAVES TOMORROW, SO I FELT SORT
OF BAD.

BUT I COULDN'T EVEN LOOK AT MY PARENTS.

THEY THINK THEY'RE SO SNEAKY.

RIGHT IN THE MIDDLE OF DINNER, DAD EXCUSES
HIMSELF TO USE THE BATHROOM.

THERE'S A PERFECTLY GOOD BATHROOM
DOWNSTAIRS, BUT HE GOES UPSTAIRS AND USES THE ONE
UP THERE. OR SO HE SAYS.

I KNOW WHAT HE'S DOING.

HE'S IN MY ROOM, CHECKING MY COMPUTER.

SEARCHING THE DRAWERS.

LOOKING UNDER MY BED FOR JOURNALS OR NOTES.

STARING OUT THE WINDOW AND WONDERING —
WHAT'S THIS KID UP TO?

WELL, GOOD LUCK, DAD. YOU'RE NOT GOING TO
FIND ANYTHING. YOU KNOW WHY? BECAUSE I'M
SNEAKIER THAN YOU BY A LONG SHOT. I GOT THIS
WONDERFUL TRAIT FROM YOU, MR. SECRET SOCIETY.
YOU PASSED IT DOWN AND IT GOT BIGGER AND
BETTER. YOU'RE AN AMATEUR WITH YOUR WOODEN

BIRD AND FLUSHING THE TOILET LIKE YOU THINK I'M
ACTUALLY GOING TO BELIEVE YOU'RE USING THE
BATHROOM UP THERE.

AFTERWARD, I WENT STRAIGHT TO MY ROOM AND
WROTE A HUGE, COMPLICATED, GET-IN-THE-WORST-
KIND-OF-TROUBLE EMAIL TO SARAH.

Hi, Sarah. I hope you got my note at the blue rock. It was a real
trick getting under there. I hit my head. I have a feeling you knew
how hard that delivery would be for me and chose the blue rock
to exchange notes anyway. Hey, if it puts a smile on your face, I'm
happy.

Speaking of smiling, you were doing a lot of that when you tricked
me with that Carl Kolchak video. Pop culture reference from 80s
TV = Sarah is about to play a trick, dead ahead. I should have
known. Next time I won't be such an easy target.

Okay — the good news — are you ready? I know how to get
inside Longhorn's in the middle of the night when it's closed up.

I've spent a lot of time in that place because Dad runs the fly-
fisherman's club. I know you know about the club, but I'm not sure

you've ever been aware of how often I associate with this group of misfit fishing bums. I don't talk about it because it seems the slightest bit nerdy to be heading down to Longhorn's every Thursday night to tie flies and talk about trout with old guys. At least it comes in handy now, right?

Here's how you get yourself in there after hours:

There is a window in the men's room — I know it's not painted shut because I checked it once just to see for myself. Longhorn's Grange is open on weekdays for all kinds of things, like on Tuesdays when the old ladies meet up and sew quilts in there. And no, I'm not part of the blanket-making club. My grandma was before she died, so that's how I know. I've got a fishing-themed quilt on my bed to prove it.

I think I could get in there tomorrow during the day and unlatch that window. The only way to reach it is from the top of the sink, but my leg is feeling better every day and I'm sure I can do this. Tomorrow night, if you go to the bathroom side of Longhorn's, you should be able to pull that window open and climb inside.

Bring a ladder. The window is pretty high.

Okay, second thing (did I mention that it's getting late and I'm tired — I hope I can stay awake long enough to finish this monster email). Second thing is . . .

The black door on the stage.

Years ago — this must have been when I was first attending the fly-fishing club with my dad — I wandered off from my tying vise and got up on the stage. The amps were there for the bands when they have dances, and I was turning the knobs this way and that. There's a drum set on the stage, too. They just leave it there because it's so hard to move, I guess.

So I started tap-tap-tapping on this drum set and my dad hollered at me.

I stopped.

That was when I saw the black door.

Tuesday, September 21, Midnight

I fell asleep at my desk.

This is bad.

Real bad.

I didn't finish the email to Sarah.

The screen is black on my laptop. It went to sleep a few minutes after I did, so the screen went dim, but I can't be sure that nobody came in here and saw it. All you have to do is wipe your hand across the mouse and the screen comes back on, big and bright, and I'm in huge trouble.

I moved the mouse and it came back up right where I left off.

That was when I saw the black door.

I remember what happened.

I took a break and leaned back in my chair.

I rubbed my leg because it felt like it was falling asleep.

I had turned the light off so it was totally dark except for the light from my screen.

I leaned forward again, placed my elbow on my desk, and rested my head on my hand.

That's the last thing I remember.

A COUPLE OF MINUTES LATER THE SCREEN MUST'VE GONE DARK.

I WOKE UP AND IT WAS PITCH-BLACK IN MY ROOM AND I DECIDED RIGHT THEN AND THERE THAT FALLING ASLEEP WAS JUST THE BEGINNING OF MY PROBLEMS.

THE REAL PROBLEM WAS WHAT WOKE ME UP.

OLD JOE BUSH.

HE WAS IN MY ROOM. I'M SURE OF IT.

I HEARD HIM.

I HEARD THE LEG DRAGGING DOWN THE HALLWAY.

I DIDN'T DREAM IT! I KNOW I DIDN'T DREAM IT.

YOU WANT TO KNOW HOW I KNOW I DIDN'T DREAM IT?

BECAUSE I DID SOMETHING THEN. SOMETHING I SHOULD NOT HAVE DONE. BY THE LIGHT OF MY COMPUTER MONITOR I CREPT OVER TO THE DARK SIDE OF THE MOON POSTER. THE ONE THAT COVERED THE WORDS ON MY WALL.

DON'T MAKE ME COME LOOKING FOR YOU.

I LIFTED THE POSTER OUT OF THE WAY FROM THE BOTTOM. THE TAPE WASN'T VERY STICKY, SO

IT WAS EASY. MY SHADOW COVERED THE WALL AND I COULDN'T SEE THE WORDS, SO I MOVED TO THE SIDE.

AND THERE THEY WERE.

MORE WORDS.

WORDS THAT HADN'T BEEN THERE BEFORE.

THE APOSTLE WILL SEE YOU NOW.

I TAPED THE POSTER DOWN AND CAME BACK TO MY DESK.

DID I WRITE THOSE WORDS OR DID HE?

I DON'T REMEMBER HAVING THE PEN IN MY HAND.

AND I DON'T THINK IT'S MY HANDWRITING.

EITHER I WROTE BOTH MESSAGES OR I DIDN'T WRITE EITHER ONE.

AND WHAT DOES THIS NEW MESSAGE EVEN MEAN?

THE APOSTLE WILL SEE YOU NOW.

HE'S WATCHING ME.

IT MEANS I STEPPED OVER THE LINE AND I'M NEXT.

THE APOSTLE IS DEAD. I'M DEAD.

I FEEL A CHILL THAT RUNS RIGHT DOWN THE CENTER OF MY BROKEN LEG, LIKE IT'S IN THE FREEZER AND IT'S ABOUT TO CRACK INTO A THOUSAND PIECES FROM THE

COLD. THAT KIND OF FEELING DOESN'T COME FROM

NOWHERE.

I DON'T THINK IT'S A FEELING FROM THIS WORLD. IT'S

FROM THE APOSTLE'S WORLD, JOE BUSH'S WORLD —

IT'S FROM THE KINGDOM OF THE DEAD.

I'M JUST ABOUT SURE HE WAS HERE.

EITHER THAT OR I'M GOING CRAZY.

I SENT THE EMAIL TO SARAH UNFINISHED JUST TO

GET IT OFF MY SCREEN.

I CAN'T TELL HER THIS STUFF. I CAN'T. IT'S NOT LIKE

BEING A MEMBER OF MY DAD'S FISHING CLUB. THIS IS

DIFFERENT. SHE'LL THINK I'VE LOST IT. SHE WON'T

TRUST ME ANYMORE.

I STARTED A NEW EMAIL.

Sarah — You have to turn bolts on three sides to release the black door, so bring a flat-blade screwdriver with you. Once you get it open, you'll see the stairs going down.

I'll make sure the window is open so you can get in. I'm sure you've got a plan for how to run the camera. You always do.

Gotta go — miss you. Ryan.

I TOOK A CLOSE-UP PICTURE OF MY WALL AND

PRINTED IT OUT AT MY DESK.

HAVING A PICTURE OF IT MAKES THE WORDS REAL.

I'M NOT MAKING THIS UP. I'M NOT SEEING THINGS.

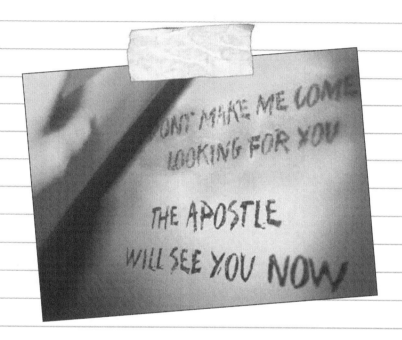

WEDNESDAY, SEPTEMBER 22, 1:00 A.M.

I CAN'T SLEEP.

265

WEDNESDAY, SEPTEMBER 22, 2:00 A.M.

I can't sleep.

WEDNESDAY, SEPTEMBER 22, 3:00 A.M.

I won't sleep.

I'm not writing on these walls.

It's someone else.

WEDNESDAY, SEPTEMBER 22, 5:00 A.M.

I ZONKED OUT FOR A COUPLE OF HOURS. THEN, WHEN I WOKE UP, I REFUSED TO LOOK BEHIND THAT POSTER AGAIN.

SARAH EMAILED ME, PRETTY UPSET. SHE WASN'T TOO KEEN ON THE LONG EMAIL AFTER WE AGREED NOT TO TAKE CHANCES. BUT THEN SHE SAID IT WAS NEARLY IMPOSSIBLE NOT TO EMAIL EACH OTHER. SHE WAS DOING IT, TOO. JUST BE CAREFUL, SHE SAID — ERASE, ERASE, ERASE. LEAVE NO TRACE. OUR RELATIONSHIP DOESN'T EXIST.

I HATE THE SOUND OF THAT.

OUR RELATIONSHIP DOESN'T EXIST.

HAVE MY PARENTS WON?

SARAH'S EMAIL WENT ON AND GOT A LITTLE BETTER. TALK ABOUT BREAKING HER OWN RULES. I'VE ALMOST NEVER SEEN HER WRITE THIS MUCH. MAYBE SHE MISSES ME AFTER ALL.

I think your idea with the window at Longhorn's is perfect. No one's up there at night, especially around that back side in the weeds, so it should work. I can already imagine the questions if Bonner catches me walking up the street with a ladder at midnight. That's not even something I want to think about. Let's see — 4 a.m. right now. I've been getting by on almost no sleep lately. I think the detective in me thinks early morning is the safest time or something — either way, I'm wide awake, so I'll haul one of my dad's old ladders up there in the next hour and hide it in the brush behind Longhorn's. Not that anyone is going behind Longhorn's to find it.

I have a feeling that crow is going to move again soon. Crossbones members probably check it every day, right? If that's true, then it sure would be nice to watch and see who takes a particular interest in it today. Or maybe we could see someone actually moving the birdie — wouldn't that be something? If we knew who that was, we'd be one step closer.

I need you to do something for me. There's a perfect spot downtown at the café. If you sit at the corner table, there's a nice view of the library right across the street. Just go in there with your journal or something and tell them you had to get out of the house. Marla won't care. She knows your mom, so I'm sure she'll be happy you're out of the house. Just sit there and drink coffee and eat pie and scribble.

I think someone will move the signal while I'm at school. There are only a few days before they burn down the dredge. Whoever is in the Crossbones can't wait much longer. They're just as interested in the dredge as we are — we just don't know why. And Gladys knows I'm snooping around. So does Bonner. They're watching me as much as I'm watching them. I think they'll move it while I'm at school so I can't see it happen.

Let's try to be as safe as we can. Every one of these emails is an invitation to get caught. Leave me a note at the blue rock and let me know what you find out. I'll stop there on my way home and check. If it's anything interesting, I'll leave you a note on the rock and we'll go from there. Sorry to send you running around, but if we're as close to some sort of Crossbones event as I think we are, we need to be extra careful.

Hang in there. Have a slice of pie for me.

Delete! Delete! Delete!

Sarah

I'M ACTUALLY SORT OF EXCITED ABOUT GETTING OUT OF MY ROOM.

I DON'T LIKE IT IN HERE ANYMORE.

I'M SITTING AT THE CAFÉ ALL BY MYSELF. I JUST GOT HERE.

RIGHT AFTER I DELETED SARAH'S EMAIL, I WENT BACK TO BED. THE SUN WAS COMING UP, WHICH MADE ME FEEL SAFER. THAT WHOLE VAMPIRE THING IS SO RIGHT ON. DARKNESS AND EVIL GO TOGETHER LIKE SPRINKLES ON CUPCAKES. IT'S AMAZING HOW MUCH CALMER I AM WHEN IT'S LIGHT.

ANYWAY, I DIDN'T WAKE UP UNTIL AN HOUR AGO, AND THEN I WENT DOWNSTAIRS AND DISCOVERED THAT MY DAD HAD DECIDED TO STAY HOME FROM WORK AND SPEND THE DAY WITH HENRY. HE (HENRY) IS LEAVING TOMORROW. MY DAD TOOK ALL OF LAST WEEK OFF FROM WORK. HE WAS SUPPOSED TO TAKE THIS WEEK OFF, TOO, BUT, ACCORDING TO HIM, "THE PLACE WAS FALLING APART." MY DAD HAS WORKED FOR THE SAME COMPANY SINCE BEFORE I WAS BORN. HE'S A MAINTENANCE MECHANIC AT A PAPER MILL, WHICH MEANS HE WORKS ON A GIGANTIC METAL MACHINE WITH A LOT OF MOVING PARTS. THE MACHINE IS WORTH A LOT OF MONEY. IF IT BREAKS DOWN, IT'S A BIG DEAL.

The problem is my dad has been there so long everyone else is younger or less experienced than he is with this dinosaur of a machine. So if it rattles or shakes funny, everyone freaks out and they call my dad.

"It's amazing they lasted a week," he said when I was down on the porch. "Took two days just to calm everyone down. But I still have time for a Cabela's run."

Yes, Dad had that sporting goods gleam in his eye. I mean, at Cabela's, the fishing section alone is bigger than some of the lakes I've been on.

"You should come with us," said Henry. He was wearing a cowboy hat I hadn't seen before.

"Where'd you get that hat?" I asked.

Henry took it off and examined it with some pride.

"Yard sale. Two bucks. Can you believe that?"

"Did you wash it?"

Henry looked at the cowboy hat as if he hadn't thought of that but probably should have,

Then he set it on his knee and looked back at me for an answer about whether or not I was going with them.

"I'm not sure I can walk that much," I lied. A trip to Cabela's sounded amazing and I totally could have done it. "But I might walk downtown and back."

My dad piped in. "I'm glad to hear you're at least thinking of getting outside. That room of yours is starting to smell funny."

The truth is — and this was actually okay with me — I could tell my dad wanted a few hours alone with his best friend on his last day in town. I could understand how important it was even if he didn't.

"You guys have a good time," I said. "Don't spend too much of my college fund."

I knew as well as my dad did how easy it was to blow months of savings at Cabela's in a matter of hours.

Dad's timing seemed to be working out really well for me, since I was supposed to be watching the crow all day from the vantage point of the

CAFÉ. BUT THEN HENRY WENT INSIDE TO RUN A DISHRAG AROUND THE RIM OF HIS NEW COWBOY HAT, AND MY DAD AND I WERE LEFT ALONE ON THE PORCH. HE SIPPED HIS COFFEE AND SET THE CUP ON A FOLDING CARD TABLE THAT HAD SEEN MORE ACTION ON THE FRONT PORCH IN THE PAST WEEK THAN IT HAD IN THE PREVIOUS YEAR.

"HOW'S THAT LEG DOING? YOU READY FOR SCHOOL?" HE ASKED.

HE DIDN'T SOUND LIKE HE WAS GOING TO BADGER ME ABOUT SARAH, SO I PLAYED ALONG.

"I THINK I'LL BE OKAY. SEEING SOME OF MY FRIENDS WILL BE NICE. IT'S GETTING A LITTLE OLD BEING HOME EVERY DAY."

"I'M GLAD TO HEAR IT. SITTING AROUND SKELETON CREEK WILL GET YOU NOWHERE."

HE PICKED UP HIS CUP AND LOOKED AT THE DRAWING ON THE SIDE. MY DAD IS VERY FOND OF A GOOD COFFEE CUP, AND THIS ONE, I HAD TO ADMIT, WAS MY FAVORITE.

IT WAS WHITE WITH AN OLD FAR SIDE CARTOON ON IT WHERE TWO DEER ARE STANDING TOGETHER AND ONE OF THEM HAS A BIG RED BULL'S-EYE ON ITS CHEST. THE

ONE WITHOUT THE BULL'S-EYE LOOKS AT THIS POOR
DEER AND SAYS, "BUMMER OF A BIRTHMARK."

I WAS THINKING HOW CLEVER THIS WAS WHEN MY DAD
SAID, "LET ME SEE YOUR PHONE."

HE KNEW I KEPT IT WITH ME A LOT OF THE TIME
AND THERE WAS NO POINT TRYING TO HIDE THE FACT
THAT I HAD IT JUST THEN, SO I GAVE IT TO HIM.

HE HAD BECOME A LOT SAVVIER WITH PHONES AND
COMPUTERS IN THE PAST FEW WEEKS. THE ACCIDENT
SEEMED TO WAKE HIM UP TO THE FACT THAT HE NEEDED
TO KNOW WHAT WAS GOING ON OR RISK MISSING
SOMETHING THAT MIGHT GET ME KILLED. IN A WEIRD
WAY THIS MADE ME FEEL LOVED, LIKE HE WAS WILLING
TO PUT IN SOME EFFORT IN ORDER TO PROTECT ME
FROM MYSELF.

BUT LIKE I'VE BEEN SAYING ALL ALONG, I'M TWO
STEPS AHEAD OF MY DAD WHEN IT COMES TO STUFF LIKE
THIS. EVERY TEENAGER IS. MOST PARENTS, EVEN ONES
LIKE MINE THAT ARE ACTUALLY TRYING TO KEEP UP,
ARE PERPETUALLY BEHIND.

HE TOUCHED SOME OF THE BUTTONS — OBVIOUSLY
CHECKING IT FOR TEXT MESSAGES FROM SARAH AND
CALLBACK NUMBERS. I'D GOTTEN PLENTY OF CALLS

274

FROM OTHER FRIENDS I WASN'T CLOSE TO BUT STAYED IN CONTACT WITH ANYWAY. BUT HE WASN'T GOING TO FIND ANYTHING FROM SARAH.

I WAS SURPRISED WHEN HE HELD THE PHONE TO HIS EAR. HE WAS USING MY PHONE TO CALL SOMEONE. NO ONE ANSWERED, SO HE HUNG UP AND HANDED THE PHONE BACK TO ME.

"NO ONE'S HOME AT SARAH'S," HE SAID.

IF SHE HAD BEEN THERE, SHE WOULD HAVE PICKED UP. CALLER ID WOULD HAVE TOLD HER IT WAS MY CELL PHONE. IT'S A LUCKY THING SHE WAS GONE.

HE DUG INTO HIS BACK POCKET AND PULLED OUT A FAT WALLET. THIS IS ONE OF THE OLD-SCHOOL THINGS I LIKE ABOUT MY DAD. I LOVE HIS OLD JEANS AND THE PREHISTORIC LEATHER BELT THAT HOLDS THEM UP, BUT THIS WALLET — I DON'T KNOW, IT SEEMS LIKE THE SORT OF THING I'D NEVER CARRY. IT'S SHAPED FUNNY, LIKE IT'S BEEN SAT ON FOR TWENTY YEARS. ITS WORN LEATHER IS DARK IN THE MIDDLE AND LIGHTER ON THE EDGES. AND WHEN MY DAD OPENS IT UP, THERE ARE ALL KINDS OF TREASURES IN THERE. PIECES OF PAPER FROM I DON'T KNOW WHERE, NOTES ABOUT FORGOTTEN THINGS, FADED PICTURES OF ME AND MOM, PENNIES AND

NICKELS THAT HAVE LEFT ROUND MARKS IN THE
LEATHER.

"HERE," HE SAID, HANDING ME A TWENTY WITH A
FOLD IN ONE CORNER. "GET YOURSELF A NEW SHIRT
WHILE YOU'RE DOWNTOWN. MIGHT COME IN HANDY FOR
SCHOOL."

HENRY BURST OUT ONTO THE PORCH WITH THE HAT
BACK ON HIS HEAD, ALL EXCITED ABOUT GETTING ON THE
ROAD. HE WANTED TO BE BACK BEFORE TWO O'CLOCK
SO THEY COULD FISH THE CREEK ONE LAST TIME. DAD
FINISHED UP HIS COFFEE, AND SOON THEY WERE GONE IN
MY DAD'S PICKUP, LEAVING THE HOUSE EMPTY EXCEPT
FOR ME. I STAYED ON THE PORCH, AFRAID TO GO UP
THE STAIRS TO MY ROOM.

I WAS STARTING TO HATE MY ROOM.

I FINALLY GOT UP THE NERVE TO ENTER THE HOUSE.
IT SHOULD HAVE BEEN NO BIG DEAL CLIMBING THE STAIRS,
BUT I TOOK IT REAL SLOW AND QUIET, LIKE SOMETHING
BAD MIGHT HAPPEN IF I WAS TOO LOUD.

SLOWLY I HEADED UP THE STAIRS, CURSING EVERY
CREAKY STEP UNTIL I REACHED THE TOP. I LOOKED
DOWN THE HALL AND THOUGHT ABOUT SEARCHING MY

DAD'S ROOM AGAIN. BUT I DIDN'T HAVE THE GUTS TO DO IT. ONCE WAS ENOUGH.

I GATHERED A COUPLE OF JOURNALS, SOME PENS, AND A COPY OF EDGAR ALLAN POE'S BEST SHORT STORIES. I FELT IN MY POCKET FOR THE TWENTY MY DAD HAD HANDED ME.

THAT, I FIGURED, SHOULD BUY PLENTY OF PIE AND COFFEE.

Wednesday, September 22, 11:30 a.m.

The waitress my mom knows isn't working today, which has led me to consume more cups of coffee than should be allowed by law. My hands are shaking. I can feel my heart racing in my chest. This can't be good for me.

Two slices of pie couldn't have helped. That's a lot of sugar. But I can't drink coffee on an empty stomach.

I've got ten bucks left.

How much am I supposed to tip this lady?

She keeps asking me if I want a refill and I keep saying yes so I'll have a reason to stay without seeming like I'm just taking up space.

How does one become a waitress in a dead-end town? I've never seen her around here before. I'd guess she's about twenty-five. Did she move here? And, if so, what the heck for?

She probably married a local who moved back here. She couldn't have known what she was getting herself into.

Bummer for her.

From where I'm sitting I can see the library, but the black crow above the door is at an angle and too far away. To my eyes, it's an indistinct blob of black above the door. I've been scouting the angle, though, and it looks to me like Dr. Watts could see the crow from the second story of his house. He's only a half block off Main Street, and his window points in the right direction.

I haven't seen anyone enter or leave the library all morning. Not even Gladys, who, I assume, is holed up inside, either reading something hugely boring or concocting some sort of scheme to get me killed. I think now is my best chance to get inside the men's room at Longhorn's. I can't remember what happens there on Wednesdays, but something is always going on in the middle of the day. I don't think it's the quilt—making club and I know it's not fly—tying.

My plan is to do this quickly and get back so I don't miss it if the crow gets moved. I want to see who does it. So I'll swing past Dr. Watts's

HOUSE AND SEE IF HE REALLY CAN CATCH A GLIMPSE OF THE FRONT OF THE LIBRARY, AND THEN I'LL GO TO LONGHORN'S AND RETURN BACK HERE. I SHOULD BE ABLE TO DO ALL THAT IN AN HOUR. MAYBE FASTER WITH THIS CAFFEINE JUMP IN MY STEP.

THAT TOOK LONGER THAN I EXPECTED. HOW WAS I SUPPOSED TO KNOW THEY WERE BUILDING TRAINS UP AT LONGHORN'S? HAVE YOU EVER STUMBLED INTO A ROOM FULL OF MODEL TRAIN ENTHUSIASTS? THOSE GUYS ARE BIG-TIME RECRUITERS, SO THEY WOULDN'T LEAVE ME ALONE. THEY'D ALL HEARD ABOUT MY ACCIDENT AND SOME OLD-TIMER TOLD THIS REALLY HORRIBLE STORY ABOUT A CONDUCTOR WHO FELL BETWEEN TWO TRAIN CARS AND HELD ON FOR DEAR LIFE WITH BOTH HANDS. HIS LEGS BOUNCED AROUND UNTIL FINALLY SOMEONE FOUND HIM AND HAULED HIM BACK TO SAFETY, BUT BY THAT TIME BOTH HIS LEGS WERE BROKEN.

So THEN THIS GUY SAYS TO ME, "LUCKY HE DIDN'T END UP UNDER THE TRAIN. THAT'S A WHOLE 'NOTHER STORY YOU DON'T EVEN WANT TO HEAR."

I HADN'T WANTED TO HEAR THE FIRST STORY, EITHER, BUT THAT HADN'T STOPPED HIM FROM TELLING IT TO ME, AND SURE ENOUGH HE TOLD ME THIS OTHER STORY ABOUT THE GUY WHO FELL UNDER THE TRAIN. I'M NOT GOING TO REPEAT IT. IT'S A BAD STORY.

ONCE THEY HAD ME STANDING THERE, I HAD TO
HEAR ABOUT THE ENGINES AND THE TRAINS THAT USED
TO RUN THROUGH TOWN AND LOOK AT ALL THEIR
MODELS AND ON AND ON. IT WAS PRETTY INTERESTING,
ACTUALLY. I WAS STANDING THERE THINKING, <u>HEY,
I COULD JOIN THESE GUYS IF I DIDN'T HAVE SCHOOL. I
COULD GET MY OWN TRAIN AND DO SOME RESEARCH ON
THIS AND THAT. THESE OLD GUYS AREN'T THAT BAD.</u>

IN OTHER WORDS, I WAS DISTRACTED.

IT WAS ABOUT THIRTY MINUTES AFTER I'D LEFT THE
CAFÉ THAT I REALIZED I WAS AWAY FROM MY POST AND
WAS PROBABLY MISSING OLD JOE BUSH HIMSELF
TURNING THE BLACK CROW ON THE STEPS OF THE
LIBRARY.

I EXCUSED MYSELF TO USE THE MEN'S ROOM.

ONCE I WAS IN THERE, I REALIZED A SINK IS A LOT
EASIER TO CLIMB ON TOP OF WHEN YOU DON'T HAVE A
LEG THAT WAS RECENTLY BROKEN INTO A BUNCH OF
PIECES. BUT I WAS DETERMINED TO GET THAT WINDOW
OPEN FOR SARAH. I MUST HAVE BEEN IN THERE A LONG
TIME, LIKE TEN MINUTES, BECAUSE I HAD ONLY JUST
UNLATCHED THE TOP WINDOW AND GOTTEN HALFWAY
DOWN AGAIN WHEN I HEARD SOMEONE AT THE DOOR

PEEKING IN, ASKING IF I WAS OKAY, HAD I FALLEN INTO THE TOILET — THE USUAL STUFF.

I SORT OF HALF FELL, HALF CLIMBED THE REST OF THE WAY DOWN AND LANDED ON MY REAR END ON THE TILE FLOOR. IT'S A MIRACLE I DIDN'T HURT MYSELF. THE SAME GUY WHO HAD TOLD ME THE TWO TRAIN STORIES HELPED ME UP AND TRIED TO MAKE ME FEEL BETTER BY COMMENTING ON HOW DIFFICULT IT MUST BE TO GO TO THE BATHROOM WITH A BROKEN LEG, ETC., ETC.

THE FUNNY THING WAS, I'D HAD ABOUT TEN CUPS OF COFFEE AND I REALLY NEEDED TO USE THE BATHROOM. BUT I'D ALREADY BEEN IN THERE FOREVER SO I MADE FOR THE DOOR AND HEADED BACK HERE, TO THE CAFÉ, WHICH IS WHERE I'M SITTING.

I WENT STRAIGHT TO THE BATHROOM.

WHEN I GOT BACK, THERE WAS A GLASS OF WATER AT MY TABLE. (MY TABLE — HOW FUNNY IS THAT? I NEVER COME IN HERE.)

"MORE COFFEE?" THE WAITRESS ASKED ME. SHE SAID IT LIKE SHE'D PREFER IT IF I FOUND SOMEPLACE ELSE TO TAKE UP SPACE ON THE PLANET. WE'D BEEN SHARING IDLE CHITCHAT ALL MORNING ABOUT SCHOOL,

MY INJURY, THE TOWN, BUT GENERALLY SHE WAS A ONE- OR TWO-WORD CONVERSATIONALIST AND THIS "MORE COFFEE?" QUESTION WAS ALL I WAS GOING TO GET.

"CAN I JUST STICK WITH THE WATER INSTEAD?" I ASKED.

SHE GAVE ME THE EVIL EYE, LIKE I WAS A FREELOADER, SO I ORDERED A THIRD SLICE OF PIE . . . AND KEPT MY EYE ON THE CROW.

IT STILL HASN'T CHANGED.

WEDNESDAY, SEPTEMBER 22, 12:58 P.M.

I can't believe what just happened.

Ten or fifteen minutes ago while I'm choking down a bite of cherry pie, guess who I see coming up Main Street —

Our friendly neighborhood park ranger. Daryl Bonner.

He walked right past the library, glanced at it, and crossed the street.

I slumped behind my journal and then thought I better not have it out or he might turn private eye on me and try to confiscate it as evidence. Can a park ranger do that? I don't know, but he's got a uniform and he's a big guy, so I didn't take any chances. I bent down and put it in my backpack, and when I glanced back up again, I heard the bell ding at the café door and watched Ranger Bonner walk toward my table.

I'm not sure if it was all the coffee I'd drunk or what, but I was super nervous.

"Hi, Ranger Bonner," I said with this shaky voice. It sounded like I'd just thrown someone under a train.

The rest of the conversation went like this:

Bonner: "Feeling better, I see."

Me: "Yes, much. Thank you, sir."

Bonner: "Seen Sarah lately?"

Me: "No, sir. I haven't seen her in a long time."

Bonner: "You know, she's still snooping around. She can't seem to leave things alone."

Me: "I wasn't aware, since I haven't seen her."

(Mind you, my voice was shaking every time I opened my mouth. No more coffee!)

Bonner: "You're sure you haven't talked to her?"

Me: "Oh, I'm sure. I'd remember that."

Bonner: "Very funny."

Me: "Not trying to be funny, sir."

He looked at me sideways and stood up. I could tell he didn't trust me.

That's all we need — Daryl Bonner following me <u>and</u> Sarah.

He made for the door without turning back, then disappeared down the block.

I drank a glass of water, went to the bathroom again, and stared at the library.

Sitting at the café was making me realize I don't want to be a spy when I grow up. Too much sitting around doing nothing.

Five more minutes just went by and I'm . . .

Oh, no. Don't tell me. This can't be.

Is that . . .

. . . my dad?

He's coming up Main on the other side of the street.

What time is it?

1:05 p.m.

He and Henry are back from the city like they said. But they should be heading for the creek.

Okay, I'm just going to slide down in this booth, watch him, and take a few notes.

He's in front of the library.

Looking both ways.

Now looking off toward Dr. Watts's house.

He's going up the steps.

Has his hand on the crow.

I can't see what he's doing!

He's down the steps and crossing the street.

COMING TOWARD ME?

He can't come in here. No way!

Here he is, right in front of the window, about to reach the door.

Hold your breath, Ryan — that always helps.

Keep your head down. Keep writing.

He's walking like he's got somewhere to be.

He's gone down the street, toward my house and out of sight.

That was way too close. If he saw me watching him, I don't know what I'd do.

Or what he'd do.

I can't see the crow. I should have brought binoculars!

Hold on. Something else is happening.

OKAY, THE PAST HOUR HAS BEEN A WHIRLWIND, BUT I'LL TRY TO EXPLAIN FAST. I COULDN'T GO BACK TO THE CAFÉ OR I'M SURE THAT WAITRESS WOULD HAVE BEEN LIKE, "WHAT IS YOUR PROBLEM?"

I CAN'T TAKE THAT KIND OF STRESS RIGHT NOW.

SO I'M SITTING AT THE STATION HOUSE. NOT UNDER THE STATION HOUSE, WITH THE BLUE ROCK, BUT ON THE STEPS LEADING UP TO THE DOOR THAT'S NEVER UNLOCKED.

I WONDER WHAT'S IN THERE?

SCATTERBRAIN!!!!

I NEED SOMEONE TO SLAP ME SO I CAN CALM DOWN.

SO HERE'S WHAT HAPPENED IN THE PAST HOUR:

I PACKED UP MY STUFF AND LEFT THE CAFÉ. I'VE NEVER WALKED AROUND IN OUR TINY, HANGING—ON—FOR—ITS—LIFE DOWNTOWN WITH SO MUCH ANXIETY. I'VE NEVER WORRIED ABOUT WHO MIGHT BE WATCHING ME. MY DAD COULD BE RIGHT AROUND THE CORNER. DARYL BONNER MIGHT BE STARING OUT FROM BEHIND A WINDOW. GLADYS MORGAN COULD COME OUT AT ANY MOMENT AND POINT HER SHOTGUN AT ME. AND THAT DR. WATTS GUY — HE MIGHT HAVE HIS BINOCULARS

TRAINED ON ME, CALL SOME THUG ON HIS PHONE, AND THEY'D FIND ME WRAPPED AROUND A TREE IN THE CREEK TOMORROW MORNING.

I TURNED DOWN A SIDE STREET AS SOON AS I WAS OUTSIDE THE CAFÉ AND WALKED AWAY FROM THE LIBRARY, TOWARD THE WOODS. THERE ARE WOODS ALL AROUND SKELETON CREEK, BUT THE CAFÉ WAS ON THE SIDE OF THE STREET OPPOSITE THE BIG MOUNTAINS. I GLANCED UP AT THEM AND SAW HOW SMALL THE LIBRARY WAS IN THEIR MONSTROUS SHADOW. ALL THOSE BOOKS DON'T ADD UP TO A HILL OF BEANS AGAINST ONE BIG MOUNTAIN. I TURNED DOWN A SIDE ALLEY AND COULDN'T STOP THINKING ABOUT A PILE OF BOOKS — LIKE EVERY BOOK EVER PRINTED — AND I WONDERED IF ALL THOSE BOOKS WOULD BE AS BIG AS THE ONE MOUNTAIN. MAKES A GUY WONDER ABOUT WHO MADE MOUNTAINS AND WHY THEY WERE MADE SO BIG.

SO ALL THESE THOUGHTS WERE RUNNING THROUGH MY HEAD, WHICH KEPT ME FROM BEING TOO NERVOUS AT THE THOUGHT OF TURNING A CORNER INTO MY DAD OR RANGER BONNER OR GLADYS READY TO SLAP ME ACROSS THE FACE WITH A COPY OF WAR AND PEACE OR LORD OF THE RINGS. BEFORE I KNEW IT, I WAS

WALKING PAST THE LIBRARY, GLANCING UP AT THE BLACK CROW AS MY THROAT TIGHTENED. IT WAS A VERY QUICK GLANCE, LIKE READING A CLOCK AND GOING BACK TO MY HOMEWORK, BUT THAT WAS ALL THE TIME I NEEDED TO SEE THAT MY DAD HAD CHANGED THE TIME.

A STRAIGHT SHOT TO MARTHA'S AT TEN PAST THE KNOB.

A STRAIGHT SHOT TO MARTHA'S AT TEN PAST THE KNOB.

A STRAIGHT SHOT TO MARTHA'S AT TEN PAST THE KNOB.

I KEPT REPEATING THOSE WORDS BECAUSE I'D MEMORIZED THEM FROM THE ALCHEMIST DIAGRAM OF 79.

BEFORE I KNEW HOW I EVEN GOT THERE, I WAS ACROSS THE STREET, DOWN A BLOCK, AND SITTING ON THE CURB, SHAKING UNCONTROLLABLY. I THOUGHT ABOUT THE MOUNTAIN OF BOOKS AND MY BODY NOT GROWING. I BREATHED THE MOUNTAIN AIR IN AND OUT UNTIL I FELT A LITTLE BETTER. IT DAWNED ON ME THEN THAT I SHOULD KEEP WATCHING FROM WHERE I SAT. NO ONE HAD SEEN ME — OR AT LEAST IF THEY HAD, THEY HADN'T STOPPED ME. MAYBE SOMETHING ELSE WOULD

HAPPEN. I STOOD AND PEEKED AROUND THE CORNER ONTO MAIN STREET. I SORT OF LEANED ON THE BRICK BUILDING LIKE I WAS PLAYING IT COOL IN CASE ANYONE WALKED PAST.

I WAITED.

FIVE MINUTES WENT BY. 1:51.

FIVE MORE MINUTES PASSED. 1:56.

PEOPLE WALKED BY THE LIBRARY, BUT NO ONE APPEARED TO LOOK AT THE CROW. NO ONE WENT INSIDE THE LIBRARY. IT JUST SAT THERE UNTIL 1:58, WHEN GLADYS MORGAN OPENED THE DOOR AND CAME OUTSIDE. SHE STOOD THERE A MOMENT LOOKING UP AND DOWN MAIN STREET.

THEN SHE LOOKED AT ME.

I DIDN'T MOVE, AND IT WASN'T BECAUSE I WANTED HER TO SEE ME. I JUST COULDN'T MOVE.

SHE STARED RIGHT AT ME AND I HALF EXPECTED TO HEAR HER WHISPER, "DON'T MAKE ME COME LOOKING FOR YOU."

BUT SHE ACTED LIKE SHE HADN'T SEEN ME AT ALL. GLADYS IS ANCIENT, SO I WAS LIKELY NOTHING MORE THAN A CATARACT-INDUCED BLOB NEXT TO A FUZZY BUILDING. STILL, IT WAS CREEPY THE WAY SHE STOPPED

292

AND HELD HER GAZE RIGHT WHERE I WAS STANDING, LIKE SHE KNEW SOMEONE WAS HIDING JUST OUTSIDE HER ABILITY TO SEE.

GLADYS TURNED AROUND, LOOKED AT THE BLACK CROW, AND WENT BACK INTO THE LIBRARY.

2:00 P.M.

I LINGERED.

I DON'T EVEN KNOW FOR SURE WHY. IT WASN'T LIKE I HAD IT ALL FIGURED OUT OR ANYTHING, BUT SOMETHING TOLD ME TO STAY. THIS LITTLE DANCE WASN'T DONE YET.

AT 2:03 P.M., MY DAD CAME BACK.

HE WALKED CASUALLY UP THE SIDEWALK AND JUMPED THE TWO STEPS TO THE LIBRARY DOOR.

HE DIDN'T SEE ME.

I WATCHED HIM REACH UP AND MOVE THE CROW, AND WHEN HE DID, I REALIZED HE WAS DOING THE JOB THE APOSTLE HAD ONCE DONE.

THE APOSTLE WILL SEE YOU NOW.

COULD MY DAD HAVE WRITTEN THOSE WORDS?

IF HE DID, HE'S CRAZY. MEET MY DAD, ESCAPEE FROM THE NUTHOUSE.

OR WAS IT WORSE THAN CRAZY?

Was it deadly?

No. I couldn't think about that.

He would've been just a kid when Joe Bush died.

A kid like me.

I walked to the blue rock so I could leave a note for Sarah. Now here I sit with the sun beating down on my head. Stress makes you do things you shouldn't. It's that whole fight-or-flight thing. I worked my leg way too hard today without even realizing I was doing it. It didn't hurt then, but it hurts a lot now.

I hope I haven't reinjured it.

I'm not looking forward to the long walk back home.

The lies I'll have to tell about what I've been doing all day.

The questions about the shirt I didn't buy with the money my dad gave me.

But wait — who's the real liar here?

My dad moved the signal, then moved it back.

Everyone in the Crossbones knew they were supposed to look between 1 p.m. and 2 p.m. on

WEDNESDAY. MAYBE THEY'VE BEEN LOOKING FOR YEARS. WHO KNOWS? PROBABLY IT'S ALL PART OF SOME ELABORATE SYSTEM. THE CROW MOVES THE FIRST TIME AND EVERYONE KNOWS IT WILL MOVE AGAIN AT 1 P.M. THE NEXT DAY? COULD BE. THAT WOULD MAKE SENSE, BECAUSE MY DAD IS GONE ALL DAY EVERY DAY. BUT DR. WATTS AND GLADYS? THEY'RE RIGHT HERE. MAYBE DR. WATTS GOES TO HIS TOP WINDOW EVERY DAY, POINTS HIS BINOCULARS AT THE LIBRARY, AND THEN GOES BACK TO WHATEVER IT IS HE DOES IN THAT OLD HOUSE OF HIS. ALL GLADYS HAS TO DO IS GLANCE OUT THE DOOR SHE STEPS THROUGH EVERY DAY.

Sarah — you're going to have to move fast. Crossbones is meeting below Longhorn's at 12:10 tonight.

I can't walk out here again. My leg is killing me.

You'll have to email me, but my guess is they'll be watching even closer. Send me a note at exactly 9:00 p.m. and let me know if you need me to do anything.

I'll turn in early, tell them I'm tired and not feeling well, and maybe they'll leave me alone.

At least I know my dad won't be home tonight.

My best guess about who you're going to see at this secret meeting? Dr. Watts, my dad, Gladys Morgan, and maybe Daryl Bonner.

Everyone else who might have shown up is already dead.

Ryan

WEDNESDAY, SEPTEMBER 22, 5:05 P.M.

SARAH IS GOING TO EMAIL ME IN A FEW HOURS, BUT RIGHT NOW I'M SITTING ON THE FRONT PORCH, TRYING TO PLAY IT COOL. THE OLD COUCH IS GETTING SOME HOLES, BUT IT'S THE MOST COMFORTABLE PLACE TO REST, OUTSIDE MY OWN ROOM. I HOPE MY MOM DOESN'T MOVE IT TO THE YARD AND TRY TO SELL IT.

DAD AND HENRY ARE STILL AT THE CREEK FISHING, WHICH DOESN'T SURPRISE ME. SOME OF THE BEST BUGS COME OUT IN THE LATE AFTERNOON AND EARLY EVENING. THEY MIGHT NOT BE BACK UNTIL 7:00 OR 8:00, ESPECIALLY IF THEY'RE TRYING TO AVOID ANOTHER DINNER LIKE LAST NIGHT. I'VE HAD THE HOUSE TO MYSELF ALL AFTERNOON AND MOM WON'T BE HOME FOR ANOTHER HOUR. I BROUGHT MY LAPTOP DOWNSTAIRS AT THREE, AND FOR THE PAST TWO HOURS I'VE BEEN DIGGING AROUND.

THREE CANS OF COKE LATER, I'VE FOUND SOME AMAZING STUFF.

I HAVE DECIDED THAT I'M OBSESSED WITH ROBERT BOYLE, ROBERT HOOKE, AND SIR ISAAC NEWTON. AS FAR AS I'M CONCERNED, THESE GUYS WERE ROCK STARS. I CAN SEE HOW A SECRET SOCIETY WOULD BE

INTERESTED IN THEM. WHO DOESN'T LOVE A MAD SCIENTIST? BUT AFTER THE RESEARCH I DID TODAY, I THINK I'M STARTING TO SEE A BIGGER REASON WHY THE MEMBERS OF THE CROSSBONES HAVE BEEN INTERESTED IN BOYLE, HOOKE, AND NEWTON.

A BRIEF HISTORY OF THESE THREE PEOPLE IS WORTH WRITING DOWN. FIRST HOOKE. ROBERT HOOKE.

MANY HISTORIANS BELIEVE HOOKE WAS THE FIRST PERSON TO USE THE WORD CELL IN RELATION TO BIOLOGY. THAT ALONE MAKES HIM LARGER THAN LIFE. IMAGINE BEING THE FIRST PERSON TO USE THE WORD PIZZA OR FOOTBALL OR MOVIE. THOSE ARE NOTHING COMPARED TO THE WORD FOR THE BUILDING BLOCK OF ALL LIFE AS WE KNOW IT (INCLUDING PIZZA, FOOTBALLS, AND MOVIES). IMPRESSIVE.

ROBERT HOOKE DID ALL THESE EXPERIMENTS WITH AIR PUMPS AND SPRINGS AND ELASTIC — A BUNCH OF REALLY GREAT STUFF. A LOT OF PEOPLE GIVE HOOKE CREDIT FOR INVENTING THE BALANCE SPRING, WHICH IS WHAT MAKES SMALL TIMEPIECES POSSIBLE. HE THEORIZED CORRECTLY ABOUT COMBUSTION DECADES

BEFORE ANYONE ELSE UNDERSTOOD IT. HE INVENTED BAROMETERS, OPTICAL DEVICES, MICROSCOPES, AND UNIVERSAL JOINTS. HOOKE WAS ONE OF THE FIRST PEOPLE TO ACCURATELY MEASURE WEATHER, TO SEE OBJECTS TOO TINY FOR THE NAKED EYE, AND SURVEY HUGE PARTS OF LONDON SO IT COULD BE REBUILT AFTER THE GREAT FIRE OF 1666. (HE ALSO FIGURED OUT SOME VERY IMPORTANT STUFF ABOUT ELASTICITY, BUT I HAVE TO ADMIT I DON'T REALLY UNDERSTAND IT.)

ONE OF SIR ISAAC NEWTON'S MOST FAMOUS LINES WAS ACTUALLY IN A LETTER HE WROTE TO ROBERT HOOKE:

IF I HAVE SEEN FURTHER IT IS BY STANDING ON THE SHOULDERS OF GIANTS.

SO THAT'S WHAT SIR ISAAC NEWTON, THE DISCOVERER OF GRAVITY, THOUGHT OF HOOKE. NOT BAD.

SIR ISAAC NEWTON IS EVEN MORE IMPORTANT THAN I REALIZED. SURE, I KNEW HE WAS IMPRESSIVE, BUT I COULD HAVE SPENT ALL DAY RESEARCHING THE THINGS HE INVENTED AND DISCOVERED AND NOT EVEN SCRATCHED THE SURFACE.

FROM GRAVITY TO PLANETARY MOVEMENTS, FROM CALCULUS TO HOW LIGHT WORKS, NEWTON WAS AT THE FOREFRONT OF SO MANY GROUNDBREAKING DISCOVERIES IT'S NO WONDER HE IS KNOWN AS THE FATHER OF SCIENCE.

AND THEN THERE WAS THE LAST OF THE THREE, ROBERT BOYLE, WHO TURNS OUT TO BE THE MOST INTERESTING.

LET'S START WITH HIS HAIR!

THE GUY HAD GUTS TO GO OUT ON THE STREETS OF LONDON LOOKING LIKE THAT. WOW. PLENTY OF WIGS TO CHOOSE FROM AT THE WIG SHOP AND HE CHOSE THE BIGGEST OF THE BUNCH.

ROBERT BOYLE WAS A SCIENTIST WITH DEVOUT RELIGIOUS BELIEFS. AFTER READING UP ON HIM, I THINK THIS WAS ONE OF THE KEY THINGS THAT MADE BOYLE UNIQUE. IT'S NOT THAT OTHER NOTABLE SCIENTISTS OF HIS TIME HAD NO FAITH, IT'S JUST THAT BOYLE WAS A CHRISTIAN FIRST AND A SCIENTIST SECOND. THE FACT THAT HE WAS HIGHLY SUCCESSFUL AT BOTH MADE HIM A POWERFUL FIGURE OF THE TIMES. HE ADMIRED GOD'S WORKMANSHIP AND SAW THE STUDY OF NATURAL SCIENCE AS A FORM OF WORSHIP. THE ONLY WAY, IN HIS VIEW, TO DISCOVER THE WORLD GOD MADE WAS TO INVESTIGATE IT. THIS SEEMS LIKE A SOUND IDEA TO ME.

AS FAR AS I CAN TELL, HE WAS A LITTLE BIT OF A NUTTY PROFESSOR. JUST ABOUT EVERYTHING BOYLE EVER WROTE WAS SHORT ON ORGANIZATION AND LONG ON IDEAS. I IMAGINE, IF HE'D HAD A CAR, THE KEYS WOULD HAVE GONE MISSING ALL THE TIME. HE WAS

CONSTANTLY REFUTING THE IDEAS OF OTHER CHEMISTS AND SCIENTISTS, AND ALTHOUGH HE WAS OFTEN RIGHT, THIS MIGHT HAVE HAD THE EFFECT OF MAKING HIM SEEM LIKE A KNOW-IT-ALL TO SOME.

HE WAS OUTRAGEOUSLY WEALTHY, PRIMARILY BECAUSE HIS FATHER WAS ONE OF THE RICHEST MEN IN IRELAND. HIS TITLE (I'M NOT MAKING THIS UP) WAS THE GREAT EARL OF CORK, BUT I DON'T THINK HE MADE CORKS OR PLUGGERS OR BOTTLE CAPS. HE LIVED IN CORK, WHICH I GUESS IS A PLACE IN IRELAND. ANYWAY, THIS MEANT BOYLE COULD AFFORD TO HIRE ASSISTANTS, INCLUDING ROBERT HOOKE — YES, THAT ROBERT HOOKE — TO WORK FOR HIM. IT WAS BOYLE'S IDEA TO EXPLORE GASES AND PUMPS, BUT HOOKE DID MANY OF THE HANDS-ON EXPERIMENTS.

MANY PEOPLE REGARD ROBERT BOYLE AS THE MOST IMPORTANT CHEMIST OF HIS TIME, WHICH MAKES THE FACT THAT HE WAS AN ALCHEMIST ALL THE MORE INTERESTING. YOU HEARD ME RIGHT — ROBERT BOYLE, THE ROBERT BOYLE, WAS A CLOSET ALCHEMIST! AND NOT JUST A HOBBY ALCHEMIST — HE WAS FAIRLY OBSESSED WITH IT. APPARENTLY, SIR ISAAC NEWTON ALSO THOUGHT A LOT ABOUT ALCHEMY,

BUT IT WAS BOYLE WHO APPEARS TO HAVE BEEN AT THE FOREFRONT OF THIS VERY SUBJECTIVE SCIENCE. AND WHILE IT'S HARDER TO FIND REFERENCES TO ROBERT HOOKE AND ALCHEMY, SOMETHING TELLS ME ALL THREE OF THEM WERE SECRETLY WORKING IN THIS AREA TOGETHER.

ALCHEMY, I'M STARTING TO LEARN, WAS THEN AND CONTINUES TO BE TODAY A CONTROVERSIAL OFFSHOOT OF "REAL CHEMISTRY." DURING BOYLE'S TIME, IT WAS VIEWED AS VOODOO CHEMISTRY WHERE CHEMICALS AND METALS WERE BROUGHT TOGETHER IN STRANGE WAYS TO ACCOMPLISH OUTLANDISH THINGS. IT WAS NOT "SERIOUS" SCIENCE.

AND HERE WE COME TO THE MOST INTERESTING THING OF ALL, THE THING THAT MAKES THE APPEARANCE OF THEIR NAMES IN THE CROSSBONES MAKE ALL THE SENSE IN THE WORLD.

ROBERT BOYLE WROTE A SECRET PAPER THAT DIDN'T SURFACE UNTIL LONG AFTER HIS DEATH. IT WAS NEVER MEANT TO BE PUBLISHED, BUT IT WAS.

THIS IS WHAT THE PAPER WAS CALLED:

AN HISTORICAL ACCOUNT OF A DEGRADATION OF GOLD MADE BY AN ANTI-ELIXIR.

If you believe this secret paper by Boyle, he was very close to figuring something out — something remarkable and kind of scary for what it could mean. Robert Boyle was very close to finding a way to turn gold into something else.

Imagine if you could change the properties of gold so it wasn't gold anymore, and then change it back again. Imagine!

What if you worked on a gold dredge and had a way to hide gold or change gold, then change it back?

It can't be possible, can it? Could Boyle and Hooke and Newton have secretly figured this out, but told no one? What if the secret is out there and someone from my little town figured it out? A process like that sure would come in handy on a gold dredge.

It might start to answer why so many members of the Crossbones ended up dead and why at least one of the dead doesn't want to leave the dredge.

I'm stuck in my room, where I just watched the last tiny speck of light from the sun disappear. Summer is fading fast. It used to stay light until almost ten out here.

Not anymore.

Mom came home at 6:00 and made me dinner. It wasn't as bad as I expected it to be. But then again, it's hard to mess up when you're making spaghetti and the sauce is out of a jar.

We sat together at the kitchen table and waited for Dad and Henry to come home.

"They're not coming back for dinner, are they?" Mom asked me. She was twirling a fork full of pasta.

"I wouldn't count on it."

Without Henry around, it was quieter. I'm beginning to think I prefer quiet. It's a lot of work, holding up my end of the conversation. Mom and I mostly sat in silence, which was okay. We talked about what I'd done all day and I told her I spent most of it at the café writing and drawing.

"That sounds nice."

"It felt good to be out of the house," I said. "I think I'm ready to get back to school. This town is awfully dull during the day with no one around."

Mom smiled. I was glad to make her think I wanted to go back to school like a normal kid, even if I wasn't too sure about it myself. There's going to be a lot of questions about the accident and what I've been doing. I could live without all the attention.

Dad and Henry finally stumbled in around 8:00, arguing about who caught the bigger fish and smelling like two guys who hadn't taken a shower in about a month.

"We're starved. What's cooking?" asked Henry.

"Whatever _was_ cooking is gone," Mom replied. "You're on your own."

Henry and my dad looked at each other, shrugged their shoulders, and went straight for the Bisquick.

"What is it with you two and pancakes?" asked my mom.

They didn't answer. Two old friends in the kitchen making the easiest of all foods. I envied them their time together like never before.

"I was out a lot today, and I'm tired," I said.

I didn't mean for it to sound like I was irritated, especially with Henry leaving and all, but I think it was obvious I saw them as a little club no one else was invited into.

"You sure you don't want a cake or two?" Henry said. "I could tell you about how I caught ten times more fish than your dad did."

"I thought you had to go visit Gerald down the road," Dad said.

Henry nodded, but then said, "Gerald can wait awhile. He'll be up late. Always is."

Gerald is another old friend of Henry's. He lives in the next town over — a town that has the distinction of having been the very last place in America to get phone service. It's even more of a dead end than Skeleton Creek. Gerald is

QUITE A BIT OLDER AND CAN'T GO FISHING ANYMORE, BUT HENRY ALWAYS VISITS HIM AT LEAST ONCE ON EVERY TRIP OUT FROM NEW YORK. THE FISHING HAD BEEN SO GOOD FOR TWO WEEKS HE'D PUT IT OFF UNTIL THE LAST MINUTE.

HENRY DID A LITTLE MORE BEGGING AND DAD NODDED LIKE HE WANTED TO SPEND SOME TIME WITH ME. SO I SAT WITH THEM ON THE PORCH FOR ALMOST AN HOUR, ACTING MORE AND MORE TIRED AS THE MINUTES PASSED, UNTIL HENRY JUMPED OUT OF HIS CHAIR SO HE COULD DRIVE THE TEN MILES DOWN TO GERALD'S PLACE. I WAS SURE MY MOM USED THE TIME I WAS ON THE PORCH TO CHECK MY COMPUTER AND MY PHONE. AT LEAST I COULD TURN IN EARLY AND THEY WOULDN'T HAVE ANY REASON TO BOTHER ME.

I CAME UP HERE A LITTLE WHILE AGO, RIGHT BEFORE THE SUN STARTED SETTING, AND RIGHT AT 9:00 I CHECKED MY EMAIL. NOTHING. I CHECKED AGAIN AT 9:01 AND THERE IT WAS, A NOTE FROM SARAH. IT WAS COOL TO THINK SHE WAS SITTING AT HER COMPUTER AND ME AT MINE, AND SOMEHOW IN THOSE SIXTY SECONDS WE'D MADE A CONNECTION. SHE CLICKED SEND,

I REFRESHED MY SCREEN, AND THERE WAS THE NOTE.
IT WAS SORT OF LIKE MAGIC, AND I MISSED HER MORE
THAN EVER.

I'm so glad you stayed at the café! Who knows what would have happened right under our noses if not for you. This is it, Ryan — something really big is happening tonight. And we're going to see it!

I'm sure I can get into the Watts place while the meeting is going on.

My parents, believe it or not, are out on a date. They should be back in about a half hour. I'll see them when they come home so they think everything is all normal. If all goes well, they'll be asleep by eleven and I'll go straight to Longhorn's, then to Dr. Watts's house. Watts has to be hiding something, and this is our best chance to find out what. He can't be two places at once, so we know he'll be out of his house. I just hope I can get inside.

The tape in the camera at Longhorn's Grange will run for about ninety minutes. Hopefully that will be long enough to catch the entire meeting. I'll start it as close to midnight as possible.

Okay — best part of all — I'll broadcast everything live for you. I can't go live with the Crossbones meeting, but I can use my other camera — the one we used to broadcast live in the dredge — to send you a feed. Go to the site at 11:30 p.m. if you can. That's when I'll start broadcasting off and on. Just be sure no one else is watching.

To get into the feed, go to my site and use the password: maryshelley.

Scared but excited! This is going to be incredible!

Sarah

I'M SCARED FOR HER.

I MEAN REALLY SCARED.

I'M NOT SURE WE SHOULD DO THIS.

I'M REALLY CLOSE TO BAILING OUT. THIS IS STARTING TO REMIND ME OF THE NIGHT I LEFT FOR THE DREDGE AND ENDED UP TRAPPED INSIDE THE SECRET ROOM.

I HATE THE WAY THIS FEELS, LIKE I HAVE NO CONTROL OVER THINGS.

ALL I CAN DO IS WATCH WHILE MY BEST FRIEND BREAKS INTO TWO PLACES IN ONE NIGHT.

AND WHAT IF SHE GETS CAUGHT? IT'S NOT HARD TO IMAGINE AN ALARM ON DR. WATTS'S DOOR GOING OFF, OR HER GETTING TRAPPED IN THE BASEMENT AT LONGHORN'S GRANGE. ONE OF THOSE THINGS COULD EASILY HAPPEN.

I WON'T BE ABLE TO DO ANYTHING BUT SIT HERE AND WATCH IT HAPPEN.

I PICKED UP MY COPY OF <u>FRANKENSTEIN</u> AND STARTED READING IT TO PASS THE TIME.

I'M AMAZED AT HOW MUCH I UNDERLINED AND TOOK NOTES IN THIS OLD PAPERBACK. THE MARGINS ARE FILLED WITH LITTLE QUESTIONS AND COMMENTS. I'VE DOG-EARED ABOUT THIRTY OF THE PAGES. I WENT BACK THROUGH, PAGE BY PAGE, AND READ SOME OF WHAT I'D UNDERLINED AND NOTED.

<u>NONE BUT THOSE WHO HAVE EXPERIENCED THEM CAN CONCEIVE OF THE ENTICEMENTS OF SCIENCE.</u> THIS STRUCK ME AS VERY INTERESTING, HAVING JUST SPENT ALL DAY READING ABOUT NEWTON, HOOKE, AND BOYLE.

<u>I SHUNNED MY FELLOW CREATURES AS IF I WERE GUILTY OF A CRIME.</u>

I CAN RELATE, DR. FRANKENSTEIN.

TWO YEARS AFTER MAKING THE MONSTER, FRANKENSTEIN DISCOVERS IT HAS KILLED HIS BROTHER. THIS IS WHEN THE DOCTOR STARTS TO REALLY GO NUTS. IN THE MARGIN I WROTE: <u>HAD HE NEVER CONSIDERED WHAT THE CREATURE MIGHT DO?</u>

A DARN GOOD QUESTION, IF I DO SAY SO MYSELF.

LATER, REFERRING TO DR. FRANKENSTEIN'S CHARACTER, I SCRIBBLED IN THE MARGIN: <u>IT SOUNDS AS THOUGH HE IS CONVINCED JUSTICE WILL PREVAIL.</u>

IT'S QUESTIONABLE WHETHER OR NOT DR. FRANKENSTEIN WAS RIGHT ABOUT THAT.

I WROTE ALL OVER THIS BOOK IN HUNDREDS OF DIFFERENT PLACES, LIKE THE STORY AND THE QUESTIONS IT RAISED IN MY MIND WERE TOO BIG FOR THE PAGES TO HOLD. THESE ARE JUST A FEW OF MY SCRIBBLES IN THE

MARGINS: What did he tell them? He has set his course on doom and power. The dead and the innocent, these are his obsession now. Was he never afraid? I am constantly afraid. Pastoral. This is the devil, I'm sure of it. He would commit another to the same misery. He has killed accidentally. The monster is innocent, because he has no remorse. The apple and the angel. Abandoned. Alone. Immortal. What's that noise?

When I look at the margin notes, I can see why some people might wonder about me. Maybe my parents are worried I'll grow up to be a reclusive weirdo who can't be in a room full of people without having his nose in a book or a journal to write things down in. And the strangest thing? I have no memory of writing these things. Maybe I did it at night, asleep, instead of trashing the walls in my room.

It's 11:30 P.M. Time to go online.

SARAHFINCHER.COM
PASSWORD:
MARYSHELLEY

Wednesday, September 22, 11:30 p.m.

Nothing. The screen is dead.

She's not there.

I wonder when my dad is going to sneak out and if my mom knows he's leaving.

He's going to leave soon.

He might already be gone.

Wednesday, September 22, 11:32 p.m.

Nothing's there.

This is starting to worry me.

Where is she?

Wednesday, September 22, 11:35 p.m.

Still no Sarah. Should I call someone?

Maybe her camera's not working. I don't know what to do!

I'm checking my email.

WEDNESDAY, SEPTEMBER 22, 11:37 P.M.

SHE SENT AN EMAIL!

I don't trust maryshelley. Someone's been trying to hack into my site, in just the last few hours. Bonner? Your dad? My parents? Doesn't matter. Maryshelley is dead. I've beefed up security. Snoopers get shut out and hit with a nasty virus. Whoever it is won't be back. Lost a few minutes on this, so I won't be live until 11:40. Cutting it close!

Use theancientmariner

S.

I'VE GOT THREE MINUTES.

THE ANCIENT MARINER. I WAS WONDERING WHEN THIS WAS GOING TO COME UP.

SARAH AND I TOOK THE SAME ENGLISH CLASS TOGETHER LAST YEAR, AND FOR SOME REASON I OBSESSED OVER THIS POEM. SHE HATED IT BECAUSE IT WAS SO WORDY AND HARD TO UNDERSTAND.

BUT I LOVED IT.

I THINK BECAUSE IT WAS SO SAD AND LONELY.

It's about how bad choices led someone astray. How he can't find home.

It's the story of a wanderer who lost his way and never came back.

I hear my dad sneaking down the stairs.

It's a ten-minute walk to Longhorn's Grange.

Sarah better hurry.

SARAHFINCHER.COM
PASSWORD:
THEANCIENTMARINER

Thursday, September 23, 12:42 a.m.

That's it. I'm calling the police.

Thursday, September 23, 12:43 a.m.

I can't do it.

I don't know why I can't call the police.

I just can't.

Who else can I ask for help?

I couldn't trust my dad even if he was here.

And my mom? Either she's in on all this or she's totally oblivious. I can't bring her in. She'd go ballistic two seconds after I mention Sarah's name.

Henry. Henry can help me. He'll understand.

I'm going downstairs.

Thursday, September 23, 1:12 a.m.

Thirty minutes ago I crept down the stairs and stood in front of Henry's door. I stood there with my hand ready to knock and then the strangest thing happened. I heard the knock, but I hadn't moved my hand. This, I felt for a moment, was the final sign that I'd gone over the edge. Scrawling on my walls, seeing ghosts, and now I'm hearing myself knock without actually knocking.

The tap-tap-tapping wasn't coming from the door in front of me. It was coming from the door behind me.

The screen door that leads outside.

Something about that tapping made me want to run back upstairs and lock myself in my room. I couldn't turn around. Cold sweat started forming on my forehead. I could feel it, like blood about to drip from a dozen small cuts on top of my head.

It was either a big, black crow tapping its beak on my front door, or it was Old Joe Bush.

He'd finished off my best friend and now he was coming for me.

"Ryan. Is that you?"

I glanced around and saw a shadow in the doorway. Luckily, I knew the voice.

Sarah.

I have never traveled so quickly and quietly at the same time. Before I even knew I'd moved from Henry's door, I was outside on the porch, holding Sarah. She was shaking like she'd just fallen through ice into a frozen lake.

We whispered in the dark on the porch and I kept thinking my mom was going to walk up any second and catch us.

"I couldn't stand it in there anymore with dead Dr. Watts," she said. "Whatever was outside went left, away from the back door. So I went out into the night the same way I came in. I ran as fast as I could."

"My dad could be here any minute."

"I kept looking back, but there was nothing there. No ghost, just darkness."

Sarah was in shock. She wasn't herself. She was like a robot, repeating what she'd seen with this choppy voice full of air. She didn't understand we couldn't be there on the porch, holding each other.

"Sarah, my dad — or my mom, for that matter — we can't get caught."

"I'll make an anonymous phone call tomorrow from the school about Dr. Watts so someone finds his dead body."

"You're okay. That's the important thing. Can you make it home without me?"

I couldn't imagine getting caught. My parents had threatened over and over again to move away and leave Sarah behind if we didn't steer clear of each other. She had to go.

Sarah reached into the back pocket of her jeans.

"I think Dr. Watts was planning to bring this with him to the Crossbones meeting. Hold on to it, will you? I think it's important."

I didn't want the envelope, but I had to get

Sarah moving. My dad was going to appear out of the dark any second. I could feel him coming up Main Street. I just knew.

"Sarah, you have to go," I said, taking the envelope out of her hand and guiding her toward the porch steps. For some reason I felt like I was pushing her toward the edge of a cliff. I hadn't even noticed she had her camera with her. It was like an appendage, this metal whirring thing stuck to her hand. She carried it around so much I hardly paid any attention.

"I'll get my other camera from Longhorn's later, like around four, before it gets light outside."

I was concerned about her, after what she'd seen. "You should get some sleep," I told her. "You've been through a lot."

She looked back at me all glassy-eyed, and I thought she might tumble down the steps.

"Gladys, your dad, and Daryl Bonner. Those three are all that's left. I wonder what they're going to say to each other?"

"You don't need to go back there tonight," I told her. "Promise me you'll get some sleep."

Sarah didn't answer me. She moved off and got swallowed by the darkness.

"Be quiet out there," I warned, maybe too late. "You might run into my dad."

Thursday, September 23, 1:31 a.m.

Timing is everything when you're deceiving your parents. If they show up at just the wrong moment, everything blows wide open. The close calls add up, until it feels like the end is inevitable. It feels like the truth is going to get out there eventually. The only question is when.

I made it upstairs with the envelope in my sweating hand without Henry opening his door. But when I turned to face my room at the top of the stairs, someone was standing in front of it.

It scared me so bad I nearly jumped down the stairwell and screamed for Henry to save me.

But then I realized it was my mom. Not necessarily a great situation, but better than having a killer standing in front of you.

"What's wrong with everyone in this house?" she said.

"I was just getting some water in the kitchen," I told her. (I hate lying all the time. It's getting way too easy to come up with what I need on a moment's notice. Lying on demand was never a skill I intended to cultivate. Honest.)

"DID YOU SEE YOUR DAD DOWN THERE?" SHE

ASKED.

AND THIS IS THE TIMING PART I'M TALKING ABOUT,

BECAUSE JUST THEN THE SOUND OF THE SCREEN DOOR

SQUEAKING DRIFTED UP THE STAIRS. MY DAD WAS HOME.

AND I COULD TELL THAT MOM HADN'T KNOWN HE'D

GONE OUT.

SHE WAS HIS PROBLEM NOW, NOT MINE.

"GET BACK IN BED," SHE SAID.

I THINK SHE FIGURED HE AND HENRY HAD SNUCK OUT

TO HAVE SOME LAST—MINUTE FUN OR SOMETHING. IT

DIDN'T MATTER TO ME. ALL I KNEW WAS THE FOCUS

WAS OFF OF ME, I WAS BACK IN MY ROOM BEHIND MY

CLOSED DOOR, AND I WAS HOLDING AN ENVELOPE THAT

WAS SUPPOSED TO ARRIVE AT A SECRET CROSSBONES

MEETING BUT NEVER DID.

Thursday, September 23, 7:15 a.m.

I had a terrible dream last night. Dr. Watts wasn't dead. He was only sleeping. Sarah turned around and Dr. Watts sat up. He'd been using the blue rock as a pillow and he picked it up and held it over his head.

"You're not allowed in here."

Sarah turned at the sound of his voice and Dr. Watts bashed my best friend in the head with the blue rock. The blue rock turned red and I woke up.

I couldn't go back to sleep for a while. There was no noise in the house. It was crazy quiet, which always makes me try really hard to hear the smallest sound. It's a bad habit, because I do hear things if I listen too carefully. I thought maybe I heard my dad's whisper, closer than it should've been from under my door. And I'm almost sure I heard the sound of a marker writing on a wall. Maybe I was half asleep — I don't know.

I'm just glad it's light outside.

There's no word from Sarah, and I'm guessing

SHE TOOK ME UP ON MY RECOMMENDATION AND LEFT THE CAMERA AT LONGHORN'S AND GOT SOME NERVE-CALMING SLEEP INSTEAD. I BET SHE WENT HOME AND COLLAPSED AND FORGOT TO SET HER ALARM. SHE MUST BE EXHAUSTED.

STILL, IT BUGS ME THAT I HAVEN'T HEARD FROM HER. I SAW THE GHOST OF JOE BUSH JUST LIKE SHE DID. IT WAS OUT THERE, AWAY FROM THE DREDGE. IT'S BEEN IN MY ROOM WHILE I'VE BEEN SLEEPING.

OF COURSE, SHE'S THE ONE WHO FOUND A DEAD BODY. NOT ME.

WHAT IF SARAH NEVER MADE IT HOME LAST NIGHT?

WHAT IF SHE WANDERED DOWN A DEAD-END STREET AND CAME FACE-TO-FACE WITH WHATEVER IT WAS WE SAW ON HER CAMERA?

I SHOULDN'T HAVE LET HER GO OUT INTO THE DARK ALONE.

A REAL FRIEND WOULD HAVE WALKED HER HOME.

SHE'S FINE.

SHE'S PROBABLY ON HER WAY TO SCHOOL, MAD AT ME FOR NOT OPENING THIS ENVELOPE.

I WAS TOO AFRAID TO TEAR IT OPEN LAST NIGHT.

I THINK I'LL WAIT UNTIL AFTER BREAKFAST.

Thursday, September 23, 10:00 a.m.

I need to get a few timing issues down straight before I open the envelope. Everything is starting to feel connected.

Okay, here goes:

Last night was Wednesday until midnight and then it was Thursday. The Crossbones met last night right after midnight.

Henry is scheduled to leave in a few hours, also Thursday. Things are going to get awfully quiet around here after that. Good thing I'll be back in school on Monday.

Another story ran in the paper this morning about burning down the dredge. They've moved it up again. It's now scheduled for "demolition by flames" on Saturday afternoon — two days from now, leaving two nights to visit it. After that, no one is visiting the dredge ever again.

I guess my point is that everything is converging. The Crossbones meeting, Dr. Watts's death, the burning down of the dredge, Henry going home, the house getting quiet, me going back to school. Where's Bonner in all of

THIS? I'M SO SURE HE'S INVOLVED IN SOME SORT OF SHADY BUSINESS WITH THIS WHOLE THING. IN FACT, I'D BET MY LIFE ON IT. I CAN'T WAIT TO SEE WHAT HE SAYS AT THE CROSSBONES MEETING.

Now, TO THE ENVELOPE.

I'M GOING TO JUST LAY THIS OUT THERE AS STRAIGHT AS I CAN, BECAUSE I DON'T KNOW WHAT ELSE TO DO WITH INFORMATION THIS IMPORTANT. WHAT WAS IN THAT ENVELOPE FEELS LIKE THE KIND OF STUFF THAT COULD GET ME KILLED. PART OF ME WISHES I'D NEVER OPENED IT AND THAT SARAH HAD NEVER FOUND IT. THE OTHER PART OF ME IS FEELING LIKE WE'RE INCREDIBLY CLOSE TO PIECING TOGETHER THE HIDDEN PAST OF THE DREDGE AND THAT THIS IS THE MOST INTERESTING AND EXCITING THING THAT'S EVER HAPPENED TO ME. I THINK IT MIGHT BE EVEN MORE INCREDIBLE THAN SARAH AND I COULD HAVE IMAGINED.

THERE WERE THREE PIECES OF PAPER IN THE ENVELOPE.

Meeting Notes

- Boyle's Formula

- J.B's trials
  and amendments

- Purpose of the code

- Systematic method for
  reclaiming the assets

CONTROVERSIAL "LOST" PAPERS BY BOYLE PUBLISHED

LONDON — British scientist Robert Boyle (1627–1691), regarded in some circles as the father of the scientific investigative methods employed by virtually all contemporary researchers, has had some of his most esoteric work come under close scrutiny with the publication of heretofore unseen works.

Revealing that Boyle spent many years dabbling in alchemy, these documents, to be published later this month by <u>Scientific Quarterly</u>'s prestigious book division, primarily concern themselves with the scientist's pursuit of turning gold into other precious and non-precious metals, and vice versa.

Reaction from British historians has been consistently negative so far, calling on <u>SQ</u> to halt publication in order to "Protect The Good Name of Sir Boyle."

Boyle's alchemical formula for separating and liquefying gold, as tested and amended by Joseph Bush and Ernest Watts, M.D.

Make a paste of equal parts antimony and stibnite, being careful with your hands and lungs. Deliquesce it, distill the deliquescence, and keep the liquid in a nonporous container (mind the alkalinity!). It will not keep its potency beyond 30 minutes, so work quickly.

Place the rocks or minerals that appear to contain gold in this liquid, and cover with a tight seal. (Be careful not to breathe the fumes at this stage.) After 20 to 25 seconds, open the container. The rocks will appear unchanged, apart from a dusty white coating, much like the coagula of dead ammoniac salt.

Move the rocks to a container of distilled water (must be distilled properly!) and the water will turn dark gray almost immediately. Wait at least 50 seconds (but no more than 80) and pour through a fine-mesh screen.

True gold will remain in the screen, in granular form.

Now grind a small measure of auric seed (granules) to a fine powder, add a drop of the liquid saved from the deliquescence process, and pour the gold granulate on top. The gold will liquefy on contact in working temperatures between 39 and 97 degrees Fahrenheit, and remain liquid for up to 17 minutes. It can be poured into a mold in sections, as it is prepared, until the mold is filled. Wait 30 minutes after the final pouring before removing the block of gold.

So basically, while Robert Boyle was trying to discover a way to change gold into something else, he actually discovered something entirely different. This is kind of common in science, I guess, searching for one answer and stumbling onto another. Boyle never did figure out how to turn copper into gold or gold into iron, but he did figure out two other very interesting things. The first was how to quickly and easily separate gold from anything else, so that gold particles embedded in rocks could be freed and purified. Second, he figured out how to chemically alter gold in order to liquefy it without the use of heat, so that particles of gold could be liquefied and gathered together into larger units without a change in temperature. All of this was done through chemical alchemy, and all of it remained secret, even after the publishing of the lost Boyle papers. It was Dr. Watts and Joseph Bush who thought to expand on Boyle's ideas and actually put them to practical use. Dr. Watts conducted the experiments, and Joseph Bush wrote the paper

AND PUT THE THEORIES TO THE TEST WITHIN THE DREDGE ITSELF.

CLEARLY, JOSEPH BUSH WAS A LOT SMARTER THAN ANYONE IMAGINED.

THE PAPERS GIVE NO DETAILS OF THE ACTUAL USE OF THESE THEORIES AND PRACTICES, SO I'M LEFT TO WONDER ABOUT A LOT OF THINGS. DID THE SECRET SOCIETY FIND OUT ABOUT THESE PROCESSES? DID JOSEPH BUSH USE THE PROCESSES ONLY TO HAVE OTHER MEMBERS OF CROSSBONES TURN ON HIM? DID THE MEMBERS OF CROSSBONES STEAL SOME QUANTITY OF GOLD FROM THE DREDGE? IF SO, WHERE DID THEY HIDE IT? AND WHY ARE SO MANY MEMBERS OF THE CROSSBONES DEAD? ARE THEY KILLING EACH OTHER OFF IN SEARCH OF WHAT — OR WHERE — JOSEPH BUSH HID? OR IS SOMEONE OUTSIDE OF CROSSBONES KILLING OFF CROSSBONES MEMBERS?

ONE THING STANDS ABOVE EVERYTHING THAT FELL OUT OF THIS MYSTERIOUS ENVELOPE — THE GHOST OF JOE BUSH. IT WANTS REVENGE, AND FOR SOME REASON IT'S TURNED ITS GAZE ON ME AND SARAH.

Thursday, September 23, 12:13 p.m.

Henry's gone, which bums me out.

Things are already getting quieter around here.

He said he wished more than ever that he could stay.

"I'd like to see them finally put an end to that thing. It's going to be quite a bonfire out there in the woods. I hope you've got a good volunteer fire department in this town."

This made me think of Sarah, since her dad happens to be a volunteer firefighter. He'll be standing there watching when it goes up. Him and all his buddies.

I wonder if they'll let me and Sarah go, and if they do, will we be able to stand next to each other while the phantom of Joe Bush gets burned into oblivion?

I say this as if he's not already dead. I wish he were alive so I could ask him a few questions.

"Tell Sarah to record it for me, will ya?" Henry asked as he gave me a good-old-boy sideways hug. He didn't seem to remember I wasn't

ALLOWED TO SEE HER. I THINK HE WAS JUST HOLDING ON, TRYING NOT TO GET UPSET AT LEAVING. A SECOND LATER HE WAS GONE, BIG OLD COWBOY HAT AND ALL, HEADING BACK TO NEW YORK. WE WOULDN'T SEE HIM AGAIN UNTIL NEXT YEAR.

TO MAKE MATTERS WORSE, I STILL HAVEN'T HEARD FROM SARAH.

I'M WORRIED SOMETHING MIGHT HAVE HAPPENED TO HER.

BUT HER PARENTS WOULD HAVE CALLED HERE.

SHE'S AT SCHOOL.

SHE'LL CONTACT ME THIS AFTERNOON, I'M SURE OF IT.

Thursday, September 23, 4:13 p.m.

My dad took Henry to the airport and my mom is at work. This house is SO silent. I took the envelope to the blue rock and left it for Sarah so she could read it. On the way back I stopped at the café for pie and coffee and stared out at the library for an hour. Then I came home, watched game shows on TV, and fell asleep outside on the porch sofa.

It's almost 4:30. I should have heard from Sarah by now. What's her plan to get the tape? What's she doing? Does she realize we only have tonight and tomorrow night and that's it? After that the dredge is gone, and all the secrets with it.

I'm tempted to call her, but that would be really dangerous.

I'll watch the History Channel instead. That'll kill an hour.

Thursday, September 23, 8:13 p.m.

This is driving me crazy. Why won't she call or email or throw a rock at my window? Nothing. Just dead air (bad choice of words). My dad and mom aren't talking much. They're taking a deep breath with Henry gone, trying to get used to the silence. Me? I'm smothered in silence! I can't take any more being alone and quiet all the time.

Thank God I start school on Monday. After that I'll talk to Sarah all I want.

We'll come up with something so my parents don't find out.

Daryl Bonner just stopped by. That park ranger's got a lot of nerve. It's ten o'clock at night! Who stops by at ten for a chat on the porch?

I crept down the stairs so I could listen, because it occurred to me that maybe he had Sarah locked up or had heard something about her. Park rangers can't lock kids up, right? That's totally against the law.

Anyway, he didn't lock her up. But he was looking for her. I couldn't hear much, but I heard enough.

"With the burn day coming up, I'm nervous she's going to try to get back in there. Why? I have no idea. Just keep an especially close eye on Ryan, will you? I'm not saying he's going anywhere, but she might try to contact him if she's got some sort of plan that includes the dredge. I sure wouldn't put it past her."

"I'll keep an eye on my boy," Dad said. "You don't need to worry about that."

I felt like a prisoner under house arrest.

What gave him the right?

But I could see why my parents were so nervous. To hear it from Daryl Bonner, Sarah was completely out of control and might drag me down with her. She was the friend no parents wanted their child to have.

If only they knew I am just as involved as Sarah is. She is out in the open, where everyone could see. But I'm lying and sneaking around every bit as much as she is.

Friday, September 24, after midnight

She's out there tonight, doing something. I know it. She's in Longhorn's or Dr. Watts's house or the dredge.

She just doesn't trust me anymore. Why is she holding out on me? Why not at least check in and say hello? I can't understand what's gotten into her.

I've never felt this alone.

Friday, September 24, 6:15 a.m.

Hallelujah — she sent me a video!

SARAHFINCHER.COM
PASSWORD:
GEORGELUTZ

344

Friday, September 24, 8:15 a.m.

Now I know why she was so quiet — and it's not because she was mad at me or had stopped trusting me. We're the same as before.

And the tape?

We have all the pieces now.

And she's right — this is our last shot.

I need to know: What is my dad up to? What was Joe Bush up to?

I have all day to think about what a nightmare this is going to be. Even Sarah looks frightened, which frightens me even more. I try to lie to myself. I try to think that maybe last time in the dredge wasn't as bad as I think it was. And there is this part of me that's so curious. What's hidden down there?

It could be something really important.

Like the evidence of a murder.

Or a stash of gold.

FRIDAY, SEPTEMBER 24, 8:23 A.M.

NINE HUNDRED BUCKS AN OUNCE. IF THERE'S EVEN ONE POUND OF GOLD HIDDEN IN A CAVE UP ON THE MOUNTAIN SOMEWHERE, IT'S WORTH FIFTEEN THOUSAND DOLLARS.

I WISH I COULD TRUST MY DAD AND MY MOM. I WISH OUR PARK RANGER WASN'T SUCH A CREEP.

BUT MOST OF ALL? I WISH THERE WASN'T A GHOST WAITING TO KILL ME WHEN I GET TO THE DREDGE.

FRIDAY, SEPTEMBER 24, 11:23 A.M.

TAKING A NAP SINCE I'LL BE UP ALL NIGHT.

FRIDAY, SEPTEMBER 24, 3:15 P.M.

BY THE WAY, THAT GEORGELUTZ PASSWORD WAS A REAL FIND. SARAH REALLY KNOWS HOW TO FREAK ME OUT. THE AMITYVILLE HOUSE WAS MESSED UP. I FEEL LIKE I HAVE A LOT IN COMMON WITH GEORGE LUTZ. I KNOW EXACTLY HOW HE FELT.

Friday, September 24, 4:43 p.m.

Daryl Bonner just knocked on the door. I tried to act like I wasn't home, but he yelled my name and it startled me. Nothing like dropping a can of Coke to alert others to your presence.

"Come on out," he said through the screen door. "I just want a word with you."

I swear this guy acts like he's a police officer, which is maybe why I'm so confused about how much authority he has. I feel like he could haul me off to jail and get away with it.

Anyway, the Coke was fizzing all over the kitchen floor, so I asked him to wait. When I got out to the porch, he was standing with his hands on his hips, staring down Main Street.

"Tomorrow, things are going to get a lot safer around here," he said. "But tonight's a different story."

"What do you mean?"

"I mean Sarah. She's just crazy enough to try and go out there again. Why are you two so interested in the dredge anyway?"

Why would he think I'd tell him?

347

"We're not," I said. "We're just bored."

"I don't believe you."

"I'm not sure what you want me to say."

"Just promise me you won't go out there tonight. Can you do that?"

I am so deep in trouble that one more broken promise won't hurt.

"I promise I won't go out there tonight," I said.

He didn't believe me.

"Trust me, Ryan. You don't want to be anywhere near there tonight. Just stay away."

I could already imagine him giving this same lecture to Sarah. She'd go along, just like I did, lying through her teeth. What gave him the right to tell us what to do anyway? He had a lot of nerve.

I began to think Sarah's idea of going at 3:00 a.m. made a lot of sense. That's so late it's almost the next day. It was our best chance to get in quietly, open the secret room, and enter the five-digit alchemy code into the cryptix.

FRIDAY, SEPTEMBER 24, 9:43 P.M.

DAD AND MOM ARE HOME. THEY'RE SITTING ON THE PORCH DOWNSTAIRS. I SAT WITH THEM FOR A WHILE AND WE TALKED ABOUT A FEW THINGS. MY DAD WAS SURPRISINGLY CHATTY.

I REALLY WISH I KNEW WHAT HE WAS UP TO.

I REALLY WISH I KNEW HE WASN'T A KILLER.

APPARENTLY, DR. WATTS'S BODY WAS FOUND — I DON'T KNOW WHETHER IT WAS BECAUSE OF A CALL SARAH MADE OR IF SOME NEIGHBOR CAME ACROSS HIM. WHATEVER THE CASE, IT'S BIG LOCAL NEWS. (IN SKELETON CREEK, ANY DEATH IS BIG LOCAL NEWS.) DAD DOESN'T LOOK TOO UPSET — BUT AT THE SAME TIME, HE DOESN'T LOOK TOO GUILTY, EITHER. AND IN THE VIDEO FROM LAST NIGHT, HE HARDLY LOOKED LIKE HE'D JUST KILLED A MAN. SO EITHER HE'S INNOCENT . . . OR HE'S AN AMAZING DECEIVER. I WANT TO BELIEVE THE FIRST. BUT I'M FEARING THE SECOND.

THEY WERE A LITTLE NICER ABOUT SARAH AND SCHOOL FOR A CHANGE, LIKE THEY KNEW WE COULDN'T DODGE EACH OTHER ENTIRELY. A GLANCE OR A HELLO WOULD BE IMPOSSIBLE TO AVOID. THEIR MESSAGE WAS CLEAR: JUST KEEP IT TO A MINIMUM AND STAY

349

FOCUSED ON YOUR WORK. DON'T GET TRIPPED UP.
COME HOME RIGHT AFTER SCHOOL.

I ASKED DAD WHAT TIME THEY WERE BURNING
DOWN THE DREDGE AND HE SAID EARLY, ABOUT EIGHT IN
THE MORNING. THAT BOTHERED ME A LITTLE, BECAUSE
IT MEANT A LOT OF PEOPLE WOULD BE OUT THERE
AT THE CRACK OF DAWN TO GET A GOOD SEAT AND SEE
THE FLAMES. WE'D HAVE TO GET IN AND OUT OF THE
DREDGE FAST.

I TURNED IN FOR THE NIGHT AND LEFT THEM SITTING
TOGETHER.

SO QUIET, THOSE TWO. I GUESS A LOT OF YEARS
MARRIED CAN DO THAT TO PEOPLE.

BUT THEY SEEM HAPPY, GENERALLY SPEAKING. MY
DAD, ESPECIALLY.

LIKE THE WEIGHT OF THE WORLD HAS BEEN LIFTED
OFF HIS SHOULDERS.

Friday, September 24, 11:13 p.m.

New email from Sarah.

Saturday, September 25, 1:30 a.m.

The password, in case someone comes in my room and finds my journal tomorrow morning because I've turned up missing, is fatheraristeus. Just go to www.sarahfincher.com and put in those letters — fatheraristeus — you'll find us.

There's nothing left to say.

It's time for me to go.

SARAHFINCHER.COM
PASSWORD:
FATHERARISTEUS

Saturday, September 25, 9:30 a.m.

It was Henry.

Bonner pulled off the mask and it was Henry underneath.

I didn't even realize the camera had stopped. I think I was in shock.

That's Sarah, writing in my journal. We're back home now.

Keep telling the story. Until I turn the camera on again.

The most interesting thing about the look on my dad's face when he realized his best friend was in the dredge at 3:30 a.m. was not his confusion. Sure, he was confused. Who wouldn't be? It was the recognition in his eyes that something was very wrong. It was the hint of an idea that Henry might have put me and Sarah at risk, might have even tried to harm us. The

WHEELS WERE TURNING IN HIS HEAD, I CAN TELL YOU THAT.

A SON KNOWS WHEN HIS DAD IS ONTO SOMETHING.

BONNER CHECKED HENRY'S PULSE. HE WAS IN BAD SHAPE, BUT HE WAS CONSCIOUS. HIS LEG WAS SHATTERED. I KNEW HOW HENRY FELT AND HOW LONG IT WAS GOING TO TAKE FOR HIM TO RECOVER. HE WAS IN FOR A LONG, PAINFUL RIDE.

WHEN HENRY GLANCED AT THE FACES HOVERING OVER HIM IN THE DREDGE, HE KNEW HE WAS CAUGHT. DAD LOOKED LIKE HE WAS GOING TO KILL HIM.

HENRY LAY THERE, BROKEN LEG AND ALL, AND STARTED TO DENY, DENY, DENY. BUT MY DAD KEPT SHAKING HIS HEAD SLOWLY SAYING, "JUST TELL ME THE TRUTH FOR ONCE."

AND THAT WAS IT. HENRY WAS READY FOR IT TO BE OVER. HE WAS FINALLY READY FOR ALL THE SECRETS TO COME OUT AFTER TWENTY LONG YEARS. HOLDING BACK THAT KIND OF TIDE MUST GET VERY TIRING.

HENRY WOULD SAY SOMETHING, THEN MY DAD WOULD FILL IN A BLANK, THEN ME OR SARAH, UNTIL ALL

THE PARTS WERE FLYING AROUND THE DREDGE,
TOGETHER IN ONE PLACE AT LAST.

HENRY WAS THE ONLY PERSON BESIDES FRANCIS
AND THE APOSTLE WHO EVER SAW JOE BUSH MOVE
THE LEVER AND REVEAL THE SECRET ROOM. HE
DISCOVERED THE SECRET ROOM WHEN THE DREDGE WAS
STILL TEARING EVERYTHING APART AND FORMING
SKELETON CREEK. HENRY HAD SUSPECTED THE THREE
MEN WERE STEALING GOLD. WHO WOULDN'T AT LEAST
TRY? IN FACT, MAKING SURE GOLD WASN'T BEING
STOLEN WAS ONE OF HENRY'S PRIMARY JOBS ON HIS
FREQUENT VISITS FROM NEW YORK. THERE WAS NO
WAY OF KNOWING FOR SURE HOW MUCH GOLD SHOULD BE
COMING OUT OF THE GROUND, WHICH MADE IT IMPOSSIBLE
TO GAUGE WITH ANY KIND OF ACCURACY WHETHER
GOLD WAS MISSING. HENRY HAD TO SNEAK UP ON THEM,
AND THAT'S EXACTLY WHAT HE DID.

IN THE MIDDLE OF THE NIGHT ON A SCORCHING-HOT
AUGUST 14 (EVEN IN PAIN, EVEN SO MUCH LATER, HE
REMEMBERED THE DATE), HENRY GOT IN THE LAKE OF
WATER THE DREDGE FLOATED IN, SWAM OVER AMID THE
POUNDING NOISE, AND BOARDED. DRIPPING WET FROM

HEAD TO TOE, HE WATCHED AS OLD JOE BUSH MOVED A HANDLE THAT DIDN'T SEEM TO HAVE ANY PURPOSE.

THE THING THAT MADE ME THE MOST ANGRY THE WHOLE TIME HENRY WAS TALKING ABOUT THIS WAS THAT IT SEEMED LIKE HE'D NEVER, EVER LIKED SKELETON CREEK OR ANYONE IN IT. FROM BEGINNING TO END, THAT HAD ALWAYS BEEN AN ACT.

THIS, FOR ME, WAS AN UNFORGIVABLE DECEPTION.

He only came back again and again for one reason.

YOU GOT IT, SARAH. GOLD.

It was only _ever_ about getting his greedy hands on the gold.

BUT FINDING THE SECRET ROOM WAS ONLY PART OF THE PUZZLE. IT WOULD TAKE A LOT MORE THAN THAT TO GET WHAT HE WANTED, BECAUSE OLD JOE BUSH WAS A REALLY SMART GUY WHO LOVED SKELETON CREEK.

Henry didn't actually say this. We figured it out this morning. We haven't slept. And Ryan's dad finally started talking.

YEAH. JOE BUSH CREATED LAYERS OF SECRECY WITHIN AN ORGANIZATION HE FOUNDED WHEN THE DREDGE SHOWED UP IN TOWN: THE CROSSBONES. ITS CHARTER MEMBERS WERE THE THREE MEN WHO WORKED THE NIGHT SHIFT TOGETHER ON THE DREDGE: JOE BUSH, THE APOSTLE, AND FRANCIS PALMER. ONLY THOSE THREE WERE AWARE OF THE LOCATION — OR EVEN THE EXISTENCE — OF THE SECRET ROOM. THE THREE WERE ABSOLUTELY SWORN TO SECRECY, AND TOGETHER THEY RECRUITED DR. WATTS, GLADYS MORGAN, AND MY DAD, PAUL McCRAY.

DR. WATTS AND JOE CREATED THE FORMULAS FOR PURIFYING AND MELTING GOLD, BUT DR. WATTS NEVER KNEW ANYTHING ABOUT A SECRET ROOM. HE WAS CONTENT TO DO THE CHEMISTRY WITH JOE AND KEEP OUT OF THE DIRTY DETAILS OF STEALING GOLD. JOE GAVE THE COMBINATION TO THE CRYPTIX TO MY DAD AND GLADYS BUT NO ONE ELSE. THEY HAD NO IDEA A SECRET ROOM HAD BEEN CREATED OR EVEN WHY.

AND EVERYONE IN THE CROSSBONES WAS GIVEN ONE PRIMARY OBJECTIVE: TO SAVE THE TOWN FROM THE EVIL OF THE DREDGE. IN DUE TIME, WHEN JOE WAS READY, ALL THE MEMBERS WOULD KNOW EVERY SECRET. BUT HE KNEW THAT WOULD HAVE TO WAIT A LONG TIME, AT LEAST UNTIL THE DREDGE WAS SHUT DOWN FOR GOOD.

THERE WAS ONE BIG PROBLEM. OLD JOE BUSH MIGHT HAVE BEEN SMART AS A WHIP, BUT HE WASN'T IMPERVIOUS TO ACCIDENTS. ACCORDING TO HENRY (BUT THEN, HOW MUCH CAN WE REALLY TRUST HIM?), OLD JOE BUSH REALLY DID DIE BY ACCIDENT. HE REALLY WAS PULLED INTO THE GEARS BY THE CUFF ON HIS PANTS. HIS LEG WAS SMASHED AND THE GEARS SPIT HIM OUT INTO THE WATER BELOW, JUST LIKE THE LEGEND SAID. AND IT HAPPENED THE NIGHT AFTER HENRY DISCOVERED THE SECRET ROOM.

ONLY JOE KNEW EVERY IMPORTANT DETAIL: THE EXISTENCE OF THE SECRET ROOM HE'D MADE, WHERE IT WAS, THE COMBINATION TO UNLOCK THE CRYPTIX, AND THE ALCHEMY FORMULA FOR PROCESSING GOLD THE WAY HE'D SECRETLY DONE IT.

Henry went straight to Francis Palmer when he could no longer turn to Joe for answers. He threatened Francis with losing his job. But Francis didn't know anything Henry didn't already know. He knew Joe spent hours and hours in the secret room. He knew where the secret room was. But that was it.

So Henry questioned Francis mercilessly and — as he told it — <u>accidentally</u> killed him. The same was true for The Apostle.

Henry said it something like this:

"They were all accidents! I never meant to hurt anyone. I scuffled with Francis up there and he fell. And that crazy Apostle, I dunked him in the river but I didn't drown him. He just slipped out of my hands and drifted downstream in the dark. It wasn't my fault he couldn't swim."

As far as Henry was concerned, very little was ever his fault.

After The Apostle died, the remaining members of the Crossbones fell quiet for

YEARS. DR. WATTS, GLADYS, AND MY DAD ALL WENT ON WITH THEIR DAILY LIVES. BETWEEN THE THREE OF THEM, THEY HAD NO IDEA A SECRET ROOM EVEN EXISTED. THEY ONLY HAD A HUNCH THERE WAS SOME GOLD HIDDEN SOMEWHERE AND THAT SOMEONE HAD KILLED THEIR FRIENDS IN SEARCH OF IT. BEST TO LEAVE WELL ENOUGH ALONE.

YEAR AFTER YEAR, HENRY CAME BACK, SEARCHING FOR CLUES. HE WAS SURE THERE WAS A STASH OF GOLD HIDDEN SOMEWHERE ON THE MOUNTAIN, AND HE WAS CONVINCED THE CRYPTIX CONTAINED A MAP THAT WOULD TELL HIM WHERE TO LOOK. IF ONLY HE COULD UNLOCK IT WITHOUT BLOWING HIMSELF UP.

ON ONE OF HENRY'S VISITS SOME KIDS WERE SNEAKING AROUND THE DREDGE AND HE CHASED THEM OFF. AFTER THAT HE NEEDED A PLAN TO KEEP SNOOPING THRILL-SEEKERS AWAY FROM THE DREDGE. SO HE CREATED THE GHOST OF JOE BUSH. ELEVEN MONTHS OUT OF EVERY YEAR IN NEW YORK GAVE HIM PLENTY OF TIME TO FIGURE THINGS OUT. EVERY YEAR HE ADDED A FEW MORE SUBTLE TOUCHES. UNDERGROUND SPEAKERS, REMOTE SWITCHES FOR

SOUNDS, IRIDESCENT MASKS AND HOODS, INVISIBLE TRIP WIRES THAT LET HIM KNOW WHEN SOMEONE WAS HEADING DOWN THE TRAIL TOWARD THE DREDGE. HE EVEN HAD HIS OWN SECRET SHORTCUT THROUGH A SEEMINGLY IMPENETRABLE FORTRESS OF BLACKBERRY BUSHES.

THINGS WERE DIFFERENT WITH ME AND SARAH. NUMBER ONE, WE WERE PERSISTENT.

I was persistent. What's this we stuff?

LIKE I WAS SAYING, WE WERE PERSISTENT. BUT THERE WAS ONE THING THAT TIPPED HENRY OFF THAT I DIDN'T KNOW ABOUT UNTIL HE MENTIONED IT. SARAH HAD BEEN GOING TO THE DREDGE AND FILMING IT FOR WEEKS BEFORE THAT FIRST VIDEO SHE SHOWED ME. SHE'D ALREADY BEEN INSIDE, ALREADY SCOUTED AROUND FOR HOURS. AND HERE'S ONE OF THE WEIRDEST PARTS OF THE WHOLE STORY: HENRY HAD SURVEILLANCE CAMERAS SET UP INSIDE AND OUTSIDE THE DREDGE. NOT ONLY COULD HE KEEP AN EYE ON IT FROM A LAPTOP HE CARRIED WITH HIM, HE COULD ALSO WATCH IT FROM NEW YORK. AND WATCH IT HE DID. YEARS OF

WATCHING THE DREDGE TURNED HENRY INTO QUITE THE
TECHNICIAN WITH THIS SORT OF THING. IF A PERSON
WALKED PAST CERTAIN PLACES IN THE WOODS ON THE
WAY TO THE DREDGE, THEY UNKNOWINGLY SET OFF
ALERTS ALL THE WAY OUT IN NEW YORK. THE BEST
I CAN UNDERSTAND IT, THERE WERE WIDE PADS BURIED A
FOOT UNDERGROUND AND THEY WERE SENSITIVE TO
PRESSURE. IF SOMEONE WALKED ON THE TRAIL, HENRY
KNEW THEY WERE COMING.

AND SO IT WAS THAT BY THE TIME HENRY
ARRIVED IN SKELETON CREEK, HE'D WATCHED SARAH
WITH HER CAMERA. HE'D SEEN HER VISITING THE
DREDGE NOT ONCE BUT SEVERAL TIMES, RECORDING ALL
KINDS OF THINGS. IT WORRIED HIM ENOUGH TO PUT HIS
WELL-WORN SCARE TACTICS INTO HIGH GEAR WHEN HE
SHOWED UP IN SKELETON CREEK.

Henry was also growing bolder because of all the
talk about burning down the dredge.

HE DIDN'T KNOW WHO ELSE WAS IN THE
CROSSBONES, BUT HE WAS SURE THERE WERE OTHERS.
HE'D SEEN LITTLE HINTS HERE AND THERE FROM MY

362

DAD. AND THERE WAS THAT ONE NIGHT, WHEN I FELL ASLEEP AT MY DESK AND WOKE UP WITH WORDS SCRIBBLED ON MY WALL WITH A PEN. I HAD THAT LIST — THE LIST OF EVERYONE WE'D DISCOVERED WAS IN THE CROSSBONES. IT WAS THAT LIST THAT SENT HENRY TO SEE DR. WATTS WHEN HE SAID HE WAS VISITING A FRIEND.

HE HAD AN EXCUSE FOR THAT NIGHT, TOO.

"I DIDN'T MEAN TO KILL DR. WATTS. I FORCED MY WAY IN, THAT MUCH IS TRUE. AND I QUESTIONED HIM. I KNEW HE HAD ANSWERS, BUT THE OLD LOON WOULDN'T TELL ME ANYTHING. I ONLY SWUNG ONE TIME, CAUGHT HIM RIGHT IN THE HEAD. BUT HE MADE ME SO MAD, ALL CLAMMED UP LIKE THAT. HE WAS FRAIL, MORE SO THAN I REALIZED. I'M SURE HE DIED OF A HEART ATTACK, NOT THAT LITTLE BUMP ON HIS HEAD."

I GUESS YOU COULD SAY HENRY'S CONFESSION WAS TEMPERED WITH QUITE A LOT OF EXCUSES. AT LEAST HE DIDN'T DO MUCH COMPLAINING WHEN IT CAME TO HIS OWN SEVERE INJURIES.

"DID YOU WRITE THOSE WORDS ON MY WALL?" I ASKED HIM.

"WHAT WORDS? WHAT ARE YOU TALKING

about?" Dad asked. He was already mad, but the idea of Henry in my room, writing on my walls, brought his anger to another level.

Henry just looked down at his broken leg and wouldn't answer. He couldn't bring himself to look at my dad, and I never knew for sure if it had been Henry or not.

Finally, Henry just about passed out from the pain. Bonner called the hospital for an ambulance.

And I got the camera working again.

There was at least one more big surprise waiting for us on the dredge. But this part is better seen than said.

WEDNESDAY, SEPTEMBER 29, 4:30 P.M.

I'M BACK IN MY ROOM ALONE. I BEGAN WRITING THINGS
DOWN IN HERE, SO IT SEEMS LIKE THE MOST LOGICAL
PLACE TO END UP.

IN SOME WAYS I'M MORE AFRAID THAN I WAS WHEN
THIS WHOLE THING STARTED. THE DANGER HAD ALWAYS
FELT AS IF IT CREPT OFF THE PAGE OF A SCARY STORY
I'D MADE UP IN MY HEAD. SURE, IT WAS SPOOKY OUT
ON THE DREDGE, BUT THERE WAS A FEELING SOMEWHERE
AT THE BACK OF MY MIND THAT IT WAS STILL A GHOST
STORY.

THINGS ARE DIFFERENT NOW.

HENRY IS OUT THERE SOMEWHERE. THEY
SEARCHED THE WOODS FOR DAYS AND FOUND NOTHING.
CHANCES ARE HE PLANNED FOR THIS AND CREATED A
SECRET WAY TO ESCAPE UNNOTICED. IT WOULD BE JUST
LIKE HIM TO THINK AHEAD. I WONDER WHAT HIS
APARTMENT IS LIKE IN NEW YORK — FULL OF
CAMERAS POINTED AT THE DREDGE — WATCHING THEM
REMOVE ALL THE HIDDEN TREASURES. I DON'T KNOW AND
NEITHER DOES HENRY, BECAUSE HE'S VANISHED INTO
THIN AIR. NO ONE HAS BEEN ABLE TO FIND HIM.

WE'VE TAKEN HIS GOLD AND LEFT HIM INJURED. HE

HATES US. AND THE WORST PART, HENRY THINKS I'M

THE CAUSE OF ALL HIS PROBLEMS.

FROM HERE ON OUT THE DANGER IS REAL.

I'M GOING TO CHANGE SUBJECTS BECAUSE I'M HOPING

IT WILL MAKE ME FEEL BETTER.

RIGHT AFTER I PULLED UP THAT FLOORBOARD ON

THE DREDGE AND DUMPED THE BLOCKS OF GOLD OUT,

DARYL TOLD US SOMETHING WE DIDN'T KNOW ABOUT HIS

DAD. PART OF ME FEELS LIKE WE SHOULD HAVE FIGURED

IT OUT ON OUR OWN A LONG TIME AGO, BUT WE NEVER

SUSPECTED.

"YOU DON'T KNOW WHO I AM, DO YOU?" HE

ASKED US.

IT WAS SARAH WHO STARTED CHIPPING AWAY AT

THE OPTIONS.

"YOU'RE NOT A PART OF THE CROSSBONES. YOU

DIDN'T HAUNT THIS PLACE. YOU'VE NEVER BEEN HERE

BEFORE THIS SUMMER. WHO ARE YOU?"

"I'VE ALWAYS SUSPECTED FOUL PLAY," SAID DARYL.

"ALWAYS. BUT I NEVER IMAGINED . . ."

"WHO ARE YOU?" SARAH REPEATED.

"I WAS A FOSTER KID IN THE CITY UNTIL I WAS

TWELVE. THAT'S WHEN THE BONNERS ADOPTED ME.

About a year after that I started going by my middle name — Daryl. I guess I was looking for a break with the past. A fresh start."

"What's your first name?" asked Sarah. She could make a really good investigative reporter. Always first with the questions.

"Joseph," said Daryl. "I'm Old Joe Bush's son."

I remember feeling light-headed for some reason, like the ghost of Joe Bush had inhabited his son and we were about to be appropriately scared out of our wits. But the moment passed and I realized something as Daryl went on. The guy had lost his dad to the dredge. He'd obviously lost his mom young, too, and he'd been through the toughest kind of childhood. But curiosity had gotten the better of him. He'd been searching for answers just like we had, only the stakes were even higher.

"Now I know the truth," he said, looking at the opening to the secret room.

All this happened before we realized we'd basically forgotten all about the cryptix and the secrets we'd uncovered. After we figured out Joe had liquefied the gold and hidden it inside the planks of the dredge itself, Daryl piped back in.

"I should have guessed he would come up with something like this. My dad was about the handiest guy in town, everybody said that. That's why they chose him to run the dredge. He was gifted with motors and cranks and all kinds of machinery. But he was also a carpenter. A really good carpenter. He built the house we lived in. I remember him bringing these planks home, saying he was fixing them or replacing them. No one would have ever guessed differently. It was his job to repair things, and they were always just planks coming out of the dredge, so even if they checked, there was nothing to find. As far as anyone else was concerned, the dredge was slowly getting a new floor that always looked better and better. But when those boards went back, the centers were gone, ready to be filled with a block of pure gold. I guess my old man was pretty smart."

The diagram of the dredge we found in the secret room was very detailed. It showed every floorboard on both floors of the dredge. The ones Joe Bush had filled with gold were colored in with a pencil. There weren't very many empty planks yet to be filled in. In other words, the dredge was a ship of gold. There were hundreds of hidden gold bars.

A year after New York Gold and Silver abandoned dredge #42 in Skeleton Creek, the town bought it for a dollar. There was some talk of turning it into a tourist attraction, but it never materialized. Who wants to walk way out into the woods and look at an old hunk of wood and metal? Nobody, that's who.

But it ended up being the best investment Skeleton Creek ever made.

I got an update from my dad when I came home today. So far they've pulled 1,400 pounds of gold out of the dredge. Every floorboard they pull up has another ten or twenty pounds of pure gold hidden down the middle. The price of gold is high these days, pushing a thousand dollars

AN OUNCE. MY DAD CARRIES A CALCULATOR IN HIS POCKET, ADDING UP THE NUMBERS OVER AND OVER.

"AT A THOUSAND DOLLARS AN OUNCE WE'RE AT SIXTEEN THOUSAND PER POUND OF GOLD," HE TOLD ME EARLIER TODAY. "DO YOU REALIZE HOW MUCH MONEY WHAT THEY'VE FOUND IS WORTH? OVER TWENTY-TWO MILLION BUCKS."

"IT'LL REACH THIRTY MILLION BEFORE THEY'RE DONE TEARING IT APART," I SAID. I'D STUDIED THE DIAGRAM CAREFULLY. THERE WAS A LOT MORE TO BE FOUND.

THIRTY MILLION DOLLARS' WORTH OF GOLD. CAN YOU IMAGINE? AND IT WAS ALWAYS RIGHT THERE, SITTING IN THE WOODS JUST WAITING FOR SOMEONE TO FIND IT.

EVEN THE DREDGE WON'T COME OUT TOO BADLY IN THE END. THERE ARE ALREADY PLANS IN THE WORKS TO BUILD A WOOD-PLANK TRAIL FROM MAIN STREET ALL THE WAY OUT TO THE DREDGE WITH SIGNS ALL ALONG THE WAY DESCRIBING THE AMAZING STORY SARAH AND I UNCOVERED, GHOSTLY SOUNDS AND SITES INCLUDED. THE FACT THAT HENRY HAS GONE MISSING WILL ONLY ADD TO THE URBAN LEGEND AND BRING IN

EVEN MORE TOURISTS. SOME PEOPLE SAY THEY HOPE HE NEVER COMES BACK AND NEVER GETS FOUND.

I AM NOT ONE OF THOSE PEOPLE.

THERE'S TALK OF REBUILDING THE DOWNTOWN AND TURNING SKELETON CREEK INTO A WORLD-CLASS FLY-FISHING AND SIGHTSEEING DESTINATION, WITH THE CREEK AND THE DREDGE AS ITS CENTERPIECE. THIRTY MILLION DOLLARS OUGHT TO COVER IT.

MY DAD'S PLANNING TO OPEN A FLY SHOP, SINCE THE TOWN IS "GIFTING" MY PARENTS AND SARAH'S PARENTS FIVE PERCENT OF WHATEVER COMES OUT OF THE DREDGE.

OH, AND THEY'RE GIVING SARAH AND ME ENOUGH MONEY TO ATTEND ANY COLLEGE WE WANT AFTER GRADUATION. WE'RE CURRENTLY ON THE HUNT FOR A UNIVERSITY KNOWN FOR EXCELLENCE IN BOTH WRITING AND FILMMAKING. I CAN ONLY IMAGINE WHAT KIND OF TROUBLE WE'LL GET INTO WHEN WE SHOW UP ON CAMPUS.

EVERYONE IN SKELETON CREEK SEEMS TO BELIEVE WE CAN TURN THIS PLACE AROUND. STILL, FOR ME, THE TOWN WASN'T THE MOST IMPORTANT THING THE DREDGE GAVE ME BACK.

What I got back, what really matters, is my best friend. They can have all the money as long as they let me and Sarah stay together, which it appears they are going to do. I suppose it would be hard to justify keeping us apart, seeing as how we saved Skeleton Creek and all.

I'm talking to my dad more these days, and he's talking, too. The fly shop will be good for us, a common interest we can share. Plus he'll be around a whole lot more, doing something he loves.

He doesn't talk about Henry. I can't imagine how it would feel for your best friend to betray you like that, to lie about so much for so long. It has softened my dad about me and Sarah, but he's going to have a hard time trusting like that again.

We've both learned a lot about the risks and rewards of friendship.

One of the nice things about being a writer is that writing is always there for me when I need it. During the past few weeks, through all the trauma and loneliness and fear, writing has been

MY REPLACEMENT BEST FRIEND. I'VE SPENT MORE TIME WRITING DURING THE LAST TWENTY DAYS THAN I DID DURING THE HUNDRED DAYS BEFORE THAT. WRITING WAS A COMFORT. I FEEL I OWE IT SOMETHING IN RETURN.

BUT THE PENDULUM IS SWINGING THE OTHER WAY NOW, AND I SUSPECT I'LL BE WRITING A LOT LESS FOR A WHILE. SARAH AND I HAVE SOME CATCHING UP TO DO. THERE'S SCHOOLWORK. I'LL BE DRIVING SOON. I HAVE A STRONG FEELING SARAH WILL WANT TO MAKE A STAB AT LOCATING HENRY, AND I CAN'T LET HER DO IT ALONE.

BUT I KNOW WRITING WILL BE HERE WHEN I NEED IT, AND THIS IS A GREAT COMFORT TO ME AS I VENTURE BACK OUT INTO THE WORLD FULL-TIME.

WE'RE HOSTING A BARBECUE ON THE PORCH TONIGHT, WHICH MEANS I HAVE TO WRAP THIS UP AND GO HELP MY MOM. PRETTY SOON DARYL BONNER AND GLADYS MORGAN WILL BE HERE ALONG WITH A WHOLE BUNCH OF OTHER TOWN FOLKS. SARAH WILL BE HERE WITH HER PARENTS AND HER NEW CAMERA. MY DAD WILL MAN THE GRILL. LATER ON, WHEN THE BUGS START HATCHING AND THE SUN TIPS BEHIND THE MOUNTAINS, I'LL TAKE SARAH TO THE CREEK SO I CAN TEACH HER HOW

TO CAST A FLY ROD. MAYBE WE'LL WALK OUT TO THE DREDGE AND TAKE A LOOK AROUND, OR UP TO LONGHORN'S GRANGE TO RETRIEVE HER DAD'S LADDER OUT OF THE TALL WEEDS.

I CAN'T HELP THINKING ABOUT THAT BLUE ROCK WE PAINTED WHEN WE WERE KIDS AND THE SIMPLE QUESTION SHE ASKED ME.

I WANT TO PAINT THE ROCK, DON'T YOU WANT TO PAINT THE ROCK?

WITHOUT SARAH, I'M NO DIFFERENT THAN THE LEGEND OF OLD JOE BUSH. I'M LIKE A GHOST, ALONE IN MY ROOM, MAKING UP STORIES AND KEEPING TO MYSELF. IT'S LIKE SARAH HAS AHOLD OF MY HAND, PULLING ME FORWARD. SHE'S LOOKING BACK AT ME WITH THE SAME QUESTION IN HER EYES OVER AND OVER AGAIN.

I WANT TO LIVE, DON'T YOU WANT TO LIVE?

I DO, SARAH.

I DO.

PATRICK CARMAN's
SKELETON CREEK
☠ THE ☠
CROSSBONES

PC STUDIO

A couple of days ago I walked past a parked car I'd never seen before. The owner had slapped a crooked blue bumper sticker on the trunk.

Just because you're paranoid doesn't mean people aren't really out to get you.

I have never read a truer statement in my life.

MONDAY, JUNE 20, 12:03 A.M.

I AM SURE SOMEONE OR SOMETHING IS OUT TO GET ME.
WHATEVER IT IS ESCAPED FROM THE ABANDONED
DREDGE AND HAS LEAKED OUT INTO THE REST OF THE
WORLD.

<u>IT'S LOOSE, IT'S ANGRY, AND IT'S LOOKING FOR ME.</u>

I HAVE A BAD HABIT OF ALLOWING THOUGHTS LIKE
THIS TO FILL MY MIND IN THE MIDDLE OF THE NIGHT.

<u>IT WANTS TO GET ME.</u>

THERE WAS A TIME WHEN I THOUGHT I TURNED
TERRIBLE THINGS OVER IN MY MIND BECAUSE I READ AND
WROTE TOO MANY SCARY STORIES. (NOTE TO SELF:
START WRITING ABOUT UNICORNS AND BUNNIES.) THE
LOGIC WAS PRETTY STRAIGHTFORWARD: I READ ABOUT
ZOMBIES, THEREFORE I DREAMT ABOUT WALKING DEAD
PEOPLE WITH ARMS THAT FELL OFF. I WROTE STORIES
ABOUT GHOSTLY BEINGS, SO NATURALLY I ASSUMED
SOMETHING CREEPY WAS STANDING OUTSIDE MY WINDOW
WITH A CHAIN SAW.

IT'S A GOOD THING I'M OLDER NOW. I'M WISER. I'VE
GOT A BETTER SENSE OF HUMOR. I CAN HANDLE
WHATEVER COMES MY WAY.

But this is <u>real</u>, and I can prove it.

You'll see. I'll <u>make</u> you see.

I just thought of a sick story about a

giant red bunny and a one-eyed unicorn.

Hang on.

MONDAY, JUNE 20, 1:15 A.M.

OKAY, I'M BACK. AND BUMMED OUT. SOMETIMES THE <u>IDEA</u> FOR A STORY IS SO MUCH BETTER THAN THE STORY ITSELF. SUCH IS THE CASE WITH A ONE-EYED UNICORN GOING TOE-TO-TOE AGAINST A SEVEN-FOOT RABBIT-MAN. THEN AGAIN, DARK HUMOR IS LIKE BLACK MEDICINE FOR MY FEARS. IT KEEPS ME FROM SCREAMING IN THE LONELY HOURS OF THE NIGHT.

MOVING ON . . .

I FEEL I SHOULD RECAP WHAT GOT ME INTO THIS MESS IN THE FIRST PLACE. IT'S GOOD SHORT STORY PRACTICE, IF NOTHING ELSE.

<u>FIRST, THE SEVEN-WORD VERSION:</u>
HAUNTED BY GHOST, FOUND GOLD, SAVED TOWN.

<u>AND THE SLIGHTLY EXPANDED, FAR MORE USEFUL VERSION:</u>
MY BEST FRIEND, SARAH, AND I DISCOVERED THE PRESENCE OF A GHOST OUT IN THE WOODS. THE GHOST WAS CALLED OLD JOE BUSH, AND IT WAS REAL. THE

WOODS WERE HOME TO AN ABANDONED DREDGE, WHICH
WAS HAUNTED BY THE GHOST AND PROTECTED BY A
SECRET SOCIETY CALLED THE CROSSBONES. MY DAD
WAS A CROSSBONES MEMBER, THOUGH I QUESTION TO
THIS DAY HOW MUCH HE REALLY KNEW. A CERTAIN
SOMEONE I WILL NOT NAME (HIS NAME IS FORBIDDEN IN
SKELETON CREEK) WENT TO GREAT LENGTHS TO KEEP
PEOPLE AWAY FROM THE DREDGE. HE WENT SO FAR
AS TO EMBODY THE GHOST OF OLD JOE BUSH, AND I'M
CONVINCED HE WENT CRAZY IN THE EFFORT. AFTER A
WHOLE LOT OF INVESTIGATING AND ONE MAJOR INJURY,
SARAH AND I DISCOVERED THE REASON WHY THE
DREDGE WAS BEING PROTECTED: ITS FLOORBOARDS WERE
FILLED WITH FORTY MILLION DOLLARS' WORTH OF GOLD.
SARAH AND I WERE CREDITED WITH FINDING THIS LONG-
LOST STASH AND WERE FORGIVEN OUR TRANSGRESSIONS,
LIKE LYING IN THE FIRST DEGREE, SNEAKING AROUND
BEHIND OUR PARENTS' BACKS, ACTING LIKE RECKLESS
TEENAGERS, NEARLY GETTING KILLED. THE GHOST OF
OLD JOE BUSH IS GONE NOW. IT TOOK THE IMPOSTER
AND THE CROSSBONES WITH IT.

I DON'T KNOW WHY I'M WRITING ALL THIS DOWN
AFTER ONE IN THE MORNING. FOR ALL I KNOW THE

GHOST OF OLD JOE BUSH IS STANDING IN MY DRIVEWAY, THINKING ABOUT HIS OPTIONS: RIP THE FRONT DOOR OFF ITS RUSTY HINGES? OR QUIETLY WALK THROUGH THE WALLS AND HOVER OVER MY BED?

I AM GOING TO CLOSE MY EYES.

I CAN DO THIS. I CAN GO TO SLEEP. I CAN TURN MY MIND TOWARD SOMETHING OTHER THAN THE GHOST OF OLD JOE BUSH.

I AM THINKING HAPPY BUNNY THOUGHTS.

MONDAY, JUNE 20, 9:00 A.M.

I ALWAYS FEEL BETTER IN THE MORNING, LIKE THE LIGHT OF DAY HAS TRAPPED MY FEARS UNDER A PILE OF DIRT. AT LEAST THEY'RE BURIED UNTIL NIGHTFALL.

IT'S OFFICIALLY SUMMER, I HAVE A LITTLE BIT OF CASH, AND I LOVE EGGS AND HASH BROWNS. THESE FACTS HAVE DRIVEN ME OUT OF MY BEDROOM AND INTO A BOOTH AT THE CAFÉ ON MAIN STREET. I'VE EMPTIED MY POCKETS ONTO THE SCUFFED GREEN TABLE AND TAKEN STOCK OF MY PATHETIC FINANCIAL CONDITION: TWELVE DOLLARS, FIFTY-FIVE CENTS. AND I DON'T GET ANOTHER INFUSION OF MOOLA UNTIL FRIDAY.

HOW CAN I HAVE A GIANT PILE OF MONEY IN THE BANK AND BE SO BROKE AT THE SAME TIME?

GOOD QUESTION.

THE TOWN GOT MOST OF THE GOLD ME AND SARAH FOUND, WHICH WAS FAIR, I SUPPOSE. THE UNFAIR PART? WHAT GOLD I <u>DID</u> GET TO KEEP WAS PLACED IN A TRUST. I CAN'T TOUCH IT UNTIL I TURN EIGHTEEN, WHICH FEELS LIKE A MILLION YEARS FROM NOW.

WHAT THIS MEANS IS TECHNICALLY MY SOCIAL STATUS HAS GONE <u>DOWN</u> SINCE I SAVED THE TOWN FROM RUIN. EVERYONE ELSE IN SKELETON CREEK IS EITHER

DRIVING A NEW PICKUP TRUCK, RENOVATING A HOUSE, OR HAULING A BIG-SCREEN TV THROUGH THE FRONT DOOR. A FAIR NUMBER ARE DOING ALL THREE AT THE SAME TIME.

THE SPENDING SPREE IS COURTESY OF MAYOR BLAKE, WHO'S NEVER LIFTED A FINGER TO DO MUCH OF ANYTHING BESIDES OPEN A PEPSI CAN. HE GAVE EVERY FAMILY, INCLUDING MY OWN, ONE HUNDRED THOUSAND DOLLARS. HE CALLED IT A "STIMULUS PACKAGE" AND ENCOURAGED EVERYONE TO BLOW IT AS FAST AS THEY COULD. ONE THING ABOUT MAYOR BLAKE — HE'S GOOD AT FIRING OFF HIS MOUTH AND GETTING EVERYONE EXCITED. WHETHER IT'S TURNING THE DREDGE INTO A HAUNTED ATTRACTION OR BUILDING A NEW VISITORS' CENTER, THE GUY CAN REALLY YACK IT UP. PEOPLE AROUND HERE ARE PERPLEXED BY SO MUCH CHATTER; IT CONFUSES THEM INTO DOING STUPID THINGS (LIKE SPENDING A HUNDRED GRAND IN NO TIME FLAT).

EVEN AFTER THEY GAVE ME AND SARAH A BIGGER WAD OF DOUGH THAN ANYONE ELSE GOT, THERE WAS STILL MORE THAN TEN MILLION LEFT. A LOT OF NEW FOLKS ARE RUNNING FOR MAYOR SO THEY CAN DECIDE HOW TO SPEND IT, AND THE POPULATION HAS BALLOONED FROM

SEVEN HUNDRED TO SEVEN HUNDRED AND FOURTEEN, A REVERSAL OF DECADES IN THE OTHER DIRECTION.

SITTING IN THE CAFÉ, SIPPING A COLD CUP OF COFFEE, MY THOUGHTS HAVE TURNED TO SARAH. WE USED TO START EVERY SUMMER WITH PLANS ABOUT WHAT KIND OF TROUBLE WE WERE GOING TO GET INTO.

BUT THAT'S GOING TO BE A LITTLE CHALLENGING THIS TIME AROUND, BECAUSE NOW SARAH'S GONE.

I GUESS HER PARENTS LOOKED AT THE MONEY AS A TICKET OUT OF SKELETON CREEK, BECAUSE THEIR HOUSE WAS UP FOR SALE THE SAME DAY THE CHECKS LEFT THE MAYOR'S OFFICE. I DON'T KNOW — I GUESS I CAN HARDLY BLAME THEM. IT'S STILL A DEAD-END TOWN, AND ME AND SARAH DIDN'T EXACTLY GIVE THEM A LOT OF REASONS TO HANG AROUND. ALMOST GETTING KILLED WITH YOUR BEST FRIEND DOES SEND UP A LITTLE BIT OF A RED FLAG. IT WOULDN'T SURPRISE ME IF MY PARENTS AND HER PARENTS HAD A SECRET MEETING.

MY DAD: ONE OF US IS GOING TO HAVE TO MOVE OUT OF TOWN BEFORE OUR KIDS GET THEMSELVES KILLED.

SARAH'S DAD: I'VE GOT FAMILY IN BOSTON. I COULD FIND WORK THERE.

385

MY DAD: I'D LIKE TO OPEN A FLY SHOP, MAKE A GO
OF IT.

SARAH'S DAD: I'LL TALK TO MY WIFE.

I BET THAT'S EXACTLY HOW IT WENT DOWN,
FOLLOWED BY A FOR SALE SIGN POUNDED INTO
THE MUD IN FRONT OF HER HOUSE.

WITH SARAH GONE, THINGS CHANGED. WE EMAILED
AND TALKED TO EACH OTHER ONLINE, BUT THE
MESSAGES THINNED TO A FEW LINES HERE AND THERE.

THREE MONTHS AFTER SHE LEFT, I GOT A NOTE
THAT FELT LIKE THE BEGINNING OF THE END.

Hey, Ryan,

I was accepted into summer film school at UCLA, so at least I'll be back
on the West Coast for a week. I never thought I'd escape Skeleton Creek.
I know how it feels there.

Get out or get dead — that's my advice.

S.

It was just the kind of email I didn't need. Not only had Sarah escaped Skeleton Creek without me, but to make matters worse, she felt sorry for me. Get out or get dead? Wow, talk about a two-by-four in the face. That one hurt.

Still, I really miss her. She filled a lot of space, and that space has turned empty.

This is probably why the summer feels so aimless. Our plans were never really our plans. They were her plans.

I have no idea what to do with myself with the summer laid out before me. I have this nagging feeling that only one thing could ever bring us close to each other again.

Our friendship has always had its foundation in the thrill of danger and secrets. Even when we were little kids, it was always about sneaking around behind everyone's back. Skeleton Creek was full of rubes, and it was our job to pull one over on them.

It feels like those days are over.

Unless something happens.

Unless the thing that drove us apart is, in the end, the one thing powerful enough to bring me and Sarah back together.

Unless the ghost of Old Joe Bush returns.

Monday, June 20, 9:40 a.m.

I know that sounds crazy.

The ghost is gone. Everyone says the ghost is gone.

But if he is, why can I still feel his presence?

If he's disappeared, how do I know he's still here?

Monday, June 20, 9:45 a.m.

I swear, the waitress just tried to look over my shoulder.

I'm so tired of feeling watched.

One second.

Monday, June 20, 9:49 a.m.

The dredge still sits out there in the woods, same as it ever was, and I never go out there. Tourists seem to like it, which is what prompted Mayor Blake to push the idea of a haunted attraction. Sort of like a haunted house. I think this is a terrible idea, and I've said as much. But who's going to listen to a sixteen-year-old, even if he did save the town?

A fresh cup of coffee and I still have a little time before I have to open the fly shop. That should be enough time to address the most important thing I took from the dredge that night. It wasn't the hordes of gold we found hidden in the floorboards, secretly stashed by Joe Bush long before he was pulled into the gears and drowned in the water below. No, it was something much smaller and infinitely more dangerous.

The last thing Sarah recorded in the dredge was a shot of the floor. If you look at that video, you'll see the same thing everyone else saw: an envelope. It's one of the great mysteries

OF THE DREDGE, AND ONE OF THE REASONS PEOPLE STILL THINK IT'S HAUNTED. BECAUSE YOU KNOW WHAT? NO ONE CAN FIND THAT ENVELOPE. IT'S AS IF IT NEVER EXISTED.

PEOPLE ASK ME ABOUT IT FROM TIME TO TIME. I JUST SHRUG AND SHAKE MY HEAD.

I DON'T FEEL LIKE LYING ANYMORE.

BUT I ALSO DON'T FEEL LIKE SAYING, "THE ENVELOPE? YEAH, I HAVE IT. I KEPT IT. HEY, SOMEONE'S GOTTA KEEP A LID ON THIS NIGHTMARE."

SO, YEAH, I TOOK THE ENVELOPE. IN ALL THE CONFUSION THAT NIGHT, I SLIPPED IT INTO MY POCKET AND DIDN'T TELL ANYONE, NOT EVEN SARAH. THEN I HID IT IN THE BACK OF ONE OF MY DESK DRAWERS AND TRIED TO FORGET. I THOUGHT MAYBE — JUST MAYBE — IF I DIDN'T ACKNOWLEDGE ITS EXISTENCE, IT WOULDN'T HAVE ANY POWER. IT WOULD SIT BACK THERE AND ROT LIKE AN OLD APPLE CORE.

BUT IT DIDN'T ROT. INSTEAD, IT BLOOMED IN MY IMAGINATION, AND A MONTH LATER I COULDN'T STAND LEAVING IT ALONE ANY LONGER. LIKE THE DISTANT, HOLLOW VOICE OF THE UNDEAD HIDDEN BENEATH OLD FLOORBOARDS, THIS GHASTLY THING WOULD NOT SHUT UP.

WHAT'S INSIDE? IT ASKED, SCRATCHING THE BACK OF MY BRAIN WITH ITS CLAWS.

I LAY THERE, NIGHT AFTER NIGHT, WONDERING WHAT HAD BEEN LEFT BEHIND, UNTIL FINALLY I COULDN'T STAND IT ANY LONGER.

A DISTANT THUNDER ROLLED OVER THE MOUNTAIN AT HALF PAST TWO IN THE MORNING AS I PULLED THE DRAWER ALL THE WAY OUT AND TOOK OUT THE DREADED ENVELOPE. RACING BACK TO MY BED, I FELT THE EVIL EYE OF OLD JOE BUSH WATCHING ME COWER BENEATH THE COVERS. WAS IT THE GHOST, OR WAS IT THE MAN, STANDING OUTSIDE MY WINDOW? I WOULD HAVE SWORN SOMETHING WAS THERE, TOUCHING THE GLASS AT MY SECOND-STORY WINDOW, AN ICY BREATH FOGGING THE PANE.

I TORE THE ENVELOPE OPEN AND HELD ITS CONTENTS IN MY HAND.

ONE CARD, TWO SIDES. THE WORK OF A MADMAN IF EVER THERE WAS!

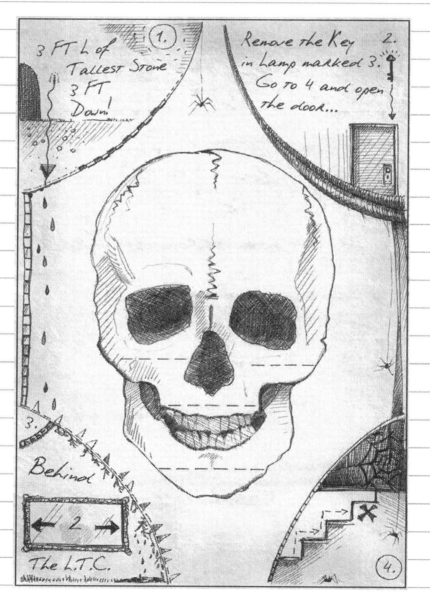

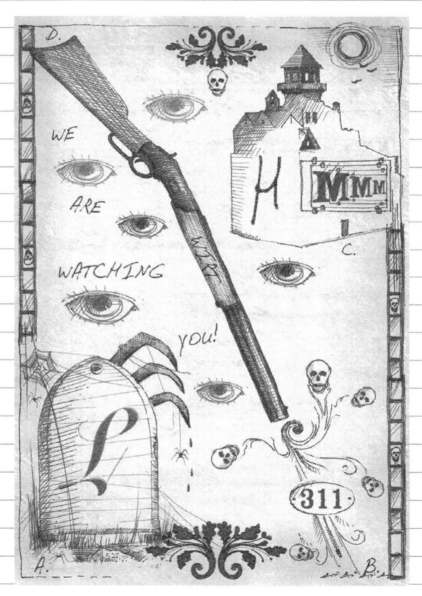

As a whole, I came to call this crazy thing I'd found the Skull Puzzle, because that's what it was: skulls and tombstones and guns. A puzzle of the dead.

I spent the next few months trying to figure out what the clues on the card meant. Many months, and a giant ZERO to show for my efforts. I searched online endlessly, all hours of the night, until I woke up one morning and realized the contents of the envelope had become my obsession.

I should have left the envelope at the back of my drawer, as I'd planned to do. Or better yet, I should have left it in the forsaken dredge where it belonged. Maybe the ghost of Old Joe Bush would have emerged from his watery grave and pulled it into the mud where it belonged.

But no. I had it now.

MONDAY, JUNE 20, 10:10 A.M.

THERE CAME A NIGHT WHEN I DECIDED TO PUT IT BACK.
I HAD THE FEELING IT WAS CURSED, THAT IT WOULD SEND
MY MIND SPINNING INTO OBLIVION IF I KEPT IT. AGAINST
ALL MY BETTER JUDGMENT, I TOOK TO THE WOODS
BEHIND SKELETON CREEK AND MADE THE LONG WALK
ALONE. BUT WHEN I STOOD BEFORE THE DREDGE IN THE
DEAD OF NIGHT, I WAS SO SCARED I COULDN'T BRING
MYSELF TO GO INSIDE. I RAN BACK THROUGH THE
WOODS, TREE LIMBS SLAPPING ME IN THE FACE, AND
COLLAPSED ON MY BED.

YOU HAVE TO UNDERSTAND: I ALMOST DIED THERE.

IT'S HARD TO GO BACK TO A PLACE WHERE YOU
ALMOST DIED.

AS I WENT TO MY LAPTOP IN SEARCH OF SOME
UNATTAINABLE COMFORT, I KNEW DEEP IN MY BONES
THAT I WOULD FIND A MESSAGE FROM SARAH. I CAN'T
SAY WHY, OTHER THAN TO ADMIT MY BELIEF THAT I AM
CONNECTED TO SARAH IN AN OTHERWORLDLY WAY.
SAY WHAT YOU WILL, BUT I FELT TRUE TERROR AT THE
DREDGE. THE SAME PANIC SARAH FELT ON THE NIGHT SHE
FIRST SAW THE GHOST OF OLD JOE BUSH. MY FEAR,
SO CLOSELY LINKED TO HER OWN, CALLED OUT TO HER.

I REALIZE EMAIL IS A DIGITAL INVENTION LACKING IN
DRAMATIC REALITY, BUT THIS WAS ONE MESSAGE THAT
PRODUCED FEELINGS I WILL NEVER FORGET.

Hi, Ryan,

I had a dream you were at the dredge without me and it made me
sad. I miss you. I miss our secrets. There must be something we could
do to get the magic back. But what?

S.

I EMAILED HER BACK IMMEDIATELY.

Sarah,

I can bring that feeling back. Tell no one, especially your parents.

R.

I attached the two images and had to wait only nine minutes for her reply. We spent the rest of that first night instant messaging, emailing web sites and images, whispering into our cell phones. By the time the sun came up, we'd spent five hours in constant communication.

Like the ghost of Old Joe Bush, we were back.

If only I'd known then what I know now, I never would have encouraged Sarah to go down this path with me. I never would have taken that envelope in the first place.

It was what they wanted, and we had it.

We didn't even know they were paying any attention.

The Crossbones were watching us.

We've made some progress, which I will explain after I get off work, but in the meantime, there's something to watch.

She's uploading videos again. Same web address, new passwords. It's different this time around, and I'm still getting used to it. Sarah never shows her face. I wish I could see her, but I understand why she's changed her recording methods. Nothing on the internet is safe, and videos get captured and posted all the time. She's much more comfortable behind the camera, not in front of it, but it's more than that.

Sarah is scared, just like I am.

She doesn't want the wrong people seeing her. She's even altered the way she sounds. It's almost her voice, but not quite. Kind of gives me the creeps, if you want to know the truth.

Sarah's first video is up there, a disturbing recap of everything that's happened so far to us. If I'm gone and you've stumbled onto this journal, maybe you need to see what happened

AT THE DREDGE. MAYBE YOU NEED AN INTRODUCTION
TO THE CROSSBONES BECAUSE, LET ME TELL YOU,
THEY MATTER. EVEN IF YOU ALREADY KNOW ABOUT
THESE THINGS, HER TELLING IS WORTH A LOOK.

DON'T WATCH IT WITH THE LIGHTS OFF.

ALWAYS BE ON GUARD.

SARAHFINCHER.COM
PASSWORD:
MRSVEAL

As soon as I got that password from Sarah, I Googled it and found a digital copy of a short story called "A Relation of the Apparition of Mrs. Veal." Who knew Daniel Defoe, the same guy who wrote Robinson Crusoe (a fave of mine), also wrote a ghost story? "The Apparition of Mrs. Veal" is a short story about a lady who sees a woman wandering around on the day after her death. Not the most chilling thing I've ever read, but interesting in that it is said to have been taken from actual events.

I can relate.

Watching the entire story of what happened to us in three minutes is like seeing my life flash before my eyes. All those events happened over a period of only a few weeks, but looking back, it feels like a much bigger chunk of my life. I guess some memories are burned in forever while others blow away like leftover ash.

MONDAY, JUNE 20, 5:46 P.M.

I JUST SPENT THE DAY AT MY SUMMER JOB — A
PRETTY GOOD GIG, ALL THINGS CONSIDERED.

MY PARENTS SAVED HALF OF THE MONEY THEY
GOT FROM THE GOLD AND SUNK THE REST INTO A FLY
SHOP, WHERE I AM GAINFULLY EMPLOYED AT A RATE
WELL BELOW MINIMUM WAGE ALONG WITH ANOTHER
YOUNG GUY NAMED SAM FITZSIMONS (EVERYONE
CALLS HIM FITZ). MY DAD IS CONSTANTLY REMINDING
ME THAT MY PAY IS WELL BELOW WHAT FITZ MAKES
BECAUSE IT INCLUDES ROOM AND BOARD. THIS IS A
TOTAL CROCK AND PROBABLY AGAINST THE LAW, BUT
I'LL TAKE WHAT I CAN GET.

ACTUALLY, HIRING FITZ WAS MY IDEA. MY DAD
MADE ME TRY OUT FOR THE FOOTBALL TEAM BACK IN
OCTOBER AND I WAS CURSED TO MAKE THE C SQUAD.
THE ONE GOOD THING THAT CAME OUT OF THE
EXPERIENCE WAS FINDING A GUY WHO WAS JUST AS
INEPT AT SPORTS AS I WAS. FITZ AND I RODE THE BENCH
TOGETHER, TOOK HITS FROM THE A SQUAD AS
PRACTICE DUMMIES, AND TALKED ABOUT FISHING
THROUGH ENDLESS FRIDAY NIGHTS OF NO PLAYING TIME.
WHEN FOOTBALL CAME TO AN END A COUPLE OF

403

MONTHS AGO, I STARTED PESTERING MY DAD TO HIRE THE GUY WHO'D SAT NEXT TO ME FOR THREE MONTHS OF WINTER GAMES.

"CAN HE TIE A FLY AND CAST A ROD?" WAS MY DAD'S ONLY QUESTION, WHICH I ANSWERED HUGELY IN THE AFFIRMATIVE. FITZ WAS A FISHING NUT, AND MY DAD WANTED CHEAP, EXPERIENCED, LOCAL LABOR. MY FOOTBALL BUDDY FIT THE BILL. FITZ WAS LIKE A LOT OF SIXTEEN-YEAR-OLD GUYS WHO LIVED IN THE MOUNTAINS: GOOD WITH A GUN, A FISHING ROD, AND A CAMPFIRE. AND CHEAPER THAN CHEAP TO EMPLOY, BECAUSE ALL HE REALLY WANTED TO DO WAS SPEND ALL HIS MONEY IN THE FLY SHOP, ANYWAY. A REAL WIN-WIN FOR MY DAD.

A LITTLE MORE ABOUT FITZ:

HE LIVES A FEW MILES OUTSIDE OF TOWN IN A TRAILER WITH HIS DAD — A SITUATION NOT AS UNCOMMON AROUND HERE AS ONE MIGHT IMAGINE. HIS DAD'S A LOGGER, WHICH IS MORE THAN LIKELY WHY HE'S DIVORCED. (LIFE LESSON: WOMEN DON'T DIG IMPOVERISHED WOODSMEN WHO SHOWER TWICE A WEEK.) FITZ RIDES AN OLD MOTORBIKE HELD TOGETHER BY DUCT TAPE AND CHICKEN WIRE AND NEVER WEARS A

HELMET. WE'RE A LITTLE SHY ON COPS AROUND HERE, AND EVEN IF WE HAD ANY, I DOUBT THEY'D CARE ABOUT TEENAGERS JOYRIDING IN THE BACK OF PICKUP TRUCKS OR RACING AROUND WITHOUT HELMETS ON. IT'S KIND OF PAR FOR THE COURSE IN SKELETON CREEK, IF YOU GET MY DRIFT.

FITZ'S MOTORCYCLE BURNS OIL, WHICH MEANS YOU CAN OFTEN SMELL HIM COMING BEFORE HE SHOWS UP. EVEN THOUGH I TELL HIM I DON'T MIND THE SMELL, HE WON'T LET ME RIDE IT. ONE OF THESE DAYS I'M GOING TO LIFT HIS KEYS AND DO COOKIES IN THE GRAVEL BEHIND THE FLY SHOP, BECAUSE, ACTUALLY, IT'S A SWEET BIKE. IT HAULS.

WHEN FITZ TALKS, IT'S ALMOST ALWAYS ABOUT FISHING AND HUNTING, WHICH IS A LITTLE WEIRD. THE ONLY BUMMER ABOUT HAVING HIM AROUND IS HE'S A VERY GOOD FISHERMAN AND AN EVEN BETTER FLY TIER. PLUS, HE'S A PEOPLE PERSON, UNLIKE ME. (GENERALLY SPEAKING, I PREFER NOT TO TALK WITH ANYONE I DON'T KNOW UNLESS I'M FORCED INTO IT.) I HAVE A HUNCH MY DAD IS GOING TO USE HIM A LOT TO TAKE TOURISTS FISHING AND LEAVE ME IN THE SHOP. IF THAT HAPPENS, I WILL HAVE TO KILL FITZ, BECAUSE I

CANNOT STAND THE IDEA OF FISHING STORIES IN WHICH I
AM NOT A PARTICIPANT.

I'M GOING DOWNSTAIRS FOR DINNER. THEN IT'S TIME
TO WRITE DOWN HOW ME AND SARAH ACCIDENTALLY
SUMMONED A GHOST AND A SECRET SOCIETY BACK INTO
OUR LIVES.

MONDAY, JUNE 20, 10:15 P.M.

I GOT ROPED INTO A FEW HOURS ON THE STREAM WITH FITZ AND MY DAD AFTER DINNER, BUT I'M FINALLY BACK. FITZ LANDED A MONSTER OUT OF THE BIG HOLE AT MILE 7, BUT IT WAS PRETTY SLOW OTHERWISE, AND I GOT SKUNKED. MY MIND WAS ON OTHER THINGS.

I WISH I COULD TELL FITZ WHAT'S GOING ON. I MEAN, WHAT'S REALLY GOING ON. BUT THAT'S NOT WHERE WE ARE RIGHT NOW. LIKE WITH MOST OF MY FRIENDS. I HAVE PLENTY OF PEOPLE I COULD HANG OUT WITH, OR PLAY VIDEO GAMES WITH, OR TALK ABOUT HOMEWORK WITH. BUT FRIENDS I CAN TELL EVERYTHING? JUST SARAH, AND EVEN HER, NOT REALLY. WHICH IS PROBABLY WHY I SPEND SO MUCH TIME WITH THESE NOTEBOOKS. IT'S EASIER THAN GETTING OTHER PEOPLE INVOLVED.

I NEED TO GO BACK AND RETRACE HOW I ENDED UP IN THE SITUATION I'M IN, BECAUSE REALLY, I DON'T KNOW EXACTLY HOW IT HAPPENED. IT'S BEEN THREE WEEKS SINCE I TOLD SARAH ABOUT THE SKULL PUZZLE. SHE CALLS IT THE SKULL. EITHER WAY, IT'S FULL OF SURPRISES.

"THE SKULL SAYS THIS AND THE SKULL SAYS THAT," SHE'LL TELL ME. OR "I THINK THIS IS WHAT THE SKULL IS TRYING TO TELL US."

407

JUST LIKE EVERY OTHER TIME BEFORE, SHE'S GOT A WAY OF TAKING THE LEAD.

AS I WRITE THIS, SARAH IS DRIVING FROM CHICAGO.

BECAUSE OF THE SKULL.

I KNOW, CRAZY.

HERE'S HOW IT HAPPENED, AS BEST I CAN STRING IT ALL TOGETHER.

ABOUT A WEEK AFTER I SENT SARAH THE SKULL PUZZLE, SHE EMAILED ME AN IDEA THAT I HADN'T THOUGHT OF. I'D BEEN LOOKING AT THOSE IMAGES FOR MONTHS, FEELING STUMPED BY THE WEIRD COLLECTION OF SYMBOLS AND NUMBERS. BUT SARAH'S DAD WAS A HUNTER AND MINE WASN'T. TURNS OUT THAT WAS THE TRIGGER THAT BLEW MY WHOLE LIFE APART.

Hi, Ryan,

I've been thinking about the gun. That word on the barrel — Wirt — it's not what we thought. I looked up all the gun manufacturers again, and this time, I cross-checked owners and company owners. Ryan — it's not *Wirt*, it's *Winchester*. I kept focusing on the founder, Oliver

Winchester, but that was a dead end. But guess what his son's name was? William Wirt Winchester. So we know it's a Winchester gun! That's good, right?

Not much, but something.

S.

BY THE TIME I GOT THIS EMAIL FROM SARAH, I'D HAD THE SKULL FOR A LONG TIME. AT SOME POINT ALONG THE WAY I SCANNED IT AND TOOK IT APART, SEPARATING EACH ITEM INTO ITS OWN FILE.

HERE'S THE RIFLE AGAIN:

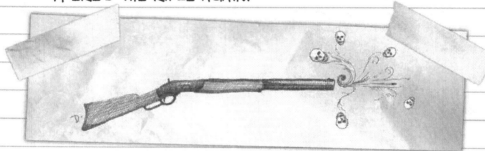

I DO NOT LIKE GUNS OF ANY KIND, AND THIS ONE IS NO EXCEPTION. I SEARCHED THE NAME WILLIAM WIRT WINCHESTER, AND BEFORE THE NIGHT WAS OVER, I KNEW WHAT I'D GOTTEN MY HANDS ON. SARAH AND I BOTH KNEW. THE EMAILS FLEW BACK AND FORTH AS WE MADE PROGRESS. IT WAS LIKE WE'D BEEN LOST IN THE WOODS AND HAD SUDDENLY FOUND THE RIGHT TRAIL.

Sarah,

Did you look up his name? If you do you'll find he was married to — get this — a lady named Sarah. That's crazy, right? And she was crazy. Her husband and her kid both died, and she had piles of money. She basically owned half the Winchester gun company during the Civil War. Can you imagine how many guns they sold? Hang on — I'm diving back in.

Ryan

Ryan,

The Winchester House in San Jose, California — freaky! I love it! I think it's even better than our own haunted dredge. Get this: Sarah (Winchester) started building the house after she got all that money and basically never stopped building. She believed that there had to be enough rooms to hold all the people who had ever been killed by a Winchester gun. Fat chance, Sarah — you'd need a house as big as Mexico for that. She came close! The Winchester House is gigantic and it's filled with doors that lead to nowhere, secret passageways, and lots of confirmed ghost sightings.

This is getting good.

S.

Sarah,

I got it. Check out this piece of the Skull Puzzle:

The part I blew up is marked with a number 4, which probably means it's a match for the letter D at the end of the gun:

The stairs don't make any sense. They end at the ceiling. The Winchester House is full of crazy stuff like this — you said so yourself. My guess? If we could figure out a way to find this exact spot in the house, we'd find one part of what we're looking for.

We could fill in one of the dotted lines on the Skull Puzzle and we'd be on our way to solving this thing.

R.

MONDAY, JUNE 20, 10:47 P.M.

It's getting late, but I don't care. I have to get this all down.

Just in case something happens.

It didn't take us long to figure out that what I'd found was a key to a series of places where paranormal activity had been recorded. Someone had created a haunted treasure map . . . but where did it lead and what was it for? In my darkest thoughts, I could only imagine one place a map like that would take me, and that was six feet underground, with a tombstone over my head.

This was a map of the dead, made by a guy who'd lost his mind.

Henry.

There, I said it.

Henry, who betrayed my family, my town, and me. Henry, who disappeared like a ghost. Henry, the traitor. Henry, the threat.

This was Henry's doing. The Skull Puzzle came out of his twisted mind and landed in his pocket.

BUT WHEN DID HE MAKE IT — BEFORE OR AFTER HE WAS
TAKEN OVER BY THE GHOST OF OLD JOE BUSH?

LOOKING AT EVERYTHING THROUGH A GHOSTLY
LENS SHARPENED OUR SEARCH DRAMATICALLY. DURING
THAT SAME NIGHT, SARAH AND I FIGURED OUT ONE OF
THE OTHER CLUES ON THE SKULL: THE STRANGE HOUSE
WITH AN H AND THREE M's ON IT.

BEFORE WE APPLIED THE HAUNTED FILTER, THESE
IMAGES COULD HAVE MEANT A MILLION DIFFERENT
THINGS. THE BUILDING COULD HAVE BEEN A HOUSE OF
PANCAKES FOR ALL WE KNEW. OR, MORE LIKELY,
HOUSE OF THE DEAD OR HOUSE ON HAUNTED HILL.
ALL WE HAD WAS AN H, A BUILDING, AND A MIRROR
REFLECTING THE LETTER M OVER AND OVER AGAIN.
SARAH AND I STARTED THINKING OF IT AS THE HOUSE

Ryan,

I got it I got it I got it! Sometimes YouTube isn't a total waste of time. I found a video while doing a search for haunted mirrors and BANG — I found it! I can hardly type this, I'm shaking so much. Just watch the video and then let's risk a call. It's 2:30 a.m. here, so your parents have to be asleep. Call me when you're done watching!!

S.

OF MIRRORS, WHICH GAVE US THE DIRECTION WE WERE LOOKING FOR.

SHE SENT A LINK THAT HAD SOME GUY GIVING A GUIDED TOUR OF A HOTEL CALLED THE DRISKILL. FIVE MINUTES IN, I KNEW SARAH WAS RIGHT. FIRST OFF, THE DRISKILL IS TOTALLY HAUNTED, PROBABLY THE MOST HAUNTED HOTEL IN AMERICA. THERE ARE DOZENS OF GHOST STORIES ABOUT THIS PLACE, AND ONE OF THEM HAS TO DO WITH MIRRORS. THERE ARE THESE GIANT ONES IN THIS ONE ROOM, ALL OF THEM MADE BY SOME RICH DUDE IN MEXICO FOR CARLOTA, HIS LADY FRIEND. AND HIS NAME? MAXIMILIAN — THAT'S MAX WITH AN M, JUST LIKE IN THE MIRROR ON THE DRAWING.

NOW THE SPOOKY PART! THIS TOUR GUIDE WAS TELLING A STORY ABOUT WHAT HAPPENS IF YOU GO UP THERE TO THE MAXIMILIAN ROOM ALL BY YOURSELF AND LOOK STRAIGHT INTO ONE OF THE MIRRORS. WHAT IT DOES IS REFLECT TO AN IDENTICAL MIRROR ON THE OPPOSITE WALL. THEN IT REFLECTS BACK AGAIN, SO YOU BASICALLY LOOK INTO A NEVER-ENDING SERIES OF SMALLER AND SMALLER MIRRORED IMAGES OF YOURSELF. AND INTO THAT ENDLESS COLLECTION OF YOU AND ONLY YOU WALKS CARLOTA! SHE JUST APPEARS, OUT OF NOWHERE, STARES AT YOU, AND THEN YOU'RE DEAD. OKAY, THE DEAD PART I MADE UP, BUT YOU MIGHT DIE WHEN YOU RUN SCREAMING FOR YOUR LIFE, TRIP, AND FALL DOWN THE STAIRS.

THE CONNECTING IMAGE ON THE SKULL PUZZLE IS THIS ONE:

415

This seemed pretty straightforward. There's an image of a person behind the two. It's soft, but it's there. Carlota! The rest also makes sense in the context of five mirrors on one wall. The two and the arrows mean there are two mirrors on either side, so that would make it one of the two middle mirrors. "Behind the L.T.C." has to mean "Behind the Left Top Corner."

Wow. We were getting pretty good at this puzzle stuff. The answers we were finding had to fill in the dotted lines in the Skull.

Four words, four haunted places — and we'd found two of them.

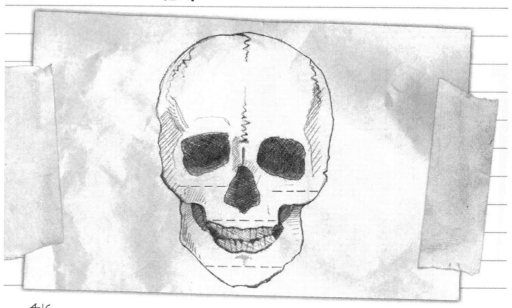

SORRY. HAD TO STOP THERE BECAUSE I HEARD DAD IN THE HALL.

I WISH I COULD TELL HIM ABOUT ALL THIS. BUT I KNOW I CAN'T.

HE WOULDN'T UNDERSTAND. HE'D TELL ME TO STOP. BOTH HIM AND MOM — THEY NEVER UNDERSTOOD WHAT SARAH AND I WERE UP TO. (OR MAYBE DAD KNEW ALL TOO WELL — BUT I DON'T WANT TO THINK ABOUT THAT.) THEY WERE GLAD WHEN SARAH LEFT. THEY THOUGHT IT MEANT I WOULD STOP DOING THINGS LIKE THIS — STAYING UP ALL NIGHT, DIGGING INTO PLACES I SHOULD LEAVE ALONE.

MOM AND DAD, IF YOU'RE THE FIRST PEOPLE WHO FIND THIS — IF SOMETHING'S HAPPENED — KNOW THAT THERE'S NO WAY YOU COULD HAVE STOPPED ME. IT'S NOT YOUR FAULT. I JUST HAVE TO DO THIS. IT DOESN'T EVEN FEEL LIKE A CHOICE. THE MYSTERY FOUND ME. AND THE ONLY WAY TO GET RID OF IT IS TO SOLVE IT.

OKAY, BACK TO THE SKULL PUZZLE. THE NEXT DAY I KNOCKED OFF THE THIRD OF THE FOUR LOCATIONS: THE HORNED TOMBSTONE WAS MINE. THIS WAS THE ONE IMAGE WE SHOULD HAVE FIGURED OUT

SOONER, BECAUSE WHAT SAYS <u>HAUNTED</u> MORE THAN A TOMBSTONE? BUT THERE ARE AN AWFUL LOT OF CEMETERIES OUT THERE FULL OF A LOT OF ZOMBIES AND GHOSTS, SO HOW WERE WE TO KNOW WHICH ONE THIS PARTICULAR TOMBSTONE REFERRED TO?

THERE WAS AN L ETCHED ON THE STONE, BUT THAT COULD MEAN A LOT OF THINGS. IT WAS MY MOM, BELIEVE IT OR NOT, WHO HELPED ME SOLVE THIS ONE.

I TOOK THE SCAN I HAD AND CAREFULLY CUT OUT THE L, NO HEADSTONE. I ALSO ISOLATED THE REPEATING HORN THAT STUCK OUT OF THE RIGHT SIDE. AFTER PRINTING THEM BOTH ON ONE PIECE OF PAPER, I WENT AND SAT ON THE PORCH WITH THE NOTEBOOK I WRITE MY STORIES IN.

Mom was sipping an iced tea with lemonade, otherwise known as an Arnold Palmer, the heat of summer dropping her to the old couch like a sack of potatoes. I opened my journal and set the piece of paper on the scuffed coffee table. Bingo. I'd opened up the world of my notebooks to my mom, a rare occurrence. She wasted no time asking me what I was working on.

"A ghost story," I said. This was the most common of answers, which is to say it gave my mom no information. She picked up the piece of paper and gave it a long once-over.

"A haunted farm?" she asked. "Please don't cut people up with the blades."

"The what?" I asked.

"The plow blades. Don't put them in the hands of a monster and cut people up. You're above that. I didn't raise a blood-spilling novelist."

I asked her to tell me what she was talking about, and a few seconds later I was good and educated about how a farmer plows a field. The repeating horns on the tombstone weren't horns at all — they were the blades of a plowshare,

THE KIND THAT GET PULLED BY A HORSE. OLD—SCHOOL, FOR SURE, BUT A DIRECTION I HADN'T TRIED.

IT DIDN'T TAKE ME LONG TO FIND MYSELF ONCE AGAIN EMAILING SARAH.

Sarah,

You're not going to believe this, but I figured out the horned tombstone. Those aren't horns! They're blades from a plow, and this tombstone is in a cemetery that's only a fifteen-hour drive from your front door!

It's called the Bachelor's Grove Cemetery, and it's a perfect match. There's a pond on the grounds and a farmer was pulled in there by his crazy plow horse. And guess what drove the plow horse nuts? A lady in white — the letter L — who wandered across the horse's path and sent it into a wild rage. The farmer haunts the place along with the lady and the horse, a triple threat, plus about a hundred other undead creatures of the night. It's a seriously bad place.

And guess where it is? Bachelor's Grove, Chicago. Like I said, fifteen hours from your front door. It's abandoned, so no one will be around. Unless you count the dead people.

Ryan

THE REALLY HORRIBLE PART ABOUT THE HORNED TOMBSTONE WAS THE PART OF THE SKULL THAT REFERRED TO WHERE THE CLUE WOULD BE HIDDEN. SARAH POINTED THAT OUT IN HER NEXT EMAIL, WHICH SHOWED UP ABOUT AN HOUR AFTER I SENT MINE.

R—

You do realize that even I'm not thrilled about digging three feet deep in an abandoned cemetery, right? You may have finally found something even I won't do.

S.

SHE WAS TALKING ABOUT THIS:

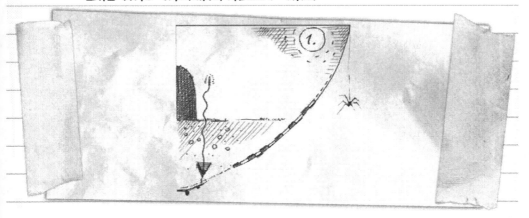

Not a fun message, even in broad daylight. Whatever this pointed to would need to be dug up in a cemetery. Totally verboten in Ryan's playbook, but it would need to be done.

Are there laws about stuff like this? I mean, could Sarah go to jail for digging up a cemetery? More important, could Sarah die from digging up a cemetery? I think that's possible. I was just glad she was far enough away from the rest of the places to make it impossible to track them all down.

At least that's what I thought until she told me the incredibly stupid plan she'd come up with.

MONDAY, JUNE 20, 11:48 P.M.

THIS TIME, SHE CALLED ME, MIDDLE OF THE NIGHT,
PHONE VIBRATING MY BRAIN AWAKE FROM UNDER MY
PILLOW.

"I CALLED YOU SIX TIMES," SHE STARTED. "YOU
ARE ONE HEAVY SLEEPER."

"SORRY. WHAT'S WRONG?"

"NOTHING'S WRONG. I JUST COULDN'T WAIT TO TELL
YOU THE GOOD NEWS."

"IT'S SUMMER AND IT'S FOUR THIRTY IN THE
MORNING," I REMINDED HER.

"NOT IN BOSTON. HERE IT'S SEVEN THIRTY AND I
JUST ATE OATMEAL WITH MY PARENTS."

"AND I CARE ABOUT THIS WHY?"

"BECAUSE THEY SAID YES. I GUESS TURNING
SEVENTEEN OPENED A FEW DOORS FOR ME."

I SAT UP IN BED, BECAUSE I KNEW WHAT THIS YES SHE
WAS TALKING ABOUT MEANT.

"YOU'RE NOT SERIOUS," I SAID.

"OH, YEAH, I'M SERIOUS. HAUNTED ROAD TRIP."

I COULDN'T BELIEVE IT. I MEAN, I REALLY COULDN'T
BELIEVE IT. SARAH AND I HAD TALKED ABOUT IT, BUT
THIS WAS UNBELIEVABLE. MY PARENTS WOULDN'T EVEN

423

LET ME DRIVE DOWN THE HILL FOR A CHEESEBURGER WITHOUT MAKING SURE I HAD MY GPS PHONE ON RED ALERT SO THEY COULD TRACK MY EVERY MOVE. MAN, SARAH WAS LUCKY.

SARAH HAD WORKED IT TO THE HILT, TELLING HER PARENTS THAT IT WOULD BE THE BEST STUDENT PROJECT EVER IF SHE COULD DRIVE TO SUMMER FILM SCHOOL IN CALIFORNIA AND MAKE A DOCUMENTARY ALONG THE WAY. SHE WOULD STOP AT INTERESTING LOCATIONS, VISIT WITH DIFFERENT FAMILY MEMBERS COAST TO COAST, AND CREATE THE COOLEST VIDEO DIARY ANY FILM SCHOOL TEACHER HAD EVER SEEN. IT WAS GOING TO BE AMAZING.

"TURNS OUT I HAVE RELATIVES SPREAD OUT ALL OVER THE COUNTRY," SARAH TOLD ME. "I'M ONLY STAYING IN TWO HOTELS. THE REST IS AUNTS, UNCLES, AND MY PARENTS' OLD COLLEGE ROOMMATES. JUST DRIVE, EAT, FILM. OH, AND MAKE A FEW STRATEGIC STOPS ALONG THE WAY."

IT WASN'T EXACTLY A STRAIGHT SHOT, BUT IT WAS CLOSE. BOSTON TO CHICAGO, THEN AUSTIN, AND FINALLY CALIFORNIA: BACHELOR'S GROVE CEMETERY, THE DRISKILL HOTEL, THE WINCHESTER HOUSE.

"I'LL HAVE TO CUT SOME CORNERS HERE AND THERE TO STAY ON SCHEDULE, BUT I'VE GOT SEVEN DAYS TO GET ACROSS AMERICA BY CAR. THEY TOTALLY BOUGHT IT!"

THERE WAS ONLY ONE PROBLEM: WE DIDN'T KNOW WHERE THE LAST LOCATION WAS. THERE WERE FOUR THINGS TO FIND, AND WE'D ONLY FOUND THREE. THE MEANING OF THE NUMBER 311 CONTINUED TO ELUDE US, AND THE LONGER IT TOOK TO FIGURE OUT, THE MORE LIKELY SARAH WOULD HAVE TO BACKTRACK OR CHANGE COURSE.

"I'LL HANDLE THINGS ON THE ROAD," SHE TOLD ME. "YOU JUST FIND THAT LAST LOCATION BEFORE I END UP A THOUSAND MILES ON THE OTHER SIDE AND CAN'T

MAKE IT BACK IN TIME. REMEMBER, EVERY MILE IS DOUBLE IF I'M BACKTRACKING, AND THERE'S VERY LITTLE ROOM FOR ERROR. MY PARENTS WILL FREAK IF I DON'T SHOW UP ON TIME WHERE I'M SUPPOSED TO."

WHEN I HUNG UP THE PHONE, I WAS ONE PART JEALOUS, ONE PART EXCITED, AND FIVE PARTS SCARED OUT OF MY SHORTS.

WE WERE ABOUT TO UNLOCK A MESSAGE THAT WOULD LEAD TO TROUBLE OF THE WORST KIND. I WAS SURE ABOUT THIS, AND SO WAS SARAH. WE BOTH KNEW IT WAS A BAD IDEA, BUT WE COULDN'T HELP OURSELVES.

AND DO YOU WANT TO KNOW WHY WE KNEW IT WAS A BAD IDEA?

BECAUSE THE GHOST OF OLD JOE BUSH WAS WATCHING US. HE KNEW WHAT WE WERE UP TO.

WE KNEW THIS BECAUSE HE SENT US A MESSAGE YESTERDAY. A VIDEO. TO OUR PERSONAL EMAILS.

IT WASN'T GOOD.

IF YOU WANT TO SEE IT FOR YOURSELF, YOU CAN FIND IT AT SARAH'S SITE. BUT BE WARNED — IT'S NOT RIGHT. IT MIGHT KEEP YOU UP AT NIGHT.

426

SARAHFINCHER.COM
PASSWORD:
FACEINTHEMIRROR

TUESDAY, JUNE 21, 7:00 A.M.

You're hiding something, aren't you, Ryan McCray? Something of mine, maybe? Something I left behind. Don't be surprised if HE comes looking for you. I won't be able to stop him. Even I can't protect you from that one.

It will burn, burn, burn and you won't get it out.

The ghost of Old Joe Bush is back. Not Henry — some other version of him, and, man, is he not happy.

He will get you! — I think he is Henry, and the ghost of Old Joe Bush is trying to warn me, not the other way around.

Burn, burn, burn! I think he means that what's to come will be seared into my memory, never to fade away. Whatever wild ride I'm in for, I'll remember it when I'm ninety . . . as if I have any chance of living that long.

Riddles upon riddles — that's what you get when you're dealing with a lunatic wrapped in a ghost.

I realize I should tell someone about this. I really do. There's a madman out there sending

428

ME VIDEOS AND I'M NOT RUNNING TO MY PARENTS? IT'S HARD TO EXPLAIN, BUT I THINK WHAT'S GOING ON HERE IS VERY DEEP. I THINK I HAVE A CONNECTION TO OLD JOE BUSH THAT MAKES ME DO THINGS I WOULDN'T OTHERWISE IMAGINE ON MY OWN. ME AND JOE BUSH HAVE A LOT IN COMMON. BOTH OF US ARE (OR WERE) KNOWN FOR SNEAKING AROUND AND HIDING THINGS. I WANT MY LIFE TO BE EXCITING, BUT I'M STUCK IN SKELETON CREEK. I THINK JOE FELT THE SAME WAY. TRAPPED, PARANOID, FORCED TO KEEP SECRETS HE DIDN'T WANT TO BE IN CHARGE OF. IT MAKES ME WONDER IF I'LL BE A GHOST SOMEDAY, HAUNTING SOME OTHER KID IN SOME OTHER SMALL TOWN. IT SOUNDS A LITTLE BORING, IF YOU WANT THE TRUTH. DAYS AND NIGHTS FILLED WITH STANDING AROUND DOING ALMOST NOTHING. ANYWAY, THE POINT IS, I DON'T KNOW WHERE THIS IS ALL LEADING, BUT SOMETHING TELLS ME I SHOULD DO THINGS THE WAY I'VE ALWAYS DONE THEM: SECRETLY, AT LEAST UNTIL I KNOW WHAT'S REALLY GOING ON, AND WHO I CAN REALLY TRUST.

SARAH IS OFFICIALLY ON THE ROAD. I COULDN'T TALK HER OUT OF IT, AND TONIGHT SHE ARRIVES IN CHICAGO. SHE'LL HAVE TO VISIT THE CEMETERY

AFTER DARK, WHICH POSES CERTAIN PROBLEMS. SHE
HAS AN AUNT AND UNCLE WHO LIVE ABOUT AN HOUR
OUTSIDE OF THE CITY AND THEY'RE EXPECTING HER
FOR DINNER. SHE'LL NEED TO SNEAK OUT OF THE HOUSE
AFTER EVERYONE IS ASLEEP, DRIVE TWO HOURS TO THE
CEMETERY, DIG UP WHATEVER IS HIDDEN THERE, AND GET
BACK BEFORE DAWN.

THAT MEANS THE GRAVE DIGGING WILL ALMOST
CERTAINLY HAPPEN AFTER MIDNIGHT, WHICH IS
BASICALLY BEYOND MY ABILITY TO IMAGINE. ALONE
IN AN ABANDONED CEMETERY AT NIGHT, DOING
UNSPEAKABLE THINGS — IT DOESN'T GET ANY SCARIER
THAN THAT, AND MY BEST FRIEND WILL BE DOING IT
ALONE.

THAT IS, IF SHE DOESN'T GET CAUGHT SNEAKING OUT
OF HER UNCLE'S HOUSE.

It's two or three in the afternoon wherever Sarah is, and she just texted me at work.

<u>Stopped for a late lunch, 2 hours to go. Waffle House!</u>

Living in the West, I have never experienced a Waffle House. It's Sarah's favorite fast-food restaurant because it serves breakfast all day and it's dirt cheap. She says the grits are to die for and the waffles are a crispy slice of heaven. Plus, the characters that hang out at the Waffle House tend to be chatty, older gentlemen with time on their hands. She doesn't outright talk to many of them, because she doesn't have to. They're generally on a first-name basis with the waitresses, and the conversations run thick.

This is how Sarah describes it:

"There's something right about hearing old memories from an old voice, the smell of waffles in the air while I sip my coffee. It's magic."

Actually, I think it's Sarah that's magic. Most people wouldn't see anything special about a place like that; they'd miss what really matters. But Sarah sees the loneliness and the longing and the two-dollar-and-fifty-cent comfort. She knows what to look for.

Tuesday, June 21, 1:15 p.m.

I used my lunch break to text back and forth with Sarah, something my dad strictly prohibits in the shop. He has a frightening aversion to text messaging in general.

"It's a phone," he has said more than once while I tap out a note on the tiny keyboard. "It's for making calls, not for writing novels."

I wouldn't say the world is passing my dad by, but he's easily two steps behind at all times. He has no patience for the things he sees no use for, so rather than endure his wrath, I take my break walking down Main Street while I hold a conversation with Sarah.

Sarah: Rest stops are gross.

Me: Please don't tell me more.

Sarah: I'm an hour from my uncle's house!

Me: Nervous about tonight?

Sarah: Got my grave digger in the trunk. A brand-new shovel. At least I have a weapon if I need it.

ME: MIGHT DO BETTER WITH A HAMMER. THE UNDEAD DON'T GO DOWN WITHOUT A FIGHT.

SARAH: IS THIS CONVERSATION SUPPOSED TO MAKE ME FEEL BETTER?

ME: JUST TAKE IT SLOW AND BE CAREFUL. NOTHING CRAZY. IF YOU SHOW UP AND IT DOESN'T FEEL RIGHT, GET THE HECK OUT OF THERE FAST.

WALKING AND TEXTING AT THE SAME TIME HAS A WAY OF PUTTING ME IN THE CROSSHAIRS OF SOMEONE I COULD HAVE AVOIDED IF I'D BEEN PAYING ATTENTION. WHEN I LOOKED UP FROM THAT LAST TEXT, WHICH TOOK QUITE A WHILE TO TAP OUT, I WAS FACE-TO-FACE WITH GLADYS MORGAN, THE TOWN LIBRARIAN. IF YOU ARE FAMILIAR WITH GLADYS, THEN YOU KNOW HOW SCARY THIS WOMAN CAN BE. SHE'S TALL AND BIG-BONED, WHICH MATCHES HER TOWERING PERSONALITY. A SMILE ALMOST NEVER APPEARS ON HER WRINKLED FACE.

"THAT'S THE DUMBEST INVENTION IN THE HISTORY OF DUMB IDEAS," SHE INFORMED ME. "BE CAREFUL YOU DON'T WALK INTO THE STREET. YOU'RE LIKELY TO GET RUN OVER BY A TOURIST DOING THE SAME THING BEHIND THE WHEEL OF A CAR."

"Thanks, Miss Morgan. I'll keep that in mind."

"Don't patronize me, Mr. McCray. It will come back to haunt you."

Sitting on the bench outside the library, writing all this down, I realize that a Waffle House in Minnesota would be a great place to drop Gladys Morgan and forget to pick her up. Let her bug someone else for a change.

Tuesday, June 21, 2:12 p.m.

Some guy just called the shop on his way into town with three buddies after hearing the evening hatch was on. They want guides for the big river an hour to the east. Four customers means two rafts and two guides, and my dad just chose me over Fitz.

This presents a serious moral dilemma for me. If I back out, then Fitz gets the gig and I'm stuck in the shop all night. Under normal circumstances, this would be a catastrophe. I like Fitz, but there's no doubt we're in a summer—long competition for guiding gigs. It's fifty bucks a pop plus tips and it's time on the water. I've been fly—fishing my whole life, and the water has a certain pull that can't be explained. Saying no to an evening hatch with big trout sipping the surface is very nearly beyond my comprehension. Especially given the fact that putting Fitz on a boat when I was asked first sends a certain message to my dad. This could become an unwelcome pattern pretty fast. I

COULD BE SITTING IN THE SHOP ALL SUMMER LONG

WATCHING THE CLOCK TICK WHILE FITZ IS OUT EARNING

A LOT MORE MONEY AND HAVING THE TIME OF HIS LIFE.

STILL, IT WAS NO CONTEST. THERE WAS NO WAY I

COULD LET SARAH SHOW UP AT A CEMETERY WITHOUT

HAVING ME ON THE PHONE TO KEEP HER CALM.

So I TOLD MY DAD I HAD A STOMACHACHE, A

HEADACHE, AND I'D JUST THROWN UP IN THE BATHROOM.

"IT'S JUST NERVES. YOU'LL BE FINE," WAS HIS

ANSWER.

FITZ WAS VISIBLY BUMMED OUT. HE WANTED THIS

GIG AS BAD, OR WORSE THAN I DID, SO I TOLD MY DAD I'D

BE HAPPY TO LET FITZ HAVE THE FIRST GO OF THE

SUMMER AND TAKE THE NEXT RUN. UNFORTUNATELY

FOR ME, MY DAD WOULD NOT BUDGE. I COULD SEE IT IN

HIS EYES. HE WAS TAKING HIS OWN KID OUT ON THIS

ONE WHETHER I LIKED IT OR NOT, AND THAT WAS FINAL.

MY ONLY OTHER OPTION WAS TO FALL DOWN

OUTSIDE AND BREAK MY ARM OR STICK A FLY HOOK IN

MY FOREHEAD, AND I WASN'T EVEN SURE THOSE OPTIONS

WOULD TIE ME DOWN IN THE SHOP FOR THE EVENING.

NOPE, I'LL BE LOADING A BOAT OFF THE WATER AT

DARK ON A RIVER WITH NO CELL SERVICE AT 9:00, AND I WON'T BE BACK IN A PLACE WHERE I CAN CONTACT SARAH UNTIL AT LEAST 10:30.

WHICH IS 12:30 A.M., SARAH'S TIME.

I TRIED TEXTING SARAH, BUT SHE WOULDN'T TEXT BACK. THEN I CALLED, BUT SHE DIDN'T PICK UP. I COULDN'T DO ANYTHING BUT LEAVE HER A VOICE MESSAGE.

I GOT ROPED INTO A RIVER RUN — TRIED TO GET OUT OF IT BUT COULDN'T — PLEASE FORGIVE ME. I'LL TEXT YOU THE SECOND I GET BACK. <u>BE CAREFUL!</u>

SARAH WAS GOING TO HAVE TO DO THIS ALONE, JUST LIKE WHEN THIS WHOLE NIGHTMARE STARTED.

I HOPE SHE DOESN'T DRIVE OVER HERE AND HIT ME WITH HER SHOVEL.

BEST NIGHT OF FISHING EVER. NORMALLY, I'D BE ECSTATIC ABOUT CATCHING TWO DOZEN LUNKERS IN ONE TRIP, BUT TONIGHT, IT WAS AGONIZING. THE BETTER THE FISHING GOT, THE LONGER I KNEW WE'D STAY ON THE RIVER. EVEN AFTER I PULLED THE RAFT TO THE SHORE AT DARK, DAD LET THEM FISH FOR ANOTHER FORTY MINUTES. I KEPT CHECKING MY PHONE — NO SERVICE! — PRACTICALLY PULLING MY HAIR OUT WITH FRUSTRATION. I'M FINALLY GETTING A CHANCE TO PUT THE NIGHT'S EVENTS ON PAPER, BUT I'M SO TIRED FROM WORK I CAN HARDLY KEEP MY EYES OPEN. ROWING FOR FIVE HOURS TAKES A LOT OUT OF A GUY, BUT I HAVE TO WRITE THIS DOWN WHILE IT'S FRESH IN MY HEAD.

FIRST THINGS FIRST: MY DAD IS ONTO US. I MESSED THAT UP BIG-TIME.

"IF YOU'RE TRYING TO REACH SARAH, YOU CAN FORGET IT," HE SAID AFTER THE THIRD TIME HE CAUGHT ME CHECKING FOR CELL SERVICE.

WHEN HE CAUGHT ME A FOURTH TIME, HE SAID, "THIS IS THE LAST TIME YOU BRING THAT THING. DO YOUR JOB."

But the fifth time was the kicker. He didn't have to say anything, because the look on his face told me everything I needed to know. It was the same look he gave me when I was getting into real trouble with Sarah last year. It's a very specific look — not impatience or frustration, but something far worse: distrust. He's only ever looked at me that way when it involved Sarah. He knew we were back in serious contact, and he suspected we were doing something that might get us killed.

Later, when we were alone at the shop and were putting away the rafts and the gear, he came up next to me in the dark and gave me a real earful.

"I'm not going to be happy if you and Sarah are up to your old tricks again. Don't do anything stupid."

I covered as best I could, but I knew he was only one phone call away from talking to Sarah's dad and discovering she was on her way

TO CALIFORNIA. HE'D SMELL TROUBLE AT THAT POINT, NO DOUBT, BUT THERE WAS NOTHING I COULD DO TO STOP HIM.

THANKFULLY, DAD WAS EVEN MORE TIRED THAN I WAS WHEN WE FINALLY ARRIVED BACK AT THE HOUSE AT 10:45. WE FOUND A NOTE FROM MOM, AND TWO PLATES OF FRIED CHICKEN AND COLESLAW IN THE FRIDGE. I TOOK MINE UPSTAIRS TO MY ROOM SO I COULD FINALLY BE ALONE.

I LOOKED AT MY PHONE LIKE IT MIGHT REACH OUT AND TRY TO STRANGLE ME WITH GUILT, WHICH IS BASICALLY WHAT HAPPENED.

SEVEN TEXT MESSAGES, THREE CALLS, ONE VOICE MAIL. ALL OF THEM MISSED, ALL OF THEM FROM SARAH.

FIRST, THE AWFUL STRING OF TEXT MESSAGES:

9:47 P.M.
I'M HERE! DROP ME A TEXT, LET ME KNOW YOU'RE ALONE. I WANT YOU ON THE PHONE SO YOU CAN HEAR ME SCREAMING.

9:52 P.M.

WHERE ARE U?????????? NO WAY YOU'RE STILL ON THE RIVER.

9:58 P.M.

SERIOUSLY, RYAN. THIS ISN'T FUNNY. CALL ME. IT'S CRAZY DARK OUT HERE.

10:10 A.M.

TRIED CALLING TWICE. I'M AT THE END OF A DIRT ROAD. HEADLIGHTS ON TOMBSTONES. I DON'T THINK I CAN DO THIS.

10:14 A.M.

I CAN DO THIS.

10:21 A.M.

I'M GOING IN, YOU BIG CHICKEN!!!!

10:24 A.M.

ABOUT TO GET REALLY DIRTY. CAN'T TYPE WITH MUDDY FINGERS. IF MY PHONE RINGS NOW, I WILL JUMP OUT OF MY SHOES. DON'T CALL.

I HAVE NEVER FELT AS HELPLESS, LAME, AND GUILTY AS I DID READING THOSE MESSAGES, UNLESS YOU COUNT THE VOICE MAIL FROM SARAH:

"WHY DOES THIS FEEL FAMILIAR? BECAUSE YOU DID THE SAME THING AT THE DREDGE LAST YEAR! DO YOU HAVE ANY IDEA HOW SCARY IT IS STANDING ALONE IN AN ABANDONED CEMETERY AT MIDNIGHT WITH A SHOVEL IN YOUR HAND? NO, I GUESS YOU DON'T, SINCE YOU BAILED ON ME!

"DOESN'T MATTER — I GOT WHAT WE CAME FOR. I SHOULD BE BACK AT MY UNCLE'S PLACE BY 2:30 A.M., GRAB A FEW HOURS OF SLEEP, THEN I'LL CONVERT THIS THING. I'M NOT EVEN GOING TO TELL YOU WHAT IT IS. THAT'S THE PRICE YOU PAY FOR FISHING WHILE I'M DIGGING UP A GRAVE SITE. SWEET DREAMS. AT LEAST I'M ALIVE!

"OH, AND YES, THAT WAS THE CREEPIEST THING I'VE EVER DONE IN MY LIFE."

WOW. COULD I FEEL ANY WORSE? I DON'T THINK SO. IT'S A LITTLE OVER THE TOP THROWING IN THAT "DIGGING UP A GRAVE SITE" COMMENT, BECAUSE THAT'S

NOT WHAT SHE HAD TO DO. DID SHE? I'M PRETTY SURE
SHE ONLY HAD TO DIG A HOLE AT A CEMETERY. THAT'S
NOWHERE NEAR AS SCARY AS UNEARTHING AN ACTUAL
GRAVE. I'M ALMOST SURE I WOULD HAVE BEEN FINE
DIGGING A HOLE. I WOULD HAVE PRETENDED IT WAS MY
BACKYARD.

THE COMBINATION OF A HYPERACTIVE GUILT
COMPLEX AND NOT KNOWING WHAT SHE'D DUG UP WAS
KILLING ME. WHAT IF IT WAS AN ARM BONE OR A SKULL
OR MORE GOLD?

IT COULD BE ANYTHING.

BUT I DIDN'T HAVE THE GUTS TO CALL HER, KNOWING
THAT SHE'D BE DRIVING, AND TIRED DRIVER + MIDDLE OF
THE NIGHT + ANSWERING CELL PHONE = TROUBLE. IT'S
BAD ENOUGH I'VE LET HER DOWN, SO IT'S BEST I DON'T
CONTRIBUTE TO HAVING HER SWERVE OFF THE ROAD ON
HER WAY BACK TO CHICAGO.

I TEXTED HER ONCE, BUT THAT WAS IT.

I'M SO SORRY. THE HATCH WAS ON AND MY DAD
WOULDN'T CALL IT A NIGHT. I WAS STUCK!

SHE STILL HASN'T TEXTED ME BACK OR CALLED ME.

Maybe she's asleep.

Or maybe she got caught.

I wish I could be sure.

If I know Sarah, she'll be ringing my cell on her time zone, not mine, which means I'll probably hear from her by 5:00 a.m.

It's one call I know better than to miss.

WEDNESDAY, JUNE 22, 4:23 A.M.

That was cruel, even after I missed the grave-digging event. Sarah called me at 4:13 A.M. and woke me out of a dead sleep. Note to self: Do not eat fried chicken at 11:00 P.M. and neglect to brush teeth. Totally gross.

Sarah hadn't gone to sleep like she said she was going to. That girl is wired after midnight — she can keep going, and going, and going. I've come to realize that her favorite time to edit video is the middle of the night, when everyone else is dreaming (or, in my case, having nightmares). After sneaking back into her uncle's guest room around 3:00 A.M. her time, she went straight to work on a video that contains footage I never would have expected.

The first half of the video is clearly something she'd been working on for a while. I think she may actually be planning to use this trip as a documentary film project for real, because the first part is the history of the cemetery, complete with ghostly sightings. After that, she includes her own experience

DIGGING IN THE DIRT. WATCHING IT, MY GUILT CAME
RUSHING BACK FULL FORCE.

But the most interesting part of the video?
The reveal of what she found. In some ways, it
makes total sense. I should have seen it coming.

There was a box.

And inside that box?

Our first clue that the Crossbones are a
lot more dangerous then we'd thought.

The Apostle is back . . . and spookier
than ever.

This you GOTTA see.

SARAHFINCHER.COM
PASSWORD:
THELADYINWHITE

WEDNESDAY, JUNE 22, 8:42 A.M.

I HAVE TO HAND IT TO SARAH — SHE'S GETTING REALLY
GOOD AT MAKING THESE VIDEOS. BACK IN THE DAYS OF
THE DREDGE, HER VIDEOS WERE STILL STRAIGHT-UP
HOME-MOVIE QUALITY, BUT THIS WAS DIFFERENT. THIS
WAS THE FIRST TIME I THOUGHT, HOLY COW, SARAH COULD
ACTUALLY BE A HOLLYWOOD FILMMAKER SOMEDAY.
IF I DIDN'T KNOW BETTER, I WOULD HAVE SAID THE
DOCUMENTARY FOOTAGE OF THE CEMETERY WAS REAL.
IT SURE GAVE ME THE CHILLS. BUT THAT WAS NOTHING
COMPARED TO SEEING THE A-POSTLE AGAIN. THAT GUY
ALWAYS MADE MY SKIN CRAWL. SEEING HIM AGAIN AND
REALIZING WHAT HIS ROLE IN THE CROSSBONES WAS
ONLY SERVED TO HEIGHTEN MY DREAD.

    I NOW KNOW THREE THINGS I DIDN'T KNOW BEFORE:

    — SOMETIME IN THE PAST, THE A-POSTLE'S
PRIMARY ROLE WAS TO DOCUMENT THE
HISTORY OF THE CROSSBONES. FOR WHATEVER
REASON, HE BROKE THIS DESCRIPTION INTO
DIFFERENT PARTS AND HID THE TRUTH IN VARIOUS
LOCATIONS OF HIS OWN CHOOSING.

— THE CROSSBONES IS OLD. IT WAS ORIGINALLY COMPRISED OF "SUPER-PATRIOTS" WHO BECAME CONCERNED THAT AMERICA'S EXPERIMENT IN DEMOCRACY WAS IN DANGER FROM THE BEGINNING.

— THEY HAD A THREE-PART MISSION:

1) PRESERVE FREEDOM
2) MAINTAIN SECRECY
3) DESTROY ALL ENEMIES.

TROUBLING NEW INFORMATION, FOR SURE, AND A LOAD OF NEW QUESTIONS:

— WAS THE APOSTLE A LOT MORE IMPORTANT THAN I ORIGINALLY GAVE HIM CREDIT FOR?

— WAS THERE SOMETHING MORE TO HIS DEATH THAN WHAT SARAH AND I UNCOVERED?

— WHAT HAD THE APOSTLE BEEN DOING IN SKELETON CREEK?

— WHAT SECRETS DID THE CROSSBONES KEEP AND WHAT ENEMIES DID THEY DESTROY?

— And, possibly of greatest importance, what does my dad have to do with all of this? He's got the birdie tattooed on his arm, just like the A-postle has on his hand. Sarah made sure to point that out in her own clever but twisted way. My dad was in the Crossbones. Is he still?

Sarah is back on the road, heading for her next haunted tour stop, and I still haven't had any luck figuring out the last location she has to visit. This, I'm afraid, is a big problem.

She'll be in St. Louis by noon, Memphis by 5:00 p.m., and she's due in Little Rock, Arkansas, before dark. Her mom's college roommate lives there, and Sarah is hoping to put in some time at the Bill Clinton Library as part of her video project for camp. The faster she moves, the more likely we're never going to figure out what the number 311 stands for.

I PUT ON SOME PINK FLOYD AND LIE IN BED,
STARING AT THE CLUES.

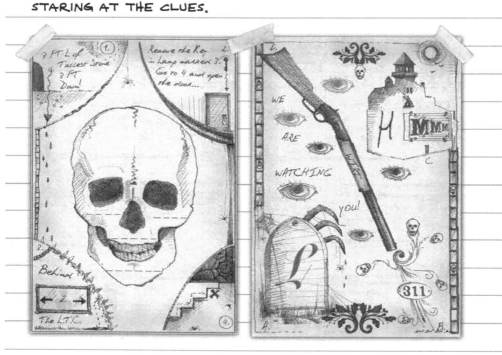

I THINK ABOUT THE CROSSBONES' THREE—PART MISSION:
1) PRESERVE FREEDOM 2) MAINTAIN SECRECY
3) DESTROY ALL ENEMIES.

ME AND SARAH FIT A LITTLE TOO COMFORTABLY
INTO NUMBER THREE.

DESTROY ALL ENEMIES.

THE MESSAGE IS CRYSTAL CLEAR: WE'RE A
THREAT TO THE CROSSBONES, SO THEY HAVE TO GET
RID OF US. IT FEELS LIKE SARAH'S TAKEN A BASEBALL

BAT TO A HORNETS' NEST AND NOW SHE HAS TO KEEP
MOVING, OUTRUNNING THE SWARM AS SHE HEADS WEST.

THE BOX SARAH DUG UP WAS BIG AND HEAVY. I'M
ACTUALLY SURPRISED SHE WAS ABLE TO GET IT OUT OF
THE GROUND BY HERSELF, NOW THAT I UNDERSTAND
WHAT WAS INSIDE: AN OLD—STYLE 8MM FILM
PROJECTOR AND A REEL OF FOOTAGE. SHE'D POINTED
THE PROJECTOR ON A WHITE WALL AND USED HER OWN
CAMERA TO CAPTURE THE IMAGE TO GET IT ONTO HER
COMPUTER — NOT THE MOST HIGH—TECH METHOD, BUT
IT HAD WORKED JUST FINE.

MY GUESS? THE REST OF THE LOCATIONS WILL
HAVE MORE REELS OF FILM, BUT NO PROJECTOR.

WE HAVEN'T HEARD THE LAST OF THE APOSTLE.

Wednesday, June 22, 11:00 a.m.

My dad just chose Fitz to guide the river today.

"No need to worry about me, Mr. McCray," Fitz said. "I don't even <u>have</u> a cell phone."

<u>Dude</u>, I wanted to say. <u>Remember who recommended you for the job</u>?

In fairness, once my dad was out of the room, Fitz turned to me and said, "Sorry about that. But you know how it is when you're stuck in the shop and the fish are biting. It's rough."

This, I remembered, was what Fitz and I had in common. It wasn't his fault my dad could only take one of us. Had we been able to go out, all three, it would have been fantastic, because we all knew the water better than we knew most things on land.

"It was pretty awesome," I admitted, without telling him why I'd been so distracted.

Under normal circumstances, I would have been jealous of Fitz for getting time on the river while I was going to be sitting bored in the fly shop all afternoon. But if today is anything like yesterday, they'll be out until

LATE. AN EMPTY SHOP AND AN INTERNET CONNECTION IS EXACTLY WHAT I'VE BEEN HOPING FOR. STILL, MY DAD DIDN'T HAVE TO TELL FITZ I'D CONSTANTLY CHECKED MY PHONE YESTERDAY. THAT WAS HITTING BELOW THE BELT.

"BEST FISHING OF THE YEAR AND YOU'RE STUCK IN THE SHOP," FITZ SAID AS HE LOADED BOXES OF FLIES. "BEEN THERE, DONE THAT!"

OKAY, THAT HURT. BUT TURNABOUT WAS FAIR PLAY. I COULD ALREADY SEE HOW THE SUMMER WAS GOING TO GO. MY DAD WOULD PLAY ME AND FITZ AGAINST EACH OTHER ON EVERY FRONT. HOW MANY FISH DID YOU CATCH? HOW MANY FLIES DID YOU TIE? UNFORTUNATELY FOR ME, WHILE I'M FITZ'S EQUAL ON THE FOOTBALL FIELD (WE ARE BOTH PATHETIC LOSERS), HE IS THE BETTER FISHERMAN. I LOVE FISHING, BUT I DON'T <u>LIVE</u> IT. FITZ IS MORE IN THE MOLD OF MY DAD: THERE'S FISHING, AND THEN THERE'S EVERYTHING ELSE. THEY'RE BOTH AT A WHOLE DIFFERENT LEVEL OF ENTHUSIASM.

I'VE ALWAYS WONDERED WHAT IT WOULD BE LIKE TO HAVE A BROTHER. YOU CAN'T BE AN ONLY CHILD WITHOUT WONDERING. IMAGINE THAT — ANOTHER

McCray in the house. It wouldn't even matter if
it was an older brother or a younger brother.
There'd still be that competition.

I helped them pack up the supplies, and my
mom stopped by with a cooler full of sandwiches,
cans of soda, and homemade chocolate chip
cookies.

"Looks good, Mrs. McCray," Fitz commented
as he peered into the cooler. "You sure make a
mean lunch."

<u>Give it a rest</u>, I thought.

"I brought you a sack of the same," my mom
then said, handing me a white paper bag with a
lunch in it. "See you for dinner?"

"Not likely," Dad answered for me. "If this is
anything like last night, it'll be cold chicken and
slaw again. We'll be out until at least an hour
after dark, and I want Ryan here to help us
unload."

Here again, I think my dad thought this was
something of a punishment, when really he had
given me free rein of the shop to help Sarah.
This was going to be perfect.

OR AT LEAST THAT'S WHAT I THOUGHT. THEN HE GAVE ME A PIECE OF PAPER WITH A LIST OF FLIES HE WANTED TIED BEFORE HE GOT BACK. IF YOU'VE NEVER SEEN OR TIED A FLY FOR FISHING, LET ME TELL YOU, MAKING THEM IS NO PICNIC. YOU START WITH A BLANK HOOK AND A TABLE FULL OF MATERIAL — FEATHERS, FUR, STRING, GLUE — SERIOUSLY, LIKE A MILLION OPTIONS, ALL SO YOU CAN MAKE WHAT ESSENTIALLY AMOUNTS TO A FANCY FISHING LURE. MY DAD HAD JUST GIVEN ME A WHOPPER OF AN ORDER FOR A WHOLE SLEW OF THESE THINGS:

— 2 DOZEN GOLD-RIBBED HARE'S EARS, SIZE 10 AND 12 MIXED

— 3 DOZEN ORANGE STIMULATORS, SIZE 14

— 1 DOZEN WOOLLY SPECIALS, NUMBER 8

— 2 DOZEN PURPLE PARACHUTE ADAMS, SIZE 12

THIS WAS, NO DOUBT, ANOTHER REMINDER OF HOW I JUST WASN'T CUTTING IT IN THE SHOP. FITZ WAS A KNOWN FLY-TYING MACHINE. EIGHT DOZEN FLIES, WHICH REPRESENTED ABOUT TWO HUNDRED DOLLARS FOR THE SHOP IN SALES, WAS NOTHING FOR FITZ.

"I can bang out a couple dozen before we leave if you want," Fitz told my dad.

Now he'd done it — he'd gone too far. I was smoldering with resentment, mostly because I knew he could whip together a dozen perfect flies a lot faster than I could tie six crappy ones.

"He's got all day and half the night," my dad said. "And no cell phone to distract him."

Uh-oh. This was bad. Dad held out his hand expectantly. Mom made a beeline for the door, because she knew I'd try to pit my parents against each other. She was gone before I could yell, "Mom, come on, tell him! How am I going to call you when I need a diaper change?"

I gave my dad my most seething look and removed the battery from my phone, handing him the rest. He turned away, mumbling something about how we were past all that. Fitz gave me a hopeless shrug, like he knew better: No matter how much parents tell you they won't read your texts, they will. It's written into the laws of parental physics. They can't help themselves, even if they did say they wouldn't do it.

After they took off, I felt a little better about one thing: My dad clearly hadn't called Sarah's dad yet. If he had, he would have mentioned it. No way could he know Sarah was on the road all by herself without saying something to me. Actually, this added up. When the hatch was on at the river, my dad was like a trout zombie: fish, eat, sleep, repeat. His mind was totally gone.

The shop was quiet and I had ninety-six flies to tie, which was a colossal enterprise for a guy Fitz likes to call "fumble fingers." He's totally right. He can tie about a dozen flies an hour, especially the easy ones, which is all my dad gave me (another not-so-subtle message about my lack of skill in this department). The list I got was like fly-tying 101 for beginners, but I'd be lucky to get in eight an hour, which meant if I didn't stop to use the bathroom or eat a cookie, I'd still be at it when they returned after dark.

So I started tying flies while several unanswerable questions ran through my head.

459

— What the heck does 311 mean?

— How angry is Sarah going to be when she finds out I've gone dark again?

— How in the world am I ever going to tie ninety-six flies without falling asleep?

Wednesday, June 22, 3:00 p.m.

Four hours, one sandwich, and thirty-seven flies. Not bad! I feel I'm slightly ahead of schedule and I have an idea about the number 311. I can't call Sarah from the shop phone because I know my dad will check the call list when he gets back in. We don't even <u>have</u> a home phone anymore, just cell phones in our pockets, so that's a bust. This leaves me at a bit of an impasse when it comes to reaching Sarah, who is surely almost to Memphis by now.

I'm closing the shop and walking down the street.

I think Gladys Morgan might be able to help me with the numbers. She's been around here forever and a day, since the time when the A-postle walked up and down the sidewalks all day trying to convert people. If anyone around here would know what the A-postle had been up to, it would be old Gladys.

Wednesday, June 22, 4:39 p.m.

I've just spent more than an hour not tying flies, which puts me way behind schedule, but it was totally worth it.

I figured out what 311 means. Or, more accurately, Gladys Morgan figured it out for me. This is huge — it means we have all four locations. It means there's a chance we might actually be able to solve whatever this crazy thing is.

The number 311, shot violently out of the Winchester like a bullet on the battlefield. It could have meant so many things. For all I knew, it was somehow attached to the Winchester.

462

Old wrinkly Gladys steered me straight on that in a hurry once I got to the dusty library and started peppering her with questions. I had to handle it carefully, because like my dad, she had been part of the Crossbones. Who knew what she'd do if she found out I was digging up Crossbones history?

"So, Miss Morgan, have you ever thought of the number three-one-one in a spooky sort of way?" I asked her.

"You're a mixed-up child," she began. "Shouldn't you be minding the shop?"

"It's a slow day. I just needed a break."

"And you come down here to bother me? What are you up to?"

"I'm not up to anything. I'm just bored is all."

"I highly doubt that."

She sat there stewing for a good twenty seconds before saying another word, and even then, it wasn't an answer.

"Numbers can be deceiving."

"What's that supposed to mean?" I asked.

No reply, so I switched tactics.

"Did you know the A-postle back in the day? The preacher up the road said the A-postle knew something about what the numbers meant."

A huge lie — and about a preacher, no less. I felt my toes getting warm, like I'd sunk one level closer to a lake of fire.

Gladys was as old as the dredge. If anyone knew about the A-postle it would be her.

"Sure, I knew the A-postle. A highly annoying little man, if you ask me. He was always yelling at everyone he met."

"I don't understand."

And then she looked at me real funny, like she was trying to see inside my head.

"He preached fire and brimstone, which is always more believable when it's screamed in your face, or so he thought. He used to say those numbers now and again, like he was taunting someone. A very odd duck, the A-postle. I'm glad he's gone."

I made her back up and tell me more. Had he said anything else about the numbers?

"This can't lead to anything good."

"It led to forty million in gold last time."

Not a bad answer, if I do say so myself.

Gladys let out a deep breath and shook her head.

"He didn't just say the numbers, he said something more. He'd be preaching along like he always did with that Bible in his hand and suddenly he'd stop and yell 'three-one-one door goes SLAM and you're dead!' And he'd slam his hand on the Bible real hard. No one liked him."

"So I've heard."

Gladys shot me an accusing look and I knew I'd gotten dangerously close to her Crossbones radar. Before she could start asking me questions, I hightailed it for the shop.

When I got back, I found two out-of-towners standing outside looking for free fishing tips. I steered them in the right direction as fast as I could, then jumped on the shop computer and typed the Apostle's phrase into Google.

<u>311 door goes SLAM and you're dead!</u>

It felt all wrong typing it in there, like I'd said some sort of incantation and the ghost of

Old Joe Bush was about to wander in, summoned from the dead.

But Google felt differently about those words. It returned a link that made me whisper the word <u>bingo</u> the second I saw it.

<u>Haunted High Schools</u>

About ten seconds later, I gave up on the idea of not using the shop phone to call Sarah.

Wednesday, June 22, 5:12 p.m.

311 was a classroom number at a high school built in the 1800s. The room was said to be haunted. The door locked on its own. Unexplained sounds came from inside when no one else could get in. This was all very interesting, and, even better, now I knew where the Apostle had hidden what we needed to find. And it wasn't inside the school, it was outside, where Sarah could get to it without being seen (I hoped).

Remove the Key in Lamp marked 3. Go to 4 and open the door....

I knew what this meant, and it was good! There must be lights outside, ones that had been there a long time. Sarah wouldn't have to wait until morning; in fact, that would be exactly

WHAT SHE <u>WOULDN'T</u> WANT TO DO. SHE'D NEED TO
SNEAK ONTO THE GROUNDS WHEN IT WAS DARK, FIND THE
LAMP MARKED <u>3</u> (WHATEVER THAT MEANT), GET THE
KEY, AND PROCEED TO THE NUMBER <u>4</u>, WHERE SHE'D
OPEN THE DOOR. THIS CLUE WOULD BE A LOT BETTER
IF IT MADE SENSE, BUT SARAH IS SHARP ON HER FEET
AFTER MIDNIGHT, SO THERE'S A CHANCE SHE'LL FIGURE
IT OUT. AND THIS TIME, I'LL BE RIGHT THERE WITH HER.

THE ONE REALLY BAD THING ABOUT ROOM 311?
IT'S IN SPRINGFIELD, MISSOURI, WHICH IS IN THE
OPPOSITE DIRECTION OF THE WAY SARAH HAS BEEN
DRIVING ALL DAY.

SHE PICKED UP HER PHONE AND STARTED IN ON ME
BEFORE I COULD TELL HER WHAT I'D FOUND.

"WHERE HAVE YOU BEEN? DO YOU HAVE ANY
IDEA HOW MANY TIMES I'VE TRIED TO CALL? NOT
A GOOD TIME TO LEAVE ME HANGING, RYAN. NOT A
GOOD TIME!"

I APOLOGIZED ABOUT FIFTY TIMES AND TOLD HER
WHAT HAD HAPPENED WITH MY DAD. MY DAD WAS ONTO
US, OR AT LEAST GETTING SUSPICIOUS, AND WE NEEDED
TO BE CAREFUL. ONCE I GOT HER SETTLED DOWN, SHE
WAS JUST HAPPY TO HEAR MY VOICE, WHICH MADE <u>ME</u>

HAPPY. IT WAS LIKE WE WERE THE ONLY TWO PEOPLE IN THE WORLD, SECRETLY GOING ABOUT OUR BUSINESS. IT WAS A GOOD FEELING, BUT IT ALSO MADE ME MISS HER MORE THAN EVER.

WHAT I REALLY WANTED TO DO? JUMP IN MY MOM'S MINIVAN AND DRIVE IN SARAH'S DIRECTION UNTIL WE COLLIDED. I'D HAVE DRIVEN THIRTY HOURS STRAIGHT TO FIND HER IF I THOUGHT I COULD GET AWAY WITH IT.

I HEARD NOISE IN THE BACKGROUND AND ASKED SARAH WHERE SHE WAS, BRACING MYSELF FOR THE BAD NEWS.

HOW FAR COULD SHE HAVE GOTTEN? HOW MUCH TIME HAD WE LOST?

"STEAK 'N SHAKE," SHE SAID. "THE FUNNY THING ABOUT THIS PLACE? I DON'T THINK THEY MAKE STEAKS. PRETTY GOOD GRILLED CHEESE, THOUGH."

ALL THESE WEIRD RESTAURANTS! WHERE ARE THE McDONALD'S AND THE BURGER KINGS?

"TONIGHT I'M HITTING THE CRACKER BARREL FOR ALL-NIGHT BREAKFAST. THAT PLACE MAKES A MEAN OMELET."

"WHAT STEAK 'N SHAKE ARE YOU AT? I MEAN, WHAT CITY?"

"Memphis. I'm ahead of schedule by half an hour."

I heard her slurping on a milk shake and wanted to guess what flavor it was, but time was of the essence. (I'd have guessed chocolate.)

"Look, Sarah, I've got some good news and some bad news," I told her. I went on to give her the same good and bad news I've already written down once before, and she sort of freaked out on me.

"Central High School in where?"

"Springfield, Missouri."

"Hang on."

I heard her set the phone down on the counter and riffle through some papers, probably maps of the region. A few seconds later, she was back.

"That's three hundred miles in the opposite direction, but at least it's not in Montana. Things could be a lot worse."

Some weird part of me wanted to remind her that the best fly-fishing in the world was in Montana, and I'd have been happy to bolt out there and catch a few fish while actually making

470

myself useful to our little endeavor, but I let it slide. We figured out it would take five hours for her to drive from Memphis to Springfield, by which time it would be late at night. She was supposed to be in Little Rock before dark, but that wasn't going to happen.

"I'll cover," she said. "I don't think my parents will send the cavalry just yet."

We made a plan: Sarah would leave straight away for Springfield and find the hotel nearest to the school. While she drove, I'd figure out what she should do when she got inside. Tomorrow morning she'd get into the school as early as possible, then head for Little Rock a day late.

"Sorry, Sarah, this isn't going quite like I thought it would."

"Funny, it's going EXACTLY how I expected. That's what makes it perfect! Don't worry — this is going to be great. You're doing recon, I'm out in the field — we make a perfect team."

I understand what she meant, but deep down inside, I still feel like such a loser. I wish I could

BE THE ONE TO DRIVE ALL NIGHT, CHASING DOWN URBAN LEGENDS, FUELED ON HAMBURGERS AND MILK SHAKES. BEING BORED IS ONE THING, BUT FEELING TRAPPED IS A WHOLE DIFFERENT LEVEL OF LAMENESS. SARAH IS OUT THERE, LIVING LARGE, AND WHAT AM I DOING? TYING A BUNCH OF STUPID FLIES AND WATCHING THE PAINT DRY.

WE TALKED ABOUT THE PHRASE WITH THE LAMP AND THE NUMBERS AND SHE AGREED: SHE'D HAVE TO GET OVER THERE AT NIGHT, WHEN NO ONE WAS AROUND.

"TONIGHT, HAUNTED SCHOOL, SPRINGFIELD," SARAH SAID. I COULD TELL SHE WAS UP AND MOVING. "I CAN HARDLY WAIT."

AND THEN SHE WAS GONE. I STILL HAVE FIFTY-NINE FLIES TO TIE. SARAH HAS HER PARENTS TO FOOL AND A FIVE-HOUR DRIVE TO NAVIGATE. WITH ANY LUCK AT ALL, WE'LL BOTH SUCCEED BY THE TIME MY DAD GETS OFF THE RIVER AND GIVES ME MY PHONE BACK.

WEDNESDAY, JUNE 22, 8:45 P.M.

I JUST GOT A CALL FROM FITZ THAT UNDER NORMAL CIRCUMSTANCES WOULD PUT ME IN A PRETTY GOOD MOOD. THE CALL COULD ONLY MEAN ONE THING, WHICH WAS PERFECTLY CLEAR BY THE FRUSTRATED SOUND OF FITZ'S VOICE.

"THE HATCH TOTALLY DIED. SLOWEST DAY ON THE RIVER IN WEEKS. TALK ABOUT SOME UNHAPPY FISHERMEN."

"THAT BAD?" I ASKED HIM.

"YOU HAVE NO IDEA. WE COULD HAVE THROWN WORMS SLATHERED IN WD-40 OUT THERE AND IT WOULD HAVE PRODUCED THE SAME RESULT: NADA."

LEGEND IN OUR NECK OF THE WOODS IS THAT FISH LOVE WD-40 MORE THAN LIFE ITSELF. THEY'D BEAT EACH OTHER UP TRYING TO HOOK THEMSELVES, BUT I'D NEVER TRIED IT.

THIS WAS TAILOR-MADE FOR GLOATING RIGHTS. I GO OUT AND CATCH FISH AFTER FISH, FITZ HEADS OUT THE VERY NEXT DAY AND GETS SKUNKED. IT SHOULD HAVE BEEN MUSIC TO MY EARS, BUT MY PILE OF FLIES WAS ONLY SIXTY-ONE DEEP. I HAD THIRTY-FIVE TO GO AND MY FINGERS WERE ALREADY RAW FROM TYING.

"Better luck next time," was all I could muster.

"We'll be back at the shop in about twenty. Want some help finishing those flies?"

Fitz didn't have to ask if I'd finished — he'd seen my work before and knew the results all too well. He guessed I'd finished seventy, which made me feel even worse than I already did. At least my night was going to end a little earlier than expected and I could get my phone back.

It's cool Fitz is willing to help me out, especially after I showed him up on the river.

Here's hoping I can hit seventy before he walks in the door.

Wednesday, June 22, 9:38 p.m.

When he got back, I traded Fitz jobs, unloading and cleaning the boats while he whipped off twenty-six flies in record time. My dad was none the wiser. I guess if Fitz and I were truly competitive, he would've found a way to let my dad know. But everything remained between us. When Fitz was through, he told me to keep practicing on those flies, and I told him to keep practicing on that fishing. Then he got on his old motorcycle and took off, a stream of blue smoke trailing him in the moonlight. I knew just how he felt — I'd been there. Nothing makes you more tired than rowing a boat all day and listening to people complain about not catching fish. It's murder.

Before I could get my phone back from my dad, he looked at my fly-tying handiwork and found some of it wanting. I had to admit — there were twenty-six perfect little guys in the pile, but the rest were gimps. Half of them probably wouldn't even float.

"I COULD SPRAY THEM WITH WD-40," I SAID

LAMELY, HOPING TO GET HIM SMILING.

HE HANDED ME MY PHONE AND SMILED.

"CAN'T BE GOOD AT EVERYTHING. I THINK FITZ IS

BAD LUCK ON THE WATER. WORST DAY OF THE YEAR."

I FEEL BAD ABOUT HOW GOOD IT FELT TO HEAR MY

DAD SAY THAT. IT ISN'T FAIR TO FITZ, BUT I SURE DON'T

WANT TO GET IN THE HABIT OF SITTING AROUND THE

SHOP ALL SUMMER WHEN I COULD BE OUT FISHING. FITZ

COULD TIE, AND IT WAS STARTING TO LOOK LIKE I'M

"GOOD LUCK" ON THE RIVER.

NOW IF ONLY THAT GOOD LUCK COULD MAKE ITS

WAY TO SPRINGFIELD, MISSOURI.

I HAVE NO DOUBT THAT SARAH NEEDS IT.

Thursday, June 23, 12:03 a.m.

By the time I finally called Sarah she was sitting in her car across the street from the school. She'd been waiting a while and was impatient, so our conversation was brief. A minute after I reached her, Sarah was wandering on the grounds searching the bottom of every lamppost she could find. Some of them were new, because the school had been added on to, but there was an entire wing that still had the old facade and a few statues of patriarchs that Sarah said "looked real, like they were planning to climb off their pedestals and drag me down the street."

She found a row of lampposts that looked like they could have been placed there quite a while ago, and then she was feeding me information that felt right.

"Okay, there's a bunch of these, like eight or so, and they have big bases on them. It's like they're tall and skinny, but wide at the bottom. They're not numbered, but they're in a row. That's good, right?"

I told her to count from one end of the row until she got to the third one, then see if there was some sort of latch or metal door at the base.

"Dang it," she said, louder than I thought was a good idea.

There was a small metal door, probably for getting access to the wiring, but it required one of those Allen wrenches to get in. Sarah cursed herself for not bringing tools, then ran across the school grounds to her car, where she kept a toolbox in the trunk.

After what seemed like an hour, she returned to the lamppost, fumbled around with a bunch of different sizes, and found the right one. When she finally got it open, she put her hand inside and felt around.

"It feels like I might get electrocuted in there," she told me. "Can you say Frankenstein?"

I had a terrible urge to tell her the electrocution bit is only in the movie, not in the book, but this was probably not the right time to go all literary on my best friend. I controlled

MY URGE TO TALK ABOUT MARY SHELLEY AND STUCK
TO THE BUSINESS AT HAND, WHICH WAS GETTING SARAH
OUT OF HARM'S WAY AS FAST AS I COULD.

"JUST BE CAREFUL — IT'S NOT GOING TO HURT YOU."

"EASY FOR YOU TO SAY. YOU'RE AT HOME WITH
THE DOORS LOCKED AND I'M SEARCHING THE GROUNDS
OF A HAUNTED SCHOOL."

"POINT TAKEN. TRY REACHING UP INTO THE SPACE
WHERE NO ONE WOULD EVER THINK TO FIND SOMETHING."

I COULD HEAR HER DOING HER BEST, IMAGINED HER
ARM IN THERE UP TO HER ELBOW AS SHE TRIED TO FIND
A HIDDEN KEY. WHAT IF SHE REALLY DID GET
ELECTROCUTED? WHAT IF THERE WERE LOOSE WIRES
IN THERE AND SHE FRIED HER WHOLE DANG ARM OFF?

"GOT IT!" SHE YELLED. WHEW.

I YELLED "NICE!" A LITTLE TOO LOUD AND MY
MOM WOKE UP. I COULD TELL, BECAUSE SHE SHOUTED
"YOU OKAY, RYAN?" DOWN THE HALL.

I DIDN'T ANSWER. MY MOM IS A HEAVY SLEEPER,
AND SHE HATES TO GET OUT OF BED AT NIGHT. ONCE
SHE'S UP, SHE'S UP FOR LIKE AN HOUR. I COULD IMAGINE
HER STARING AT THE CEILING, HOPING SHE'D ONLY
THOUGHT SHE'D HEARD ME YELL, HOPING SHE COULD

STAY WHERE SHE WAS. SARAH WAS YAMMERING IN MY EAR BUT I STAYED PERFECTLY STILL AND QUIET. WHAT IF MY MOM WAS SNEAKING DOWN THE HALL, STANDING AT MY DOOR? I WATCHED FOR A SHADOW UNDER THE DOOR FOR A FULL MINUTE, THEN BREATHED A SIGH OF RELIEF. SHE HAD TO BE ASLEEP AGAIN.

SARAH HAD FOUND A SMALL METAL BOX, HELD INSIDE ON A HOOK, UP WHERE NO ONE WOULD EVER HAVE A REASON TO LOOK.

THIS WAS GETTING GOOD.

I WHISPERED TO HER, "MOM'S ON ALERT, GOTTA STAY LOW. LISTEN, THOSE STATUES OF PEOPLE, HOW MANY ARE THERE?"

"I WAS THINKING THE SAME THING, AND YOU'RE RIGHT — THERE ARE FOUR."

"THEN YOU KNOW WHAT TO DO."

REMOVE THE KEY IN LAMP MARKED 3. GO TO 4 AND OPEN THE DOOR. . . .

I HEARD SARAH RUNNING, HER BREATH HEAVIER THAN IT NEEDED TO BE. SHE WAS STARTING TO GET SCARED OR NERVOUS, I COULD TELL. I TALKED HER DOWN, TRIED TO MAKE HER FEEL BETTER, BUT SHE WAS STARTING TO FEEL THE PRESSURE.

"I don't like it out here, Ryan. Something doesn't feel right."

"Just stay calm. You can do it. There must be some sort of small door with a key entry somewhere at the base."

She told me there was, but that her hands were shaking so badly she couldn't get the key in. Also, the keyhole was totally blocked with crusted old chewing gum.

"Use the smallest Allen wrench you've got and clean it out."

This was a good tip, because a ring of Allen wrenches has sizes that are like metal toothpicks, perfect for clearing away old gum.

"Someone's here. I can feel it. I'm turning my camera on."

I tried to tell her no, just stay focused on the keyhole, but she wouldn't listen.

Everything went quiet. I called her name, but there was nothing. Even her breathing had stopped.

Then the phone went dead.

481

Thursday, June 23, 12:13 a.m.

I tried calling back twice, but it went straight to voice mail. I paced in my room. Was she seeing things? Was there really someone out there? What was going on?

My phone buzzed with a text message.

He's here.

I typed back as fast as my fingers would fly.

Who? Get out of there!

Her reply was the last thing I wanted to see. Ever.

Old Joe Bush. He's here.

This was as close as I've ever come to screaming in my room. Actually, I did scream, but I got my pillow first and held it against my face.

A few seconds later, my phone rang, and Sarah was back.

"Tell me you were messing with me. Please, Sarah, tell me you were kidding."

"I'm back in my car. I'm safe, but I wasn't kidding. He was there, Ryan. He was right there, standing in the shadows."

"It could have been anyone." I said these words more out of hope than reality. I knew Old Joe Bush was still out there. I'd seen him myself.

"My camera was on, so I'll show you. Right now, I'm getting out of here. This is crazy, Ryan. Like really crazy."

And then she started laughing. She was thrilled and scared to death all at once. Sarah Fincher loved this kind of ride, where the stakes were high and the shocks were off the charts. But even this one got to her more than usual. She was laughing, but it was a hair shy of turning into crying. I knew her well enough to know that much.

Someone was watching us. Someone knew.

And that someone was out there with my friend, keeping an eye on what was his.

"I got it. I got what we were supposed to find."

Those were the last words Sarah said before stepping into the hotel lobby.

THURSDAY, JUNE 23, 12:21 A.M.

SARAH WAS CALM WHEN SHE CALLED BACK FIFTEEN MINUTES LATER. SHE WAS IN HER HOTEL ROOM, AND I COULD TELL SHE'D HIT THE WALL. SHE WAS SAFELY TUCKED AWAY IN A LOCKED ROOM. WE BOTH FELT BETTER.

SHE'D GOTTEN THE SMALL METAL DOOR OPEN AND HAD FOUND ANOTHER SMALL REEL OF FILM, WHICH MEANT THE A-POSTLE WAS ABOUT TO START TALKING AGAIN.

AND THERE WAS SOMETHING ELSE.

SARAH'S PARENTS WERE MORE UPSET THAN SHE'D EXPECTED, AND THEY WANTED TO KNOW EXACTLY WHERE SHE WAS AND WHY SHE'D DRIFTED OFF COURSE.

"NOT A GREAT PHONE CALL EARLIER TONIGHT," SHE TOLD ME. "I THOUGHT THEY WERE GOING TO MAKE ME TURN AROUND AND HEAD BACK HOME."

SHE'D CALLED THEM AT AROUND 9:00 TO TELL THEM SHE'D MADE A MISTAKE IN ST. LOUIS AND WAS HEADED TOWARD SPRINGFIELD INSTEAD OF LITTLE ROCK, BUT HADN'T REALIZED IT UNTIL SHE FOUND HERSELF FOUR HOURS OFF COURSE.

"The part that stung the most was them thinking I was actually that dumb," she went on. "I mean, seriously, do they really think I'd drive four hours in the wrong direction without doing it on purpose?"

They weren't "onto us," as I'd been so worried about. No, they were something far worse in Sarah's book: They were worried their daughter was an idiot. I tried to convince her that having her parents think she's dumb is actually kind of useful in this particular situation.

"You can make as many mistakes as you want. They'll just think you have a bad sense of direction."

"Ryan, you don't get it," she corrected me. "This was the only slipup they're going to allow. They got me a hotel room here, but only after grilling the front desk lady like she was a convicted felon. So embarrassing. If this happens again they're pulling the plug. My dad said so."

Not good. Not good at all, since there were

AT LEAST A COUPLE MORE TIMES ON THIS JOURNEY
WHERE SHOWING UP ON TIME WOULD REQUIRE A SMALL
MIRACLE.

SHE WAS ROAD WEARY. TOO MUCH JUNK FOOD,
TOO MANY HEADLIGHTS IN THE FACE, AND NOT NEARLY
ENOUGH SLEEP HAD PUSHED SARAH TO THE BRINK.

NOW I'M EXHAUSTED, TOO. IT'S TIME TO GET SOME
SLEEP.

IF I CAN.

Thursday, June 23, 8:00 a.m.

Sarah was up very early. I can tell because she posted another video before hitting the road for Little Rock.

This thing is scary in so many ways.

There's her troubling documentary about the words 311 door goes SLAM and you're dead! I never liked that phrase to begin with, but now I don't want to hear it again for as long as I live.

Then there's a new message from the A-postle, which is stranger than the first.

But the most terrible part, by a mile, was what her camera caught while she was at the school. I had no idea what she'd seen. She hadn't told me. Nope, not good old Sarah — she had wanted to show me so I could be just as scared as she was.

This video changed everything, and I don't recommend continuing with this journal until you see it.

The stakes just got a lot higher.

SARAHFINCHER.COM
PASSWORD:
SLAM

THURSDAY, JUNE 23, 9:24 A.M.

I UNDERSTAND WHY SHE DIDN'T TELL ME. I THINK SHE
WAS IN SHOCK, BUT ALSO I THINK SHE THOUGHT
SERIOUSLY ABOUT TURNING FOR HOME. SHE SAYS SHE'S
ON HER WAY TO LITTLE ROCK, THAT SHE'LL TAKE A
BREAK WHEN SHE GETS THERE AND DECIDE IF SHE WANTS
TO KEEP GOING. SHE'LL BE THERE BY EARLY
AFTERNOON, GET SOME REAL REST — AND THEN
WHAT? TURN FOR BOSTON OR AUSTIN, TEXAS?
HOME IS SAFE. AUSTIN IS THE DRISKILL, THE MOST
HAUNTED HOTEL IN AMERICA. I'D ENCOURAGE HER TO
QUIT AND GO HOME OR JUST DRIVE STRAIGHT THROUGH
TO UCLA AND FORGET ABOUT THE APOSTLE AND
EVERYTHING ELSE.

BUT I KNOW SHE WON'T LISTEN TO ME.

NEITHER ONE OF US CAN TURN BACK NOW.

WE'RE IN TOO DEEP.

I'M NOT GOING TO TAKE THE TIME TO RECAP THE
DOCUMENTARY FOOTAGE ABOUT THE SCHOOL — THAT'S
GOING TO STAY IN VIDEO FORM ONLY. BUT I WILL LAY
OUT THE NEW INFORMATION WE HAVE ABOUT THE
CROSSBONES AND THE MESSAGE THE GHOST OF OLD
JOE BUSH SENT.

First Joe, then the Crossbones.

I've heard of these things that are like benevolent spirits, ghosts who are there to protect or warn us, not to bring us harm. If I believe in ghosts at all, I sure want to believe in that kind. Here's what it said: I'm not here to harm you. Quite the opposite. Keep going, but tell no one. It would only anger him more. You've awakened the Raven.

Okay, first off, who the heck is the Raven? I know the poem, and Sarah has used it as a password, but apparently the Raven is also a person or a being of sorts who's angry at us. Just what we need — a giant black bird gunning for us. What if it's bigger than me? I don't even want to think about the beak on a raven that big.

The most interesting thing about that footage, though? Old Joe Bush might be on our side. I've had some experience with this sort of thing, and it adds up. Henry pretended to be the ghost of Old Joe Bush, but that doesn't mean the ghost never existed to begin with. Whether this thing has taken over Henry or Henry isn't

EVEN IN THE PICTURE AND THIS GHOST IS REAL, THE SAME THING IS TRUE: THE REAL JOE BUSH WAS A GOOD GUY. HE WAS ALL ABOUT PROTECTING THE TOWN FROM THE VERY BEGINNING.

I THINK HE'S TRYING TO PROTECT ME AND SARAH NOW.

BUT PROTECT US FROM WHAT?

THE RAVEN — WHATEVER OR WHOEVER THAT IS.

SECTION TWO OF THE FOUR SECTIONS OF THE PUZZLE SHOWED ITSELF IN THE VIDEO, JUST AS THE FIRST ONE HAD. THE WORD IS GROUND. PUT IT TOGETHER WITH THE FIRST WORD, UNDER, AND IT MAKES ANOTHER WORD: UNDER — GROUND. UNDERGROUND.

IT DOES NOT HAVE A NICE RING TO IT.

THE LAST PLACE I WANT TO BE WHEN THIS THING GOES DOWN IS UNDERGROUND.

AS TO THE CROSSBONES, IT GETS WEIRDER BY TURNS, AND SO DOES THE APOSTLE. IT'S CLEAR TO ME NOW THAT THE APOSTLE WAS NEAR THE TOP OF THE CROSSBONES HIERARCHY AND TOOK IT UPON HIMSELF TO DOCUMENT WHAT HE KNEW. ALSO, HE WAS DISGRUNTLED. THESE CLUES HE'S LEFT ARE SOME SORT OF INSURANCE AGAINST THE CROSSBONES, A WAY OF

SAYING, HEY, TREAT ME WITH SOME RESPECT OR I'LL TELL EVERYONE WHAT YOU'VE DONE. MY FINGER IS ON THE TRIGGER, SO DON'T MESS WITH ME.

THE A-POSTLE VIDEO ALSO CONNECTS THE CROSSBONES TO THOMAS JEFFERSON, WHOM THEY DISTRUSTED. THEY WANTED TO DESTROY THE FORMER PRESIDENT, TRYING ON THREE OCCASIONS: SETTING HIS HOUSE ON FIRE, DRIVING HIM INTO BANKRUPTCY, AND — THE THIRD ITEM IS ONLY HINTED AT, BUT IT SOUNDS LIKE IT HAS SOMETHING TO DO WITH TAKING JEFFERSON'S ASSETS. AND FINALLY, THE A-POSTLE HAS OPENED THE DOOR TO THE DREDGE AND WHY IT MATTERED. THE NEW YORK GOLD AND SILVER COMPANY WAS A CROSSBONES INVENTION. ALL THAT GOLD, INCLUDING THE RICHES DUG OUT OF SKELETON CREEK, WAS CROSSBONES GOLD.

I THINK THE A-POSTLE WANTED MORE THAN THEY WERE WILLING TO GIVE HIM. HE GOT GREEDY.

UNFORTUNATELY FOR HIM, HE MIGHT HAVE BEEN A LITTLE TOO LOUD FOR HIS OWN GOOD.

HE ENDED UP FLOATING FACEDOWN IN THE RIVER, AND WHO TOOK CREDIT FOR THAT LITTLE "ACCIDENT"?

HENRY.

Little doubt remains: Henry and the Apostle were big-time members of the Crossbones.

They were enemies in the end.

If there were three at the top of this shadowy organization, I'd have to guess the third person was the Raven.

The big question this raises for me right now: How is my dad involved?

A bad thought has entered and I can't stop rolling it over in my head.

What if my dad is the Raven?

Thursday, June 23, 2:30 p.m.

Me and Fitz went down the street for a burger and fries at the café and talked about fishing, fishing, and more fishing. Why the hatch was off so severely we didn't even go out today. What makes a good fly and a bad fly (the person making them, obviously), biggest fish ever, most fish in a day, an hour, and a minute (three in one minute, although I think he's lying). Fitz could talk about the arcane business of hooking a trout like my mom could talk about Bon Jovi.

I mention this because my mom is a product of the 1980s and she will not stop listening to music from her "era." Journey is a particular favorite. Also Asia, Def Leppard, REO Speedwagon, and Styx. But Bon Jovi is the king of '80s rock and roll in my mom's view, the perfect antidote after a long day at work. I've heard this one song, "Livin' on a Prayer," at least five million times.

My mom has two friends from college who live in Seattle and the three of them are going to a Bon Jovi concert next Tuesday night. It's

ALL MY MOM HAS TALKED ABOUT FOR DAYS, AND I MENTIONED THIS FACT TO FITZ, WHICH PRODUCED A GOOD RESULT:

"THAT DUDE IS LIKE A HUNDRED YEARS OLD, RIGHT? HE MUST HAVE SOLD HIS SOUL TO THE DEVIL."

"ALL I KNOW IS SHE'LL BE GONE MONDAY TO WEDNESDAY AND I'M LOOKING FORWARD TO IT. ME AND DAD EAT OUT, WATCH TV, AND FISH UNTIL MIDNIGHT. IT'LL BE SWEET."

"SOUNDS LIKE HEAVEN. SAY YOU'LL INVITE ME."

"IT'LL COST YOU FOUR DOZEN FLIES WITH MY NAME ON 'EM. BUT YOU CAN'T MAKE THEM PERFECT, THEY HAVE TO BE ALMOST PERFECT. OTHERWISE MY DAD WILL KNOW YOU DID IT FOR ME."

"DEAL."

IT WAS NICE TO KNOW I COULD CASH IN ON FORTY-EIGHT FITZ-TIED FLIES WHENEVER I WANTED. IT REPRESENTED HOURS OF WORK, AND IT WAS TIME I WANTED ACCESS TO IN CASE I GOT LEFT IN THE FLY SHOP ALONE ANYTIME SOON. I THOUGHT ABOUT THAT AND CHANGED TACTICS.

"THIS IS AN UP-FRONT PAYMENT DEAL, FITZ," I CONCLUDED. "I'M GOING TO NEED THOSE FLIES BY

TOMORROW MORNING, JUST TO BE SAFE. NEVER KNOW WHEN I MIGHT NEED THEM."

"THE ONLY PROBLEM I SEE IS MAKING THEM IMPERFECT. THAT'S GONNA REALLY TEST MY SKILLS."

I LIKE FITZ. HE'S INTO THE SAME THINGS I AM AND HE'S FUNNY. I HAVE A FEELING THE NEXT FOOTBALL SEASON WAS GOING TO BE A HOOT WITH THIS GUY DURING THE LONG RIDE ON THE BENCH.

IT'S NOT THE SAME AS HAVING SARAH AROUND, BUT IT'S SOMETHING.

Thursday, June 23, 8:00 p.m.

After the lunch break, my dad and I hit the river for a few hours to see if things had improved and found that they had. We weren't guiding anyone, but the fish were slamming dry flies on the surface of the water again, so things were looking up. Chances were pretty good the weekend would produce some serious fishermen heading in from Boise or even Portland.

Fitz tied all the flies he owed me while we were gone, which shouldn't have surprised me, but it did. He showed the results when my dad wasn't looking and I had a hard time finding the imperfections.

"Trust me, Ryan — these aren't perfect. I'd lose all respect for myself if I gave these to your dad."

"Did I mention we caught more fish than you could shake a stick at?"

"You did, and you're a loser."

Me and Fitz had great shop banter. It was really enjoyable. I had forty-eight flies in my backpack, a friendly doofus for a shop mate, and

A SUCCESSFUL DAY OF FISHING UNDER MY BELT. I COULD

ONLY HOPE THAT SARAH HAD ENJOYED HER DAY

IN LITTLE ROCK AS MUCH AS I'D ENJOYED MINE IN

SKELETON CREEK.

FOR DINNER I WENT HOME AND TALKED TO MY

MOM, WHO WAS BLARING BON JOVI ALL THE WAY OUT

INTO THE STREET. NO AMOUNT OF BARBECUE IS WORTH

THIS TORTURE, AND I TOLD HER AS MUCH WHILE SHE

FLIPPED BURGERS.

"NO ONE ELSE IN TOWN WANTS JOE BONJY

BLARING DOWN THE STREET THROUGH THE SCREEN DOOR."

I HAD LONG SINCE STOPPED CALLING THIS GUY BY HIS

REAL NAME AND MY MOM HATED IT.

"BON JOVI IS A LEGEND. ONE DAY YOU'LL

REALIZE THAT AND THANK ME FOR INTRODUCING YOU

TO SOME REAL MUSIC."

FAT CHANCE, MOM. CAN I PLEASE JUST GET MY

CHEESEBURGER? AND FOR THE SAKE OF TEENAGERS

EVERYWHERE, PLEASE STOP DANCING ON THE PORCH.

I WATCHED IN HORROR AS MY MOM RAISED THE

SPATULA LIKE A DRUMSTICK AND STARTED WAILING ON

THE GRILL, THEN I RETURNED TO DRAWING IN MY

JOURNAL. I'D ONLY ENCOURAGED HER BAD BEHAVIOR.

BEST TO STAY QUIET UNTIL MY DAD CAME HOME AND
MADE HER SHUT DOWN THE CONCERT.

I HAD BEEN DRAWING A MAP OF WHERE SARAH HAD
BEEN, WHERE SHE WAS GOING, AND WHAT SHE WAS
FINDING. SHE WAS MAKING SOME SERIOUS PROGRESS, NO
DOUBT, BUT THE LONGEST ROAD WAS AHEAD OF HER AND
IT WORRIED ME. A DAY OF CHILLING IN LITTLE ROCK,
ARKANSAS, MIGHT HAVE KILLED THE WHOLE EXCURSION,
AND SHE'D BEEN OMINOUSLY QUIET ALL DAY. I WAS
GIVING HER SOME SPACE, NOT BUGGING HER, LETTING HER
OFF THE GRID FOR A FEW HOURS.

THIS IS THE MAP I DREW:

SARAH'S ROAD TRIP
7 DAYS

BOSTON

CHICAGO

ST. LOUIS

SAN JOSE

SPRINGFIELD

PHOENIX

LITTLE ROCK

MEMPHIS

LOS ANGELES

SAN ANTONIO

AUSTIN

DAY 1 - 983 miles / 15 hours
DAY 2 - 820 miles / 14 hours
DAY 3 - 300 miles / 5 hours
DAY 4 - 620 miles / 10 hours
DAY 5 - 950 miles / 15 hours
DAY 6 - 700 miles / 11 hours
DAY 7 - 940 miles / 5 hours

4-99

I sat on the porch eating my burger, waving flies off my Doritos.

All I could think of was Sarah.

Will she move toward me or away from me come morning?

Friday, June 24, 8:04 a.m.

Maybe I shouldn't be so excited, but I am — Sarah is on the road again, and she's headed straight for Austin, Texas. She got an early start and should arrive at the Driskill Hotel by 5:00 in the evening. After that she'll need to keep going until she reaches San Antonio, where another one of Mrs. Fincher's siblings lives. Mrs. Fincher comes from a big family: three sisters, two brothers. They scattered like buckshot out of Skeleton Creek years ago, which, so far, has been really convenient for Sarah.

This is really working — we're doing it. Or more accurately, Sarah is doing it. I'm like a far-removed copilot and it's killing me more every day. What I want more than anything in the world is to be out there with her, or even out there going in a different direction — anything that will get me out of this town and into something exciting.

I'm starting to sound more like Sarah every day, and that's fine by me. The people, the music,

THE LONG, BORING DAYS IN THE FLY SHOP — I GUESS
IT'S ALL STARTING TO DRIVE ME MAD WITH ROAD
TRIP ENVY.

We've DONE OUR RESEARCH ON THE DRISKILL,
AND SARAH WARNED ME THAT GETTING A
DOCUMENTARY ABOUT IT WAS KIND OF UNLIKELY SINCE
SHE'S GOING TO BE GETTING INTO SAN ANTONIO LATE
AND RIGHT BACK ON THE ROAD SATURDAY MORNING
FOR THE LONG HAUL TO PHOENIX. AFTER THAT, IT WAS
ANOTHER LONG DRIVE TO SAN JOSE FOR THE FINAL
LOCATION — THE WINCHESTER HOUSE — AND THEN
SHE'D HAVE TO MAKE IT BACK TO LA FOR THE START
OF FILM SCHOOL ON MONDAY AT 10:00 A.M. AN
ALL-NIGHTER WOULD BE REQUIRED SOMEWHERE IN
THERE OR SHE'D NEVER MAKE IT.

My DAD SURPRISED ME WITH WHAT I'M SURE HE
THOUGHT WAS STUNNINGLY GOOD NEWS, BUT IT WAS
MORE OF A MIXED BAG THAN HE REALIZED.

"SOMEONE WENT BACK TO BOISE AND SPILLED THE
BEANS ABOUT THAT DAY WE HAD LAST WEEK. YOU
KNOW, LUNKER DAY," MY DAD BEGAN. HE WAS EATING
STEEL-CUT OATS, A NEW HABIT TO OFFSET THE GREASY
SUMMER BARBECUE FARE WE'D BEEN ENJOYING. "GROUP

502

of four emailed this morning. They bit on the multiday."

"When?" I asked.

"Tuesday and Wednesday — the fish better be biting."

My dad had put together this insane two-day fishing package with streamside camping along a seventeen-mile stretch of river. Under normal circumstances I'd sooner die then have him pick Fitz to man the second boat and serve the fried chicken, but this time, I couldn't think of anything I wanted less.

"Your mom will be in Seattle at that concert, so I can hardly leave you home. You got the gig. We'll leave Fitz in the shop and he'll tie a million flies while we're gone."

My heart sank. Not only was I going to have to take back my invitation to Fitz and give back all the imperfect flies he'd tied for me, I was going to be on the river at a critical time. What if Sarah needed me and I was totally out of range for two days? She was scheduled to be at film camp by then — but still, knowing Sarah,

IF THERE WAS A FIFTH LOCATION, SHE'D CALL IN SICK FOR A DAY OR TWO AND OFF SHE'D GO.

I KNEW MY DAD BETTER THAN TO QUESTION HIS DECISION. IF I OFFERED UP FITZ, HE'D DIG IN HIS HEELS AND USE HIS STERN VOICE: OH, YOU'RE GOING. DON'T EVEN TRY TO GET OUT OF IT.

THEN HE DROPPED ANOTHER BOMBSHELL.

"TALKED TO SARAH'S DAD LAST NIGHT. HOW COME YOU DIDN'T MENTION SARAH WAS DRIVING ACROSS AMERICA ALL BY HERSELF?"

I HAD TO THINK ON MY FEET, BECAUSE FOR SOME UNKNOWN, STUPID REASON I HAD NEVER PREPARED FOR THIS PARTICULAR MOMENT.

"THAT'S JUST THE KIND OF THING SHE DOES, DAD. I TALK TO HER WHEN SHE GETS BORED, BUT IT'S HER DEAL. SPEAKING OF WHICH — I DO HAVE A LICENSE, YOU KNOW. HOW COME I NEVER GET TO DRIVE ACROSS THE COUNTRY?"

PUT SOME HUMOR IN THERE, THAT'S THE TICKET.

MY MOM ACTUALLY LAUGHED OUT LOUD AT THAT ONE, LIKE I'D LOST MY MIND. MY DAD REELED OFF ALL THE REASONS WHY I WASN'T DRIVING ANYWHERE FAR AWAY SOON, AND HOW I SHOULD APPRECIATE THE

504

DRIVING I DID GET TO DO: <u>SHE'S A YEAR OLDER THAN YOU, HER PARENTS ARE IDIOTS, SHE'S GOT FAMILY STREWN ALL OVER THE DANG COUNTRY, BE HAPPY YOU GET TO DRIVE THE TRUCK TO THE RIVER.</u>

THIS WAS GOOD. I HAD EFFECTIVELY DIVERTED THEIR ATTENTION AWAY FROM MY OVERAMBITIOUS DRIVING FRIEND AND ONTO THEIR CONCERNS ABOUT ME DRIVING AT ALL. MISSION ACCOMPLISHED, FOR THE MOMENT. MY DAD GAVE ME THAT SUSPICIOUS LOOK AGAIN, BUT HE ALSO HAD <u>TROUT BUM</u> WRITTEN ALL OVER HIS FACE. THERE WAS A LOT TO PLAN WITH AN OVERNIGHTER, AND HIS WHEELS WERE TURNING. NOT ENOUGH ROOM IN THAT HEAD OF HIS FOR TOO MANY BIG THINGS, AND FOR THE MOMENT, HIS BURGEONING BUSINESS WAS TAKING PRECEDENCE OVER WORRYING ABOUT SOME CRAZY TEENAGER DRIVING IN OUR GENERAL DIRECTION.

FRIDAY, JUNE 24, 2:00 P.M.

MY DAD FELT SORRY FOR FITZ AND TOOK HIM OUT ON
THE RIVER ALL DAY, BUT NOT BEFORE SPILLING THE
BEANS ABOUT NEXT WEEK'S TRIP. FITZ THREATENED TO
TAKE HIS FLIES BACK, BUT WHEN I HANDED THEM OVER
AND HE TOOK A LONG LOOK AT THEM, HIS FACE
SOURED. HE'S A REAL FLY SNOB.

"KEEP 'EM. YOU'RE GOING TO NEED A LOT OF
GEAR ON THAT OVERNIGHTER."

MY DAD HAD ALREADY ASSIGNED ANOTHER FOUR
DOZEN FOR THE DAY, SO THIS WAS MUSIC TO MY EARS.
WITH FITZ'S IMPERFECTS IN HAND, I COULD LOUNGE
AROUND ALL DAY IF I WANTED TO, HELP THE OCCASIONAL
CUSTOMER, AND BASICALLY CHILL UNTIL SARAH SHOWED
UP IN AUSTIN AT AROUND 3:00 P.M. MY TIME.

THEY PULLED OUT OF THE SHOP PARKING LOT AT
NOON, AND I STARTED DOING SOME SERIOUS RESEARCH
ON THE DRISKILL HOTEL. SINCE SARAH WON'T BE
DOING A DOCUMENTARY ON THIS, I'M RECORDING MY
FINDINGS HERE, WHILE IT'S STILL LIGHT AND I'M FEELING
REASONABLY SAFE.

I'VE PREVIOUSLY MENTIONED THE PART ABOUT THE
MIRRORS AND HOW LOOKING INTO THEM WILL REFLECT

506

THIS DEAD LADY WHO WILL LATER APPEAR IN YOUR NIGHTMARES FOR THE REST OF YOUR LIFE. SORRY, I WANTED TO SCREAM THAT, BECAUSE IT'S JUST SO WRONG. ANYWAY, THE DEAD LADY IN YOUR DREAMS IS ONLY THE HALF OF IT. THE DRISKILL HAS HAD MORE CONFIRMED PARANORMAL EVENTS THAN JUST ABOUT ANY OTHER PLACE IN THE COUNTRY. HERE ARE A FEW OF THE CREEPIER ONES:

— THERE WAS A KID WHO STAYED THERE A LONG TIME AGO WHO HAD THIS RED BOUNCY BALL. SHE SNUCK OUT OF HER PARENTS' ROOM AND STARTED BOUNCING IT DOWN THIS TREMENDOUSLY LONG STAIRCASE, THEN SHE FELL ALL THE WAY TO THE BOTTOM AND BROKE HER NECK. I GUESS SHE WAS ALL TANGLED UP AT THE BOTTOM, VERY GRUESOME. NOW THE SECOND-FLOOR LADIES' ROOM, THE STAIRCASE, AND THE LOBBY ARE HAUNTED BY THE SOUND OF A BOUNCING BALL AND A GIRL WHISPERING IN YOUR EAR.
— THE ORIGINAL OWNER OF THE HOTEL LOVED THE PLACE BUT WENT TOTALLY BANKRUPT

TRYING TO BUILD IT. THE GUY SMOKED CIGARS LIKE A MADMAN, AND SOMETIMES THE SMELL OF SMOKE JUST SHOWS UP IN DIFFERENT PARTS OF THE HOTEL FOR NO REASON WHATSOEVER. <u>CIGAR</u> SMOKE. IT'S A NONSMOKING HOTEL.

— THE HOUSTON BRIDE IS ANOTHER CONFIRMED SIGHTING. SHE'S A LADY WHO KILLED HERSELF IN ONE OF THE ROOMS AFTER HER FIANCÉ CALLED OFF THEIR WEDDING. SHE'S BEEN SEEN TRYING TO ENTER ROOMS WITH BAGS FULL OF STUFF, APPARENTLY BOUGHT WITH HIS MONEY AS REVENGE. THE ROOM SHE STAYED IN WAS NAILED SHUT FOR A WHILE, BUT SHE STILL SHOWS UP AND KNOCKS ON THE DOOR, TRYING TO GET IN. OR AT LEAST HER GHOST DOES.

NOTHING TOO SCARY — I MEAN, NOTHING THAT SOUNDS LIKE YOU'D END UP ZOMBIFIED FOR STAYING AT THE DRISKILL, BUT SOME PRETTY SPOOKY STUFF, NONETHELESS. SARAH NEEDS TO AVOID A VARIETY OF SPIRIT CREATURES AND THE HOTEL STAFF, FIND THE HALL OF MIRRORS, AND FIND THE FILM REEL. I HOPE SHE

DOESN'T KNOCK A MIRROR OFF THE WALL. THAT'D BE
BAD LUCK, AND WE SURE DON'T NEED IT.

THE REEL OF FILM WILL BE BEHIND THE TOP LEFT
CORNER, ACCORDING TO THE SKULL PUZZLE:

WOULD THE GHOST OF OLD JOE BUSH SHOW HIS
FACE AT THE DRISKILL? I DON'T THINK SO, NOT IN THE
LIGHT OF DAY, WHEN SARAH WOULD BE IN THERE. THAT
JUST SEEMS HIGHLY UNLIKELY.

FRIDAY, JUNE 24, 6:00 P.M.

WRONG! YOU HAVE GOT TO BE <u>KIDDING</u> ME. THE DRISKILL HOTEL HAS ANOTHER GHOST, AND IT'S <u>MY</u> GHOST, THE GHOST OF OLD JOE BUSH. SARAH GOT IN AND MADE IT TO THE HALL OF MIRRORS WITHOUT A PROBLEM. SHE FOUND THE MIRROR SHE WAS LOOKING FOR AND SHE GOT THE REEL OF FILM, WHICH WAS CAREFULLY HIDDEN BEHIND THE MIRROR. THEN SHE TURNED AROUND AND POINTED THE CAMERA AT THE MIRROR ON THE OTHER SIDE, AND THINGS WENT OFF THE RAILS.

YOU HAVE TO SEE THIS TO BELIEVE IT. PLEASE, JUST GO LOOK AT WHAT SARAH RECORDED.

THERE'S MORE ABOUT THE CROSSBONES — BUT MOST IMPORTANT, HE'S FOLLOWING HER.

THE GHOST OF OLD JOE BUSH WAS THERE.

SARAHFINCHER.COM
PASSWORD:
HALLOFMIRRORS

FRIDAY, JUNE 24, 11:00 P.M.

My day of work at the fly shop is over, I've put in some time with my mom on the porch, and Sarah is safely tucked away in San Antonio with her aunt. Tomorrow, Sarah will drive the entire day, fifteen hours to Phoenix, and I'll endure a Saturday at the shop, the only day when it's actually crawling with customers. The fish are biting, so we're going to sell a lot of flies and gear and give a lot of advice.

But none of that matters tonight, because tonight has nightmare written all over it. That video from Sarah was a bone chiller. Seeing the ghost of Old Joe Bush in that mirror, the way he moved, the way he whispered. It had to be real, right? I mean, there's no other answer. How else could it just show up like that? The only other answer besides TERRIFYING GHOST would be . . . I don't even know. Maybe there are secret rooms behind those mirrors where the Crossbones have their meetings and plan the demise of the human race. Who knows?!

A FEW THINGS I DO KNOW — SOME GOOD, SOME BAD:

— I DO NOT WANT TO STAY AT THIS HOTEL.
EVER.
— IT'S OFFICIAL: THE A-POSTLE WAS IN A
MAJOR FIGHT WITH THE OTHER LEADERS OF THE
CROSSBONES.
— THE SKULL PUZZLE THAT HENRY HAD IN
HIS POCKET WAS MADE BY THE A-POSTLE. HE
SHOWED IT IN THAT FOOTAGE. AND THE PUZZLE
LEADS TO SOMETHING BIG THE CROSSBONES
DON'T WANT FOUND.
— MY DAD IS NOT PART OF THIS ORGANIZATION,
WHICH IS A HUGE RELIEF. THE FACT THAT HIS
SECRET GROUP, USED TO PROTECT THE DREDGE,
WAS ALSO CALLED THE CROSSBONES WAS A
TACTIC USED BY THE A-POSTLE TO GAIN POWER.
IT WAS A WARNING TO CROSSBONES LEADERS —
EITHER GIVE HIM WHAT HE WANTED, OR HE'D
REVEAL EVERYTHING. LEAKING THE VERY
NAME OF THE CROSSBONES TO JOE BUSH WAS
THE BEGINNING OF A DANGEROUS GAME.

— And that dangerous game, I'm pretty sure, led to Henry taking him down to the river. They must have fought, because that event ended with the Apostle drowning. It also landed the Skull Puzzle in Henry's pocket. Only now the Apostle's puzzle has found its way to my pocket, and I'm one step away from figuring out where it leads.

— And last, the word PORT, which I can now add to UNDER and GROUND. This confuses me a little bit. I still think wherever this thing is hidden is underground, but those three words together could be UNDER PORT GROUND or PORT UNDERGROUND or GROUND UNDER PORT. No matter how it slices and dices, these three words lead to a port of some kind, so we're talking near water.

I sure hope the Winchester House proves more helpful.

Sarah is convinced that all roads lead to Thomas Jefferson. The Crossbones hated him and wanted him destroyed. They tried to kill him and drove him into financial disaster. What else could they have done to ruin his life? That part remains a mystery, but I have a feeling we're going to find out more when Sarah arrives at the Winchester House.

The last stop on her whirlwind tour will be the strangest, and her timing couldn't be better. She'll sleep over in Phoenix at a hotel predetermined by her parents, and finish the drive on Sunday. She's expected in LA on Sunday night for check-in at the dorm on UCLA's campus, then the film camp starts Monday morning.

Our plan for getting Sarah into LA Sunday night is a little on the shaky side, and it involves cutting out of Phoenix very, very early. Here's how it's going to work:

— Sarah will go straight to sleep in Phoenix when she arrives there at around 9:00 p.m. tomorrow night (Saturday).

— She's going to get up at 4:00 a.m. and start driving. It's ten hours to San Jose, so she should be there by around 2:00 p.m.

— Back on the road by 4:00 p.m. for a slightly late but reasonable UCLA arrival at 9:00 p.m.

I'm tired, but I'm also afraid of whatever nightmare will be waiting for me once I close my eyes. I'd call Sarah, but she's asleep for sure. Fitz doesn't have a phone. My parents are out.

Another solitary late night in Skeleton Creek.

I really need to get a life.

Saturday, June 25, 3:10 p.m.

Nothing much to note. Sarah is on the move, heading for Phoenix. We talked this morning and she sounded upbeat but just as confused as I am. She's excited about film camp, but she's even more excited about getting to the Winchester House and finding whatever's hidden at the top of a set of stairs that leads to nowhere.

I'm with her.

SUNDAY, JUNE 26, 9:11 A.M.

It's dreadfully quiet. Sunday mornings are like that in Skeleton Creek. At least I don't have to listen to Bon Jovi.

I'd write more, but there's nothing going on around here worth mentioning, and Sarah is doing pretty much nothing but driving and listening to music. She's bored, I'm bored. I bet even the ghost of Old Joe Bush is bored. Probably sitting in a tomb somewhere playing cards with some other dead people while we get our act together.

Sunday morning makes me think of the Apostle in a different way. The guy was nuts, for sure, or maybe just acting nuts, but either way, he went to church on Sundays. My parents aren't the churchgoing sort, but Sunday mornings are sacred in their own way for us. It's silent, for one, almost like everyone is tiptoeing around. And the porch is a favorite spot. While some people from town walk by with their Bibles in hand giving us sideways glances that say <u>you</u> <u>should be going to church</u>, you heathens! we just

SIT THERE DRINKING OUR COFFEE AND READING WHATEVER IT IS WE WANT TO READ.

It's spiritual in its own way. We do set the world aside for a few hours. We talk slower, quieter, nicer. And what is the church, anyway? My dad is fond of saying, "It sure ain't no building, I can promise you that," and this strikes me as a small but meaningful pearl of wisdom.

Me, I think heaven is on the river. It's where I feel my connection to whoever made all this stuff. It's where I find peace. Casting is my prayer, for what little it's worth. There's nothing more mysterious and beautiful than a wild fish in a mountain stream. It lives a secret life in a world I can never know, but if I can catch it, I can hold it in my hand for a moment. After that, I can bash its head in or let it go. As you might imagine, I let them all go. I don't want to upset the balance of nature.

This is what happens in Skeleton Creek when the world outside goes silent and my best friend is driving, driving, driving. I start talking about

THE MEANING OF LIFE, WHICH APPARENTLY HAS

SOMETHING TO DO WITH FISH.

The Winchester House can't show up fast

ENOUGH. A few more hours and she'll be there.

Too bad I'll be at the shop with Fitz while my

DAD TAKES THE DAY OFF TO LOUNGE ON THE PORCH

TAKING NAPS AND READING THE Sunday Boise paper

(it's a whopper).

FITZ DOESN'T MIND IF I TALK ON THE PHONE WHILE I'M WORKING, BUT I'M NERVOUS ABOUT MAKING CALLS TO SARAH WHILE HE'S STANDING THERE. HE'S A PRETTY ALOOF SORT OF GUY, VERY FOCUSED WHEN HE'S SITTING IN FRONT OF HIS FLY-TYING VISE OR READING UP ON SOME ARCANE CASTING TECHNIQUE, BUT STILL, I WOULDN'T WANT HIM KNOWING ABOUT WHAT ME AND SARAH ARE UP TO. THE FEWER PEOPLE WHO KNOW, THE BETTER.

SO IT WAS KIND OF ALARMING WHEN FITZ CALLED ME OUT.

"HOW'S SARAH DOING?" HE ASKED ME.

AT FIRST I THOUGHT HE WAS JUST, YOU KNOW, MAKING SMALL TALK, SO I BRUSHED IT OFF WITH A SIMPLE "PRETTY GOOD, AS FAR AS I KNOW."

"WISH I HAD A CELL PHONE. DAD WON'T GET ME ONE. SAYS IT'S TOO EXPENSIVE."

"IT IS," I CAUTIONED HIM. "HALF THE MONEY I MAKE IN THIS PLACE GOES TO COVERING MY MONTHLY BILL."

"MUST BE NICE TO KEEP UP WITH HER ON THE ROAD."

AT FIRST, THIS SEEMED LIKE A NORMAL-ENOUGH QUESTION. BUT THEN I WONDERED: HOW DID FITZ KNOW about Sarah's trip? I didn't say anything, and Fitz looked up from his work on a perfect parachute adams, a hard fly to tie just right.

"You know your dad still worries about you guys," he said. "He told me himself."

So that was it. My dad was using river time to get Fitz into the loop, probably hoping to use this fly-tying fish-face to infiltrate my wall of silence.

"Look, Fitz, my dad's paranoid as all get-out. He blows everything out of proportion. She's driving to film camp in LA, no big whoop."

"I'm thinking maybe you're the one who's paranoid. Your dad is just worried about you, is all."

Okay, this was starting to annoy me. He couldn't outfish me, so he was trying to be my dad's best friend?

But then he went for the jugular, and it sort of shut me up.

"You have no idea how good you have it around here," he said. "I barely see my dad, and when I do, he doesn't have much to say. He couldn't care less about football _or_ fishing."

It was the first time since I'd met him that I actually felt sorry for Fitz. His dad never came around. In fact, I'd never even met his dad. He logged up in the forest for a living, and let me tell you, cutting down trees pays even worse than owning a fly shop, and it takes even more time.

All the same, I stayed quiet about Sarah. Texting only, which was big-time inconvenient once she arrived at the Winchester House.

Me: Can't talk, at the shop, Fitz is here.

Sarah: You're SO missing out. This place is the best. Huge, weird, awesome.

Sarah: And they don't care if I use my camera!

Me: Did you find the stairs to nowhere?

Sarah: Hold your horses.

Me: I hate this.

Sarah: Price you pay for staying home.

ME: Not fair.

SARAH: Neither is digging up a grave alone at midnight.

ME: Ouch.

SARAH: I'm peeling off from the group. Hang tight.

Four minutes went by before she was back.

SARAH: That was close. Almost got caught.

ME: What? Did you get it???

SARAH: I got it.

And that was it. She had the last clue the Apostle had left behind in her hot little hands, and it was only 2:42.

Ahead of schedule.

LONGEST DAY OF MY LIFE. THERE IS NOTHING MORE FRUSTRATING THAN HAVING A REEL OF 8MM FILM SITTING IN THE BACKSEAT OF A CAR THAT YOU CAN'T WATCH UNTIL YOU GET TO AN OUTLET, PLUG IN THE DANG PROJECTOR, AND POINT IT TO A WALL. SO ANNOYING. SARAH HAD THE GALL TO DRIVE BACK TO LA FIRST AND CHECK INTO HER DORM ROOM. SHE WAS ARRIVING AT THE UCLA CAMPUS JUST AFTER 8:00 P.M. HER ROOMMATE WAS A LOCAL GIRL WHO WASN'T SCHEDULED IN UNTIL MONDAY MORNING, WHEN THE WEEKLONG CAMP WOULD BEGIN, SO THE ROOM WAS ALL HERS.

DURING THE NEXT HOUR SHE CALLED ME TWICE, ONCE TO LET ME KNOW SHE'D DONE ALL THE PLEASANTRIES AND LANDED IN HER ROOM SAFELY, THE SECOND TIME AFTER WATCHING THE LAST APOSTLE VIDEO. IN TYPICAL MADDENING SARAH FASHION, SHE WOULDN'T TELL ME WHAT IT REVEALED, ONLY THAT SHE'D FIGURED OUT WHERE THE LAST LOCATION WAS BY WATCHING THE APOSTLE. I BADGERED HER FOR INFORMATION, BUT SHE WASN'T HAVING ANY OF IT.

"Give me a few hours and you'll have your chance" was all she'd say.

I knew better than to push Sarah. If I texted her too many times for answers she'd make me wait until morning. She was a filmmaker and this was her big finale. For Sarah, spilling the beans on the phone would be like me reading the last page of a book while I was still in the middle of the story. I got that, but it didn't make me any less crazy.

I spent the next three hours staring at the Skull Puzzle and the map, wondering where this was all leading and how Sarah would get to the last location. One thing was for sure: It would have to wait a week, because there was no way we could spring her from camp now that she was in. We'd been incredibly lucky to get her there without finding our way into serious trouble.

At 11:30 p.m., a text message showed up on my phone.

Check your email. I'm a zombie — totally wiped out — me go sleep now.

I COULD HARDLY BLAME HER. SEVEN DAYS, FIVE THOUSAND MILES, AND FOUR HAUNTED LOCATIONS — SARAH HAD DONE TEN TIMES THE WORK I HAD, AND SHE DESERVED SOME REST BEFORE WHAT WAS SURE TO BE A GRUELING WEEK OF FILMMAKING.

I FIRED UP MY SARAH—ONLY GMAIL ACCOUNT AND FOUND HER MESSAGE.

Ryan,

I uploaded everything to my site in one chunky video as usual. The Winchester House had the best story of them all. I could have spent a week on that short documentary, but there just wasn't any time. You've also got the footage of me finding the reel, which was tucked into the edge of the stair. (I had to pry up a piece of molding, so hopefully I don't get busted somewhere down the road.) The Apostle is at the end.

I hate to be the one to tell you this, Ryan, but I think you're up to bat.

You'll see what I mean when you watch the video.

Zzzzzzz.

S.

What was _that_ all about? I had a bad feeling the last location was going to be right here at home in Skeleton Creek, the one place I didn't want it to be. It would mean I'd be the one digging a grave at midnight or some other kind of unthinkable horror.

Unfortunately for me, the news was even worse.

Rainsford.

Nice password, Sarah. The main character from "The Most Dangerous Game," a short story we'd both read in the same junior high class a few years ago. We'd both loved the idea: Rainsford lands on an island and finds he's being hunted like a wild animal. Did Sarah think I was about to be Rainsford in our story? And if so, who was going to do the hunting? The Raven, Winchester's ghost, or some other creature of the night?

You'll have to watch the video to find out. That's what I had to do.

SARAHFINCHER.COM
PASSWORD:
RAINSFORD

MONDAY, JUNE 27, 12:14 A.M.

It doesn't take Sherlock Holmes to figure out I'm in big trouble.

The final location is closer to me than it is to Sarah. Those four words: UNDER, PORT, GROUND, LAND — could only spell out one place: PORTLAND UNDERGROUND. I wrote the words onto the Skull Puzzle and stared at them:

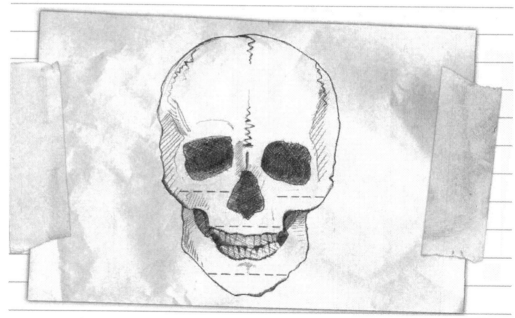

Even if we could wait a week, which I don't think we can, Portland is a solid fifteen-hour

DRIVE IN THE WRONG DIRECTION FOR SARAH. THERE IS NO WAY TO GET HER THERE, EVEN AFTER CAMP ENDS.

So REALLY, IT WOULDN'T MATTER IF WE WAITED A WEEK OR A MONTH. SARAH WOULDN'T BE ABLE TO DO IT.

THIS TIME, THE TASK IS GOING TO FALL TO ME.

I'M GOING TO HAVE TO LEAVE SKELETON CREEK, MAKE THE SEVEN—HOUR DRIVE TO PORTLAND, AND FIND WHAT WE'VE BEEN LOOKING FOR.

I HAVE A BAD FEELING ABOUT THE GHOST OF OLD JOE BUSH ON THIS ONE. THE FIRST TIME I SAW HIM, I'D JUST GOTTEN DONE CLIMBING A LONG SET OF STAIRS UP INTO THE RAFTERS OF THE DREDGE. THIS TIME, IF HE SHOWS UP AGAIN, I'LL BE UNDER THE EARTH IN AN ANCIENT TUNNEL.

IT FEELS LIKE I'M ABOUT TO WALK INTO MY OWN GRAVE AND NEVER RETURN.

MONDAY, JUNE 27, 8:20 A.M.

I KNOW WHAT I NEED TO DO, BUT I SO DO NOT WANT TO
DO IT. I LEFT HOME EARLY THIS MORNING AND CAME
BACK DOWN TO THE CAFÉ TO THINK. TODAY IS GOING
TO BE BUSY AT THE SHOP, GETTING EVERYTHING READY
FOR THE TWO-DAY RIVER RUN. IT'S A TRIP I'VE
DECIDED I CAN'T MAKE, EVEN THOUGH THE THOUGHT OF
LETTING FITZ HAVE MY SLOT IS NEARLY KILLING ME.

WHAT CHOICE DO I HAVE? THE STARS HAVE
ALIGNED, AND EVEN THOUGH I'M BOUND TO GET INTO
SOME SERIOUS TROUBLE OVER THIS, I HAVE NO CHOICE.
MY DAD WILL BE GONE ALL DAY TUESDAY AND
WEDNESDAY. LATER TODAY HE'LL DRIVE MY MOM TO
THE BOISE AIRPORT SO SHE CAN FLY TO SEATTLE. SO
WHAT DOES THAT MEAN? IT MEANS I COULD BE ALL
ALONE TUESDAY AND MOST OF WEDNESDAY. NO ONE
WILL BE BACK AT THE HOUSE UNTIL EIGHT OR NINE
WEDNESDAY NIGHT. THIS IS PROBABLY MY ONLY
CHANCE.

I CAN'T BELIEVE I'M EVEN HAVING THIS
CONVERSATION WITH MYSELF. AM I HONESTLY WILLING
TO FAKE AN INJURY, GET IN MY MOM'S MINIVAN, AND
DRIVE TO PORTLAND? IF I DO THIS AND THEY CATCH

ME, I MIGHT NEVER DRIVE AGAIN. THEY'LL TAKE AWAY MY LAPTOP AND MY PHONE. MY RELATIONSHIP WITH SARAH WILL DRY UP IF WE CAN'T STAY CONNECTED, AND MY SUMMER WILL TURN ISOLATED AND LONELY. FITZ WILL OUTFISH AND OUT—FLY—TIE ME ALL SUMMER. IT WILL BE DEPRESSING.

AND ALL THIS SO I CAN COMPLETE AN INSANE JOURNEY.

IT'S AN AWFUL LOT TO RISK, BUT I'VE DECIDED IT'S WORTH IT.

NOW MORE THAN EVER IT'S PAINFULLY OBVIOUS THAT SARAH IS WORLDLIER THAN I AM. SHE'S IN LA AT FILM SCHOOL, FOR CRYING OUT LOUD. SHE JUST DROVE ACROSS THE ENTIRE COUNTRY! AND SHE'S RIGHT. THIS IS GOING TO BE GOOD FOR ME. SCARY, BUT GOOD FOR ME. I NEED TO GET OUT OF THIS PLACE, DO SOMETHING WILD. I NEED TO BE THE ONE WHO FACES HIS FEARS FOR ONCE.

I'VE PRINTED OUT A COPY OF THAT LAST SHEET OF PAPER THE APOSTLE HELD UP, AND I KNOW WHAT IT IS. IT'S HOW TO GET INTO THE PORTLAND UNDERGROUND AT NIGHT. IT'S HOW TO FIND WHAT I'M LOOKING FOR ONCE I'M DOWN THERE.

HERE COMES FITZ ON HIS OLD MOTORCYCLE.
TIME TO PUT PHASE ONE OF MY PLAN INTO
ACTION.

MONDAY, JUNE 27, 9:15 A.M.

It's good to make your friends happy once in a while, even if it means you'll be staring a ghost in the face for doing it. I limped out of the café and onto the sidewalk as Fitz pulled over. Blue smoke from the tailpipe drifted into my face and I about gagged. The combination of aromas from the café and his oil-spewing motorcycle was not the rosiest mix.

"Did you hook your toe or what?" Fitz asked me. I swear, Fitz cannot imagine anything in life not being somehow related to fishing.

"Fell down the stairs at home, reinjured it," I lied. I'd already tried this lie out on my mom and dad, and they'd both fell for it hook, line, and sinker. (Oh, no. I'm becoming Fitz. Note to self: No more fishing metaphors.)

"That's a bummer. Rowing for two days is gonna kill."

"Don't I know it — which is why I'm not going. Looks like you got the gig."

"No way! You serious?"

Fitz was beaming. There is nothing a trout bum loves more than leaving the world entirely behind and basically living on the river for days, not hours in a row. He was happier than I'd ever seen him before, which actually felt pretty good.

The good feeling went away pretty quick when I fake-hobbled back into the café and slumped down in my booth.

Was I really doing this?

How in the world did I even end up in this situation? Voluntarily giving up the best fishing trip of the year, lying to my parents, taking risks like I'd never taken before — it all added up to a serious case of the crazies.

Sarah and I were right back where we always ended up.

On the edge of disaster.

MONDAY, JUNE 27, NOON

My mom is on a plane to Seattle. Her piece-of-junk minivan is parked in the gravel on the side of the house. The tires are pretty bald, which makes me nervous. Will that thing even make it to Portland and back?

Maybe I should take the bus.

MONDAY, JUNE 27, 3:00 P.M.

FITZ JUST TOOK OFF TO CLEAR THE TRIP WITH HIS DAD, WHICH MEANS HE'S GOING TO BE GONE FOR A WHILE. THEY CUT TREES UNTIL DARK JUST LIKE WE FISH UNTIL DARK, AND MY DAD'S LEAVING BRIGHT AND EARLY. FITZ KNOWS THE GENERAL AREA WHERE HIS DAD IS CUTTING, BUT NOT EXACTLY. HE COULD BE GONE FOR A FEW HOURS, DURING WHICH TIME I'LL HAVE TO GIMP AROUND THE SHOP AND WINCE IN PAIN AS MUCH AS POSSIBLE WHILE I HELP MY DAD PACK FOR THE FLOAT TRIP.

I HATE MAINTAINING A LIE ALMOST AS MUCH AS I HATE TELLING IT IN THE FIRST PLACE. EVERY STEP I TAKE IS A REMINDER OF HOW I'M FLAT-OUT DECEIVING MY PARENTS.

MY DAD IS GOING TO KILL ME IF I GET CAUGHT.

MONDAY, JUNE 27, 7:00 P.M.

IT TOOK FITZ FOREVER TO GET BACK, BUT HE'S A GO.

EVERYTHING IS SET.

TOMORROW MORNING, MY DAD WILL DRIVE THE TRUCK TWO HOURS UP INTO A NO-CELL ZONE, ONE RAFT IN THE BED OF THE TRUCK AND THE OTHER PULLED BEHIND. HE'LL PICK UP FITZ ON THE WAY, SO THE OLD MOTORCYCLE DOESN'T GET LEFT IN FRONT OF THE SHOP HALF THE WEEK. THE TRUTH IS, I THINK MY DAD BELIEVES IF IT'S SITTING THERE WHILE HE AND FITZ ARE GONE, I'LL BE TEMPTED TO GO JOYRIDING ALL OVER TOWN. ACTUALLY, UNDER DIFFERENT CIRCUMSTANCES, THAT WOULD PROBABLY BE TRUE. I'D LOVE TO RIDE THAT THING, BUT FITZ IS VERY PROTECTIVE.

THE FOUR GUYS MY DAD IS GUIDING WILL FOLLOW IN THEIR OWN CAR, THEN THEY'LL SPEND AN HOUR DOING THE SONG AND DANCE TO MOVE A RIG TWENTY MILES DOWNSTREAM. UNLOAD THE BOATS, DRIVE BOTH RIGS DOWN, LEAVE THE TRUCK BEHIND. WHEN THE TRIP IS OVER, THEY'LL LOAD UP THE BOATS AND MY DAD WILL DRIVE UPRIVER WITH ONE OF THE CLIENTS TO GET THEIR CAR. I KNOW, COMPLICATED, BUT IT'S THE ONLY

539

WAY TO RUN TWENTY MILES OF RIVER WITHOUT A LONG WALK AT THE END.

THE LAST THING FITZ SAID TO ME BEFORE HE TOOK OFF FOR HOME WAS THANKS. HE REALLY DID APPRECIATE THAT I'D GOTTEN MY LEG ALL BENT OUT OF SHAPE JUST IN TIME FOR WHAT MIGHT BE THE ONLY OVERNIGHT FISHING TRIP OF THE ENTIRE SUMMER.

I COULDN'T BEGRUDGE THE GUY. I'D HAVE FELT THE SAME WAY, I SUPPOSE. BUT IT WAS A LITTLE LIKE WATCHING YOUR FRIEND GET INJURED IN THE BIGGEST FOOTBALL GAME OF THE YEAR SO YOU COULD TAKE HIS SPOT ON THE TEAM.

IT'S NOT THE KIND OF THING YOU SHOULD THANK SOMEONE FOR.

My mom called twice to check on me, which made me feel like a ten-year-old. Sarah's right; I gotta get out of here. I'm sixteen, not ten, and I'm suffocating in Skeleton Creek. Sarah was smart to get out while she still could. Me, I'll probably be running the fly shop and sitting on the front porch feeding my parents soup through a straw when I'm fifty.

There's no denying the facts.

1) I am lame.

2) I'm too chicken to leave town and I might not go through with it.

Luckily for me, right when I was feeling most sorry for myself, Sarah sent me an email. It was maybe the best email I've ever gotten in my life.

Dear Ryan,

I was going to call you but I thought it would be better if you could have this in writing, even though writing really isn't my thing. First day of camp was fine.

541

Um, actually, I'm lying, and I can't lie to you.

The first day of film camp was awful. Everyone here is amazing, Ryan. What was I thinking, coming to this stupid thing? Did I actually think a small-town girl from nowhere could hold her own against people from LA, the film capital of the world? I kid you not, there's a thirteen-year-old kid here who understands filmmaking a billion times better than I do. His sample project was like *The Usual Suspects* meets *Paranormal Activity*, so you can imagine what the people in my own age group are bringing to the table.

Lighting, setting up, script writing, directing actors, angles, shot selection, tone — Ryan, I'm in big trouble here. I don't know anything about any of those things. I just point and shoot and cut and blend. Being here has made me realize something I never knew before.

I'm a hack.

Okay, end of pity party. Let's talk about you instead.

I know what you're thinking. You're not sure if you can go through with it. Well, you can. YOU, Ryan McCray — you can do this. Is there a chance you'll get in big trouble? Sure there is, but it's worth the risk. And you've earned the right to find whatever the Crossbones are hiding. Just think — if this leads to something connected to Thomas Jefferson, we could be returning something to the world that shouldn't be buried underground.

You could change the course of history. All it's going to take is a little courage and a minivan.

It's your time, Ryan. Don't let it pass you by.

Sarah

SHE'S RIGHT; I CAN DO THIS.

I WILL DO THIS.

TOMORROW, LIFE CHANGES FOR ME.

I'M LEAVING SKELETON CREEK.

I WROTE HER BACK.

Thanks for inviting me to the first annual Sarah Fincher pity party. I think about one of these a decade is enough, because Sarah, you're going to blow everyone away. I'm sure of it. Give yourself a day or two, be a sponge, take it all in. It's only going to make you better. I predict you'll leave there at the top of the class, because you have something a lot of people don't have: something to say.

I'm getting in my mom's car in the morning and heading to Portland.

Count on it.

R.

TUESDAY, JUNE 28, 10:00 A.M.

I KNOW, I KNOW, I KNOW! I SHOULD HAVE LEFT BY NOW.
IF I'M NOT CAREFUL IT'S GOING TO BE DARK BEFORE I
GET THERE AND THAT WILL BE A DISASTER. NO WAY
AM I GOING DOWN THERE ALONE AT NIGHT. I'M NOT
EVEN SURE I COULD GET IN THERE AT NIGHT. THE MAP
THE APOSTLE SHOWED SEEMS TO INDICATE THAT I
COULD, BUT WAS DRAWN, WHAT, FIFTY YEARS AGO?
I DOUBT THAT ENTRANCE EVEN EXISTS ANYMORE.

LAST NIGHT I HAD A NIGHTMARE OF OLD JOE
BUSH FOLLOWING ME DOWN A CORRIDOR WITH AN AX. I
WAS STANDING IN BLACK TAR UP TO MY KNEES, TRYING
TO RUN AWAY, BUT HE JUST FLOATED CLOSER AND
CLOSER. WHEN I GOT DOWN ON MY KNEES AND FELT
THE TAR FILLING MY LUNGS, I WOKE UP COVERED IN
SWEAT. I WAS TOO AFRAID TO GET OUT OF BED, SO I
JUST LAY THERE SHIVERING IN THE DARK. A LIGHT
BREEZE BLEW MY CURTAIN AWAY FROM THE WINDOW,
AND I SAW HIM.

HE WAS THERE. IT WAS NO SHADOW OR TREE LIMB.
THE GHOST OF OLD JOE BUSH WAS WATCHING ME,
HIS HEAD BIGGER THAN EVER IN THE BLACK NIGHT. HE

WAS STARING AT ME WHILE I CLIMBED OUT OF A TAR-
FILLED DREAM, WONDERING WHAT I WAS GOING TO DO
WHEN MORNING CAME.

I TURNED AWAY AND COULDN'T BRING MYSELF TO
LOOK BACK. I JUST LAY THERE, TEXTING SARAH OVER
AND OVER: He'S HERE. He'S HERE. He'S HERE.

BUT SHE NEVER ANSWERED.

SOMEHOW, AGAINST ALL MY EFFORTS TO STAY
AWAKE, I FELL BACK ASLEEP IN THE EARLY MORNING
BEFORE LIGHT AND DIDN'T WAKE BACK UP UNTIL MY DAD
WAS POUNDING ON THE DOOR AT EIGHT, YELLING FOR
ME TO GET UP. SKELETON CREEK WAS AN EARLY
MORNING TOWN; IT WAS PART OF THE CULTURE. WAKING
UP AT EIGHT WAS WHAT LAZY CITY FOLKS DID.

"I'M LEAVING IN FIFTEEN — LET'S GO OVER THE
RULES ONCE MORE," HE SAID, OBVIOUSLY NOT PLEASED
I'D SNOOZED SO LATE. HE DIDN'T TRUST ME WITH THE
SHOP WHILE HE WAS GONE, BUT I WAS ALL HE HAD.

I WAS GOING TO LET HIM DOWN, THAT WAS A FACT,
AND IT LEFT A HOLLOW FEELING IN MY GUT.

WHEN I SHOWED UP ON THE PORCH DOWNSTAIRS IN
MY SHORTS AND A WRINKLED T-SHIRT, MY DAD GAVE

ME MY MARCHING ORDERS FOR THE MILLIONTH TIME.
NO DRIVING, BRING A LUNCH SO THE SHOP STAYS OPEN,
DON'T BUG YOUR MOTHER.

"I DON'T THINK I'LL HAVE TO WORRY ABOUT BUGGING
MOM. I BET SHE'LL CALL ME TEN TIMES TODAY."

IT WAS TRUE. SHE HARDLY EVER LEFT TOWN, AND I
WAS GOING TO BE HOME ALONE. I MADE THE MISTAKE
OF FOLLOWING MY DAD AS HE WALKED DOWN THE
STEPS OF OUR PORCH TO HIS PICKUP.

THE LIMP WAS GONE, FORGOTTEN IN A SEA OF
BLACK TAR THE NIGHT BEFORE.

"LOOKS LIKE YOUR LEG IS FEELING BETTER," DAD
SAID. WAS HE SUSPICIOUS OR JUST SURPRISED? I
COULDN'T TELL.

"IT STILL HURTS, BUT YEAH, IT'S STARTING TO
BOUNCE BACK."

"TOO LATE TO CHANGE PLANS OR I WOULD, CHAMP.
LAY LOW, GET BETTER, WE'LL GET YOU OUT THERE ON
THE NEXT ONE."

AS MY DAD OPENED THE SQUEAKY DOOR TO HIS
OLD TRUCK, I FELT A DEPTH OF GUILT THE SIZE OF THE
HINDENBURG. HE ACTUALLY FELT BAD FOR ME FOR
MISSING OUT. HE'D CALLED ME CHAMP, A RARE TREAT.

And I was about to deceive him big-time. Here he was leaving me in charge of the fly shop, and I wasn't even going to be here.

All I could think of at that moment was that it wouldn't be worth it. No matter what I found out there, I'd lose my dad's respect and trust in the process.

That's why it's taking me so long to pull out of the carport.

I'm sitting in the van, staring out the window. My hands are shaking.

I've been sitting here for almost an hour.

TUESDAY, JUNE 28, 12:11 P.M.

I'M LEAVING.

Tuesday, June 28, 3:00 p.m.

It's a seven-hour drive to Portland if I don't stop, and I just stopped. Sarah had her Steak 'n Shake, her Waffle House, her Cracker Barrel. Me, I'm at the Kmart loading up on everything I forgot. I packed food for the road, since the smell of fast food in a car makes me want to barf. I was so stressed this morning I forgot to bring a shovel. I loaded my backpack with every kind of tool I could think of: screwdrivers, files, a hammer, a hatchet (for protection against zombies and vampires), but I'd neglected to bring a shovel. I found a folding one for camping that fits in my backpack, grabbed one of the sandwiches I made and a Mountain Dew, and I'm heading back on the road. Should hit Portland by 8:00 p.m.

My mom is on schedule. She has called my cell phone five times.

I've lied each time. As far as she's concerned, I'm sitting in a fly shop in Skeleton Creek.

549

TUESDAY, JUNE 28, 7:00 P.M.

BAD, BAD, BAD, BAD NEWS! THIS VAN HASN'T BEEN MORE THAN AN HOUR OUT OF SKELETON CREEK IN FIVE YEARS, AND NOW I KNOW WHY. BECAUSE IT'S A PIECE OF JUNK! I'M STUCK AN HOUR OUTSIDE OF PORTLAND AT SOME GAS STATION ADDING OIL. THE ATTENDANT GAVE ME FOUR MORE CANS AND SAID, "SHE'S A LEAKER, BUT THERE'S NOT MUCH YOU CAN DO ABOUT IT UNLESS YOU WANT TO REPLACE THE TRANSMISSION, WHICH WOULD COST TWICE AS MUCH AS THIS THING IS WORTH."

HE TOLD ME TO STOP EVERY HUNDRED MILES AND POUR IN ANOTHER CAN, AND THAT I SHOULD BE PREPARED FOR THE WHOLE THING TO GO BELLY—UP AT ANY MOMENT.

NOT WHAT I NEEDED.

I CALLED AND TEXTED SARAH, BUT SHE'S LOCKED DOWN IN CLASS. ALL I GOT WAS THIS TEXT AT 4:00 P.M.:

PICK UP CELL = GET YELLED AT. STAY CALM! I'M OFF THE GRID UNTIL BREAK AT 8

PERFECT.

550

TUESDAY, JUNE 28, 8:30 P.M.

Just stopped to load a can of oil and use the bathroom. Last rest stop before Portland. The burning oil smell of the engine makes me sick. Either that or it's my nerves.

It's going to be dark in an hour.

At least my mom is at the Bon Jovi concert, where she'll stop calling me every hour.

It's the little things that keep a guy going.

TUESDAY, JUNE 28, 9:50 P.M.

DRIVING IN TRAFFIC IS — WOW — HARDER THAN I THOUGHT IT WOULD BE. I'M AMAZED I DIDN'T PLOW RIGHT INTO THE BIG RIVER THAT CUTS THROUGH DOWNTOWN PORTLAND. AT LEAST I GOT HERE IN ONE PIECE AND FIGURED OUT HOW TO PARALLEL PARK. IT HELPED THAT THERE WERE THREE SPOTS IN A ROW, BUT STILL. I HAVE PARKED!

THE TRICK NOW IS GETTING OUT OF THE CAR, WHICH I DO NOT THINK I CAN DO.

OIL IS LEAKING ONTO THE PAVEMENT. I CAN SMELL IT. IN MY IMAGINATION, I CAN SEE IT HISSING AS IT HITS THE HOT PAVEMENT.

I'LL NEVER FORGET THAT SMELL.

Sarah called me, or I would have left sooner. No, seriously, I would have. Really, what does it matter? The Portland Underground is closed, anyway. It's dark outside. When I go in just doesn't matter. Maybe I'll wait until midnight, make it as creepy as I can. If I'm going to overcome my deepest fears, I might as well go all the way.

She encouraged me in the best way she knew how: by telling me she wouldn't be surprised if I turned for home without ever going underground.

I reminded her that, technically, even if I could get in, it would be breaking and entering. The Portland Underground is city property. They give tours down there and stuff, so it's not like it's totally abandoned.

TUESDAY, JUNE 28, 11:53 P.M.

I couldn't do it. After staying in the car until almost 11:00 p.m., I walked the three blocks to Chinatown and realized, um, yeah, not a great place to hang around at night. Lots of shady-looking characters and all-night bars. And it gets worse. The place where the Apostle showed a secret entrance? There's a building sitting on top of it. It must not have been there fifty years ago, but this makes it official: I'm not getting in there unless I take one of the tours.

If something big is hidden underground, I won't be able to remove it without getting caught.

WEDNESDAY, JUNE 29, 2:00 A.M.

MORE BAD NEWS. IT'S PILING UP, WHICH MAKES ME FEEL MORE THAN EVER THAT I MADE A BIG MISTAKE COMING HERE. AFTER I MOVED THE CAR TO A TRUCK STOP ON I-5 AND ATE PANCAKES FOR DINNER AT THE ALL-NIGHT DINER, I DECIDED I BETTER ADD MORE OIL TO THE CLUNKER. MY HANDS GOT ALL GROSS AND I WENT FOR THE GLOVE BOX, HOPING TO FIND AN EXTRA RAG OR OLD NAPKINS IN THERE. WHAT I FOUND INSTEAD TOOK MY BREATH AWAY. I SAT IN THE DRIVER'S SEAT NUMB, UNABLE TO MOVE.

THERE WAS A CELL PHONE IN THERE AND IT WAS ON. I'D NEVER SEEN IT BEFORE, AND THERE WAS ONLY ONE REASON WHY IT WOULD BE IN MY MOM'S GLOVE BOX: GPS.

MY PARENTS HAD PUT IT THERE SO THEY'D KNOW IF I DROVE OUT OF TOWN. I KNEW HOW THESE THINGS WORKED. ALL A PERSON HAD TO DO WAS GO ONLINE AND PUT IN THE CELL PHONE NUMBER. IT WOULD SHOW WHERE I WAS WITHIN ABOUT TWENTY FEET.

WHAT A SINKING FEELING.

THEY KNEW WHAT I WAS DOING.

My mom, she knew where I was. She'd always known.

Maybe that's why she kept asking me: Where are you? What are your plans?

How many times had I lied to her while she sat staring at a hotel computer screen, knowing good and well I was not minding the fly shop in Skeleton Creek?

What a disaster.

On the off chance that she hadn't actually checked the thing yet, I turned it off. If it didn't work, they couldn't prove I'd gone anywhere.

Lies upon lies upon lies. It never stops with just one.

One is always just the beginning. Count on it.

Wednesday, June 29, 10:00 a.m.

The first Underground tour starts in an hour, and I'm parked a block away. At this point, if I'm extremely lucky, I'll get back to Skeleton Creek before dark. One flat tire and I'm hosed. My dad is picking my mom up at the airport at 8:00 p.m., then it's ninety minutes to the house. 9:30 p.m. is the latest I can go.

Wait until they find out I drove all the way to Portland and back. What a fun conversation that's going to be.

Signing off until I finish the task at hand.

Underground tunnels full of black tar, here I come.

WEDNESDAY, JUNE 29, 1:12 P.M.

HORRIBLE, HORRIBLE, HORRIBLE! IT WAS BAD DOWN THERE. HE WAS THERE.

I DON'T HAVE TIME TO WRITE, GOTTA DRIVE OR I'LL NEVER MAKE IT BACK IN TIME!!

I'M FREAKING OUT.

THE UNTHINKABLE HAS HAPPENED, BUT AT LEAST I CAN TAKE COMFORT IN MY JOURNAL, SINCE I'M NOT DRIVING.

BLOW OUT. FOURTEEN HOURS ON FOUR BALD TIRES — I SHOULD HAVE KNOWN BETTER.

THIS IS GOING TO SET ME BACK ANOTHER HOUR WHILE I'M STUCK IN PENDLETON, OREGON. BY SOME MIRACLE I BLEW THE FRONT RIGHT TIRE NEXT TO AN OFF-RAMP AND ROLLED RIGHT OFF THE FREEWAY INTO A GAS STATION. THE ATTENDANT TOLD ME I WAS A MORON FOR DRIVING A HUNDRED YARDS ON A FLAT. IT'S AMAZING WHAT ADULTS WILL SAY TO A TEENAGER. IF IT WEREN'T FOR THE FACT THAT I WAS IN SUCH A RUSH AND THE TIRE HAD BEGUN SHREDDING OFF THE RIM, I'D HAVE BURNED RUBBER RIGHT OUT OF THAT PLACE FOR THE INSULT. NOT THAT MY MOM'S MINIVAN CAN BURN RUBBER, BUT I DREAMT IT COULD AS I STARED AT THIS GOOD-FOR-NOTHING MECHANIC. THERE WERE ALSO SIX-FOOT FLAMES SHOOTING OUT OF THE TAILPIPE IN MY DREAM, WHICH TORCHED HIS STUPID MUSTACHE OFF.

NINETY-TWO BUCKS AND AN HOUR — THAT'S WHAT IT'S GOING TO TAKE, WHICH WILL LEAVE ME WITH BARELY ENOUGH GAS MONEY TO GET HOME.

SARAH KNOWS EVERYTHING. I TOLD HER ALREADY. SHE CALLED IN SICK TODAY AND STAYED IN HER ROOM JUST SO SHE COULD BE THERE FOR ME. WHAT A FRIEND — I MEAN, REALLY. I HADN'T DONE THAT FOR HER EVEN ONCE ON HER LONG TREK ACROSS THE COUNTRY. SHE SAID NOW SHE KNOWS HOW I FEEL WHEN SHE GOES OUT AND DOES CRAZY THINGS. IT'S NOT AS FUN AS SHE THOUGHT IT WOULD BE. IN FACT, IT WAS WAY WORSE THAN DOING THINGS HERSELF — AT LEAST THAT'S WHAT SHE SAID. IT WAS THE FIRST TIME WE'D WALKED IN EACH OTHER'S SHOES, AND I THINK WE BOTH HAD A LOT MORE SYMPATHY FOR THE OTHER FROM THAT POINT ON.

I RECORDED BITS AND PIECES OF MY HARROWING TRIP UNDERGROUND ON MY PHONE. EACH ONE WAS LIKE THIRTY SECONDS OR SOMETHING, SMALL ENOUGH TO EMAIL. I SENT THEM TO SARAH WHILE I WAS RUNNING TO THE CAR. IT WAS THE LAST THING I DID BEFORE TEARING OUT OF PORTLAND AND HITTING THE HIGHWAY FOR HOME. I DIDN'T EVEN KNOW WHAT WAS ON THOSE

SMALL FILES — IT COULD'VE BEEN NOTHING, BUT SHE POSTED THEM ALREADY. I THINK IT'S JUST IN HER NATURE TO CUT THINGS UP, MAKE THEM BETTER, AND PUT THEM ON HER SITE. SHE FELT BAD FOR ME, I COULD TELL. AND SHE WAS SCARED. I THINK DOING THE WORK MADE HER FEEL BETTER.

I WISH I HADN'T SAT ON THIS CURB AND WATCHED.

SARAHFINCHER.COM
Password:
MAGIC8BALL

WEDNESDAY, JUNE 29, 4:23 P.M.

WHEN YOU'RE UNDERGROUND, IT DOESN'T MATTER IF
IT'S DAY OR NIGHT OUTSIDE. IT'S COLD DOWN THERE,
SHADOWS BOUNCE ON THIN LIGHT, AND YOU CAN'T STOP
THINKING ABOUT HOW YOU'RE GOING TO GET OUT WHEN
THE TROUBLE STARTS.

I DID A GOOD JOB OF LOSING THE GROUP WHEN I
REALIZED WHERE I WAS ON THE A-POSTLE'S MAP. NO
ONE SEEMED TO CARE ABOUT THE DISHEVELED
TEENAGER WHO'D GONE MISSING. THE ROUTE THE
A-POSTLE SENT ME ON LED QUICKLY TO A ROPED—OFF
AREA SCREAMING WITH NO ADMITTANCE SIGNS. IN THAT
SECTION THE WALLS CAME IN CLOSE AND THE LIGHT WAS
ALMOST NONEXISTENT. I FISHED MY FLASHLIGHT OUT OF
MY BACKPACK AND KEPT AT IT, TWISTING AND TURNING
AS THE CEILING GOT LOWER AND LOWER. BY THE TIME
I REACHED WHAT APPEARED TO BE THE LAST TURN, I
COULDN'T HEAR THE TOUR GUIDE'S VOICE ANYMORE AND
I WAS SLOUCHED OVER LIKE AN OLD MAN.

I WAS LOST IN A LABYRINTH OF UNDERGROUND
TUNNELS, ALONE IN THE DARK.

OR SO I THOUGHT.

563

Now that I'm sitting on the hot June pavement, staring at my phone and watching the video footage I captured, I realized something: I wasn't just having a mental breakdown.

The ghost of Old Joe Bush really was there. My paranoid brain didn't make that up.

He was sitting on a wooden crate, staring off to the side, moving in that otherworldly way he has — fast, then slow, then fast again. His voice was sand and dirt, as if it hadn't had a drop of water in a decade. And if I'm not mistaken, this thing had definitely turned benevolent. In other words, this ghost wanted to help me. It wanted to protect me. Who am I to care if it's Henry or some possessed version of Henry or not Henry at all? The point is, if I tell my dad or the cops or whoever, there's a chance me and Sarah might end up all alone out here.

And according to the ghost of Old Joe Bush, we're in real danger. Because this other guy, the Raven, doesn't mess around.

Apparently, we've upset him and he's out for blood. The fact that I found what I came for in the Portland Underground is a real problem.

I know this in part because of what I was told down there, but even more because of what I found down there, which I refuse to write in this journal until I get safely back to Skeleton Creek.

I'm not even sure what it is.

All I know is I gotta get home and fast or I'll be grounded for the rest of my life.

Who am I kidding? When my dad finds out what I did, my life as I know it will be over.

WEDNESDAY, JUNE 29, 10:10 P.M.

ONE FLAT TIRE AND A WHOLE LOT OF OIL LATER, I'M
FINALLY HOME. UNFORTUNATELY, I'M NOT THE ONLY
PERSON WHO'S HERE. I'VE PULLED OFF TO THE CURB ON
MAIN STREET AND I CAN SEE MY DAD'S PICKUP SITTING
IN THE DRIVEWAY.

    IS THERE A WORSE FEELING THAN STARING AT YOUR
DAD'S TRUCK, KNOWING HE'S INSIDE, KNOWING YOU'RE IN
TROUBLE? IF THERE IS, I HAVEN'T FELT IT.

    IT MIGHT BE A WHILE BEFORE I GET BACK TO MY
JOURNAL, AND IT'S A FAIR BET THEY'LL TAKE MY
PHONE AND MY LAPTOP THE SECOND I WALK IN THE
DOOR. ONE LAST TEXT TO SARAH, THEN IT'S TIME TO
FACE THE MUSIC.

    I'M HOME SAFE. HOPE TO BUST THIS THING WIDE
OPEN WITHIN THE HOUR BUT I MAY NOT HAVE A PHONE.
HOLD TIGHT!

    SEE YOU ON THE OTHER SIDE.

Thursday, June 30, I don't know what time it is and I don't care

I'm alone again, and this time, it's a good thing. A lot has happened in the past twenty-four hours, all of which I just got done telling to Sarah. So that's the first thing — they gave me my phone back. It's funny how finding something incredible — like gold or treasure — will cover a multitude of lies and deceptions.

When I got home, my parents freaked out, but not in the way that I expected them to. They didn't yell at me or start taking my things — they did the opposite. My mom hugged me, hard, for a long time. She kept saying how sorry she was that she'd left me home alone. My dad touched me on the shoulder, and when I looked at him there were tears in his eyes. I wouldn't have imagined they'd be that worried, but the truth was, they still hadn't recovered from almost losing me on the dredge. What kind of crazy son did they have? How much longer would I even be alive? I'd made it clear I was a reckless kid, untrustworthy, heading for the rocks.

It was the first time in my life that I felt something deeper than guilt. I felt remorse. Remorse for making my parents feel as if they might lose me at any moment. They'd done a good job raising me, but I had to imagine that I was making them feel like they were the lamest parents on earth. What kind of parents raise a son who can't stop putting his life at risk?

The lovefest lasted about a minute, then the hammer came down and I was reminded that, yes, my parents did know how to discipline me. Not only was I going to have this new and crummy feeling of remorse for a while, I was also getting grounded and working at the fly shop with no pay until every hour I'd left the shop closed had been made up times ten (my dad's logic being that we'd lost a lot of sales while I was out joyriding). There were two places I could go: home and the fly shop. By some miracle of good luck, they let me keep my phone and my laptop, and for this I was incredibly thankful. Not being able to tell Sarah what was going on for days on end would have been impossibly hard.

After the hugs and the consequences, I came clean about Portland. I wouldn't call it squeaky clean, but I told them a lot. I did not, however, mention the road trip Sarah had been on and the many stops she'd made. I shortened my story by a long shot and stuck to only the facts I absolutely needed to share, which were these:

— I found an encoded message in the dredge, but I didn't tell anyone about it. (Technically, this is true.)

— The message has been lost, so I can't show it to anyone. Sorry about that. (This one is a stretch, unless you count "under my mattress" as lost. But I couldn't show the Skull Puzzle to just anyone. I had to keep it safe.)

— Part two of the message was hidden in Portland, which is why I had to go there. It felt important. (Again, technically true.)

— I found what I went looking for, and it led right back where I started: Skeleton Creek.

— The Crossbones is older and more mysterious than anyone imagined. They stole things and hid them. I think I may have found one of these things. (I did not go into any detail about the Crossbones. There was more to find, and I didn't want anyone trying to stop me.)

My dad was curious about a lot of what I'd said, but mostly, he was interested in one thing.

"What do you mean you <u>found</u> something?"

I could tell what he was thinking: <u>The last time my son discovered a hidden stash of whatever, it ended up being worth forty million dollars.</u> Maybe he was thinking about expanding the fly shop, I don't know, but his tone had changed. Ryan McCray, the guy who saved the town from ruin, had found something else. This could be good.

It was 10:40 at night, but I went ahead and set things in motion, anyway.

"We're going to need to talk with Gladys Morgan," I said.

"WHAT IN THE WORLD DO YOU WANT WITH HER?" MY MOM ASKED.

"SHE'S GOT THE KEYS TO THE LIBRARY, AND I NEED TO GET IN THERE."

MY DAD WAS ALREADY PULLING OUT HIS CELL PHONE, LOOKING AT ME LIKE <u>WHAT ELSE DO YOU NEED, SON? CAN I GET YOU A COKE?</u> IT WAS BIZARRE, BUT IT GAVE ME THE FREEDOM TO REALLY GO FOR IT.

"I'M GOING TO NEED A CROWBAR AND THE BIGGEST HAMMER YOU CAN FIND. AN AX MIGHT BE HELPFUL."

"HONEY, GET THE BOY AN AX," MY DAD SAID, AND THEN HE WAS AT THE TINY SKELETON CREEK PHONE BOOK (IT WAS A PAMPHLET, REALLY), DIALING GLADYS MORGAN'S HOME PHONE.

IT WAS KIND OF HILARIOUS WHEN SHE ANSWERED. MY DAD HAD TO PULL THE PHONE AWAY FROM HIS EAR, AND EVEN I COULD HEAR HER YELL, "WHO IN THE BLANKETY BLANK BLANK IS CALLING ME IN THE MIDDLE OF THE NIGHT?!"

THERE'S SOMETHING DARN FUNNY ABOUT AN OLD LIBRARIAN WITH A POTTY MOUTH. EVEN MY DAD WAS SMILING.

We walked down Main Street carrying the tools we were going to need: I had the ax, my mom had the crowbar, and my dad had a sledgehammer. We must have looked like a gang in search of a midnight rumble. I imagined we were walking in slow motion, like in a movie trailer, which was just dumb enough to make me smile.

If Gladys Morgan was concerned when we'd called, she was downright out of her mind with worry when we showed up carrying tools of destruction.

"You're not coming in here with an ax and a giant hammer! Forget it!"

The time had come, there on the steps, to spill some of the beans.

"Gladys," I said, "your library has something very important in it. It's been there a long time, since before you showed up, and I think you'll be pleased if you let me rip the floor apart."

Gladys barred the door with her body and looked at my dad like his son had lost his marbles. We couldn't get her away from the

DOOR UNTIL MY DAD CALLED THE MAYOR, A KNOWN NIGHT OWL, AND TOLD HIM WHAT WAS GOING ON. MAYOR BLAKE IS MAYBE THE MOST OPPORTUNISTIC PERSON I'VE EVER MET, AND THE IDEA THAT SOMETHING ELSE OF SERIOUS VALUE MIGHT BE HIDDEN IN GLADYS'S LIBRARY WAS ALL HE NEEDED TO HEAR. THE BUILDING WAS OWNED BY THE CITY, HE HAD HIS OWN KEYS, AND HE WAS THERE IN UNDER FIVE MINUTES.

GLADYS WAITED ON THE FRONT STEPS, TOO DISTRAUGHT TO LOOK, WHILE MY MOM COMFORTED HER AS THE AX CAME DOWN. MY DAD IS ABOUT AS GOOD AS ANYONE I KNOW AT RIPPING THINGS APART, AND HE MADE QUICK WORK OF THE OLD FLOORBOARDS. ONCE WE HAD A HOLE IN THE MIDDLE OF THE SMALL ROOM, THE MAYOR WENT TO WORK WITH THE CROWBAR, PRYING UP BOARD AFTER BOARD. WHEN THE OPENING WAS FOUR FEET IN DIAMETER, WE WERE ALL DOWN ON OUR KNEES PEERING INSIDE.

THERE WAS A GIANT TRUNK DOWN THERE, TOO BIG FOR ONE GUY TO LIFT OUT, BUT THE ADRENALINE WAS PUMPING AND SO THE MAYOR AND THE FLY-SHOP PROPRIETOR OF SKELETON CREEK HEAVED IT UP INTO THE LIBRARY IN NO TIME.

WHEN THEY OPENED IT UP, THERE WAS A SEVERE CASE OF DISAPPOINTMENT WRITTEN ON BOTH THEIR FACES. MY DAD LOOKED AT ME AS IF I'D JUST BANKRUPTED THE FAMILY. THE MAYOR WAS ASHEN. NOT ONLY HAD HE DESTROYED A PERFECTLY GOOD FLOOR, HE'D ALMOST CERTAINLY INCURRED THE WRATH OF THE CANTANKEROUS TOWN LIBRARIAN, A VERY BAD MOVE.

IT WAS GLADYS WHO SAVED ME.

I PULLED AN ENVELOPE OUT OF MY POCKET, THE SAME SIZE AND SHAPE AND COLOR AS THE ONE I'D FOUND ON THE DREDGE. ONLY THIS ONE HAD BEEN HIDDEN IN THE PORTLAND UNDERGROUND FOR WHO KNEW HOW LONG. I TOOK OUT THE CARD INSIDE AND SHOWED IT TO MY LIBRARIAN.

X MARKED THE SPOT ON THE FLOOR OF THE TOWN LIBRARY, WITH THE WORDS:

JEFFERSON LIBRARY, 287 VOLUMES.

GLADYS MORGAN LOOKED AT THE CARD, THEN THE TRUNK OF BOOKS, THEN THE CARD.

IF I DIDN'T KNOW BETTER, I WOULD HAVE SWORN SHE ALMOST FAINTED AND FELL INTO THE GAPING HOLE WE'D JUST CREATED IN HER FLOOR.

She pulled one of the books out — perfect condition — then another and another. She ran her weathered fingers over the spines.

The mayor, sensing all was not lost, ventured a question.

"Are you going to punch me, Gladys Morgan?"

She didn't answer. In fact, I don't recall how long she remained quiet, but eventually she broke her silence and smiled like I had never seen her smile before. It was the smile of a person who loved books and had found a rare and priceless treasure of words.

The Crossbones had tried to burn Jefferson's house to the ground. They'd tried to drive him into bankruptcy more than once. Those things didn't do him in, but there was one thing they knew he loved more than anything in the world: books. The Jefferson Library became the nation's library eventually, the very beginning of the Library of Congress. But to this day — almost two hundred years later — 287 books from that library had remained missing.

THE MOST PRECIOUS BOOKS OF THE 6,487-VOLUME

COLLECTION HAD NEVER BEEN FOUND.

UNTIL NOW.

ME AND SARAH HAD FOUND THE RAREST

COLLECTION OF BOOKS IN THE COUNTRY — THE MISSING

BOOKS FROM THE THOMAS JEFFERSON LIBRARY —

HIDDEN BENEATH OUR OWN CRUMMY LITTLE LIBRARY

ALL THIS TIME.

YOU HAVE NEVER SEEN A PROUDER LIBRARIAN IN

ALL YOUR LIFE.

COULD THERE BE A MORE PERFECT DAY TO REVEAL OUR DISCOVERY TO THE REST OF THE WORLD? I DON'T THINK SO. INDEPENDENCE DAY, OUR MAYOR CALLED A PRESS CONFERENCE ON THE STEPS OF OUR TOWN LIBRARY. GLADYS STOOD ON ONE SIDE, I STOOD ON THE OTHER, AND THE TV CAMERAS ROLLED. NOT ONLY WAS SKELETON CREEK HOME TO A HAUNTED DREDGE FILLED WITH GOLD, IT WAS ALSO THE RESTING PLACE OF THE NATION'S MOST-SOUGHT-AFTER COLLECTION OF MISSING BOOKS. WHAT WAS IT WORTH? PRICELESS, HE GUSHED.

THE BOOKS WOULD BE RETURNED TO THE LIBRARY OF CONGRESS AND THE HOLE IN THE FLOOR OF OUR QUAINT LITTLE ROOM OF BOOKS ON MAIN STREET WOULD NEVER BE FILLED. THE AX THAT FLEW AND CROWBAR THAT PRIED WOULD REMAIN RIGHT WHERE THEY'D BEEN USED. IT WOULD, IN TIME, BECOME A LOCATION AS IMPORTANT AS THE HOME OF THE LIBERTY BELL OR THE OREGON TRAIL. A TOURIST ATTRACTION EVERY FAMILY SHOULD SEE AT LEAST ONCE IN THEIR LIFETIME.

Mayor Blake really knew how to lay it on thick, which I suppose is a good thing to have in a mayor. I had a feeling he was going to sail through the next election without much trouble.

I felt bad about Gladys's floor, but she didn't seem to mind. Soon they'd move the library somewhere else and give her a real book budget. We might even get some books on tape and a computer in there, which, I had to admit, made me feel pretty good, too.

There was just one thing I didn't feel great about as people streamed up the steps to shake my hand. Sure, we'd solved a major mystery right under our parents' noses. And it was true we'd given something back to the world that had long been lost. But it didn't change the fact that Sarah was going to have to drive home in a few days. It didn't change the fact that the ghost of Old Joe Bush had given me one more envelope that night underground in Portland. It was a black envelope, old and marred at the edges.

Inside? Another puzzle.

Only this time, it was no Skull Puzzle.

In place of the skull was a black raven.

We'd made him angry, this Raven, whoever he or it was.

There were five more places to go, none of which I'd figured out yet, and Sarah was going to have to visit them on her return trip to Boston. It was the only way.

She'd find the ghost of Old Joe Bush out there.

She'd find the Raven out there.

And she'd uncover the last secret of the Crossbones.

My guess? Whatever it is sits right under our noses. All roads lead back to Skeleton Creek in the end, I'm sure of it.

But the most terrifying part of all? The part that will give me nightmares for weeks after?

I know who the Raven was, and I know what he carried around with him.

I figured it out that night, walking toward the library with my dad and my mom, carrying an ax that would rip open the past.

"FITZ NEVER SHOWED UP FOR THE FISHING TRIP," MY DAD SAID AS WE WALKED. "HE UP AND QUIT AT THE LAST SECOND, LEFT ME HIGH AND DRY. LONGEST TWO DAYS OF MY LIFE TRYING TO GUIDE FOUR FISHERMEN BY MYSELF."

COULD IT HAVE BEEN FITZ OUTSIDE MY WINDOW THAT LAST NIGHT BEFORE I LEFT, WATCHING ME, WONDERING WHERE I MIGHT GO THE NEXT DAY? ALL I COULD THINK OF THE SECOND DAD TOLD ME ABOUT FITZ WAS THAT SMELL. THE SMELL OF BURNING OIL ALL THE WAY TO PORTLAND. AND THEN I KNEW: IT WAS FITZ WHO HAD PUT THE GPS PHONE IN THE GLOVE BOX. (I'D ASKED MY PARENTS ABOUT IT, AND THEY HAD NO IDEA WHAT I WAS TALKING ABOUT.) HE'D FOLLOWED ME ALL THE WAY OUT OF TOWN ON THAT CRAZY MOTORCYCLE OF HIS. IT WAS THAT BIKE OF HIS I'D SMELLED, NOT MY MOM'S JUNKER. THANK GOD I'D LOST HIM WHEN I TURNED OFF THAT CELL PHONE, BECAUSE IF I HADN'T, WHO KNOWS WHAT MIGHT HAVE HAPPENED IN THE UNDERGROUND.

I MIGHT NEVER HAVE MADE IT OUT OF THERE ALIVE.

MONDAY, JULY 4, 4:00 P.M.

I RODE MY BIKE OUT TO FITZ'S TRAILER, BUT I KNEW I
WOULDN'T FIND ANYONE AT HOME. THE MOTORCYCLE
WAS GONE AND SO WAS THE TRUCK FITZ'S DAD USED TO
HAUL WOOD OUT OF THE FOREST. THE SORRY LITTLE
MOBILE HOME WAS ABANDONED, BUT ON THE STEPS
THERE WAS A FLY BOX, THE ONE FITZ ALWAYS CARRIED
AROUND IN HIS FISHING VEST. I OPENED IT UP AND FOUND
A NOTE INSIDE.

Ryan,
    Maybe we'll see each other again sometime, but I doubt
it. My dad, he asked me to keep an eye on you. He's not
someone you say no to. I was supposed to figure out where
you were going. I was supposed to take whatever you found
and bring it to my dad. But I lost you out there. My motorbike
isn't as fast as your mom's minivan. Not knowing where you
were headed to might have been a good thing in the end.
    But my dad was angry. _Really_ angry.
    He says we're leaving in the middle of the night and
we're not coming back.
    He says I failed to live up to the family name.

Look, Ryan, you don't know my dad. He's not a nice guy.
I think you might have set him off.
Be careful. If I can swing a little help, I will. I'll
find a way to get in touch.
Keep tying flies — you'll get better. It just takes
practice.
Fitz

MY DAD WASN'T THE ONLY ONE CARRYING AN AX.
THERE WAS A CERTAIN MAN OF THE WOODS, A LONER,
A WOODCUTTER. THE DAD OF THE ONLY FRIEND I HAD
IN TOWN.

A GUY WHO CALLED HIMSELF THE RAVEN.

THE LAST THREE CROSSBONES MEMBERS AT WAR:
THE APOSTLE, HENRY, THE RAVEN.

ONE OF THEM DEAD, ONE OF THEM GONE OFF HIS
ROCKER, ONE OF THEM AFTER ME.

THREE HIDDEN TREASURES: THE GOLD, THE
JEFFERSON BOOKS, AND WHAT?

I wish I could say I know all the answers, but I don't.

I rode my bike back into Skeleton Creek, Fitz's old fly box in my shirt pocket, and thought about how far I was from safe.

My journey wasn't over yet.

SARAHFINCHER.COM
PASSWORD:
MISTERSMITHERS

PATRICK CARMAN's

SKELETON CREEK

☠ THE ☠
RAVEN

PC STUDIO

ARE YOU NEW TO SKELETON CREEK?

IF SO, MY BEST FRIEND, SARAH FINCHER, HAS A SECRET PLACE WHERE A LOT OF OUR STORY IS POSTED IN THE FORM OF VIDEOS.

SCARE EASILY? LEAVE THE LIGHTS ON.

SARAHFINCHER.COM
PASSWORD:
BRINGMEUPTOSPEED

IN AN HOUR THE WORLD WILL TURN DARK AND STILL.
ANYONE WHO'S EVER CAMPED IN THE REMOTE
WILDERNESS KNOWS WHAT I'M TALKING ABOUT. THERE
ARE NO STREETLIGHTS IN THE WOODS. NO LAMPS,
STOREFRONTS, OR GLOWING LAPTOP SCREENS. THESE
THINGS ARE A COMFORT, EVEN IN A TOWN AS SMALL AS
SKELETON CREEK, BUT I WON'T HAVE ANY OF THEM
ONCE THE SUN GOES DOWN.

YOU MIGHT SAY, "YEAH, BUT THERE ARE STARS.
ISN'T THAT THE SAME AS A BILLION FLASHLIGHTS? AND
THERE'S THE MOON — THAT THING IS HUGE." TRUE, ON A
CLEAR NIGHT WITH A FULL MOON IT'S NOT AS DARK IN
THE WOODS, BUT THAT'S NOT THE KIND OF NIGHT I'M
ABOUT TO SUFFER. I CAN ALREADY HEAR THE THUNDER
CLAPS TEN MILES OR SO OFF IN THE DISTANCE. A
STORM IS COMING AND CLOUDS ARE GATHERING
OVERHEAD.

THERE WILL BE NO STARS OR MOON TONIGHT.

MY DAD AND I LEFT SKELETON CREEK EARLY
THIS MORNING IN ORDER TO GET AWAY FROM ALL THE
CRAZINESS IN TOWN. FOR THE PAST WEEK, THE PHONE
HAD BEEN RINGING OFF THE HOOK FOR INTERVIEWS, AND

NEWS VANS HAD PULLED INTO TOWN FROM PORTLAND AND SEATTLE. FIRST, I'D FOUND GOLD ON THE DREDGE, THEN I'D DISCOVERED THE MISSING JEFFERSON LIBRARY RIGHT UNDER OUR NOSES. NO ONE KNEW HOW MUCH HELP I'D GOTTEN FROM SARAH, BECAUSE I COULDN'T TELL ANYONE. (SHE'S FAR TOO VALUABLE WORKING IN SECRET, AT LEAST UNTIL AFTER SHE MAKES THE LONG DRIVE HOME FROM LA TO BOSTON.) NOPE, THIS ONE WAS ALL ON ME. I WAS TURNING SKELETON CREEK INTO A TOWN KNOWN FOR ITS HIDDEN TREASURES, AND MY DAD THOUGHT IT BEST TO GET ME OUT OF DODGE BEFORE MY HEAD TURNED FREAKISHLY BIG.

"NOTHING LIKE ROUGHING IT TO PUT THINGS INTO PERSPECTIVE," HE'D SAID. "LET'S YOU AND ME HIGHTAIL IT FOR THE RIVER."

HE DIDN'T HAVE ANYTHING TO WORRY ABOUT, BECAUSE I DON'T HAVE ANY SPACE IN MY HEAD TO DWELL ON HOW AMAZING I AM. I'M PREOCCUPIED WITH MORE IMPORTANT THINGS, LIKE HOW I'M GOING TO STAY ALIVE FROM ONE DAY TO THE NEXT.

I'D DEVISED A COVER FOR HOW I'D COME TO FIND THE MISSING JEFFERSON LIBRARY BOOKS HIDDEN UNDER GLADYS MORGAN'S LIBRARY. INSTEAD OF A NOTE

HENRY LEFT IN THE DREDGE, IT WAS A SIMPLE MAP I'D FOUND WHILE HELPING DISGORGE FORTY MILLION IN GOLD FROM THE FLOORBOARDS. I HADN'T SHOWN THE MAP TO ANYONE BECAUSE . . . WELL, I JUST HADN'T. NO ONE SEEMS TO CARE ABOUT A LITTLE DECEPTION WHEN YOU'RE THE BEARER OF GOOD NEWS.

I FEEL PARANOID AND UNPROTECTED SO FAR AWAY FROM HOME. THE RAVEN, HENRY, THE GHOST OF OLD JOE BUSH — IT'S LIKE I'M BEING FOLLOWED BY AN ARMY OF ZOMBIES DEAD SET ON TRACKING ME DOWN.

IT ALL COMES DOWN TO THE SECRET CROSSBONES SOCIETY, AND THREE SHADOWY FIGURES AT ITS CORE.

FIRST, THERE'S THE APOSTLE, THE CROSSBONES RECORDER. HIS CREEPY VIDEOS MADE IT CLEAR THAT CROSSING THE APOSTLE CAME WITH A PRICE: HE'D REVEAL YOUR SECRETS TO THE REST OF THE WORLD. SARAH FOUND FOUR HIDDEN APOSTLE MESSAGES ON HER DRIVE FROM BOSTON TO LA, WHICH WAS WHAT LED US TO DISCOVER THE MISSING BOOKS FROM THE JEFFERSON LIBRARY. THESE BOOKS WERE A CROSSBONES TREASURE, BUT THE APOSTLE LED US RIGHT TO THEM FROM BEYOND THE GRAVE.

THEN, THERE'S THE GHOST OF OLD JOE BUSH, WHO ISN'T REALLY A GHOST AT ALL, BUT MY DAD'S FORMER FRIEND, HENRY. WHEREABOUTS UNKNOWN. I CAN'T SAY FOR SURE WHOSE SIDE HENRY IS ON, BUT TWO THINGS ARE CERTAIN: HE'S STILL OUT THERE AND HE'S SCARIER THAN EVER.

AND FINALLY, THERE'S THE RAVEN. THE MUSCLE. THE POWER. THE REALLY BAD DUDE. EVERY SECRET SOCIETY NEEDS ONE, AND THE CROSSBONES IS NO EXCEPTION.

I'VE THWARTED THE CROSSBONES ENOUGH TO KNOW: THE RAVEN WILL WANT ME DEAD. IT'S THE QUICKEST WAY TO STOP ME.

MY DAD DIDN'T EXACTLY DO ME ANY FAVORS BY DRAGGING ME DOWN THE RIVER ON A RAFT INTO THE MIDDLE OF NOWHERE. THE REALLY BAD THING ABOUT CAMPING IN THE DEEP OF THE WOODS? UNLESS YOU COUNT A SLEEPING BAG, THERE'S NO PLACE TO HIDE ONCE THE SUN GOES DOWN. MY FEARS CAN COME AT ME FROM WHATEVER DIRECTION THEY WANT.

HERE'S ANOTHER THING ABOUT CAMPING: THERE ARE AT LEAST FOUR WAYS TO DO IT, ONLY ONE OF WHICH QUALIFIES AS REAL CAMPING IF YOU ASK MY DAD.

How to camp, according to my dad, with actual fireside quotes included:

Option 1 (lamest): Use a Cabin

Dad: "The only way this counts as camping is if there's no indoor plumbing or beds, the nearest help is at least an hour drive down a dirt road, and the place is crawling with termites."

Option 2 (a near tie for lameness with option 1): Use an RV

Dad: "I think I just threw up."

Option 3 (barely not lame): Camp with a Tent in a Campground

Dad: "There's a guy delivering firewood for five bucks a box from the back of a golf cart. Why not bring a big-screen TV and a Lay-Z-Boy while you're at it?"

Option 4 (officially roughing it): Pack into a Remote Location, Fend for Your Life

Dad: "Give me three matches, my fishing gear, and some tinfoil. I'll live out here for a month and a half."

WHICH IS HOW I FOUND MYSELF SETTING UP MY PACK TENT ON THE EDGE OF THE RIVER FIVE MILES DOWNSTREAM FROM TOWN, NOWHERE NEAR A HAMBURGER OR A CELL TOWER. I'D BARELY ROLLED OUT MY SLEEPING BAG BEFORE MY DAD WAS CALLING ME TO THE EDGE OF THE WATER . . . AS HE ALWAYS DOES.

"READY FOR THE FLIP?" HE ASKED. I NODDED, KNOWING BEFORE HE FLIPPED THE COIN UP IN THE AIR THAT I HAD NO CHANCE. I'D LOST SEVENTEEN OUT OF SEVENTEEN COIN FLIPS ON SEVENTEEN OUT OF SEVENTEEN TRIPS DOWN THE RIVER, AND THINGS WERE NOT ABOUT TO CHANGE.

"HEADS," I CALLED, JUST TO GIVE MYSELF A FIGHTING CHANCE.

"SORRY, SPORT, IT'S TAILS. SEE THERE?"

THE LIGHT WASN'T VERY GOOD AND THE SHOW WAS AWFULLY FAST, BUT IT DID LOOK LIKE TAILS. DOES HE CARRY A TWO-TAILED NICKEL AROUND IN HIS POCKET AND USE SOME SLEIGHT OF HAND? I WOULDN'T PUT IT PAST HIM. MY DAD LOVES FLY-FISHING ENOUGH TO PULL ONE OVER ON HIS OWN KID, THAT MUCH IS FOR SURE. LOSING THE FLIP MEANT HE'D BE CATCHING OUR DINNER WHILE I ROUNDED UP FIREWOOD, AND THE LIGHT WAS FADING FAST.

For all his talk, my dad is often woefully unprepared in the wild. If it's fly-fishing you're looking for, he's your man. The boat is crammed full of fly boxes and other "essential trout gear." This is because he spends four hours getting the fishing gear ready, looks at his watch, and spends his last ten minutes packing everything else he'll need. When I leave to hunt for firewood I will be armed with only my wits and a hatchet, the blade of which is duller than a butter knife.

Looking up into the sky, I sense what's coming. By midnight it's going to start raining. In fact, from the smell of the air, I'd guess it's going to hail golf balls, the kind that will shred a pup tent and leave me trembling in my sleeping bag.

Better get with it so I don't end up traipsing around in the woods after dark and bump into a bear . . . or someone who's out to get me.

MONDAY, JULY 11, 11:30 P.M.

I'M BACK AT THE CAMPSITE IN MY ONE-MAN TENT. THE
FIRE HAS ALL BUT GONE OUT — A FEW GLOWING EMBERS
ARE ALL THAT REMAIN — AND ALL I CAN SAY IS THIS:
    WHAT I DISCOVERED OUT THERE IS GOING TO MAKE
THIS THE LONGEST NIGHT OF MY LIFE.
    HE FOUND ME, OR I FOUND HIM.

MONDAY, JULY 11, 11:32 P.M.

Noises outside.

MONDAY, JULY 11, 11:35 P.M.

I think it's gone. Maybe it was just the wind. I don't know whether to look or stay inside. Praying.

I'M NOT CLOSING MY EYES UNTIL DAWN.

MY CELL PHONE ISN'T GOOD FOR A SIGNAL, BUT IT DOES THROW OFF A SOFT BLUE LIGHT, WHICH IS THE ONLY LIGHT I HAVE INSIDE MY TINY TENT. DAD IS ALREADY SNORING IN HIS OWN COCOON FIVE FEET AWAY.

OKAY, I'M GOING TO WRITE DOWN WHAT HAPPENED SO I DON'T FORGET ANY OF THE DETAILS. NOTE TO SELF: SET UP AN OVERNIGHT RECORDING CAMERA IN MY ROOM WHEN I GET HOME IN CASE I GET AN UNWELCOME VISITOR IN THE MIDDLE OF THE NIGHT. AND BRING THE HATCHET TO BED WITH ME.

FOR SOMEONE WHO LIVES IN THE MOUNTAINS I HAVE A SURPRISINGLY BAD SENSE OF DIRECTION. I GET TURNED AROUND EASILY, WHICH IS EXACTLY WHAT HAPPENED AS I MEANDERED OUT IN THE WOODS IN SEARCH OF FIREWOOD. I'D FOUND A PRETTY HEFTY ARMFUL OF FALLEN TWIGS AND BRANCHES AND SET IT DOWN, GLANCING IN EVERY DIRECTION AS I TURNED IN A CIRCLE.

WHERE WAS I? WHICH WAY HAD I COME FROM?

THE WOODS GREW MENACINGLY QUIET, AND THEN I
HEARD THE SOUND OF WOOD BEING SPLIT. SURELY IT
WAS MY DAD, TIRED OF WAITING FOR MY RETURN AS HE
SET UP A FIRE TO COOK THE FISH HE'D CAUGHT. I PICKED
UP MY COLLECTION OF BUSTED BRANCHES AND TWIGS
AND STARTED IN THE DIRECTION OF THE SOUND. IT WAS
FARTHER OFF THAN I EXPECTED, BUT THE SOUND KEPT
GETTING LOUDER, SO I KEPT AT IT. I CAME TO THE EDGE
OF A CLEARING, WHERE A SINGLE, GIGANTIC TREE STOOD
ALONE IN THE GATHERING GLOOM. AND THEN IT STRUCK
ME: MY DAD DIDN'T HAVE THE HATCHET. I HAD THE
HATCHET.

It's not him I hear chopping.

THERE, AT THE BASE OF THE TREE, WAS THE
CLOAKED FIGURE OF A MAN. WHOEVER IT WAS WORE
AN OVERSIZED, BLACK RAIN SLICKER THAT RAN FROM
HIS KNEES ALL THE WAY UP OVER HIS HEAD. THE HOOD
WAS PULLED LOW OVER HIS FACE, A BLACK TUNNEL
THAT LED TO EYES I COULDN'T SEE. HE HAD THE
BIGGEST AX I'VE EVER SEEN — IT HAD TO BE FIVE
FEET LONG WITH A BLADE AS WIDE AS MY HEAD. HE
SWUNG AS IF IN SLOW MOTION, BROAD AND POWERFUL,
SLAMMING AGAINST THICK BARK. I KNEW ENOUGH ABOUT

WOODCUTTING TO KNOW THAT EVEN WITH AN AX THAT BIG IT WOULD TAKE HOURS TO BRING DOWN SUCH A MONSTER, AND THE CLOAKED FIGURE HAD ONLY JUST BEGUN.

A THUNDER CLAP, LOUD AND CLOSE, BLASTED INTO THE VALLEY. I DROPPED THE WOOD I'D GATHERED, DASHING BEHIND A TREE FOR COVER. I THOUGHT ABOUT RUNNING, WHICH IS WHAT I SHOULD HAVE DONE. INSTEAD, I TOOK OUT MY PHONE AND HIT THE RECORD BUTTON, THEN PEERED AROUND THE EDGE OF THE TREE.

THE THUNDER CLAP HAD COVERED THE SOUND OF THE DROPPING WOOD. THE FIGURE CONTINUED SWINGING THE GREAT AX.

AND THEN, WITHOUT WARNING, HE STOPPED.

LIGHTNING FILLED THE SPACE BETWEEN US AND I SAW THAT HE WAS WATCHING ME. AND WORSE, HE WAS SHARPENING THE BLADE AGAINST A STONE, SPARKS FLYING AS THE SOUND OF THUNDER ARRIVED, AS IF ON CUE.

MY BACK AGAINST THE TREE, CHEST HEAVING, I THOUGHT ONCE MORE OF RUNNING. NIGHT WAS CLOSE AT HAND, AND THE LAST THING I WANTED WAS TO BE LOST IN THE DARK WITH AN AX-WIELDING MANIAC ON

MY TRAIL. I WAITED FIVE SECONDS, TEN, FIFTEEN. THE
SOUND OF SHARPENING HAD STOPPED AND THE CHOPPING
HADN'T STARTED UP AGAIN. MAYBE HE'D GIVEN UP ON
THE BIG TREE. MAYBE HE HADN'T SEEN ME AFTER ALL.
MAYBE HE'D GONE BACK INTO THE GLOOM.

WHEN I PEERED AROUND THE EDGE OF THE TREE
ONCE MORE, HOPING TO FIND MYSELF ALONE IN THE
WOODS, THE HOODED MAN HAD CREPT MUCH CLOSER.
HE WAS CLOSE ENOUGH TO HIT ME WITH THE AX IF HE'D
WANTED TO.

AND THEN HE SPOKE.

"STORM'S COMIN'."

HIS VOICE WAS RASPY AND COLD, HIDDEN UNDER
THE CLOAK, AND I DIDN'T KNOW FOR SURE IF HE
MEANT THE STORM OVERHEAD OR SOMETHING ELSE.
HIS KNUCKLES WHITENED ON THE AX HANDLE — AN AX I
NOW REALIZED WAS PAINTED BLACK.

"GONNA BE A BIG ONE," HE WENT ON. "DANGEROUS.
NOT LIKE THE ONES BEFORE."

I JUST STOOD THERE, SPEECHLESS, STARING AT THE
BLADE.

"BETTER TAKE COVER."

600

He lifted his head in the direction from which I'd come, as if to tell me where I'd find my dad and the camp we'd set up, and then he turned and walked away. I was struck then by how ghostlike he was as he passed by the huge tree and kept on until he disappeared into the shadows.

I looked at my hand, which still held my phone.

I'd recorded the whole encounter.

But even a recording won't answer the big question I have:

Was that the Raven?

MONDAY, JULY 11, 11:47 P.M.

I MADE IT BACK TO CAMP, GRABBING UP PIECES OF WOOD
AS I RAN, AND SHOWED UP TO FIND MY DAD HAD
ALREADY BUILT A FIRE FROM WOOD SCRAPS AND
COOKED THE FISH.

   "I WAS JUST ABOUT TO COME LOOKING FOR YOU,"
HE SAID, STARING AT THE PALTRY COLLECTION OF
TWIGS I'D GATHERED UP. HE LOOKED INTO THE NIGHT
SKY. "STORM'S COMIN'."

   HE USED THE EXACT SAME WORDS AS THE MAN IN
THE WOODS — STORM'S COMIN' — WHICH SENT A CHILL
DOWN MY SPINE, ALL THE WAY INTO MY BOOTS. WE
ATE QUICKLY, THREW TARPS OVER BOTH OUR TENTS,
AND HUNKERED DOWN FOR WHAT WOULD BE A LONG,
SLEEPLESS NIGHT.

   STORMS IN THE MOUNTAINS OFTEN PASS THROUGH
QUICKLY ON THEIR WAY TO SOMEWHERE ELSE, AS IF
THEY'RE LATE FOR A POKER GAME AND THEY'VE
ONLY STOPPED BY LONG ENOUGH TO PUT OUT YOUR
FIRE. THIS WAS JUST SUCH A STORM — QUICK AND
BRUTAL — HERE AND GONE IN TWENTY MINUTES FLAT.
WIND WHIPPED THE TENTS, A MIX OF RAIN AND HAIL
PUMMELED THE TARP, AND ALL THE WHILE I THOUGHT

ABOUT THE FIGURE I'D SEEN IN THE WOODS AND THE MESSAGE HE'D DELIVERED.

THE RAVEN.

THE MORE I THINK ABOUT IT, THE SURER I AM.

THE FINAL PLAYER IN THE CROSSBONES GAME HAS FOUND ME.

BUT WHAT DOES HE WANT FROM ME?

MONDAY, JULY 11, 11:51 P.M.

NEVER MAKE THE MEAN GUY MAD.

   IT WILL COME BACK TO HAUNT YOU.

   I NEED TO CALM MYSELF DOWN. I AM TRYING TO
FIND SOME GOOD SIDE IN ALL THIS. AT LEAST IF THE
RAVEN IS NEAR, HE CAN'T BE IN LA, SO SARAH IS
SAFE FROM THE SWING OF A BLACK AX.

   IT'S THE RAVEN'S JOB TO CLEAN UP MESSES, GET
RID OF PROBLEMS, PROTECT CROSSBONES INTERESTS
AT ALL COST.

   ONE OF THE FIRST THINGS I THOUGHT OF WHEN I
SAW THE RAVEN WAS FITZ, MY BUDDY WHO USED TO
WORK AT THE FLY SHOP. THE RAVEN IS HIS DAD, SO
OBVIOUSLY I'M WORRIED ABOUT HOW FITZ IS DOING.
ARE THE TWO OF THEM LIVING UP HERE IN THE WOODS
OR SOMETHING? DOES FITZ COME DOWN TO THIS
VERY BANK ON THE RIVER AND CATCH FISH WHEN I'M
NOT HERE?

   I JUST PEERED OUTSIDE THE SLIT OF MY TENT,
THINKING I MIGHT JUST SEE FITZ STANDING THERE,
CASTING HIS LINE OVER THE WATER IN THE DARK. BUT
THERE WASN'T ANYONE THERE.

I can hear the river but I can't see it. Funny how something I love so much during the day can turn so deadly. Like a black sludge drifting past, waiting to pull me under.

I could drown just like the Apostle and Old Joe Bush before him.

Water can be evil that way.

There's one more thing I need to say before I stop writing for the night and start staring at the ceiling of my tent, waiting for the ax to come down.

Fitz gave me an envelope before he and his dad left the trailer they lived in. Inside was a piece of paper he should not have given me — because it belonged to his dad.

Now that I think I've met the Raven, I understand what a risk it was to take that piece of paper.

Storm's comin'.

Gonna be a big one. Dangerous. Not like the ones before.

Better take cover.

605

I THINK THE RAVEN MIGHT KNOW I HAVE THIS PIECE OF PAPER.

I THINK HE MIGHT FOLLOW ME RIGHT BACK INTO TOWN AND USE THAT BLACK AX TO BUST DOWN MY DOOR AND GET IT BACK.

Tuesday, July 12, 3:00 a.m.

Longest. Night. Ever.

TUESDAY, JULY 12, 8:00 P.M.

MADE IT TO DAWN WITHOUT GETTING KILLED (VERY PLEASANT SUNRISE), FELL ASLEEP ON THE RAFT, WOKE UP AT THE TAKEOUT. BLEARY-EYED, I HELPED MY DAD LOAD THE BOAT AND THE GEAR ONTO THE TRAILER, WHICH MY MOM HAD SHUTTLED DOWN THE RIVER FOR US.

"YOU'RE LOOKING PRETTY HANGDOG, CHAMP," DAD COMMENTED WHEN WE PULLED INTO TOWN AND THE TRUCK CAME TO A STOP IN FRONT OF OUR HOUSE. "HOW ABOUT I PUT STUFF AWAY FOR ONCE AND YOU TELL MOM TO WRESTLE UP SOME DINNER? LOOKS LIKE THINGS HAVE CLEARED UP NICELY AROUND HERE."

I DIDN'T HESITATE, THIS BEING THE FIRST TIME IN MEMORY I'D BEEN LET GO WITHOUT HAVING TO CLEAN UP AFTER A TRIP. WHICH IS HOW I GOT TO WHERE I AM NOW: SITTING ON THE FRONT PORCH WHILE MY MOM COOKS UP A LATE DINNER FOR ME AND DAD.

APPARENTLY, MY DAD WAS RIGHT ABOUT GETTING OUT OF DODGE: THE REPORTERS HAVE MOVED ON,

LEAVING PHONE NUMBERS, IF WE HAPPEN TO THINK OF A
SCOOP TO GIVE THEM. PROBABLY THEY GOT BORED OF
OUR THREE RESTAURANTS AND ONE BAR, OR MAYOR
BLAKE DROVE THEM HALF CRAZY WITH HIS AMBITIONS
FOR THE TOWN. EITHER WAY, BESIDES A LIST OF
REPORTERS TO CALL BACK, I'M A FREE MAN.
SKELETON CREEK IS BACK TO NORMAL, AT LEAST
FOR THE MOMENT.

"YOU SHOULD HAVE SEEN GLADYS MORGAN TAKE
TO THE PRESS," MY MOM TOLD ME. "I'VE NEVER KNOWN
THAT WOMAN TO TALK FOR SO MANY MINUTES IN A
ROW IN ALL MY LIFE."

WE CHATTED ABOUT THE BOOKS AND THE TOWN
LIBRARIAN, THE FISHING AND THE STORM THAT BLEW
THROUGH, BUT I COULDN'T BRING MYSELF TO MENTION
THE MAN IN THE RAIN GEAR. I COULDN'T TELL HER
OR MY DAD. I DON'T EVEN KNOW WHY. I MEAN
REALLY — WHY NOT TELL THEM? I GUESS IT FEELS
LIKE ONCE I DO IT'LL LEAD TO SARAH, AND WHEN THAT
HAPPENS EVERYTHING WILL COME CRASHING DOWN
AROUND US.

I DON'T FEEL LIKE A LIAR. MORE LIKE A

WITHHOLDER OF CERTAIN FACTS. I HAVE TO BELIEVE THERE'S A DIFFERENCE. THEN AGAIN, IT'S JUST LIKE A LIAR TO MAKE A DEADLINE FOR WHEN HE'LL START TELLING THE TRUTH.

WE JUST NEED A LITTLE MORE TIME TO BRING THIS CROSSBONES THING TO A CLOSE. A WEEK, MAYBE TWO, AND I'LL TELL THEM EVERYTHING. IT'S JUST THAT FIRST I HAVE TO GET SARAH BACK HOME WITH A FEW UNSCHEDULED STOPS ALONG THE WAY — STOPS I HAVEN'T EVEN FIGURED OUT YET.

AS SOON AS I CAN SCARF DOWN SOME DINNER, I'VE GOT SOME WORK TO DO. FOR STARTERS, I'M PUTTING THE WEBCAM ON MY LAPTOP INTO FULL SWING STARTING TONIGHT. EVEN IN LOW-RES RECORDING MODE IT'LL FILL HALF MY HARD DRIVE OVERNIGHT, BUT AT LEAST I'LL KNOW IF SOMEONE IS WATCHING ME. WITH ALL THESE NEW PEOPLE FLOATING IN AND OUT OF TOWN AND THE RAVEN HIDING IN THE WOODS, WHO KNOWS WHO MIGHT TRY TO SET UP THEIR OWN SURVEILLANCE ON ME?

I need to reach out to Sarah as fast as I can. Her film camp runs four more days, then she's driving back home to Boston. I need to email her the Raven sighting I recorded, get her take on the man in the rain slicker. But I also need to send her a scan of the <u>other</u> Raven. Being up all night in a tent at least gave me a chance to really look at it carefully. It's no less confusing than the Skull Puzzle, which led us to the missing Jefferson library books. Maybe this Raven Puzzle will lead to an even bigger mystery.

It's two sided, same as last time. But somehow, it's even scarier looking than the Skull Puzzle.

Flames, haunted roads, castle towers, a nickel? Where does a guy begin solving a puzzle like this? There is one image that's a dead giveaway: the nickel. That's Thomas Jefferson's old home, Monticello. It's in Virginia. At least we know one of the locations the Apostle is trying to lead us to, even if

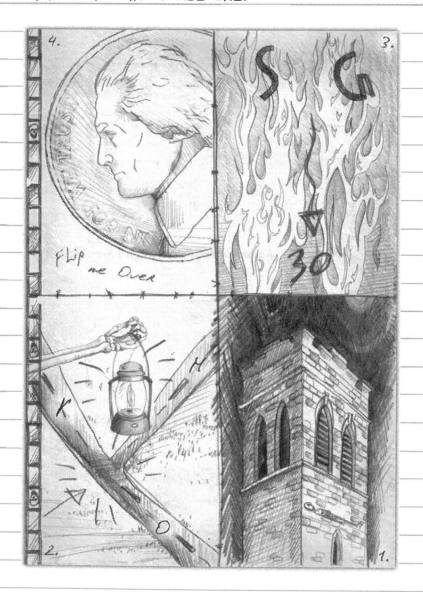

THIS IS A SCAN OF SIDE TWO:

Sarah will have no idea where to look once she gets there.

The skull from the earlier puzzle has been replaced by a raven, the four corners by clues I can't even begin to understand. Ghost Room floors, stone markers, wisps of wind — the Apostle's methods of recording definitely lean into the bizarre. But there is one encouraging bit of news on this side of the Raven Puzzle: the words.

West to East and Follow the Trail of the Apostle! tell me that long ago, the Apostle was on a journey very much like the one Sarah is on now. Originally, he went east to west, which we already knew. But now we're finding out he also traveled west to east, dropping clues on his way back. Which means Sarah can do the same thing.

If we can figure out what the clues mean, Sarah can follow the trail of the Apostle all the way back to Boston.

And we might just find the most valuable Crossbones treasure of them all.

My worries?

The Apostle is trying to trick us.

The ghost of Old Joe Bush will haunt our every move.

And the Raven will try to stop us.

TUESDAY, JULY 12, 10:00 P.M.

I FINALLY GOT TO MY ROOM AFTER A DINNER OF COLD
CHICKEN, POTATO SALAD, AND RED JELL-O WITH TINY
MARSHMALLOWS FLOATING INSIDE. I FIRED UP THE LAPTOP
AND FOUND TWO EMAILS FROM SARAH. QUICKLY, I READ
THEM, DELETED THEM, AND SCRUBBED THE MEMORY FOR
TRACES OF CONTACT. MY PARENTS HAVE BACKED OFF
A LITTLE ON THEIR FEELINGS ABOUT ME COMMUNICATING
WITH SARAH, BUT JUST THE SAME, I CAN'T TAKE ANY
CHANCES THEY MIGHT BE CHECKING IN ON ME.

Ryan,

I wish I could have been there when they smashed up the library. I'd
have paid top dollar to watch Gladys Morgan freak out. Word is out
about the books you found. Jefferson library — nice — we're kind of
amazing, I guess. Wish I could be there to take some of the credit. My
parents are like, "Did you hear about Ryan McCray?" I wanted to say,
"Um, yeah, I know all about it. I found most of the clues!" But we both
know I couldn't do that.

I took your voice mail seriously, Ryan. What did Fitz give you? What
makes you think it will lead to something else? Don't leave me
hanging!

Film school is getting better. I'm holding my own. My last video beat the socks off the one from this eleven-year-old prodigy who's been schooling me. Three more days and it's good-bye Hollywood, back in the car for the long haul to Boston.

Call me the second you get off that stupid river! It's getting lonely out here without you.

Sarah

THIS IS THE PROBLEM WITH LONG-DISTANCE COMMUNICATION. MOST OF IT HAPPENS DIGITALLY. VOICE MAILS, EMAILS, TEXT MESSAGES — THOSE ARE THE CURRENCY OF MY SECRET ONGOING CONNECTION TO SARAH FINCHER. ADD TO THAT THE ISOLATION OF THE RIVER OUTSIDE SKELETON CREEK AND THE INSANE SHOOTING SCHEDULE SARAH IS KEEPING AND IT'S A MIRACLE WE TALK AT ALL. THE BEST I COULD DO BEFORE LEAVING WITH MY DAD HAD BEEN A QUICK MESSAGE.

Don't tell anyone you were involved. Fitz left me something we need to talk about. Heading for the river — not by choice! — will email the moment I get back.

SARAH'S SECOND EMAIL WAS MORE BLUNT.

WHERE ARE YOU? And don't tell me you're still fishing. Not buying it. S.

I SENT SARAH THE RAVEN VIDEO, ALONG WITH THIS NOTE:

Sarah,

Sorry I disappeared. My dad made me do it!

Are you ready for another haunted road trip? I've attached scans of what Fitz left for me. Looks like we have our work cut out for us.

And it gets worse.

The Raven found me.

I attached a video that speaks for itself.

Miss you TONS. Be careful out there. Hope filming is going well.

R.

Tuesday, July 12, 11:11 p.m.

11:11, a bad omen. I hate when I look at the clock and find numbers doubled up like that. Gives me the creeps.

Sarah must have been sitting at her computer editing video clips when I emailed because she responded less than twenty minutes later.

She posted the video of the Raven in the woods. Seeing what I recorded, along with the additions Sarah made from past sightings, just about knocked me off my chair. At the end, she starts analyzing the Raven Puzzle.

It appears she's already hot on the Apostle's trail.

If something's happened to me, and someone is reading this after I've disappeared (or worse), get to a computer and take a look.

You can meet the Raven for yourself.

It will help you realize what we're up against.

SARAHFINCHER.COM
Password:
MELANIEDANIELS

WEDNESDAY, JULY 13, 11:00 A.M.

No rest for the weary.

My dad was pounding on my door at 7:00 and yelling for me to get out of bed, breakfast was on the table. Sometimes I hate that he opened a fly shop in town financed by a fraction of the gold I found on the dredge. Maybe if I'd left that gold there I'd still be sleeping right now and my dad would be out of town at his old job. Times like these, it feels like the world is caving in on me, like I need a secret corner where I can be alone with my thoughts.

After I watched Sarah's video last night I tried to stay awake, but I was just too exhausted from the night before. The good thing about being that tired? I slept like the dead, just what I needed. I was refreshed, ready to figure this thing out while my dad is away from the shop all day on a float.

When I left the house this morning, my mom gave me a list of reporters to call.

"Get it done, kiddo. If you don't, they'll just keep calling the house," she told me, shaking her

HEAD. "THE MAYOR IS THE WORST OF THE BUNCH. HE CALLED FOUR TIMES YESTERDAY LOOKING FOR YOU."

WHY AM I NOT SURPRISED? FIRST THE DREDGE, NOW THE JEFFERSON LIBRARY BOOKS. MAYOR BLAKE IS A SHAMELESS PROMOTER WHEN IT COMES TO GETTING SKELETON CREEK ON THE MAP. A LOT OF FOLKS ARE STARTING TO WONDER IF HE'S GUNNING FOR A BIGGER POSITION, LIKE MAYOR OF BOISE OR GOVERNOR OF THE ENTIRE STATE. I CAN ALREADY IMAGINE THE PLATFORM HE'D RUN ON:

CITY INCOME IN SKELETON CREEK UP 10,000 PERCENT. JOB GROWTH THROUGH THE ROOF. TOURISM EXPLODING.

HE WON'T MENTION THAT ANY OF THIS HAD TO DO WITH MY FINDING THOMAS JEFFERSON'S MISSING BOOKS, AND MILLIONS IN GOLD. SOMEHOW, LIKE EVERY POLITICIAN, HE'LL MAKE IT SOUND AS IF HE HAD AN AWFUL LOT TO DO WITH IT.

MY DAD TOOK OFF WITH A RETIRED COUPLE FOR A FEW HOURS, MUMBLING TO HIMSELF ABOUT WHAT A DAY IT WAS GOING TO BE WITH TWO PEOPLE BORED ENOUGH TO TRY FLY-FISHING FOR THE FIRST TIME. HE GUESSED THEY'D BE EXPERTS AT TANGLING UP THEIR LINES AND

CASTING INTO THE TREES. IT'S ALWAYS A TOUGH DAY ON THE RIVER WITH A HUSBAND AND WIFE WHO DON'T KNOW WHAT THEY'RE DOING. I ACTUALLY FELT SORRY FOR HIM AS HE LEFT, LEAVING ME TO WATCH THE SHOP ALL DAY. HE WAS NICE ENOUGH NOT TO MAKE ME TIE FLIES WHILE HE'S GONE, WHICH IS SAYING SOMETHING SINCE HE'LL PROBABLY GO THROUGH A DOZEN AN HOUR WITH THOSE TWO. LOOKING AT THE LIST OF REPORTERS I WAS SUPPOSED TO CALL DIDN'T EVEN MAKE ME WANT TO TRADE WITH HIM — IT WAS THAT BAD ON A RAFT WITH AN OLD COUPLE, ZERO FISHING EXPERIENCE BETWEEN THEM.

THE FIRST INTERVIEW WAS WITH THE PHILADELPHIA ENQUIRER, A NICE LADY WHO WAS MORE EXCITED THAN I WAS ABOUT THE DISCOVERY OF THE BOOKS. SHE HAD A COOL ACCENT AND SHE LAUGHED A LOT. APPARENTLY, SHE'D BEEN AN AMATEUR SLEUTH FOR YEARS HERSELF AND ENVIED MY FINDING SUCH AN IMPORTANT TREASURE. TWO MORE EAST COAST PAPERS, THE ASSOCIATED PRESS, THE OREGONIAN, THE SEATTLE TIMES, THE BOISE HERALD — ALL OF THEM ASKING THE SAME QUESTION OVER AND OVER AGAIN: HOW'D YOU KNOW WHERE TO LOOK?

I DODGED THIS LINE OF QUESTIONING BETTER WITH EVERY PHONE CALL I MADE, BUT IT WAS HARD NOT TO LIE. MOSTLY, I PLAYED DUMB JUST TO BE SAFE, WHICH MADE ME A SUPER LAME INTERVIEWEE (THIS TENDS TO SHORTEN UP THE CONVERSATIONS).

I'VE STILL GOT THREE MORE PAPERS TO CALL, SMALLER ONES, I THINK, BUT I'M STARVING. PLUS, I WANT TO GO LOOK AT THE GAPING HOLE IN THE LIBRARY FLOOR AGAIN.

WEDNESDAY, JULY 13, 1:21 P.M.

The hole is still there.

It's still boring, too.

Why anyone would think ripped-up floorboards in an old library would make a good tourist attraction is beyond me, but if someone can sell it, that someone is Mayor Blake. And he's got enough money in the Skeleton Creek coffers to put a nice rope around it and go all interactive, so that will help.

Wait — speaking of Mayor Blake, he just walked into the fly shop.

And he's not alone.

WEDNESDAY, JULY 13, 2:00 P.M.

"THIS HERE'S MR. ALBERT VERN," THE MAYOR SAID WHEN HE CAME IN. HIS SOUTHERN ACCENT HAS KICKED UP A NOTCH, A SURE SIGN HE REALLY IS THINKING ABOUT RUNNING FOR HIGHER OFFICE. "YOU'LL NEVER GUESS WHERE HE'S FROM. GO ON NOW, GUESS!"

I GUESSED HE WAS FROM THE BOSTON RED SOX, RECRUITING ME TO PLAY BASEBALL.

ALBERT VERN LOOKED AT ME AS IF TO SAY, "QUITE A MAYOR YOU'VE GOT HERE. YOU WOULDN'T HAPPEN TO KNOW HOW I COULD GET AWAY FROM HIM, WOULD YOU?"

"THE WASHINGTON POST!" THE MAYOR TOLD ME, COMPLETELY PROUD OF HIMSELF FOR HOBNOBBING WITH NATIONAL MEDIA. "MR. VERN IS FROM THE WASHINGTON POST! AIN'T THAT SOMETHING ELSE? RIGHT HERE IN SKELETON CREEK. AND IT GETS BETTER — HE'S STAYING FOR THE WHOLE WEEK!"

I NODDED AND TRIED TO ACT FRIENDLY, BUT MY INSIDES WERE CHURNING. IN FACT, THEY'RE STILL CHURNING. I DON'T NEED A BIG-CITY REPORTER HANGING AROUND, WATCHING MY EVERY MOVE. IF HE'S WORKING FOR THE POST, HE MUST BE PRETTY GOOD AT SNOOPING OUT THE TRUTH.

"Do you have any golden stone flies with rubber legs?"

This was the first thing Albert Vern asked me, which led the mayor to glance at him like he'd lost his way coming through town and needed directions. It didn't take long for me to realize Albert Vern was an outdoorsman when he wasn't reporting.

"I can hardly wait to get out on the river" were his next words, the mayor's cue to leave us fishermen alone.

"You two get to know each other. That's real good. I'll be just outside, checking my messages."

Mr. Vern sighed with relief when Mayor Blake was gone, explaining that he'd already endured a tour of the town and an exhaustive description of recent events.

"Tell me what's working and I'll take a dozen," he said, explaining that he'd long been a traveling reporter for the Post, casting a line on rivers from New York to western Canada. "I could tell you a fishing story or two."

628

I WAS REALLY STARTING TO LIKE THIS GUY. NO
TOUGH QUESTIONS, JUST A REQUEST FOR THE BEST FLIES
WE HAD TO OFFER.

"SOMETHING WRONG WITH YOUR BACK, MR.
VERN?" I ASKED, STARTING TO WARM UP TO A FELLOW
WRITER. HE WAS TWISTING AROUND LIKE THERE WAS A
KINK IN HIS SPINE.

"THREW MY BACK OUT PICKING UP MY BAG AT
THE AIRPORT — HAPPENS ALL THE TIME. I'M
USED TO IT."

"HOW LONG DOES IT LAST?" I ASKED. THE POOR
GUY LOOKED FEEBLE, LIKE I COULD KNOCK HIM DOWN
WITH MY PINKIE FINGER.

"USUALLY A DAY OR TWO. BUT I THINK THE
MOUNTAIN AIR IS HELPING. I'LL BE FINE."

A REAL TROUPER, THIS GUY, WHICH I ALSO LIKED,
BUT THEN THE QUESTIONS STARTED.

"SO YOU'RE THE ONE WHO FOUND THE MOST
FAMOUS MISSING BOOKS IN THE WORLD?"

I BEGAN PICKING OUT FLIES, DROPPING THEM INTO A
PLASTIC CONTAINER.

"IT WAS AN ACCIDENT, REALLY. I JUST HAD A
FEELING, MR. VERN."

He laughed and I could tell it jolted his back by the look on his face that followed.

"Well, I hope you have the same feeling about those flies you're picking out. I'd like to land some fish tonight."

He asked me to call him Albert and hoped we could go fishing together one evening, just talk about this and that. He was more interested in a vacation than a story, or so he said. Casting, he told me.

I have to be very careful with this guy. I can imagine slipping up and saying something I shouldn't or being just stupid enough to show him the Raven Puzzle if I need help. The river has a way of lulling my senses to sleep.

Before I could worry too much, Mayor Blake rang the bell on the door, returning from checking the messages on his phone. Albert Vern paid for his flies, and the two of them left for pie. The shop would be quiet for at least an hour — the perfect time to do some research.

For once, I wanted to beat Sarah to the punch.

WEDNESDAY, JULY 13, 4:12 P.M.

BINGO ON THE FIRST LOCATION! AND MORE GOOD
NEWS TO BOOT.

First, THE DRAWINGS I FIGURED OUT.

THE GHOST ROOM:

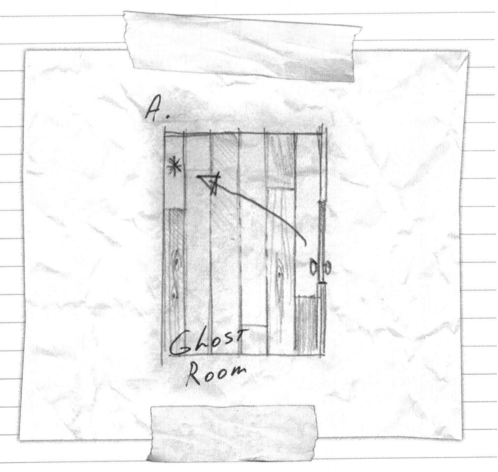

631

And THE TOWER WITH THE SKELETON INSIDE:

An hour of searching online for skeletons in churches and castles led me nowhere. Turns out there are thousands of castles, even more churches, and . . . let's see . . . billions of

SKELETONS. NOTHING WORTH REPORTING ON GHOST

ROOMS, EITHER. I WAS AT A DEAD END, AND I ACTUALLY

THOUGHT ABOUT DOING SOME WORK AROUND THE SHOP.

LUCKILY, EDGAR ALLAN POE CAME TO THE RESCUE.

THE OLD DUDE SAVED ME ONCE AGAIN.

I HAD BEEN LOOKING MOSTLY AT THE TOWER AND

THE SKELETON, BECAUSE THAT WAS MARKED NUMBER 1.

MY HOPE WAS THAT NUMBER 1 MEANT CLOSEST TO THE

WEST COAST: THE FIRST STOP ON SARAH'S JOURNEY

BACK HOME.

THE IDEA OF A SKELETON LYING IN A STONE BUILDING

STARTED TO GET ME THINKING ABOUT "THE CASK OF

AMONTILLADO," A WICKED COOL POE STORY I'VE READ

AT LEAST A DOZEN TIMES. IT'S A STORY WHERE ONE GUY

LURES ANOTHER GUY DOWN INTO THIS CHAMBER, THEN

CHAINS HIM UP DOWN THERE (YIKES!). AFTER THAT, THIS

NUT JOB BUILDS A STONE WALL IN FRONT OF THE OPENING,

SO THERE'S, LIKE, THIS SMALL ROOM WITH A MAN CHAINED

UP INSIDE. THE GUY STARTS FREAKING OUT, BUT THE

STONES ARE PRETTY THICK SO NO ONE CAN HEAR HIM

SCREAMING. I GUESS HE GOES CRAZY AND STARVES TO

DEATH BEHIND THE WALL OR TONS OF RATS FIND HIM. AT

LEAST THAT'S WHAT I THINK HAPPENS.

EITHER WAY, IT TOTALLY CLUED ME IN! THE
SKELETON IN THE TOWER WASN'T JUST LYING THERE.
IT WAS <u>IN</u> THE WALL, JUST LIKE IN THE STORY. SO I
STARTED SEARCHING FOR MASONS WHO WENT MISSING,
GHOST STORIES REVOLVING AROUND MISSING PEOPLE,
LEGENDS OF PEOPLE BEING BURIED ALIVE IN TOWERS AND
CHURCHES.

THE CRAZY THING ABOUT WHAT I DISCOVERED?
THE STORY OF THIS TOWER HAS SOME EERIE
SIMILARITIES TO THE MADE-UP STORY OF
"A-MONTILLADO." AND THERE'S A LOT OF INFORMATION
OUT THERE ABOUT IT, TOO.

THE TOWER IS PART OF ST. MARK'S CHURCH IN
CHEYENNE, WYOMING.

BUILDING ON THE CHURCH STARTED IN 1868, AND
THE MAIN STRUCTURE WAS FINISHED WITHOUT ANY
DISTURBANCES. EIGHTEEN YEARS LATER, PEOPLE STARTED
CLAMORING FOR A BELL TOWER. THEY WANTED A
REAL SHOWSTOPPER, SOMETHING NO ONE IN THE AREA
COULD BUILD, SO THEY IMPORTED TWO MASONS FROM
SWEDEN WHO KNEW WHAT THE HECK THEY WERE DOING.
JUST LIKE IN POE'S STORY — TWO GUYS!

IT GETS BETTER.

634

So these two masons worked on the tower for a while until one day the church parson, Dr. Rafter, came by to check on the work. When he did, there was only one mason, not two, and the one guy was acting strange.

The next day? Both masons were gone. (Cue thunderbolt.)

It was more than thirty years before they started building again, which is when the real trouble started. The new masons heard unexplained hammering in the walls and words they couldn't understand drifting into the air. Churchgoers swore they heard a whispered message they could understand:

There is a body in the wall!

Jump ahead to 1966, when a very old man showed up at the church to confess his sins. He confessed (I'm not making this up!) that when he was a young mason, he and a fellow Swede were hired to build the tower, but his friend fell down the stone stairs leading to the basement and broke his neck. Afraid he'd be tried for murder, the remaining mason stuffed the body

AGAINST ONE OF THE UNFINISHED WALLS. THEN HE USED
CEMENT AND STONES AND BASICALLY BUILT THIS DEAD
GUY INTO THE TOWER ITSELF.

I GOTTA SAY . . . THAT'S JUST WRONG. AND SO
EDGAR ALLAN POE IT'S NOT EVEN FUNNY.

THE REVERSE SIDE OF THE RAVEN PUZZLE HAS
THIS DRAWING:

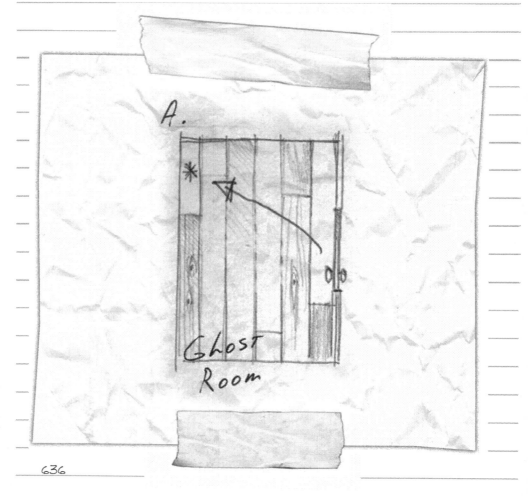

The Ghost Room. That's a real place in St. Mark's Church. Upstairs in the tower, a room where voices come through the walls. And under one of the floorboards?

A message from the Apostle.

Dad's here. Dang. Gotta go.

WEDNESDAY, JULY 13, 10:07 P.M.

WHEN MY DAD GOT BACK FROM THE RIVER HE PUT ME TO WORK UNLOADING THE BOAT. THE RETIRED COUPLE HAD BROKEN A SHOP RECORD, LOSING THIRTY-ONE FLIES ON THEIR WAY DOWN THE RIVER. TO TOP IT OFF, THEY LOST A FLY ROD — NOT ON A BIG FISH, WHICH WE WOULD HAVE CHEERED. NO, THE HUSBAND JUST DROPPED IT RIGHT IN THE RIVER AND LET IT FLOAT AWAY. HOW IS THIS EVEN POSSIBLE, YOU ASK? IT REQUIRES A RARE SET OF CIRCUMSTANCES, BUT IT DOES HAPPEN.

FIRST, YOU NEED A BEGINNER WHO'S SURE HE CAN OUTFISH HIS BEGINNER WIFE.

SECOND, THAT GUY NEEDS TO BE SITTING IN THE BACK OF THE RAFT, WHERE THE OARSMAN CAN'T SEE HIM WITHOUT TURNING AROUND. (THAT'D BE MY DAD.)

AND LAST, YOU NEED A CLUMSY PERSON KNOWN FOR DROPPING EXPENSIVE THINGS OFF OF BUILDINGS AND INTO RIVERS AND THEN TRYING TO HIDE IT FROM EVERYONE FOR APPROXIMATELY THIRTY SECONDS.

THAT'S ABOUT HOW LONG IT TAKES FOR A TWO-HUNDRED-DOLLAR FLY ROD TO VANISH FROM VIEW IN A MOVING RIVER.

On the upside, they paid for the rod and were good tippers, which made my dad feel a little better.

"I should have known what was happening. It was real quiet for about twenty seconds. Never a good sign," my dad said. "Why don't they just tell me when they drop a fly rod? I could swim out and get it."

"If it was you and mom on the boat, would you tell?" I asked.

My dad rubbed the stubble on his chin and smiled. "Good point."

He milled around the shop, checking messages and sales on the till.

"I hear you had a visitor from the Washington Post."

I asked him how he knew about Albert Vern and he said the mayor had left three messages on his phone while he floated out of cell range.

"Sounds like this guy's a fisherman."

After that my dad informed me that the mayor had offered to pay full price for an all-day float down the river.

639

"But only if you guide him," my dad added.

I could hardly say no. Number one, a day on the river with someone who knows how to fish and loves doing it is hard to come by when you're a guide. A large percentage of gigs are with people who have no business being on a river to begin with. And the guy seemed pretty cool, so why not?

"I could use a day in the shop after today," my dad said, sounding a little worse for the wear. "You go, I'll tie up three dozen flies and set up a new guide rig. It'll be a win-win."

At that moment, all I really wanted to do was stay in the shop and do research all day. The faster we figured out all the locations Sarah would need to visit, the sooner we'd know if it was even possible.

The trail led to something, somewhere. Could be an even bigger stash of gold for all we knew.

I got through dinner and "porch time" with my mom while the lazy summer evening took my dad into dreamland. When I got to my room I set the webcam on my laptop to record

640

THROUGHOUT THE NIGHT, AND CALLED SARAH. SHE
PICKED UP ON THE FIRST RING AND I EXPLAINED
EVERYTHING ABOUT THE HAUNTED CHURCH LOCATION
BEFORE SHE COULD GET A WORD IN EDGEWISE.

"CHEYENNE, WYOMING," SHE SAID. "NOT EXACTLY
ON THE WAY HOME, BUT NOT TOO FAR OFF THE PATH,
EITHER."

I EXPLAINED THAT I'D RUN THE NUMBERS — IT WAS
ELEVEN HUNDRED MILES FROM LA TO CHEYENNE.
ABOUT SIXTEEN HOURS BY CAR.

"HOW COME YOU GET ALL THE CUSHY GIGS AND I
HAVE TO DRIVE LIKE A MANIAC ALL OVER KINGDOM
COME?" SHE ASKED.

"AT LEAST YOU DON'T HAVE TO DEAL WITH
REPORTERS AND RETIRED FISHERMEN," I SAID. THEN I
DESCRIBED ALBERT VERN AND TOMORROW'S FISHING
EXPEDITION.

"DON'T TRUST REPORTERS," SHE WARNED. "HE
SOUNDS LIKE A SMOOTH OPERATOR. SPILL THE BEANS
AND WE'LL NEVER GET TO THE END OF THE APOSTLE'S
TRAIL."

I AGREED COMPLETELY, BUT WHAT I WAS REALLY
WORRIED ABOUT WERE THE OTHER LOCATIONS AND HOW

SHE WAS GOING TO CONVINCE HER PARENTS TO GO OFF ROUTE ON THE WAY BACK TO BOSTON.

MY MOM KNOCKED SOFTLY ON THE DOOR AND I HUNG UP BEFORE SHE ENTERED WITHOUT BEING INVITED IN. SHE'S LIKE THAT, MY MOM. THE VERY SOFT KNOCK ISN'T SO MUCH A COURTESY AS AN EXCUSE TO SAY, "I WARNED YOU I WAS COMING IN — DIDN'T YOU HEAR ME KNOCKING?"

SHE ASKED TO SEE MY PHONE, WHICH SURPRISED ME, SINCE I'D GOTTEN THE FEELING THEY WERE SLACKING ON KEEPING AN EYE ON ME. I SHOULD HAVE KNOWN BETTER. THERE WAS NO HIDING WHO I'D CALLED.

"MUST BE HARD, HAVING HER AS CLOSE AS LOS ANGELES."

"IT'S OKAY," I LIED.

"JUST DON'T DO DOING ANYTHING STUPID, OKAY? YOU KNOW HOW YOUR FATHER WILL REACT IF THINGS GET OUT OF HAND AGAIN."

"GOT IT. NO PROBLEM."

SHE HANDED BACK MY PHONE, BUT NOT BEFORE SAYING I SHOULD RECONSIDER RECONNECTING WITH MY OLD FRIEND. "REMEMBER HOW MUCH TROUBLE YOU both got into before?" she asked. As if I was about to forget.

Still, I could tell she understood. Your best friend is your best friend, and besides, how much trouble could we get into when we lived so far apart?

Actually, quite a bit.

Thinking about it now, I realize this is where it gets kind of scary. Like, maybe we really <u>are</u> stepping over a line we shouldn't. Part of me says, <u>Hey, Sarah is seventeen, what's the big deal?</u> She drove all the way out to LA by herself. She's an independent kind of girl. Her mom and dad aren't strict like mine. But another part says we shouldn't be pulling one over on our parents the way we are.

I called her back, and Sarah's answer, regarding the detour on the way home, was: "I already talked to them and they're fine with it."

Sarah had already called and asked about sidetracking to different locations. The haunted road trip documentary had been a big hit at the camp and her instructor was hoping for part two

ON THE WAY BACK. SARAH HADN'T PICKED ALL HER LOCATIONS YET, BUT SHE DEFINITELY WANTED TO VISIT ST. MARK'S CHURCH.

"IT'S IN THE RIGHT GENERAL DIRECTION," SARAH EXPLAINED. "AND HOW MUCH TROUBLE CAN I GET INTO IN WYOMING, ANYWAY?"

I GOT THE FEELING SHE WAS PRETTY GOOD AT CONVINCING HER PARENTS TO LET HER STRAY A LITTLE BIT. AS FAR AS THEY COULD TELL, SHE WAS BEING RESPONSIBLE. WHAT I WOULDN'T GIVE FOR PARENTS LIKE THAT. I'M LUCKY MY DAD WILL LET ME RUN THE RIVER, LET ALONE GET IN A CAR AND DRIVE ACROSS THE COUNTRY LOOKING FOR HAUNTED HOUSES.

TURNS OUT SARAH WAS ALSO MAKING SOME PROGRESS OF HER OWN ON THE RAVEN PUZZLE.

"I'M NOT A HUNDRED PERCENT SURE, BUT I THINK I KNOW WHAT'S GOING ON WITH THE SECOND LOCATION. LET ME WORK ON IT SOME MORE AND I'LL EMAIL YOU."

IN CLASSIC SARAH FASHION, SHE WOULDN'T BUDGE ON ANY DETAILS. SHE ONLY TOLD ME THAT IF SHE WAS RIGHT, THEN THEY WERE INDEED HEADING BACK EAST ON THE APOSTLE'S TRAIL.

The last thing she said had me a little
worried.

"He's here," she told me.

"Who is?"

"Him. The ghost of Old Joe Bush, Henry,
whoever."

"How do you know?"

"I just do. I can feel it. I think he's
following me."

"Oh."

Oh? Was that the best I could do?

What do you say when your best friend tells
you she thinks a man possessed by a ghost is
following her across the country?

THURSDAY, JULY 14, 2:20 A.M.

I JUST WOKE UP AND I FEEL LIKE SOMEONE HAS BEEN WATCHING ME.

NOT A GOOD FEELING.

Thursday, July 14, 6:30 a.m.

Bad! Bad! Bad!

Three hours of lying in bed and finally the sun started coming up at 5:00 a.m. so I could set foot on my floor without being terrified something would pull me under the bed. Sarah and I both have that sixth sense, where we can feel it when we're being watched, and crawling out of bed a half hour ago, I was sure someone had been in my room. There's a big part of me that wishes I hadn't set my webcam to record through the night. Then I could just <u>imagine</u> what was in my room. There would be a part of me that could think it was a cat or the wind blowing, that nothing sinister had taken place.

But I did record with my webcam. I even used that funky night-vision setting that turns everything green and shadowy.

My spook meter told me that something had happened around 2:00 a.m., so I stopped the six hours of footage I had at around 1:50 a.m. and slowly worked through the next ten minutes.

Nothing at 2:00 a.m.

Nothing between 2:00 a.m. and 2:05 a.m.

At 2:06 a.m., all the blood drained out of my face.

The door creaked open, and then, for, like, ten seconds, nothing.

Then it moved into the room and leaned over the desk.

The Raven had entered my house.

The picture went black for a moment, then he was back, towering over my bed, staring at me in that huge, hooded rain slicker.

The camera went dark again, longer this time. When the picture came back, the Raven had moved to my bookshelf. A few seconds later he was gone.

There's something awful about being watched in my sleep. It's like I'm helpless. I can't defend myself against a giant ax if I'm asleep!

I'll tell you one thing: No more sleeping without a baseball bat or the hatchet from the camping supplies.

I just hope I don't accidentally swing at my dad or my mom if they check on me after midnight.

648

I SENT SARAH THE WEBCAM FOOTAGE. MAYBE SHE CAN DO SOME ENHANCEMENTS AND SEE SOMETHING I DIDN'T. HE WAS LOOKING FOR THE RAVEN PUZZLE AT MY DESK AND ON MY BOOKSHELF, I'M SURE OF IT.

DID HE TAKE ANYTHING?

DID HE KNOW I WAS RECORDING HIM?

AND MOST IMPORTANT, IS HE PLANNING TO OFF ME IN MY SLEEP?

WHEN I LOADED MY EMAIL TO SEND THE WEBCAM VIDEO, THERE WAS A LONG MESSAGE WAITING FOR ME FROM SARAH.

Ryan,

I know what the second clue means. Totally figured it out. The really good news? It's in the southeast corner of Kansas, heading in the right direction. And it's only a few hours from Little Rock. Remember when I came out here? Little Rock is where my mom's old college roommate lives. I can stay there again. It's all working out.

So here's the deal with the second location, which has the greatest name in the history of haunted locations: the Spooksville Triangle. Nice! Here's that section of the Raven Puzzle:

2.

See how each of the three roads have a letter on them? That was the giveaway. K is for Kansas, M for Missouri, and O for Oklahoma. That means the location is right where the three states meet. After I figured that out, it was easy finding the Spooksville Triangle. It's everywhere online! A very well known haunt.

The skeleton hand with the lantern represents the ghost, but you'll have to look it up on your own. I gotta go make a movie!

More soon,

Sarah

We're getting good at this. Two days with the puzzle, and three locations down:

— Monticello, Jefferson's old haunt in Virginia
— St. Mark's Church in Cheyenne, Wyoming
— The Spooksville Triangle, corner of Kansas, Missouri, and Oklahoma.

I have no idea what we're supposed to do at any of these places or what we'll find, but it's a good start.

I spent fifteen minutes online, and Sarah was right; there's a ton of stuff about the Spooksville Triangle out there. Legend has it that a girl wandered away from her parent's farmhouse and got lost, so the mom went out at night with a lantern searching for her. But the little girl never turned up. Now people go out there and see the Spooksville light, this unexplainable ball of orange that floats around in the field. Thousands of people have seen it, but no one has been able to explain what it is. The

GHOST OF THE MOM, OUT THERE WITH THE LANTERN,
STILL LOOKING FOR HER DAUGHTER? IT WOULD
SEEM SO.

THE SKELETON HAND HOLDING THE LANTERN
OBVIOUSLY REPRESENTS THE MOM, THE THREE ROADS

REPRESENT EXACTLY WHAT SARAH SAID. THE OTHER
SIDE OF THE PUZZLE MAKES SENSE, TOO:

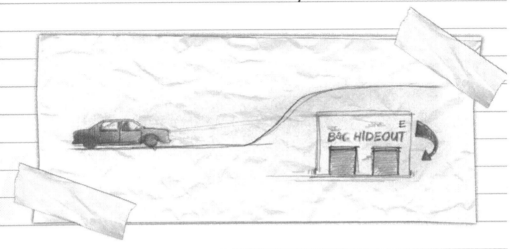

THE CAR AT THE BOTTOM OF THE ROAD — THAT'S
JUST LIKE THE LEGEND SAYS. IF YOU PARK ON THIS
DESERTED ROAD WHERE IT RISES IN FRONT OF YOU,
THAT'S WHERE YOU'LL SEE THE LIGHT AT NIGHT.

THE STONE MARKED E AT THE HIDEOUT FOR
B AND C.

THERE MUST BE AN OLD BUILDING OR SOMETHING
OUT THERE THAT CAN BE SEEN FROM WHERE YOU'D
PARK YOUR CAR. AND AT THE BACK RIGHT CORNER OF
THE BUILDING? A STONE MARKED A. NOW THAT'S
WHAT I CALL PROGRESS.

MEANWHILE, I NEED TO BE AT THE SHOP EARLY AND SET UP FOR MY DAY ON THE RIVER. I'M LOOKING FORWARD TO GETTING OUT OF DODGE FOR THE DAY, BUT I'M ALSO NERVOUS. WE'LL BE FLOATING RIGHT PAST THE CAMPSITE ME AND MY DAD STAYED AT TWO NIGHTS AGO.

AND BEYOND THE CAMPSITE, THE CLEARING AND THE GIANT TREE.

AND THE RAVEN WITH HIS FIVE-FOOT BLACK AX.

I HOPE I DON'T FIND HIM STANDING IN THE RIVER UP TO HIS KNEES, WAITING FOR MY BOAT TO DRIFT BY.

HE'S BEEN IN MY HOUSE, SO I WOULDN'T PUT IT PAST HIM.

Thursday, July 14, 4:45 p.m.

Long day with a few things to report. Just got done unloading the boat and I'm at the café on Main. Ordered a burger, fries, a Coke. I don't feel like going home yet.

First off, I got a call from Sarah and she left a message, which I told her not to do unless she had to. It was nice though. I've listened to it three times.

"How are you doing? You must be freaking out. I just — I can't believe he was in your room. If I was there you could stay at my house or something. I feel terrible for you. Plus, I miss you. It's lonely out here sometimes.

"Do you think you should tell your parents? I mean, this is getting crazy, right? It might not be worth it.

"I posted that video. You can find it using the Dickens password. I think you might have missed something, unless you just didn't tell me.

"The Raven left something behind.

"Okay, call me, right? Let me know you're okay.

"Hug.

"Sarah."

It's nice to be missed. What I wouldn't give to sit up all night working out clues together. But that's not about to happen. I feel bad she's lonely. And I've been thinking the same thing all day: I need to tell my parents. The Raven stepped over the line by coming into the house. That was WAY out of bounds. I guess this entire thing will be taken up by the authorities (whoever they are) and the game of cat and mouse will come to a screeching halt. Sad, really. Sarah and I are so close to the end.

What's she mean about the Raven leaving something for me? Now I feel like I should have skipped the hamburger and gone home for dinner. At least I'd be one step closer to my laptop and whatever was left behind in my room. Then again, I'd have to endure dinner with my mom and dad, and right now, I'm afraid I'll come uncorked and tell them everything.

Quick recap of the fishing trip: It was awesome. I could stop there, but for future

REFERENCE, ALBERT VERN CAN FISH WITH ME ANYTIME. HE ARRIVED AT THE SHOP WITH THE MAYOR TWO STEPS BEHIND, HOUNDING ME TO CALL THE <u>SEATTLE TIMES</u> TO ANSWER SOME OF THEIR FOLLOW-UP QUESTIONS. IT WAS THE LAST THING I WANTED TO DO, AND ALBERT WAS COOL ENOUGH TO TELL THE MAYOR WE WERE LATE GETTING ON THE RIVER ALREADY (NOT ACTUALLY TRUE) AND THE INTERVIEWS WOULD HAVE TO WAIT. THE MAYOR, PERPETUALLY BOWLED OVER BY A REPORTER FROM THE <u>WASHINGTON POST</u>, SLINKED AWAY, BUT NOT BEFORE PLEADING WITH ME TO MAKE THE CALL AS SOON AS I GOT OFF THE RIVER. (CHECK THAT, DID IT AT THE SHOP. MORE BORING ANSWERS THAT GOT ME OFF THE LINE THREE TIMES FAST).

MR. VERN'S BACK HAD STRAIGHTENED UP AND HE WAS RARING TO GO. HE WORE A SMILE ALL DAY, FISHED LIKE A TRUE ENTHUSIAST, AND TIPPED LIKE A GRANDPARENT. (IN OTHER WORDS, HIS TIP PAID FOR MY DINNER AND THEN SOME.) HE ONLY ASKED A FEW QUESTIONS, WHICH I DEFLECTED WITH EASE. IT MIGHT BE HE'S JUST TRYING TO GET ON MY GOOD SIDE BEFORE GRILLING ME WITH THE REAL ZINGERS. MAYBE THAT'S

WHAT REALLY GOOD REPORTERS DO — SOFTEN YOU UP
BEFORE BREAKING OUT THE HEAVY ARTILLERY.

"YOU KNOW, I HAVE A MIND TO DO THIS AGAIN
TOMORROW," HE SAID WHEN WE PULLED BACK IN AND MY
DAD WAS THERE WAITING FOR US.

"THAT CAN BE ARRANGED," MY DAD ANSWERED, AND
I COULD SEE IN HIS EYE THAT ONE DAY OFF THE RIVER
WAS ONE DAY TOO MANY. IF ALBERT VERN DID GO
OUT AGAIN, IT WOULD BE WITH MY DAD AND I'D BE LEFT
IN THE SHOP.

FINE BY ME.

I JUST ATE AN ENTIRE HAMBURGER AND A PLATE OF
FRIES IN UNDER FIVE MINUTES AND BURPED SO LOUD THE
WAITRESS CALLED ME A COW. OUCH.

BETTER GET BACK HOME, SEE WHAT SARAH FOUND.

Thursday, July 14, 5:40 p.m.

Mayor Blake is getting downright annoying. When I got home he was sitting on the porch eating my mom's leftover Jell-O with marshmallows in it. He said he was there just to visit, but I knew better. Within ten seconds he was asking if I'd called the Seattle Times. If I didn't know better, I'd say he's got something up his sleeve. Maybe he's even caught up in this whole Crossbones thing. Never trust a politician.

It took forever to get rid of him and call it an early night on account of completing my best fishing day of the year. My dad grunted at me, said tomorrow would be even better, and I hightailed it for my room.

Sarah and I have a few secret passwords we've saved up in case she needs to leave one like she did on the phone. The "Dickens password" is one we've had saved up for a while: edwindrood.

I'm not going to get into what was on the video until whoever is reading this journal checks out that video. Maybe I'm dead and gone, done in by the Raven, and my exclusive story

659

HAS BEEN GIVEN TO ALBERT VERN AT THE WASHINGTON POST. WOULDN'T THAT BE SOMETHING? MR. VERN, IF YOU'RE READING THIS, YOU'RE A HECK OF A FISHERMAN. I'LL SEE YOU ON THAT BIG RIVER IN THE SKY WHERE THE FISH ARE ALWAYS BITING.

YOU MIGHT BE SENSING THAT MY MOOD HAS BRIGHTENED. I CAN'T TELL WHY UNTIL YOU WATCH WHAT SARAH POSTED. CRAZIEST VIDEO EVER.

DO THAT, THEN COME BACK. I'LL BE WAITING.

SARAHFINCHER.COM
Password:
EDWINDROOD

THURSDAY, JULY 14, 6:10 P.M.

WATCHING THAT VIDEO THE WAY SARAH EDITED IT DOWN JUST ABOUT SENT ME RUNNING THROUGH THE HOUSE SCREAMING FOR MY MOM. I WISH I WAS KIDDING. THE SECOND TIME THROUGH, WHERE SHE MESSED WITH THE LIGHTING, IT WAS OBVIOUS THE RAVEN HAD PUT A NEW BOOK ON MY SHELF.

IT DIDN'T TAKE ME LONG TO FIND IT, BECAUSE MOST OF MY BOOKS ARE PAPERBACKS.

THIS ONE IS OLD, AND IT'S GOT A HARDBACK SPINE, ONE OF THOSE CLOTH COVERS.

I SET IT ON MY DESK AND STARED AT IT FOR ABOUT A MINUTE.

THERE'S NO WRITING ANYWHERE ON THE OUTSIDE, AND THERE AREN'T VERY MANY PAGES.

MY FIRST THOUGHT? THIS THING IS LOADED WITH TOXIC YELLOW GAS THAT WILL POUR OUT THE SECOND I OPEN THE COVER, LIKE IN ONE OF THOSE ANCIENT BATMAN SHOWS. BUT CURIOSITY GOT THE BETTER OF ME AND I CAREFULLY LIFTED THE COVER.

NOTHING.

I DON'T MEAN NOTHING HAPPENED. I MEAN THERE

662

WAS NOTHING INSIDE. I FLIPPED THROUGH THE YELLOWED PAGES WITH MY THUMB AND THEY WERE ALL BLANK. IT WAS LIKE A GHOST BOOK — NOTHING ON THE SPINE, NO WORDS OR DRAWINGS OR PICTURES INSIDE. THE WHOLE THING WAS FORTY—TWO PAGES.

NEW YORK GOLD AND SILVER GAVE EACH OF ITS ASSETS A NUMBER BEFORE THE COMPANY WENT BELLY—UP A LONG TIME AGO. ONE OF ITS ASSETS WAS THE SKELETON CREEK DREDGE. AND ITS NUMBER?

42.

COINCIDENCE? SOMEHOW I DOUBT IT. WITH THE CROSSBONES, EVERYTHING IS CONNECTED. EVERYTHING HAS A MEANING.

THERE'S SOMETHING ELSE. AT THE VERY BACK OF THE BOOK, AFTER THE FORTY—SECOND PAGE, I FOUND TWO SHEETS OF FOLDED PAPER.

A DEATH THREAT FROM THE RAVEN?

I SAT THERE AND TOLD MYSELF NO MATTER WHAT KIND OF MESSAGE I WAS ABOUT TO READ I WAS ABSOLUTELY GOING STRAIGHT DOWNSTAIRS AND TELLING MY PARENTS EVERYTHING. I THOUGHT ABOUT THE CROSSBONES THREE—PART MISSION:

1) PRESERVE FREEDOM.
2) MAINTAIN SECRECY.
3) DESTROY ALL ENEMIES.

DESTROY ALL ENEMIES WAS SOUNDING VERY
POSSIBLE, WITH ME AS THE ENEMY. I HALF EXPECTED
THE RAVEN TO JUMP OUT OF THE PAGES OF THE BOOK
AND THE GHOST OF OLD JOE BUSH TO CRASH
THROUGH THE WINDOW.

THEY'D GET ME FROM BOTH SIDES.

I OPENED THE LETTER — SINGLE SPACED ON TWO
SHEETS — AND KNEW IMMEDIATELY WHO IT WAS FROM.
I'D SEEN THIS HANDWRITING BEFORE.

Hey, Ryan,
    I saw you at the clearing the other day. I was hiding
up on the ridge, keeping an eye on my dad. He's been going
into Raven mode lately, which is never a good thing.
    We're living up in this cave by the peak. Dang cold
at night. He says we won't be here much longer, but I
don't know. It feels like something's about to happen.
Something big.

There's this metal box he's been carrying around forever. He keeps it pretty close, usually under his mattress. And the key is always around his neck. Yesterday we were out chopping wood together and he sent me back to the cave to refill a jug of water. I was there alone and I knew where he'd hidden it. I mean, I didn't actually see him hide it, but I heard him piling rocks in the corner of the cave on our first night up here. He thought I was sleeping, but I wasn't.

I moved all the rocks and found the metal box, hit the lock with my ax. It took three big swings, but the lock finally busted off. I don't know why I did it. He's going to find out. He'll know it was me. I guess I was tired of the secrets. I thought maybe there was something in there that would get me out of this cave and back on the football team, know what I mean?

There were two things in the box, neither of which makes any sense. One was a completely blank piece of paper. Well, there were two words at the top, but that was it.

The words?

THE CLAUSE.

A clause with no words. What the heck does that mean?

There was also a book inside with nothing but blank pages. So the mysterious metal box had basically nothing inside.

Makes me wonder if my dad is losing his marbles.

Or maybe there's something to this stuff I can't understand on my own.

I'm giving you the book, hoping you can help me. I have no idea why it's got no words or why it's so special, but trust me: It's a Crossbones treasure. Yeah, I know about the Crossbones. Been dealing with it my whole life. I bet it's why my mom bolted before I was three. She couldn't take all the secrecy. And you know what? I'm getting pretty sick of it myself.

Let's figure this out, Ryan. Let's pull one over on these guys.

I have a feeling we don't have much time. My dad's going to check the metal box at some point, and when he finds his stuff missing, I'm not sure what will happen.

I'm going to head into town and leave the book in your room while my dad's sleeping. I can't do much from way up here in the woods, but I'll do what I can.

There's a big divot in that giant tree my dad was chopping in the grove. If you find out anything useful, leave me a note there. I'll check the tree every day.

Or maybe just drop me a note sometime. It's pretty lonely up here.

Bring this whole crazy thing to an end, will you? And watch your back. I don't know what my dad is capable of anymore.

Fish on!

Your friend, Fitz

So it wasn't the Raven, after all. It was Fitz in my room last night! He sneaked into my room in the middle of the night in his dad's rain slicker and nearly scared me half to death. Wow.

I feel sorry for the guy. Must be rough living in a cave with the Raven. It makes me wonder what I'd do if I were him. Also makes me happy I have parents who aren't cave-dwelling secret-society members. What's a guy like Fitz supposed to do? I wish he could come down out of that cave and go back to work at the fly shop.

I can't help seeing the similarities between the tree and the blue rock, where Sarah and I used to exchange private notes. Is it just me, or do I have a habit of making friends who like to keep secrets from their parents? Getting to the blue rock was easy when Sarah wanted to exchange a note, but exchanges with Fitz will be harder. I can mountain bike down the river trail, but it's over an hour to the campsite on a bike, even longer coming back upstream.

Communicating with Fitz is going to be some work.

I called Sarah and spoke in my quietest whisper as I flipped the delicate pages in the book back and forth. She couldn't believe the book was totally empty, but she was thrilled about the fact that the Raven hadn't actually broken into my house. There was a pause on both ends and I knew what she was thinking. Know why? Because I was thinking the exact same thing.

If the Raven didn't come into my house, then he hadn't crossed some imaginary line Sarah and I had both set up in our heads. We could wait a little longer before telling anyone what we were doing. We could follow the trail of the Apostle and see where it led.

All we had to do was figure out one more clue — number 3 on the Raven Puzzle — and we'd know the road Sarah would need to follow.

Somehow I had a feeling it would lead back to the empty book I held in my hand. And the clause, whatever THAT was.

Friday, July 15, 6:55 p.m.

My parents are out playing cards down the street with the Muntzes (old family friends), so I've got a couple of hours to languish in my journal. Things to write have been piling up, but the time and energy to write them down have been few and far between.

Someone blabbed about the great fishing — probably the retired couple, even though they barely caught a thing — and the shop has been humming with fishermen ever since. Albert Vern seemed to sense the crush descending on Skeleton Creek and decided to call off the second-day float and head into Portland on a different assignment. He's supposed to be back early next week, after things die down, when Mayor Blake says I better get my act together.

"Time to get this story off the griddle before it leaves town for good" was how he phrased it.

I have some major news to report, but first I just gotta write down this Gladys Morgan

MOMENT — IT'S A CLASSIC. SHE CAME INTO THE SHOP YESTERDAY DURING A BRIEF LULL. I HALF EXPECTED TO SEE HER PULL AN AX OUT FROM BEHIND HER BACK AND START TAKING SWINGS AT OUR FLOOR TO EVEN THINGS UP AFTER WHAT WE'D DONE TO HER LIBRARY. BUT THE ANCIENT TOWN LIBRARIAN HAD OTHER THINGS ON HER MIND.

"DON'T THINK FOR A MOMENT YOU CAN FOOL ME. I KNOW EXACTLY WHAT YOU'RE UP TO," SHE WARNED ME. I WAS LIKE, <u>UH-OH. WHAT DOES SHE KNOW?</u>

"IS THERE SOMETHING I CAN HELP YOU WITH, Ms. MORGAN?" I ASKED, GLANCING OVER AT MY DAD, WHO WAS STARTING TO PAY CLOSER ATTENTION THAN I WAS COMFORTABLE WITH.

"I'LL GET YOU BACK, RYAN McCRAY, JUST YOU WAIT," SHE WENT ON. SO IT WAS ABOUT RIPPING HER FLOOR APART? OR NOT?

"UM, Ms. MORGAN, I HAVE NO IDEA WHAT YOU'RE TALKING ABOUT."

SHE GLARED AT ME OVER HER BIFOCALS.

"HOW DUMB DO YOU THINK I AM?" SHE POINTED AT ME FIRST, THEN MY DAD. "START CARRYING YOUR

WEIGHT WITH THESE REPORTERS! DO YOU HAVE ANY IDEA HOW MANY CALLS I'M TAKING? HOW MANY INTERVIEWS I'VE DONE? THE MAYOR IS AT MY HEELS ALL DAY WHILE YOU FISH OR TALK ABOUT FISHING OR SELL FISHING STUFF TO A BUNCH OF FISHING IDIOTS. GET WITH THE PROGRAM!"

SHE TURNED ON HER HEELS AND STORMED OUT OF THE SHOP BEFORE MY DAD OR I HAD A CHANCE TO ANSWER HER. THEN WE BOTH STARTED LAUGHING.

"I'M STANDING RIGHT HERE!" SHE YELLED FROM THE FRONT STEPS OF THE SHOP, THE SOUND OF OUR LAUGHTER DRIFTING OUT THE FRONT WINDOWS AND INTO THE PARKING LOT.

OTHER THAN THAT, THE MOMENTS OF LEVITY HAVE BEEN RARE. I SPEND MOST OF MY TIME WORRIED ABOUT FITZ, THE GHOST BOOK, THE RAVEN PUZZLE, SNEAK ATTACKS BY THE RAVEN, BEING HAUNTED BY OLD JOE BUSH, AND MOSTLY ABOUT SARAH. SHE'S ACTING RECKLESS AGAIN AND IT'S MAKING ME NERVOUS.

SHE CALLED ME A LITTLE OVER AN HOUR AGO FROM AN ARCTIC CIRCLE SOMEWHERE IN NEVADA.

"AN ARCTIC CIRCLE IN THE DESERT," I SAID. "YOU'VE OFFICIALLY LOST YOUR MIND."

"Arctic Circle the restaurant, not the north pole or whatever. A little trivia for you: They invented fry sauce. Pretty cool, huh?"

She was slurping on a drink they serve called a Lime Rickey.

"I thought you were in LA until tomorrow morning?" I asked.

She told me the camp had ended at noon, and that she was scheduled to stay the night in the dorm, then start the drive home tomorrow. Instead, she left the second the last class got out so her parents wouldn't get suspicious.

"Wait a second. I thought you said your parents were on board," I prodded her. I got a long pause followed by a shifty answer.

"They ARE on board. They just want me off the road by nightfall, so that's kind of a problem."

"Tell the truth, Sarah. What's going on?"

She hemmed and hawed, then spilled it.

"Okay, so maybe I didn't tell them EVERYTHING. They're fine with the detours on the way home, but they won't let me drive at night. That's

CRAZY, RIGHT? LIKE DRIVING IN THE DARK IS A BIG
DEAL OR SOMETHING."

RIGHT ABOUT THEN I WAS SIDING WITH SARAH'S
PARENTS. I COULD IMAGINE HER BREAKING DOWN AT
MIDNIGHT ON THE SIDE OF THE ROAD IN THE MIDDLE OF
NOWHERE, THUMBING A RIDE INTO SOME BACKWATER
TOWN. NOT A GOOD THOUGHT.

"THEY BOOKED ME A HOTEL IN CHEYENNE FOR
TOMORROW NIGHT," SARAH EXPLAINED. "BUT IT'S A
SIXTEEN—HOUR DRIVE IF ALL I DO IS STOP TO USE THE
BATHROOM AND GRAB A SANDWICH. I WOULD'VE HAD
TO HAVE LEFT AT FIVE IN THE MORNING TOMORROW TO
GET THERE BEFORE DARK, BUT THAT WOULDN'T HAVE
GOTTEN US WHAT WE NEED, WHICH IS WHY THERE'S A
DAY MY PARENTS DON'T KNOW ABOUT."

I DID THE CALCULATIONS IN MY HEAD: SARAH TOOK
OFF FROM LA IN THE EARLY AFTERNOON, SO SHE WAS
GOING TO ARRIVE AT ST. MARK'S CHURCH BETWEEN
THREE AND FOUR IN THE MORNING TONIGHT.

"IT'S PERFECT, RYAN. THINK ABOUT IT: I'LL GET TO
OUR FIRST LOCATION BEFORE THE SUN COMES UP,
INSTEAD OF WHEN THE SUN IS GOING DOWN. I'LL FIND THE
CLUE, THEN CHECK INTO THE HOTEL EARLY AND SNOOZE

673

ALL DAY. TECHNICALLY, I'M STILL CHECKING IN BEFORE DARK. RIGHT?"

ANYTIME SOMEONE STARTS A SENTENCE WITH THE WORD TECHNICALLY, IT'S A COVER FOR A LIE THAT'S ABOUT TO FOLLOW.

"I DON'T KNOW, SARAH — IT ALL SOUNDS KIND OF DANGEROUS. WHAT IF YOUR INSTRUCTOR CALLS THEM AND SAYS YOU LEFT EARLY?"

SHE TOLD ME IT WAS LA, WHERE FREE SPIRITS ROAM, AND THAT HER INSTRUCTOR WAS A HIPPIE WHO HAD ALREADY FLED TO THE BEACH FOR THE WEEKEND. THEN SHE CALLED ME A CHICKEN.

"NAME-CALLING IS BENEATH YOU," I SAID.

"SORRY, IT'S JUST . . . COME ON, RYAN. THIS IS IDEAL. I CAN PRACTICALLY SEE THE NEXT A-POSTLE VIDEO NOW. DON'T YOU WANT TO KNOW WHAT HE'S GOING TO SAY?"

SHE WAS ON HER GAME, FOR SURE. I WAS CURIOUS. AND I WAS HOLDING US BACK, AS USUAL.

SO I DID A LITTLE CALCULATING OF MY OWN, SEEING WHERE THIS WAS GOING.

"LET ME GUESS: YOU'LL WAKE UP IN WYOMING AROUND FOUR IN THE AFTERNOON AND CALL TO CHECK in with your parents, because that's when you're supposed to be checking in."

"Now you're getting it. I'll hit the road right after I call them, which should put me at the Spooksville Triangle in Missouri by two in the morning. And I'll get plenty of sleep. This way I can be at these locations at night, when no one is around. Makes sense, right?"

It was hard to argue with Sarah's logic, but I was worried for her and told her so, especially since she'd been feeling as if the ghost of Old Joe Bush was somewhere nearby.

Her answer to that wasn't as surprising as I'd expected it to be.

"I don't know. To tell you the truth, I think he's on our side."

It's possible. Whether it's my dad's old friend Henry or a ghost or some twisted version of the two, it's possible he isn't trying to harm us anymore.

But how can we be sure?

"Just get to Cheyenne as safely as you can," I said. "And no more surprises."

I TOLD HER I'D BE AWAKE ALL NIGHT LONG, THAT

SHE COULD CALL ME ANYTIME, AND THAT SHE BETTER

CALL ME ONCE SHE GOT TO ST. MARK'S CHURCH. IF

SHE BROKE DOWN SOMEWHERE SHE SHOULD CALL ME

FIRST AND WE'D FIGURE IT OUT TOGETHER. AND IF SHE

GOT TIRED, I ADVISED HER TO STICK HER HEAD OUT THE

WINDOW AND SCREAM.

IT'S GOING TO BE A LONG NIGHT.

I'VE GOT TIME TO KILL.

I GUESS I'LL GO GRAB A FEW MOUNTAIN DEWS AND

GET BACK TO THE RAVEN PUZZLE. IF SARAH IS GOING

TO DO ALL THE EXPLORING, THE LEAST I CAN DO IS

FIGURE THIS THING OUT FOR US.

FRIDAY, JULY 15, 10:30 P.M.

THE MAYOR FOLLOWED MY PARENTS DOWN MAIN
STREET AFTER THE CARD GAME AND GAVE ME YET
ANOTHER LIST OF NEWS OUTLETS TO CONTACT WITH
FOLLOW-UP QUESTIONS. HE SAID HE'D GIVE THEM TO
GLADYS MORGAN IF I WANTED, SO I SNATCHED THE
PIECE OF PAPER OUT OF HIS HAND. I DIDN'T NEED
THE TOWN LIBRARIAN RETURNING TO THE FLY SHOP
WITH A SLEDGEHAMMER.

WHEN THE MAYOR LEFT, I SAT ON THE PORCH WITH
MY PARENTS FOR A HALF HOUR OR SO. I YAWNED
ABOUT EVERY FIVE SECONDS AND FINALLY MY MOM
TURNED TO MY DAD AND SAID, "YOU'RE WORKING THAT
BOY TOO HARD."

MY DAD THOUGHT THAT WAS ABOUT THE DUMBEST
THING HE'D EVER HEARD. HE WENT INTO ONE IF HIS
YARNS ABOUT HOW HARD LIFE HAD BEEN IN THE OLD
DAYS. IT WAS ALL I COULD DO TO NOT THROW UP.

MY DAD YAWNED AFTER THAT, THEN I DID, THEN HE
YAWNED AGAIN.

"I'VE HAD BETTER CONVERSATIONS WITH TWO
STRAY DOGS," MY MOM SAID.

A few minutes later, my dad had fallen asleep on the porch, and my mom had her nose in a book, which was my cue to call it a night.

When I got to my room, I found three text messages waiting for me, all from Sarah.

8:17 P.M.
Rest stop, making good time, sun will be down soon. I'm wide awake!

9:45 P.M.
White Castle! Need I say more?

9:52 P.M.
Almost forgot! I finished my documentaries on St. Mark's Church and Spooksville before I left camp. Got all inspired. Password is fortunato. Check 'em out.

The White Castle comment eludes me, since I've never been. Apparently, they make tiny burgers that cost, like, five cents. That girl has

GOT TO GET OFF THE ROAD. HER IDEA OF GOOD EATS IS GETTING SKETCHY.

SHE'LL BE AT ST. MARK'S CHURCH ALL BY HERSELF BEFORE THE SUN COMES UP AND INTO THE SPOOKSVILLE TRIANGLE SOON AFTER THAT. BETTER CHECK OUT THESE DOCUMENTARIES SO I KNOW EXACTLY WHAT SHE'S GETTING HERSELF INTO.

SARAHFINCHER.COM
Password:
FORTUNATO

Friday, July 15, 10:46 p.m.

Close call!

My dad just barged right in on his way to bed, acting all weird. I think Mom told him about me talking to Sarah on the phone. Not good. I barely had time to shut my laptop before he came in, and I'm sure he suspected something. I have to be more careful.

It was a long day and I'm tired, but those two videos woke me up. I still can't believe Sarah keeps going into these places all alone. She's fearless, that girl. And reckless.

A couple of things I hadn't thought of that now strike me as problems. For one thing, how the heck is she going to get inside St. Mark's church? It'll be locked at 3:00 a.m. for sure. Check out that video and you'll see for yourself: It's not like she's going to walk right in there in the middle of the night. The Ghost Room is upstairs, in the tower, so she'll need to get inside. Something tells me she's already thought this through and her answer isn't going to be a good one.

Also, the Spooksville documentary didn't make any mention of a house or a barn out there. According to the puzzle, there should be something hidden at the hideout for B and C. . . . I sort of neglected to recall we never really figured that part out. I assumed it would figure itself out once she got there, but now that we're getting closer to the location, I'm nervous this mysterious building isn't even there. Maybe it's burned to the ground or disappeared into a sinkhole, right along with a secret message from the Apostle.

Looks like I've got plenty of work to do while Sarah drives across Utah.

If I fall asleep she'll never forgive me.

Must.

Stay.

Awake.

Saturday, July 16, 1:24 a.m.

I'm always better at sleuthing in the middle of the night. There's less pressure and my senses are on red alert. I'm not sure if it's me worrying that someone is going to come smashing through my window or what, but I do go into a different mode after midnight.

I figured out the final location, the one marked <u>3</u>. Darn proud of myself on this one. I might even have to pat myself on the back a couple of times.

Many drawings to share, so here goes.

To recap what we already know, in case we're gone and someone needs to piece this thing together . . .

Location number 1 is in Cheyenne, Wyoming. It's the St. Mark's Church, where Sarah will arrive in less than two hours.

Side 1 of the puzzle was a tower with a skeleton lying inside.

1.

SIDE 2 WAS THE GHOST ROOM FLOOR WITH THE MARKER, WHERE SARAH WILL NEED TO PRY UP THE FLOORBOARD OR SOMETHING.

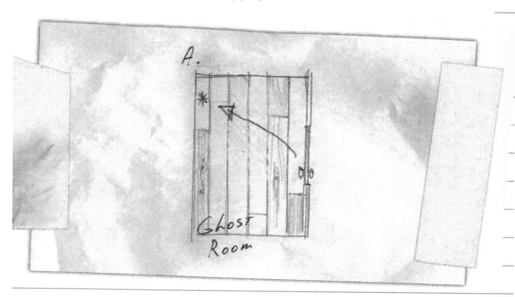

A.

Ghost Room

Okay, so we're good to go on one of the clues. Not sure how Sarah is getting in there, but if she does, hopefully we'll get another message from the Apostle.

Sarah figured out the second drawing, which looks like this:

Three roads, the lantern, the skeleton hand — it all led to the Spooksville Triangle. And the related piece from the other side of the Raven:

This drawing makes it clear that Sarah will need to park right below the rise in the road, from which we hope we'll figure out what the hideout for B and C is.

    Skipping ahead to the fourth location, it was a gimme with the nickel — Monticello, where Thomas Jefferson had lived.

    The two puzzle pieces for that one look like this:

CLEARLY, IT'S THE MONTICELLO BUILDING FROM
THE TAILS' SIDE OF A NICKEL, BUT WE'RE A LITTLE
STUMPED ON WHAT THE REST OF IT MEANS. PUT
THE LETTERS HERE? I KNOW WHERE WE'LL GET THE

LETTERS: FROM THE A-POSTLE VIDEOS AT THE
LOCATIONS, LIKE BEFORE. AND WE'LL PLACE THEM IN
THE RIGHT ORDER USING THE PLACES PROVIDED ON THE
RAVEN PUZZLE:

WHEN WE HAVE THE LETTERS AND WE PUT THEM IN
ORDER ON THE FRONT OF MONTICELLO, THIS WILL ALL
MAKE SENSE.

I HOPE.

SO NOW THE GOOD NEWS — THERE WAS ONE MORE
LOCATION TO FIGURE OUT AND IT HAD US BOTH STUMPED.
I FIGURED WE WERE BEING TAKEN BACK ACROSS THE

COUNTRY, SO I HAD A PRETTY GOOD IDEA THE
LOCATION WOULD BE SOMEWHERE BETWEEN MISSOURI
AND VIRGINIA. HERE'S A MAP I DREW WITH SOME OF
THE THINGS WE ALREADY KNEW AND THE AREA I
FIGURED I'D FIND THE LAST LOCATION:

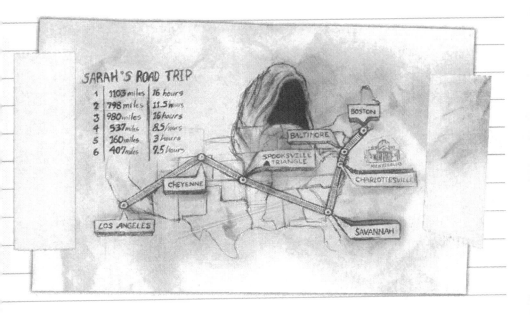

SARAH'S ROAD TRIP

1	1103 miles	16 hours
2	798 miles	11.5 hours
3	980 miles	16 hours
4	537 miles	8.5 hours
5	160 miles	3 hours
6	407 miles	7.5 hours

BOSTON
BALTIMORE
SPOOKSVILLE TRIANGLE
MONTICELLO
CHARLOTTESVILLE
CHEYENNE
LOS ANGELES
SAVANNAH

FOLLOW THE TRAIL OF THE APOSTLE.
HE WAS HEADING BACK TO WHERE IT ALL BEGAN,
BACK TO THE PLACE WHERE THE CROSSBONES WAS
BORN ALONG WITH THE UNITED STATES OF AMERICA.
THE LOCATION HAD TO BE IN THAT BOTTOM RIGHT
CORNER OF THE UNITED STATES. I SEARCHED ALL

THROUGH TENNESSEE, KENTUCKY, NORTH AND SOUTH
CAROLINA, ALABAMA, AND MISSISSIPPI FOR HAUNTED
PLACES STARTING WITH THE LETTERS S AND G UNTIL
ABOUT A HALF HOUR AGO, I LITERALLY SLAPPED
MYSELF IN THE FOREHEAD.

So stupid!

HERE'S THE DRAWING FROM THE RAVEN PUZZLE:

WHY DID IT TAKE ME SO LONG TO FIGURE
THIS OUT?

THE G IS FOR GEORGIA, WHICH IS RIGHT IN LINE

WITH A TRIP ACROSS THE COUNTRY. AND IF THE G WAS FOR GEORGIA, THEN THE S WAS FOR A CITY. A CITY WHERE A FIRE TOOK PLACE. A BIG ONE.

AS IT TURNS OUT, WITHOUT MUCH INVESTIGATING AT ALL, I FOUND THE FIRE.

SAVANNAH, GEORGIA. THE FIRE OF 1820, A FIRE THAT ENGULFED TWO-THIRDS OF THE CITY. I COULDN'T HELP THINKING SKELETON CREEK HAD SURVIVED A FIRE JUST LIKE IT IN ITS OWN PAST.

COINCIDENCE?

HARDLY!

TWO HUGE FIRES IN TWO CROSSBONES STRONGHOLDS? I THINK THEY HAD SOMETHING TO DO WITH IT. THEY BURNED JEFFERSON'S HOUSE DOWN. THESE GUYS ARE KNOWN PYROMANIACS.

THE DOWN ARROW AND THE NUMBER 30 GOT ME TO THE LOCATION. TAKE 30 AWAY FROM 1820 AND YOU GET 1790.

THE 17 HUNDRED 90 BUILDING, A HAUNTED HOTEL IN A HAUNTED CITY. AND THE MOST HAUNTED ROOM IN THAT HOTEL? LOOK NO FURTHER THAN THE CLUE ON THE OTHER SIDE OF THE PUZZLE:

Room 204. A room you can still stay in today. If you're crazy!

I don't think Sarah is crazy, but I do think she's more than willing to stay in a haunted hotel room if it gets us some answers we need. That's a no-brainer.

I'm going to take a quick break, finish drawing this map, scan it, and send it to Sarah. That way she'll have a visual. And I'm grabbing a bowl of Cheerios with a ton of sugar. I'm crashing!

Back in a sec.

SATURDAY, JULY 16, 2:00 A.M.

FINISHED THE RAVEN MAP AND SENT IT TO SARAH. WE'RE ALL DIALED IN. ALSO SLAMMED SOME SUGARY CEREAL, SO I SHOULD BE ABLE TO STAY AWAKE FOR AT LEAST ANOTHER HOUR.

    HERE'S THE FINALIZED MAP, THE JOURNEY BACK AGAIN, FOLLOWING THE TRAIL OF THE A-POSTLE:

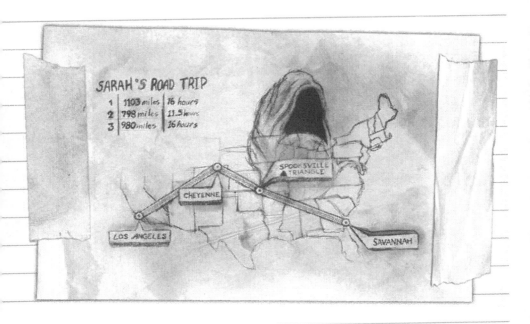

THE COOL THING IS THAT IT ENDS ON THE SAME
COAST AS BOSTON, WHERE SARAH LIVES. SHE WON'T
EVEN HAVE TO GO THAT FAR OUT OF HER WAY IN
ORDER TO MAKE ALL THE STOPS. THAT'LL HELP WITH
KEEPING HER PARENTS CALM EVEN IF SHE IS VISITING
HAUNTED LOCATIONS.

I'M GOING TO PRINT OUT MY EMAIL TO SARAH AND
PUT IT HERE IN MY JOURNAL.

I WISH I COULD STOP YAWNING!

COME ON, DUDE, YOU CAN DO THIS. ONE MORE
HOUR. STAY AWAKE.

Sarah,

I hope you're able to get this email on your phone when you stop
in the middle of the night. If so, just know I'm here for you. I'm
awake and waiting for your call. We didn't have a chance to cover
how you'll get in there, but maybe you've got that figured out.
Don't do anything too wild, okay?

I figured out the final location tonight. Figuring out locations isn't
driving across Utah drinking Lime Rickeys and eating fry sauce,

but still — I'm pretty awesome! I won't bore you with the details of how I solved it, but you should know the backstory of the place if you're going in there. I know, I know, you'll do your own research and make a killer documentary, squashing my contribution like a bug. I'll bask in my moment, however short it will be.

(Insert game show voice here) — You'll be traveling to sunny Savannah, Georgia, staying at the swanky 17 Hundred 90 Hotel. We'll even book you in the most haunted room they've got: room 204!

Okay, enough shenanigans, here's the scoop:

At one time, the hotel was a boardinghouse, where a sixteen-year-old girl used to live. (Maybe it was you in a past life! Wouldn't that be something?) Her name was Anna Powell and she was kind of naive. She fell in love with a visiting sailor, who promptly took off for the high seas, promising to return soon and marry her. Months went by. No letters, no sailor. Soon everyone agreed: He was probably married and never intended to return to a heartsick girl in Savannah. Maybe he would have returned if he'd known how distraught Anna Powell would become. One night, her heart broken to pieces, she threw herself off the balcony of the hotel to the bricks below.

Ew.

The room she jumped from? 204, the same number that resides on the Raven Puzzle. The same room you'll be staying in if we're going to find what the Apostle hid there. You'll recall there were wisps of air all around the number 204, which makes me think you'll want to search in the air vents. I bet that's where you'll find what we're looking for.

Oh, just so you know, that room is SO haunted. But we can talk about that later.

Call me!

Ryan

THERE, GOT THAT ALL IN HERE FOR POSTERITY. IF NOTHING ELSE, IT SHOWS THAT I FIGURED THIS PART OUT.

I THINK I'LL TAKE A BREAK. JUST SIT HERE AT MY DESK. MAYBE PLAY A VIDEO GAME.

I TOLD MYSELF ABOUT A THOUSAND TIMES THAT I WOULDN'T LET THIS HAPPEN. I DID PUSH-UPS. I DRANK HIGHLY CAFFEINATED BEVERAGES. I PULLED HAIRS OUT OF MY ARM. BUT IT HAPPENED ANYWAY.

I FELL ASLEEP.

NOT JUST A LITTLE, EITHER. I CONKED OUT BIG-TIME. THREE HOURS!

I AM HOPELESSLY LAME.

THERE IS ONE PIECE OF GOOD NEWS. OR MAYBE IT'S TERRIBLE NEWS. YEAH, IT'S TERRIBLE NEWS. I CHECKED MY PHONE AND SARAH NEVER CALLED ME. I MEAN, IT SUGGESTS THAT SHE DOESN'T KNOW I FELL ASLEEP, SO THERE'S THAT. BUT IT ALSO MEANS SHE'S GONE MISSING. I'LL TAKE MAD SARAH OVER MISSING SARAH ANY DAY OF THE WEEK.

RING...

SATURDAY, JULY 16, 6:30 A.M.

GREAT NEWS ON SO MANY FRONTS! THAT PHONE RING I SHOVED IN THERE AT THE END OF MY LAST ENTRY? IT WAS SARAH. APPARENTLY, WYOMING HAS SOME HUMONGOUS CELL PHONE DEAD ZONES. SHE COULDN'T GET A SIGNAL, WHICH IS WHY SHE DIDN'T CALL ME FROM ST. MARK'S CHURCH. I FEEL SLIGHTLY CONFLICTED ABOUT NOT MENTIONING THE WHOLE FALLING-ASLEEP THING, BUT SHE DIDN'T ASK AND I DIDN'T TELL.

THERE'S MORE.

SARAH PULLED IN LATE, ABOUT 4:00 A.M., AND PARKED ON A SIDE STREET. THEN SHE GOT HER CAMERA OUT AND STARTED FILMING EVERYTHING. THE SUN WAS ABOUT AN HOUR FROM COMING UP, SO THE CHURCH PARKING LOT WAS EMPTY AND NO ONE WAS AROUND. SOMEWHAT SURPRISINGLY, SHE HAD NO PLAN ONCE SHE FIGURED OUT ALL THE DOORS WERE LOCKED. ALL SHE HAD WAS A PHILLIPS SCREWDRIVER AND A PRAYER. SHE WAS COMPELLED TO SHARE THE PRAYER WITH ME:

PLEASE GOD, SHOW ME A WAY IN. WE JUST WANT TO FIGURE THIS OUT. AND I'D LIKE TO GET SOME SLEEP. I'M LIKE THE WALKING DEAD. AMEN.

698

A quick walk around the entire building yielded no better results. She was still locked out, and very soon the sun would be up over Wyoming. By 4:30 a.m., she was back in her car, discouraged and bleary-eyed. She thought seriously about heading for the hotel and crashing. No cell signal, no way in. A total waste of a thousand miles on the road.

How depressing.

And then poof! Just like that, her prayer was answered. A car pulled into the church parking lot at 4:45 a.m. An old guy stepped out of the car. He meandered, whistling an early morning tune, then unlocked the front door and went inside. Sarah stayed put as two more cars pulled up. It was like a crack-of-dawn convention at St. Mark's, and Sarah's spirits started to brighten.

"From the looks of it, this was some sort of early-bird-catches-the-worm Bible study," Sarah told me. "So I figured once they were all inside, the door would still be unlocked and I could sneak up into the tower."

She figured right. Really old people get up very early. It's like a curse or something. A few minutes later, as the sun was starting to rise, she crept through the morning shadows and into the church. Then she turned her camera on. Even I could hear the echo of voices and laughter drifting down a hallway as she turned and started walking. I could practically see the Styrofoam coffee cups, the folding metal chairs, and three old-timers gathered in a circle. She checked a couple of doors, both locked, then came to a stairway leading up.

"I knew the Ghost Room was upstairs, near the bell, so I just started hoofing it as quietly and as fast as I could," she explained, breathless with excitement. "The stairwell was dark, just a little light creeping in from the windows at the very top. About halfway up, there was a landing and an old door."

The door wasn't even shut all the way. It was open just a crack, and pushing it, the hinges creaked down the staircase. She stood stock-still, peering into the room, hoping no one had

HEARD THE SOUND. THE OPENING WAS BARELY BIG ENOUGH FOR SARAH TO FIT THROUGH IF SHE TURNED SIDEWAYS, AND ONCE SHE WAS INSIDE, THE NOISES PERSISTED. SHE FOUND HERSELF STANDING ON CREAKING FLOORBOARDS.

"TALK ABOUT A NOISY CHURCH," SHE CONCLUDED. "HAD TO BE ALL THREE OLD GUYS WERE HARD OF HEARING. BETWEEN THE DOOR AND THE FLOOR, I WAS MAKING QUITE A RACKET."

SHE SET THE CAMERA DOWN, FOUND THE FLOORBOARD SHE WAS SUPPOSED TO PULL UP, AND WENT TO WORK. SHE SAID THIS WAS THE LOUDEST THING SO FAR. NOTHING LIKE PRYING UP A PIECE OF FLOORING TO WAKE THE DEAD, BUT SHE WORKED QUICKLY AND NO ONE SEEMED TO TAKE ANY NOTICE OF WHAT SHE WAS DOING.

THEN SARAH HEARD SHUFFLING FOOTSTEPS COMING UP THE NARROW STAIRWAY.

WHAT HAPPENED NEXT SHE WOULDN'T SAY, BUT SHE GOT WHAT SHE'D COME FOR: UNDER THE FLOORBOARD, REACHING HER HAND INSIDE, A REEL OF FILM. THE APOSTLE WAS ABOUT TO SPEAK TO US ONCE MORE.

BUT THE APOSTLE WASN'T THE ONLY ONE WITH A MESSAGE FOR US.

No, it was far worse then that.

The ghost of Old Joe Bush had come up the stairs.

He'd paused outside the door, pushed it in a tad, then stopped.

Silence.

Followed by what?

SATURDAY, JULY 16, 7:20 A.M.

SARAH HUNG UP AFTER THAT. SHE WANTED TO SHOW ME EVERYTHING THAT HAD HAPPENED AND THOUGHT SHE'D NEED ABOUT AN HOUR TO PUT TOGETHER THE FOOTAGE. SHE HAD THE ANCIENT 8MM PROJECTOR WITH HER, WHICH SHE'D BROUGHT UP TO HER ROOM, SO CONVERTING THE APOSTLE MESSAGE TO VIDEO WOULD BE QUICK. SHE'D DO LIKE SHE HAD BEFORE, PROJECTING THE OLD FOOTAGE ONTO A WHITE SHEET WHILE SHE VIDEOTAPED IT.

AND SHE WAS GOING TO SEND ME A COPY OF HER ADVENTURE AT ST. MARK'S CHURCH.

I KNOW MY DAD WILL EXPECT ME OUT THE DOOR BY 7:45 A.M. IT'S SATURDAY, OUR BUSIEST DAY OF THE WEEK.

COME ON, SARAH, SEND ME SOMETHING. I'VE ONLY GOT TWENTY OR SO MINUTES. AFTER THAT I'LL BE LOCKED IN THE SHOP ALL DAY, WHERE IT MIGHT BE TOO BUSY TO SNEAK A LOOK ONLINE.

THE THOUGHT OF NOT SEEING WHAT SHE FOUND IS KILLING ME. I DON'T THINK I CAN GO ALL DAY WITHOUT KNOWING.

MAN, SHE MUST BE TIRED. MAYBE SHE FELL ASLEEP.

MY DAD JUST CALLED ME DOWNSTAIRS, BUT I FINALLY GOT AN EMAIL FROM SARAH. I YELLED DOWN THE STAIRS, TOLD MY DAD I'D BE RIGHT DOWN, AND READ HER NOTE.

Ryan,

I'm barely awake right now, so this is going to be superfast. Seeing the ghost of Old Joe Bush just about fried my brain. And the Apostle video is vintage weirdness, as expected. I posted both videos at the site and used osiris as the password.

The strangest part about what just happened?

I'm not afraid of Old Joe Bush anymore.

Me go sleep now.

S.

P.S. What's the clause? You holding out on me?

P.P.S. At the end of the video, be ready for a jolt when you look up. That's my only warning.

SARAHFINCHER.COM
Password:
OSIRIS

SATURDAY, JULY 16, 7:45 A.M.

OSIRIS: GOD OF DEATH AND THE UNDERWORLD. VERY NICE.

IF YOU ASK ME, WHATEVER FOUND SARAH IN ST. MARK'S CHURCH IS JUST AS SCARY AS EVER. AND SHE'S RIGHT ABOUT THE APOSTLE — THAT GUY IS SO OUT THERE. WATCHING HIM NEVER GETS OLD.

BUT THERE WAS SOMETHING ELSE, SOMETHING I HAVE TO CONTACT HER ABOUT. SARAH DIDN'T JUST FIND A REEL OF OLD FILM UNDER THE FLOORBOARDS IN THE GHOST ROOM. SHE FOUND A GLASS VIAL OF LIQUID, TOO. AND DO YOU KNOW WHAT WAS SCRAWLED ON THE LABEL? TWO WORDS.

THE CLAUSE.

AND BELOW THOSE TWO WORDS, FOUR MORE:

WHEN THERE IS ONE.

DAD JUST YELLED UP AGAIN. BETTER NOT LET HIM COME UP HERE.

Saturday, July 16, 3:00 p.m.

My dad let me off early after I begged for some time on the river. I don't really want to go fishing, but it's a good cover for what I need to do.

First a few notes, then I'm getting on my mountain bike and heading downstream.

I need to get a message to Fitz, and the only way that's going to happen is at the big tree in the clearing.

Okay, so a few notes before I go.

1) I don't agree with Sarah about the ghost of Old Joe Bush. Something seemed wrong this time, for sure, like Henry or possessed Henry or whoever was having some trouble breathing. But that doesn't make him any less dangerous. And seeing him reach down at her like that really bothered me. Still, I wasn't there, so I don't know what it felt like. Sarah seems to think we shouldn't do anything but keep going. Either her nerves have

707

turned to steel or she's lost her marbles, because that dude is every bit as hair-raising as he ever was, if you ask me. It is strange, though, how he never seems to come after us. He seems to be watching us, maybe even trying to help. Odd. I'll admit there is a big part of me that feels bad about not telling my dad we're seeing his old buddy Henry out in the world acting like he's completely lost it. And there's the fact that, technically, he's a fugitive. When I think about things like that, I wonder how in the world we ever got in so deep. It's like we've fallen under a spell and we can't wake up until we reach the end.

2) I have to call Sarah and leave her a message. She'll be sleeping for another hour or two, but she needs to send me that vial of liquid. She's out west, so if she can just get it in the overnight mail before she leaves, it should arrive on Monday. I have a feeling I know what it's

FOR, BUT I CAN'T SAY FOR SURE. EITHER WAY, THAT VIAL OF LIQUID NEEDS TO MAKE ITS WAY TO SKELETON CREEK PRONTO.

3) THE A-POSTLE VIDEO PROVIDED US WITH THE FIRST OF THREE LETTERS WE'RE SEARCHING FOR. NO WORDS ON THE CARDS THIS TIME AROUND, JUST SINGLE LETTERS. THE FIRST IS AN A. SO NOW THE RAVEN PUZZLE LOOKS LIKE THIS:

4) It's a little unnerving seeing that secret book in the Apostle's hand. The fact that the very same book is now in my backpack makes me feel like I've got a bull's-eye on my back with the shape of a Raven's head. He knows I have it. I can feel it. It's only a matter of time before he comes looking for it.

Phone call to Sarah made, told her to overnight the vial today — check.
Note to Fitz written — check.
Patch kit packed — check (there are a billion ways to get a flat tire on the river trail).

Ready to roll.
Here's hoping I make it back before dark without any unexpected encounters with the Raven.

SATURDAY, JULY 16, 8:16 P.M.

MY SENSE OF DIRECTION IS WACKED WHEN I GET ON THE RIVER. LET'S BE HONEST: I HAVE NO SENSE OF DIRECTION. <u>EVER.</u> YOU'D THINK I'D KNOW THE WILDERNESS LIKE THE BACK OF MY HAND, BUT IT'S ALWAYS BEEN A WEAKNESS OF MINE. I THINK YOU'RE EITHER BORN WITH A SENSE OF DIRECTION OR YOU'RE NOT. FOR ME, NORTH, EAST, SOUTH, AND WEST ARE LIKE A FOREIGN LANGUAGE. IF SOMEONE WALKED UP TO ME RIGHT NOW AND SAID, "POINT NORTH," I'D SAY, "YOU MEAN LEFT, RIGHT, OR TOWARD THE MOON? GIVE ME A CLUE HERE." I'M THAT BAD. IN FACT, WHEN I GET OLD, LIKE FIFTY, THEY'LL SERIOUSLY NEED TO TAKE AWAY MY CAR KEYS. I'LL BE JUST THE KIND OF GEEZER THAT WILL DRIVE OUT INTO THE COUNTRY AND END UP ON A DIRT ROAD IN NEVADA BY SUNRISE.

ANYWAY, THE POINT OF ALL THAT IS TO SAY, WOW, IT TOOK ME PRACTICALLY FOREVER TO FIND THAT STUPID TREE AGAIN. I ABANDONED MY BIKE AND WADED ACROSS THE RIVER, WHICH IS RUNNING ABOUT THREE FEET DEEP AT ITS HIGHEST RIGHT NOW. THE ENTIRE TIME I KEPT REPEATING TO MYSELF, <u>WHY DID YOU BRING THE GHOST BOOK WITH YOU?</u> DON'T SLIP

AND FALL IN THE WATER, YOU IDIOT! WHICH WAY IS SOUTH?

FROM THE TIME I CROSSED THE RIVER, TO THE MOMENT I FOUND THE CLEARING WITH THE MONSTER TREE, AT LEAST TWO HOURS PASSED. THEN I GOT SO NERVOUS ABOUT CROSSING THE OPEN SPACE ALONE. I STOOD IN THE TREES FOR ANOTHER TWENTY MINUTES TRYING TO GET MY NERVE UP. I HAD A STRONG FEELING THE RAVEN, HOODED AND CARRYING THAT OUTRAGEOUS AX, WAS GOING TO COME RUNNING DOWN THE RAVINE AND CHASE ME THROUGH THE WOODS.

WHEN I FINALLY DID GET TO THE TREE, I FOUND THE PLACE WHERE THE RAVEN HAD BEEN CHOPPING. IT WAS A NICE BIG DIVOT, AND TO MY SURPRISE, THERE WAS ALREADY A NOTE IN THERE. I WAS BEYOND FREAKED OUT STANDING IN THE OPEN, LIKE I WAS IN THE MIDDLE OF THE SCHOOL CAFETERIA WEARING NOTHING BUT MY UNDERWEAR. SO INSTEAD OF READING THE NOTE LIKE A NORMAL PERSON, I GRABBED IT, STUFFED MY LETTER TO FITZ INTO THE TREE, AND RAN LIKE A MANIAC. I DON'T THINK I SCREAMED WHILE I RAN, BUT I SORT OF BLACKED OUT DURING THE WHOLE RUNNING-AWAY THING, SO I MIGHT HAVE. I DIDN'T STOP UNTIL I GOT TO THE RIVER,

WHERE I REALIZED HOW OVERHEATED AND THIRSTY I WAS. AN HOUR OF RUNNING THROUGH THE WOODS WILL DO THAT TO A GUY. THAT, AND I HAD ABOUT A THOUSAND SCRATCHES AND BRUISES FROM HEAD TO TOE FROM BUSHES AND LOW-HANGING BRANCHES. THOSE THINGS STING WHEN YOU CROSS A RIVER.

NOW I'M SITTING HERE WRITING ALL THIS DOWN BECAUSE, SERIOUSLY, I'M EXHAUSTED. I NEED A BREAK OR I'LL NEVER MAKE IT OUT ALIVE.

WHEN I GOT TO THE OTHER SIDE OF THE RIVER, I FELT BETTER, LIKE I WAS OUT OF THE RAVEN'S DOMAIN AND HE COULDN'T TOUCH ME ANYMORE. STILL, THERE'S REALLY NO REASON FOR ME TO FEEL COMFORTED BECAUSE THE RIVER IS BETWEEN ME AND THE GIANT TREE. BUT FOR SOME REASON I DO FEEL CALMER NOW THAT THE TASK IS DONE.

FOUR HOURS. THAT'S HOW LONG IT TOOK ME TO GET A NOTE TO FITZ, AND I'M STILL NOT OUT OF THE WOODS YET. ON A GOOD DAY, WHEN I'M NOT TOTALLY WINDED, IT TAKES ME AN HOUR AND A HALF TO RIDE BACK UP THE TRAIL FROM HERE TO SKELETON CREEK. BUT SITTING HERE BY MY BIKE, I CAN TELL IT'S GOING TO TAKE ME A LOT LONGER. THE SUN IS ALREADY OFF

THE WATER AND I'M — WHAT? A-N HOUR FROM
SUNSET?

Not a good situation.

I should be up and moving, but I just finished a
harrowing four-hour journey and my muscles
are cramping up. Just a little more rest.

Here's what Fitz wrote to me:

Ryan,
    If you get this, you should know my dad's been talking
about moving on. He says there's no reason to stay here
much longer. He keeps talking about one more thing he has
to do, but he won't say what it is.
    I hope it doesn't have anything to do with you.
    I also hope I get to see you again, but I have a
feeling this is good-bye.
    Your friend,
    Fitz

Sort of a sad note. I feel bad for Fitz.

My note to him (I made a copy before I left
it in the tree):

Fitz,

Sarah found a vial of some sort of liquid. She's mailing it to me and I should have it Monday. I think it might be useful on "the clause," but I don't know for sure. My guess? That thing has some sort of invisible ink and whatever is in this vial will unlock it. Besides "the clause," the vial had four other words on it: "when there is one." Confusing. Does it mean "when there's a clause, the vial comes into play" or does it mean something totally different, like "when there's a number one"? Typical Crossbones doublespeak.

I'm going to leave the vial at your old trailer under the front steps. Whoever owns it hasn't rented it out again, so it's vacant. Come into town and get it late Monday night if you can.

I HOPE YOU'VE GOT SOMETHING TO READ UP THERE. MUST BE BORING.
RYAN

8:26 P.M. No MORE MR. LAZY. I GOTTA GET THE HECK OUT OF THESE WOODS AND FAST.

TIME TO RIDE.

SUN IS JUST ABOUT DOWN AND I'M SO TIRED I CAN BARELY MOVE MY LEGS. A GOOD HOUR TO GO. I USED A BUNGEE CORD TO ATTACH MY FLASHLIGHT TO THE HANDLEBARS SO I CAN SEE THE TRAIL. I HAVE THIS AWFUL FEELING I'M BEING FOLLOWED, AND WHATEVER IS FOLLOWING ME IS JUST WAITING FOR DARKNESS TO SETTLE IN. IT'S LOUD ON MY BIKE — THE SOUND OF THE WHEELS ON DIRT AND ROCKS — SO I KEEP STOPPING, LISTENING FOR SOMETHING BEHIND ME.

ONE THING I DIDN'T WRITE DOWN BEFORE THAT I SHOULD NOW. IT'S WHAT GOT ME ON MY BIKE, PEDDLING LIKE THE WIND.

ACROSS THE RIVER, STANDING ON THE SHORE.

THE RAVEN WAS WATCHING ME.

I'M ONE FLAT TIRE FROM NOT MAKING IT OUT OF THE WOODS ALIVE.

Saturday, July 16, 11:25 p.m.

Is it really 11:25 p.m.? How did that happen? How did I lose an entire afternoon and night delivering a note?

About a half hour after my last entry, I bumped into my dad coming down the trail. Scared me so bad I nearly rode right into a tree. He was relieved to find me, to say the least. All I can say is I'm glad I brought my fly box and a pack rod with me, or I'd have had zero alibi for why I was out on the trail so late. As it was, I covered pretty good.

"Your mother is worried sick," he started in. "And the mayor is about to send for the National Guard. What were you thinking?"

I went on and on about how amazing the fishing was — beyond any day I'd ever fished in my life, how I'd completely lost track of time. How sorry I was.

I felt about as small as an ant. I hated lying to him like that, but even more, I knew it was a lie I would get away with. I was using his weakness against him.

718

"That good, huh?" he said, a twinkle in his eye. He was already halfway to forgiving me, staring into the dark in the direction of the water.

Then I did the unthinkable. I held my arms out as if I were showing the size of the biggest one I'd caught, about two feet long.

"No way," he said.

I just nodded, smiled weakly, and started walking my bike next to him.

"What'd you catch him on? How long did it take to reel him in? Rainbow or brown trout?"

We talked about the mythical whale fish all the way back home as I kept feeling worse and worse. I'd promised myself I wouldn't keep telling whoppers, and there I was telling a fish story the size of Texas.

My dad smoothed things over with my mom, but she was so happy to see me it didn't take much. And the mayor, who had staked out our front porch, was so relieved he hugged me.

Yuck.

A shower, some Band-Aids, and a plate of potato salad have given me a second wind I didn't

EXPECT. ALL NIGHT LONG, I'VE BEEN THINKING OF SARAH AND HOW SHE MUST BE TRYING TO CONTACT ME. BACK IN CELL RANGE, I'D FOUND A STRING OF THREE TEXT MESSAGES. SHE'D ALSO TRIED CALLING TWICE, BUT HADN'T LEFT A MESSAGE.

4:06 P.M.
YOU DIDN'T PICK UP, SO YOU MUST STILL BE WORKING. I'M ON THE ROAD. LOOKS LIKE 1:00 A.M. AT SPOOKSVILLE IF I'M LUCKY.

8:57 P.M.
PASSING THROUGH KANSAS. FLAT. BORED. WHERE ARE YOU?

10:29 P.M.
AHEAD OF SCHEDULE, SHOULD BE THERE A LITTLE AFTER MIDNIGHT. HOPEFULLY, I'LL HAVE A SIGNAL! NOT THAT YOU'LL BE THERE TO PICK UP.

AS FAR AS SARAH'S PARENTS KNEW, SHE WAS STILL SNOOZING IN CHEYENNE, WYOMING, AND WOULDN'T

LEAVE FOR THE NEXT STOP ON HER HAUNTED TOUR UNTIL MORNING. IT WAS ALL GETTING A LITTLE HARD TO FOLLOW FROM SKELETON CREEK, BUT I UNDERSTOOD THE BASICS.

SARAH WAS STAYING WHERE HER PARENTS HAD TOLD HER TO STAY, BUT DOING IT TWELVE HOURS IN ADVANCE OF WHEN SHE WAS SUPPOSED TO DO IT. IT WAS THIS SWITCH IN TIME THAT ALLOWED HER TO VISIT THE HAUNTED LOCATIONS AT NIGHT, WHEN NO ONE WAS AROUND. SHE WAS SCHEDULED TO ARRIVE AT A SUPER 8 IN JOPLIN, MISSOURI, IN ABOUT FIFTEEN HOURS, BUT SHE'D BE THERE WAY EARLY. IT WAS A PERFECT HALFWAY POINT, A CHANCE FOR HER TO TAKE A NICE LONG REST BEFORE CONTINUING ON TO SAVANNAH, WHERE HER PARENTS, AGAINST THEIR BETTER JUDGMENT, HAD AGREED TO PAY FOR A ROOM AT THE 17 HUNDRED 90.

I TEXTED SARAH BACK, HOPING SHE WOULDN'T TRY TO READ IT WHILE DRIVING, AND WAITED.

I WAS NOT FALLING ASLEEP THIS TIME. I PUT ON SOME MUSIC, SURFED THE WEB, WAITED.

FOUR MINUTES LATER, SHE CALLED.

"Ryan! Where have you been?"

"Did you pull over?" Safety first. The last thing she needed to be doing was driving and talking on her phone. It was stressful enough knowing she was out there all alone.

"Yeah, I pulled over. Don't try to change the subject."

I explained everything as fast as I could, then asked her if she'd gotten my message and sent the vial.

"It's on the way. I even paid extra to make sure it arrives on Monday. You owe me."

She also said she'd thought about pulling an Alice in Wonderland and drinking whatever was inside, but when she twisted the top open she'd changed her mind.

"Would have been fun shrinking down to the size of a water bottle, but whatever is in there doesn't smell too good. More likely I'd have grown a third arm out of my forehead."

Thanks, Sarah, now all I can think about is

MY BEST FRIEND WITH AN ARM STICKING OUT OF HER FACE. GHASTLY.

I TOLD HER TO WATCH THE DIRECTIONS CAREFULLY, BECAUSE THERE WAS A VERY SPECIFIC PLACE SHE HAD TO PARK.

"I KNOW THE PLACE — IT'S CALLED THE MIDDLE OF NOWHERE," SHE JOKED. "CAN'T MISS IT."

SARAH LAUGHED, THEN TOLD ME SHE WAS HIGH-FIVING THE ARM STICKING OUT OF HER FOREHEAD, WHICH SHE'D NAMED JUDITH.

SHE HAD TO FOLLOW DIRECTIONS OFF THE HIGHWAY, DOWN A TWO LANE, ONTO A DIRT ROAD, AND INTO JUST THE RIGHT SPOT, WHERE THE ROAD WOULD RISE BEFORE HER:

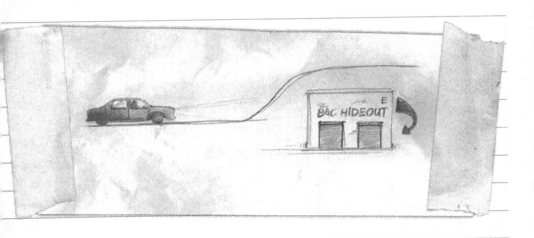

"HOPEFULLY, WHEN YOU GET THERE, YOU'LL SEE A BUILDING SHAPED LIKE THE ONE IN THE PICTURE. THAT'LL BE THE HIDEOUT FOR B AND C."

EVEN SAYING IT MADE ME SCRATCH MY HEAD. THE HIDEOUT FOR B AND C? IF THIS MYSTERY DOESN'T SOLVE ITSELF, I DIDN'T KNOW WHAT WE'RE GOING TO DO.

I TOLD SARAH ABOUT DROPPING THE NOTE TO FITZ, AND SHE SAID SHE'D TRY TO CALL WHEN SHE ARRIVED AT THE SPOOKSVILLE TRIANGLE, WHICH SHE GUESSED WOULD BE IN ABOUT AN HOUR.

THEN SHE SAID SHE WAS GOING TO LET JUDITH DRIVE, AND HUNG UP.

724

SUNDAY, JULY 17, 12:25 A.M.

AN HOUR IS A LONG TIME WHEN YOU'VE HAD THE KIND OF DAY I JUST HAD. I'M WORRIED I'M GOING TO FALL ASLEEP AGAIN. I'M GOING TO DREAM OF THE RAVEN CHASING ME THROUGH THE WOODS. HE'S GOING TO CATCH ME, AND WHEN I FINALLY SEE INSIDE THAT DARK HOOD OF HIS, THERE WILL BE A BLACK CLAW STICKING OUT OF HIS HEAD. THE BLACK CLAW WILL GRAB MY FACE AND LIFT ME OFF THE GROUND.

OKAY, I'M WIDE AWAKE NOW. I DON'T THINK THERE'S MUCH CHANCE OF ME GETTING ANY SLEEP TONIGHT WITH A DREAM LIKE THAT WAITING FOR ME.

IT'S PAST MIDNIGHT. SHE SHOULD BE GETTING INTO POSITION.

I HAVE TO REMEMBER TO SET MY WEBCAM TO RECORD AGAIN.

I THINK I JUST FELL ASLEEP WITH MY EYES OPEN, BECAUSE MY HEAD SNAPPED BACK AND I ALMOST FELL OUT OF MY CHAIR.

COME ON, SARAH. HAVE A SIGNAL. CALL ME. SOON.

Sunday, July 17, 12:35 a.m.

It's Sunday in Skeleton Creek, dark outside my window, and the world just changed in a flash.

Everything is different now. I'm not sure if I'm sad, relieved, worried, or scared. Maybe I'm all those things at once.

I'm going to relay this exactly as it happened, because there's a real possibility I'll be asked about it someday. I want to make sure I have it written down exactly as it occurred.

Sarah called me from the Spooksville Triangle at 12:27 a.m. She was parked right where she needed to be, where the desolate road rose in front of her.

"It's freakin' <u>dark</u> out here, Ryan," she said. "If I turn off my headlights it's pitch-black. How am I supposed to find a building if I can't see it?"

I thought about this for a second, then asked her if she had a flashlight.

"Of course I have a flashlight. I'm a girl alone in the dark!"

Right, of course she has a flashlight. So I asked her how she felt about getting out of the

CAR AND POINTING THE LIGHT ALONG THE SIDES OF
THE ROAD.

"DID I MENTION THE PART ABOUT IT BEING PITCH-
BLACK AND TOTALLY SPOOKY OUT HERE?"

"YOU DID."

I WANTED TO TELL HER I'D RIDDEN MY MOUNTAIN
BIKE AT NIGHT INTO THE LAIR OF THE RAVEN. I WANTED
TO TELL HER ABOUT THE CLAW DREAM I'D IMAGINED,
ABOUT THE GROVE AND THE TREE AND ALL THE
TERRIBLE, SCARY THINGS IN MY LIFE. BUT WHAT GOOD
WAS THAT GOING TO DO? SHE HAD HER OWN FEARS TO
FACE, AND TELLING HER ABOUT MINE WOULDN'T SOLVE
ANYTHING.

AND THAT'S WHEN IT HAPPENED.

THAT'S WHEN MY OLD WORLD CAME TO AN END
AND A NEW WORLD BEGAN.

"RYAN?" SARAH WHISPERED. "DON'T YOU DARE
HANG UP."

"I WON'T."

"YOU KNOW THAT LEGEND ABOUT THE LIGHT THAT
PEOPLE SEE DANCING OVER THE RISE IN THE ROAD?"

"I DO. IT'S THE LADY WITH THE LAMP, LOOKING FOR
HER LOST KID. WHY DO YOU ASK?"

"Because I just turned my headlights on. I don't see a light. I see something else."

"What do you see?"

There was a long pause as Sarah reached around and locked all the doors.

"What's going on, Sarah? Talk to me!"

"He's coming down the road."

I wanted to ask her who. But that would have been stupid. I knew who it was without her having to say.

"Get out of there! Just drive!" I yelled.

"I can't move, Ryan. He's coming for me. He's coming down the hill on that shattered leg of his."

I yelled for her to start the car and drive, then realized how stupid yelling was. What if my parents heard me? It was after midnight and they were both sound sleepers. There was my door — closed — and their door, also closed. But I'd yelled pretty loudly.

"I'm getting out of the car," Sarah said. "Don't worry. It's all going to be okay."

I WAS ON THE VERGE OF A TOTAL MELTDOWN, WHISPERING AS LOUDLY AS I FELT I COULD, "GET BACK IN THE CAR! GET OUT OF THERE!"

I HEARD THE DOOR OPEN AND SHUT. I HEARD FOOTSTEPS ON A DIRT ROAD.

SARAH? WHAT'S HAPPENING? SARAH!

WAS SHE POSSESSED? HAD SHE GONE INSANE WITH FEAR?

"RYAN," SHE WHISPERED.

"YEAH?" MY VOICE WAS TREMBLING. I WAS SURE HENRY OR THE GHOST OR WHATEVER HAD FOLLOWED MY FRIEND HALFWAY ACROSS THE COUNTRY HAD FINALLY GOTTEN HER.

BUT THEN SHE SAID SOMETHING I DIDN'T EXPECT.

"THE GHOST OF OLD JOE BUSH JUST DIED IN MY ARMS."

SUNDAY, JULY 17, 1:25 A.M.

IT'S FUNNY HOW THE MIND WORKS. AN HOUR AGO I WAS
SO TIRED I COULD BARELY KEEP MY EYES OPEN. NOW I
FEEL LIKE I'VE DOWNED FIVE CUPS OF COFFEE WITH A
RED BULL CHASER.

HENRY IS DEAD.

I HAD TO WRITE THAT DOWN, JUST ONCE, TO MAKE
IT REAL.

AND IF HENRY IS DEAD, THEN SO IS THE GHOST OF
OLD JOE BUSH. THERE WAS NEVER ONE WITHOUT THE
OTHER, AND NOW BOTH ARE LAID TO REST.

SARAH VIDEOTAPED THE ENTIRE ENCOUNTER, WHICH
SHE SAYS WAS ONE OF THE MOST HARROWING
EXPERIENCES OF HER LIFE. SEEING HIM IN THE BEAMS OF
HER HEADLIGHTS, HIS FIGURE COMING UP OVER THE ROAD,
WAS ALMOST MORE THAN SHE COULD TAKE. SHE SAYS
SHE HAD HER HAND ON THE KEY BUT COULDN'T BRING
HERSELF TO START THE CAR UP AND DRIVE STRAIGHT
AHEAD. THERE WAS A MOMENT WHERE SHE'D THOUGHT
SHE COULD DO IT, DRIVE OVER HENRY AND BE DONE
WITH IT, BUT THE MOMENT PASSED.

"WHY?" I ASKED HER. "WHY DIDN'T YOU RUN
WHEN YOU SAW HIM COMING OVER THE HILL?"

"Because he was reaching out to me, like before, at St. Mark's. And I realized then that he wasn't trying to reach out and grab me. He was trying to reach out and give me something. And there was something else. He was dying."

I asked her how she knew this and she said I would have known, too. He was moving so slowly, dragging his destroyed leg, wobbling down the hill. It was menacing in a ghostly sort of way, but she knew, deep down inside, that it wasn't a ghost at all. It was a man, a broken man.

She said I'd need to watch the video for myself to see and hear all that had happened. It was just her way to show me, not tell me. It was the only way she knew how to share the really big moments in her life. I felt a little sad for her then, because I understood what she meant. I can never tell anyone how I really feel. I always have to write it down.

And so I'll write down how I feel right now, since I won't be able to tell anyone tomorrow or the day after that or ever.

I'M SAD, IF YOU WANT TO KNOW THE TRUTH. SAD THAT HENRY WANDERED THE COUNTRY ALL ALONE, SICK AND BROKEN. I'VE ALWAYS HAD A PROBLEM WITH THAT SORT OF THING, PEOPLE BEING ALL ALONE IN THE WORLD, NO MATTER HOW BAD THEY ARE. IN MY DARKEST MOMENTS I IMAGINE MYSELF OLD AND ALL ALONE, STARING AT A TV SCREEN, WISHING IT WOULD ALL JUST COME TO AN END. MY HEART BREAKS JUST THINKING ABOUT IT.

I'M ALSO FEELING A DEEP SENSE OF RELIEF. I NOW REALIZE THAT SOMETIMES YOU DON'T KNOW HOW STRESSED OUT YOU ARE UNTIL AFTER IT'S PASSED. AFTER THE BAD PERSON IN YOUR LIFE IS GONE. AFTER THE BAD TEST IS OVER, AFTER SOME GIANT BADNESS MOVES OFF LIKE A STORM CLOUD. I DIDN'T KNOW HOW SCARED I WAS UNTIL AN HOUR AGO WHEN MY FEAR DIED RIGHT ALONG WITH THE GHOST OF OLD JOE BUSH.

HE CAN'T GET ME ANYMORE.

AND, MORE IMPORTANT, HE CAN'T GET SARAH ANYMORE.

HE'S GONE. THEY BOTH ARE. THE GHOST OF OLD JOE BUSH AND HENRY DON'T HAVE ANY POWER OVER ME ANY LONGER.

That part of my life is now in the past.

It would have been nice if they hadn't been replaced by the Raven, but I'll take what progress I can get.

I heard the same new sound in Sarah's voice, too.

"I know where the hideout for B and C is," she said.

"You're driving and talking on the phone," I said, ever the safety tzar of our lives.

"It's a dirt road after midnight. The only thing I'm going to hit is a cow."

"I feel sorry for the cow."

I asked her how she knew where the hideout was.

"He showed me."

It appeared that in the end, Henry wanted the same thing we did: to follow the Apostle all the way to the end. And that's exactly what we're going to do.

"He hasn't been reaching out to grab me," she said. "He's been trying to give me a message. Wanna hear it?"

I DID, BUT THE THOUGHT OF SARAH TALKING ON HER CELL PHONE AND READING A NOTE WHILE DRIVING DOWN A DIRT ROAD WAS MORE THAN I COULD PUT UP WITH.

"WHOA, COW!" SHE SCREAMED.

ALWAYS WITH THE JOKES, THIS GIRL.

SHE STOPPED THE CAR AT THE DESERTED TURN LEADING BACK TO THE HIGHWAY AND READ FROM THE NOTE SHE'D FOUND CLUTCHED BETWEEN HIS DEAD FINGERS. IT'S SHORT, SO IT WASN'T VERY HARD TO WRITE DOWN IN MY JOURNAL. IT WAS RANDOM, LIKE HE'D WRITTEN A LINE, THEN WAITED A WEEK TO WRITE THE NEXT — NOT SO MUCH A LETTER AS A STREAM OF UNCONNECTED THOUGHTS.

HERE IT IS, AS SARAH READ IT TO ME:

IT'S TIME TO GO, ME AND OLD JOE.

B AND C IS BONNIE AND CLYDE.

INVOKE THE CLAUSE!

I'M SORRY FOR ALL HE'S DONE.

SORRIER THAN YOU KNOW.

JOE

I've thought about what these words mean, and here are my conclusions:

— First and foremost, Henry had lost or was losing his mind. The note starts out as if it's Henry writing about him and the ghost of Old Joe Bush, and ends with Joe saying Henry is sorry. It's not clear to me Henry knew who he was at the end. As we'd suspected, something about the trauma of all those years guarding the dredge and playing the part of a ghost had gotten lodged too deeply in his brain. The guilt of all his past sins exposed and the great fall that shattered his leg only served to deepen his madness. Old Joe Bush had his leg pulled through the gears, Henry shattered his own falling in the same dredge. My guess? He was bleeding inside, needed a doctor but wouldn't turn himself in, and found his body and mind had turned against him. I think, in the end, he was neither Henry nor the ghost of Old Joe Bush. He was both.

— I BELIEVE TO THIS DAY THAT HENRY WAS A LIAR AND A THIEF, BUT I DON'T BELIEVE HE EVER INTENDED TO KILL ANYONE. HE WAS RESPONSIBLE FOR THE DEATHS OF THE APOSTLE AND DR. WATTS, AND HE NEARLY GOT ME KILLED. BUT I HAVE PERSONAL EXPERIENCE WITH THIS GUY, AND I'M TELLING YOU, THEY WERE ALL ACCIDENTS. THE BIGGEST PROBLEM HENRY HAD WAS BEING SOLD OUT TO THE CROSSBONES, WHICH MADE HIM DO THINGS HE WASN'T WIRED TO DO. I THINK HE TRIED TO SCARE PEOPLE INTO DOING WHAT HE NEEDED THEM TO DO BECAUSE HE DIDN'T HAVE IT IN HIM TO KILL IN COLD BLOOD.

— I THINK HENRY WAS TRYING TO HELP US AS ATONEMENT FOR ALL HIS SINS. THAT'S WHY HE RAN, WHY HE WOULDN'T TURN HIMSELF IN. HE PROTECTED SARAH ON HER JOURNEY WEST, EVEN AS HE WAS INCHING CLOSER TO DEATH'S DOOR. HE GAVE ME THE RAVEN PUZZLE IN THE PORTLAND UNDERGROUND. AND NOW HE'D GIVEN US THE SOLUTION TO THE B AND C HIDEOUT: BONNIE AND CLYDE. THE FAMOUS BANK ROBBERS FROM THE 1930s. WE SHOULD HAVE BEEN SMART ENOUGH TO

FIGURE THAT OUT, BECAUSE BONNIE AND CLYDE'S HIDEOUT WAS IN JOPLIN, MISSOURI, PART OF THE SPOOKSVILLE TRIANGLE.

— AND FINALLY, HE ASKS US TO INVOKE "THE CLAUSE." THIS STATEMENT IS A MYSTERY, BUT I THINK THE VIAL OF LIQUID ON ITS WAY TO SKELETON CREEK IS GOING TO SHOW US WHAT IT MEANS. HE WANTS US TO INVOKE "THE CLAUSE," SO THAT'S WHAT WE'RE GOING TO DO. I HOPE IT DOESN'T SET OFF A CROSSBONES NUCLEAR BOMB OR SOMETHING.

MY LAST WORDS ON THIS: HENRY HAD TO BE IN A LOT OF PAIN. HE LIVED A LIE HIS WHOLE LIFE AND HE WAS WANDERING THE EARTH ALONE AT THE END. HE TRIED TO MAKE THINGS RIGHT. AND NOW HE'S GONE, SOON TO BE FORGOTTEN. ALL IN ALL, THE GUY PAID A HEAVY PRICE.

REST IN PEACE.

SUNDAY, JULY 17, 1:40 A.M.

WE AGREED THAT I WOULD USE AN ANONYMOUS EMAIL ACCOUNT TO SEND IN AN ALERT WHILE SARAH CHECKED INTO HER HOTEL AND KEPT A LOW PROFILE. EVERYONE IN SKELETON CREEK HAD BEEN GIVEN AN EMAIL ADDRESS TO USE IF THEY STUMBLED ONTO ANYTHING THAT MIGHT LEAD TO FINDING HENRY, SO I KNEW JUST WHERE TO SEND IT. TOOK ME ABOUT A MINUTE TO CREATE A BOGUS GMAIL ACCOUNT AND ANOTHER MINUTE OR TWO TO TYPE IN WHAT I WANTED TO SAY.

There's a dead guy at the Spooksville Triangle in Missouri. Look it up online. You can't miss him. He's lying in the middle of the road. I think it's that crazy guy from Skeleton Creek people have been talking about. Anonymous.

WITH ALL THE OTHER ACTION FLYING AROUND SKELETON CREEK, I WAS SURE THIS NEWS WOULD MAKE IT TO THE MAYOR'S OFFICE IN NO TIME FLAT. BY MORNING, HE'D BE KNOCKING ON MY DOOR WITH NEWS OF HENRY'S DEATH. IT WOULD BE BITTERSWEET FOR

MY DAD, BUT IT WOULD ALSO ALLOW HIM TO REST EASIER KNOWING AN UNSEEN THREAT AGAINST HIS FAMILY HAD DEPARTED THE PLANET.

SARAH IS GOING TO HEAD FOR THE HOTEL IN JOPLIN, MISSOURI, AND CRASH FOR THE NIGHT. SHE'LL SLEEP LATE AND BOOK THE ROOM FOR A SECOND NIGHT, USING HER OWN MONEY. SOMETIME DURING THAT TWO-DAY BREAK, SHE'LL GO TO BONNIE AND CLYDE'S HIDEOUT AND FIND WHAT THE APOSTLE LEFT BEHIND.

HER PARENTS ARE GOING TO HEAR ABOUT HENRY FOR SURE. HOPEFULLY, THAT WON'T PUT AN END TO HER STOPS RIGHT AS WE'RE COMING TO THE FINAL LEG OF OUR JOURNEY.

Sunday, July 17, 4:05 p.m.

As I'd suspected, it was the mayor who delivered the news. About an hour ago, he landed on our front porch, where my mom and dad were reading the paper. I was inside, napping on the couch, when my mom called me out to join them.

"They found Henry," said Mayor Blake. "He's gone."

My mom seemed the most shook up at first, sitting down and staring at the old painted boards on our porch. She'd always liked Henry, and never really could bring herself to fully believe all the bad things he'd done.

"Where?" my dad asked. He, too, was moved by the news. "Where" was the only word he could muster.

"It's the strangest thing," the mayor continued. "He was out in the middle of nowhere. Someplace called the Spooksville Triangle on the border of Kansas and Missouri. What he was doing out there, I have no idea."

"How'd he die?" I asked, curious about whether or not they'd be searching for foul play.

740

The mayor said they didn't know for sure, but that it appeared Henry had never gotten medical attention after the fall in the dredge. His leg was bleeding internally, and he'd suffered a severe concussion.

"It was really just a matter of time," he concluded.

I couldn't tell how my dad was taking the news. He's a quiet guy by nature, especially so when bad things happen.

I ventured an important question.

"Who knows about this?"

The mayor could not have given me a better answer.

"I was just coming to that. The investigation is ongoing, for reasons I don't fully understand. In any case, the authorities would like us to keep this quiet for a few days until they can make an announcement. It would seem Henry had a complicated life both here and back east."

He went on to tell us that we were only being told because of all the things about Henry that were connected to our family. The

AUTHORITIES FIGURED WE DESERVED TO KNOW THERE WAS NO LONGER A MADMAN ON THE LOOSE.

IF ONLY THEY KNEW ABOUT THE AX-WIELDING RAVEN LIVING IN THE WOODS OUTSIDE SKELETON CREEK. OR MAYBE THE RAVEN IS EXACTLY WHY THEY DON'T WANT TO GO PUBLIC WITH THE NEWS JUST YET. MAYBE THEY'RE TRYING TO FLUSH OUT THE REALLY BAD GUY, AND LETTING HIM THINK HENRY IS STILL ALIVE HAS SOME PURPOSE.

EITHER WAY, IT'S EXCEPTIONALLY GOOD NEWS. I WAS LYING ON THE COUCH ALL MORNING THINKING OF HOW WE WERE EVER GOING TO KEEP SARAH ON THE ROAD ONCE HER PARENTS FOUND OUT ABOUT HENRY BEING IN THE SAME PLACE SHE WAS. THEY'D FLIP OUT FOR SURE. THEY'D MAKE HER DRIVE STRAIGHT HOME, NO MORE MAKING DOCUMENTARIES ABOUT SPOOKY PLACES. SHE'D NEVER GET TO SAVANNAH OR MONTICELLO, AND THE APOSTLE'S FINAL MESSAGE MIGHT BE HIDDEN FOREVER.

AS I GOT UP TO GO TO MY ROOM AND CALL SARAH, I HEARD MAYOR BLAKE TALKING TO MY PARENTS ABOUT HENRY. HE WAS ALREADY SPINNING IT INTO HIS PR MACHINE.

742

"I'D LIKE TO SEE IF WE CAN GET HIM BURIED HERE IN TOWN, IF YOU ALL DON'T MIND."

Another stop in the evolving Skeleton Creek tourist trap.

Yippee.

SUNDAY, JULY 17, 4:24 P.M.

Just called Sarah, but she didn't pick up. I'm sure she's catching up on her sleep, but I can't help worrying about her. I left her a voice message about word of Henry's death reaching Skeleton Creek, but that it was an open investigation not to be discussed outside of my own family.

With any luck at all, Sarah will be back in Boston before the news breaks.

Nothing to do now but wait.

Wait for a vial of liquid to show up in the mail tomorrow.

Wait for Sarah to wake up.

Wait for another message from the Apostle.

I feel like I'm crawling out of my own skin.

SUNDAY, JULY 17, 10:10 P.M.

JUST WHAT THE DOCTOR ORDERED ON A SUNDAY
THAT SEEMED TO GO ON FOREVER! SARAH DID IT TO
ME AGAIN. SHE WENT TO THE BONNIE AND CLYDE
HIDEOUT BEFORE CHECKING INTO THE HOTEL LAST NIGHT
AND DIDN'T BOTHER TO TELL ME. AFTER THAT, SHE
SLEPT UNTIL NOON, THEN SPENT THE NEXT TEN HOURS
EDITING TOGETHER A BUNCH OF NEW STUFF FOR ME TO
LOOK AT. HOLED UP IN A HOTEL ROOM IN MISSOURI
WITH NO DISTRACTIONS GAVE HER A CHANCE TO
REALLY DIG IN AND CUT SOME NICE FOOTAGE.
HERE'S THE NOTE SHE SENT ME:

Wait until you see the video of the night the ghost of Old Joe Bush
came up over the hill. If I didn't know better, I'd say it really *was* a
ghost. Henry is dead, but I'm not ready to say the ghosts have been put
to rest.

I should have called you last night, but you sounded so out of it, I figured
why worry you? Instead of going to the hotel right away, I went ahead
and drove over to Bonnie and Clyde's hideout. Everything went fine —
it was actually the easiest find yet. No ghosts, no visitors — it was all
very routine. I found the stone marked A, right at the base of the house

, in the back corner, and pried it off. In there? A burlap bag with a Crossbones birdie stamped on it. You'll have to watch the video to see what was in there and what I did with it. Crazy!

I'm giving you three videos this time — been editing nonstop! Ten hours of sleep makes me hyper-productive.

Call me after you've watched!

Password: spooksville

I can hardly wait to get on the road. Next stop, Savannah, Georgia.

Finally tired. 'Night!

Sarah

These are amazing videos — the Apostle gets close to spilling the beans about the author of the ghost book. Which begs the question . . . can there be an author of a book with no words? And seeing the ghost of Old Joe Bush one last time is kind of incredible. I'm with Sarah: if you ask me, this is one ghost that will never go completely out of existence.

SARAHFINCHER.COM
Password:
SPOOKSVILLE

I DON'T KNOW HOW SARAH KEEPS GOING. THE ROAD IS A LONELY AND SCARY PLACE, BUT SOMEHOW, SHE MANAGES TO MAKE IT LOOK LIKE SHE'S HAVING A PRETTY GOOD TIME OUT THERE. I ADMIRE THAT. IF IT WERE ME, I'D BE COMPLAINING ENDLESSLY.

ANOTHER LETTER FROM THE APOSTLE: P. SO NOW WE'VE GOT AN A AND A P — ONLY ONE LETTER TO GO. I DON'T SEE HOW ONE MORE LETTER IS GOING TO ADD UP TO ANYTHING, BUT HOPEFULLY THE APOSTLE WILL TELL US SOMETHING MORE WHEN WE SEE HIM AGAIN. FOR NOW, WE'VE GOT THE RAVEN PUZZLE FILLED IN WITH ANOTHER LETTER:

AND IN THE BURLAP SACK? ANOTHER VIAL OF LIQUID, ONLY THIS TIME THERE'S NO LABEL ON IT.

SARAH JUST SENT ME ANOTHER EMAIL. I'LL LET HER DESCRIBE WHAT WAS IN THE VIAL.

Ryan,

I couldn't wait to see what you thought — this vial's gross, right? Looks like it's filled with black tar, and it has one of those wax seals on the top. Also, it has a red ribbon on the neck that reminds me of blood (I don't know why). There's something very gothic about this vial, Ryan. Something, I don't know, sinister, I guess. I think it might be poison.

I set it in the bathroom. Couldn't stand looking at it anymore.

Sarah

I CAN SEE A STORY HERE: VIAL OF BLACK GOO CRAWLS INTO UNSUSPECTING GIRL'S EAR, TURNS HER INTO A ZOMBIE. THIS IS GETTING BAD. I HAVE TWO VIALS FILLED WITH WHAT? POISON? SOME SORT OF ALCHEMY CONCOCTION MADE BY DR. WATTS? THEY COULD BE FILLED WITH A LOT OF DIFFERENT THINGS.

Times like these, I wish I were a chemist with a laboratory in my basement.

She's sending me the vial tomorrow so it will arrive on Tuesday. By then Sarah should be all the way over to Monticello. The toughest part of her journey will be over.

Somehow, I think the hardest part of mine will just be starting.

Monday, July 18, 7:00 a.m.

My mom just knocked on my door with a message from the mayor: I'm to appear at his office at 9:00 a.m. sharp for an in-depth interview with Albert Vern of the <u>Washington Post</u> . . .

. . . and Gladys Morgan is going to join me.

"He says the reporter is stopping in for the morning, then he's on some assignment with the president. Can you believe that?"

Wow, I guess Albert Vern is even more important than I thought.

"It's now or never," my mom said.

How about never?

"Not a word about Henry," my mom added. She grilled me about Sarah — wasn't she on some road trip home from summer film school? I said I thought so, but that we really hadn't talked much lately.

My mom didn't buy it, but neither did she seem overly concerned. If only she knew that Sarah had been standing over Henry when he kicked the bucket.

I GUESS THE INTERVIEW WON'T BE THAT BAD. I MEAN, AT LEAST ALBERT VERN IS A FISHERMAN. WE STICK TOGETHER. AND IT WILL KILL SOME TIME WHILE I WAIT FOR THE MAIL TO SHOW UP SO I CAN SEE THIS MYSTERIOUS VIAL FOR MYSELF AND GET IT INTO FITZ'S HANDS.

SEEING MY MOM AND KNOWING ABOUT THIS INTERVIEW MAKES ME NERVOUS. WHEN THE GUY DELIVERS THE MAIL, HE USUALLY SHOWS UP BETWEEN 10:00 A.M. AND 11:00 A.M., WHICH MEANS HE'S PROBABLY BUZZING AROUND TOWN DURING THAT HOUR DELIVERING ALL THE MAIL—ORDER STUFF MY NEIGHBORS BUY. I CAN'T HAVE MY MOM GETTING THAT PACKAGE.

INTERVIEW STARTS AT 9:00 A.M. I'LL MAKE IT MY GOAL TO BOLT BY 10:00 A.M., JUST IN CASE. THEN I'LL WAIT ON THE PORCH FOR MY PACKAGE.

I AM NOT A SWEARING MAN, BUT IF I WAS, I'D BE CURSING UP A STORM RIGHT NOW. DANG THAT GLADYS MORGAN AND MAYOR BLAKE! NEITHER ONE OF THEM WOULD LET ME LEAVE UNTIL WE ANSWERED EACH AND EVERY QUESTION MR. VERN HAD. I COULD HAVE DONE THE ENTIRE THING IN TWENTY MINUTES FLAT, BUT OH NO, GLADYS HAD TO GO ALL HYPER-DETAIL ON ME. I'D GIVE A THIRTY-SECOND, TWENTY-WORD ANSWER, AND SHE'D FOLLOW UP WITH TEN MINUTES OF DRIVEL. IT WAS EXCRUCIATING!

HERE'S A REAL ZINGER: THE MISSING JEFFERSON LIBRARY WAS UNDER YOUR NOSE ALL ALONG. WHAT DOES THAT MEAN TO A TOWN LIKE SKELETON CREEK?

MY REPLY: WE'RE VERY PROUD. IT'S AWESOME.

GLADYS MORGAN'S REPLY: ADD TEN MINUTES OF GRADE-A BORING TO MY PERFECTLY CRAFTED ANSWER. NOW, TIMES THAT BY TWENTY QUESTIONS AND YOU'LL UNDERSTAND WHY I HAD TO RUN HOME ONLY TO ARRIVE ON THE FRONT STEPS OF MY HOUSE AT 11:04 A.M.

Luckily for me, Mom wasn't home, so now I'm sitting on those same steps with a glass vial of supersecret liquid in my front pocket. The delivery guy left it by the front door in a shoe box wrapped in brown paper. Inside the shoe box, Sarah had wrapped the vial in the equivalent of a weeks' worth of local newspapers.

Now all I have to do is get this thing out to Fitz's old trailer before noon, when my dad expects me to show up at the shop and work the rest of the day. No problem there — the trailer is on a dirt road outside of town — I can get there and back with time to spare.

I texted Sarah to let her know I got the package and she fired one right back:

On the road to Savannah. Can hardly wait! Always wanted to go there. Parents are good. They're happy I'm close to home. I'll let you know when I settle into room 204. BOO!

Love the BOO.

I HADN'T BEEN PAYING CLOSE ATTENTION TO HOW
FAR AWAY SARAH WAS GETTING. IN A FEW HOURS,
SHE'LL BE ABOUT AS DISTANT AS SHE CAN BE WITHOUT
LEAVING THE UNITED STATES.

BUMMER.

MONDAY, JULY 18, 11:50 A.M.

GOT THE VIAL IN PLACE SO FITZ CAN FIND IT. I
GLANCED THROUGH THE DUSTY WINDOWS THINKING
MAYBE I COULD FIND A PICTURE OF THE RAVEN OR
SOME OTHER CLUE. IT CROSSED MY MIND TO BREAK
IN AND LOOK AROUND, BUT MAN, THAT PLACE GIVES
ME THE CREEPS BIG-TIME. PLUS, IT WOULD BE A
DISASTER IF I GOT CAUGHT OR QUESTIONED ABOUT
A BREAK-IN AT THE OLD TRAILER. DRAWING
ATTENTION TO MYSELF RIGHT ABOUT NOW FEELS
LIKE A BAD IDEA.

I'M TEMPTED TO ASK MY DAD IF HE EVER
CROSSED PATHS WITH FITZ'S DAD, BUT I KNOW WHAT
THE ANSWER WILL BE. FITZ ALREADY TOLD ME HIS DAD
WAS RECLUSIVE, AND WHEN HE SHOPPED HE ALWAYS
WENT TO THE SAFEWAY IN BAKER CITY, DOWN
THE ROAD.

"HE'S EITHER IN THE TRAILER, IN THE WOODS,
OR DOING SOMETHING SECRET I DON'T KNOW ABOUT,"
FITZ ONCE TOLD ME. NO MATTER. EVEN IF HE DID
COME INTO TOWN, HE WOULDN'T HAVE A BLACK
HOOD ON, LOOKING LIKE AN EXECUTIONER. WHAT

GOOD'S IT GOING TO DO IF I KNOW WHAT HIS DAD LOOKS LIKE?

BY THE TIME I GET OFF WORK AT 6:00 P.M., SARAH SHOULD BE IN SAVANNAH, GEORGIA, DEALING WITH THE GHOST OF A GIRL WHO DOVE INTO PAVEMENT. OUCH.

MONDAY, JULY 18, 1:12 P.M.

ALBERT VERN JUST STOPPED INTO THE FLY SHOP TO
SAY GOOD-BYE AND ASK ME IF I WAS SURE THERE
WASN'T ANYTHING ELSE I'D LIKE TO SAY ON THE RECORD.
DAD LOOKED AT ME FROM ACROSS THE COUNTER AND I
THOUGHT FOR A SECOND HE WAS GOING TO SPILL THE
BEANS ABOUT HENRY. BUT HE STAYED QUIET AND SO
DID I. I'D SAID ALL I WAS GOING TO SAY ABOUT THE
DREDGE, THE GOLD, THE JEFFERSON LIBRARY —
ALL OF IT.

"WISH I HAD TIME TO HOOK A FEW MORE TROUT,"
VERN SAID WHEN HE REACHED THE DOOR. "KEEP
FINDING BURIED TREASURE AND MAYBE I'LL BE BACK."

AND THEN IT HAPPENED. I FREAKED OUT. I SLIPPED.
MY MIND WENT BLANK AND I JUST BLURTED IT OUT.

"YOU CAN COUNT ON IT. PROBABLY BY
TOMORROW."

ALBERT VERN WAS EYEING ME AS I SAID IT, AND
THERE WAS SOMETHING IN HIS EXPRESSION THAT MADE
ME NERVOUS. HE WAS A REPORTER AT THE TOP OF HIS
GAME AT ONE OF THE MOST PRESTIGIOUS PAPERS IN
THE WORLD. HE SMELLED SOMETHING MORE THAN A KID
BOASTING ABOUT WHAT HE THOUGHT HE COULD DO. IT

LOOKED AS IF HE'D CAUGHT THE THREAD OF A BIGGER STORY.

As the door closed behind Albert Vern, I wondered if he really was leaving town. More likely, I'd just alerted a reporter with a shovel to start digging for information.

What could he get access to? Could he get into my phone records if he wanted to? Could he get into Sarah's? What if he found all the videos? What if he figured out everything and beat Fitz to the vial?

A lot of what-ifs, all because I opened my big mouth.

Lesson learned, hopefully not too late.

759

MONDAY, JULY 18, 6:29 P.M.

SARAH SHOULD BE PULLING INTO SAVANNAH, GEORGIA, BEFORE DARK. SHE BETTER, OR HER PARENTS ARE GOING TO FLIP. I KNOW SHE SAYS THEY'RE NOT KEEPING CLOSE TABS ON HER, BUT SHE'S BEEN RIDING THE RAZOR'S EDGE OF THE RULES FOR DAYS. I'D HATE TO SEE HER PARENTS DRIVE DOWN THE COAST AND MEET HER SOMEWHERE. THAT WOULD COMPLICATE THINGS RIGHT AS WE'RE COMING TO THE END.

P.S. YOU COULDN'T PAY ME ENOUGH MONEY TO STAY IN ROOM 204 AT THE 17 HUNDRED 90 BUILDING. IT'S TOTALLY HAUNTED.

SARAH ARRIVED IN SAVANNAH AND CHECKED INTO THE ROOM. IT DIDN'T TAKE HER ANY TIME AT ALL TO FIND WHAT SHE WAS LOOKING FOR AND SEND ME AN EMAIL.

Ryan,

I don't want to take chances calling you tonight. My parents are on high alert about this place. I guess my mom did some research on the hotel and she's losing her resolve when it comes to letting me run around ghost hunting.

I have to admit, there's something spooky about this room. No matter how many lights I turn on, it still seems dark in here. I looked out the window, saw the brick sidewalk below, felt movement in the room. Maybe I'm just really tired, but I would have bet my life someone was in the room with me.

But there was no one.

I found the air duct up in the corner, used a chair and a screwdriver.

Another Apostle video — maybe the last? Hopefully, it will give us the final letter and it will make some sense. I need to set up the projector and take a look, but I wanted to email you first so you know I got it. Plus, it makes me feel better to email you. Almost like you're here.

Keep your phone handy, will ya? This room is something else. I can't shake the feeling that someone is in here with me.

I might call if I get too freaked out.

Miss you. Exhausted.

Sarah

OH, GREAT. NOW I'M GOING TO HAVE TO STAY UP PRACTICALLY ALL NIGHT IN CASE SHE CALLS. WHO AM I KIDDING? I CAN'T STAY UP ALL NIGHT TO SAVE MY LIFE. I JUST TEXTED HER TO AT LEAST SEND ME THE LETTER THE A-POSTLE LEFT IN HIS MESSAGE. I'M DYING TO KNOW WHAT IT IS.

TEXT ME THE LETTER. IT WILL GIVE ME SOMETHING TO DO. HERE IF YOU NEED ME!

A FEW MINUTES LATER:

Working on that. Someone just jiggled the handle from the outside. When I opened the door, no one was there. Eek!

Is she making that up or is someone actually following her? It's times like these I feel like running down the hall to my parents' room and confessing the whole crazy mess.

When is it the closer we get to solving a big mystery the more dangerous things seem to feel? Every day feels like one day closer to the edge of an abyss that threatens to devour both of us. Staying clear of that edge feels harder and harder, like it's got some kind of gravitational pull and it's drawing us near.

I set up my camera to record overnight, just in case, while I wait for Sarah to message me back. Then I sat at my desk and looked at the Raven Puzzle and the three letters we'd use once Sarah got to Monticello: an A, a P, and whatever letter the A-postle gave us in room 204.

MESSAGE FROM SARAH:

Hold your horses, cowboy. It takes time to
set up the old projector and feed the reel in.
Give me five.

Five minutes, which probably meant ten, and
I'd have the last letter of the puzzle. Not that
having it would solve anything. I'd gone through
the entire alphabet and it didn't matter what
letter I used, the three letters didn't make a bit
of sense. I waited, kept staring at the Raven
puzzle, pondered.
Three letters that have something to do
with Thomas Jefferson's old estate. The
solution totally eludes me.
MESSAGE FROM SARAH:

E. That's the letter the A-postle showed.
Have fun figuring it out. Looks to me like we're
dealing with an A-PE. I'm going to start
recording to video. So tired.

A-s I suspected, the third letter is only slightly helpful. I was hoping for something else, like a symbol or an entire word that would bring this whole thing together.

A--P-E. Ape.

A-pe on Jefferson's house.

A-pe on a building.

King Kong?

Oh, brother.

I feel like Charlie Brown. Total failure.

TUESDAY, JULY 19, 1:09 A.M.

I JUST HAD ONE OF THE SCARIEST MOMENTS OF MY LIFE, AND I'VE HAD SOME HUGE SCARES, SO THAT'S SAYING SOMETHING. THE MOMENT PROVIDED ME WITH THE ANSWER I'VE BEEN LOOKING FOR, THOUGH, SO I GUESS IT WAS WORTH IT. I MIGHT HAVE LOST A YEAR OF MY LIFE DUE TO STRESS OVERLOAD, BUT AT LEAST I KNOW WHAT THE A-P-E MEANS.

HERE'S HOW IT WENT DOWN.

I FELL ASLEEP AT MY DESK (PREDICTABLE, I KNOW). THEN I STARTED DREAMING, OR AT LEAST I THOUGHT I DID. SOMETIMES I CAN'T TELL WHERE THE NIGHTMARES END AND MY LIFE PICKS UP. I WAS DREAMING THAT A RAVEN WAS TAP—TAP—TAPPING ON MY WINDOWSILL.

THE RAVEN. TAPPING WITH THE EDGE OF AN AX BLADE, ABOUT TO BASH THE GLASS OUT AND CLIMB INSIDE MY HOUSE.

THE SOUND KEPT COMING AS THE POEM UNWOUND LIKE A CLOCK SPINNING BACKWARD IN MY BRAIN.

ONCE UPON A MIDNIGHT DREARY,
WHILE I PONDERED, WEAK AND WEARY

Tap tap tap. The Raven outside my window, cloaked in black, watching me sleep.

In my dream — or had I awoken? — I stood and backed up to the door, reaching for the handle.

And then the Raven spoke, first in a whisper, then loud enough for me to hear him through my window.

Ryan. Ryan! Ryan! It's me! Open the window!

After that I was fully awake, walking to the window, because it wasn't the Raven after all. It was Fitz, come to pay me a visit on his way back to the cave.

"You scared me so badly I feel like I should slap you," I said when I opened the window. "How'd you get up here?"

"It's easy," he replied. Fitz was dressed all in black with a hood over his head, so it was easy to see how I could have gotten him confused with someone else. "Climbed up on the porch rail and onto the eave."

I asked him if he'd gotten the vial, and he told me he had.

"I think it's for the clause," I said.

"I do, too."

So we agreed. He hadn't brought it with him, which he felt stupid for just then, so we couldn't know if spreading what was in the vial on the clause would reveal some hidden message or not. We both hoped it would.

"How are you doing up there? In the cave, I mean."

Fitz shrugged meaningfully, as if it hadn't been going very well and he wished he could get away. He looked off toward the street below, trying to hide the sadness in his eyes. But I could see.

"Dad's not all bad. He's confused, mostly, is what I think," Fitz said, his big shoulders leaning in on the windowsill like slabs of concrete. I'd forgotten what a big guy he was. "The Crossbones is killing him."

I hadn't ever thought of it that way before. I was simply afraid of an ax-wielding man in black who appeared to have it out for me. Henry, the

Apostle, even the Raven — maybe they were all prisoners of the Crossbones. Maybe the Crossbones made them do the things they did.

"I gotta get back before he wakes up," Fitz told me. "Long walk in the dark and all."

I wished I could go with him, but there was no way. I'd done that walk a thousand times, but rarely in the dark by myself. It would be lonely and scary.

"Sorry I can't go with you. I would if I could."

"I know you would."

Fitz smiled at me, and I thought to myself, well, at least the Crossbones won't carry on past Fitz's dad. Fitz is way too nice a guy to go that route.

A few seconds later, he was gone, promising to let me know if the vial was of any use or not.

I closed my window, locked it, lay down on the bed. Checking my phone, I saw that Sarah hadn't tried to contact me again. Maybe she, too, had conked out. She'd sounded tired in her

MESSAGES, LIKE SHE WAS ON THE VERGE OF EXHAUSTION. Hopefully, she can sleep without being bothered by whatever haunted things go on in that place.

And that's when it happened. It was while I was lying there on the bed, staring at the ceiling and wondering about my two closest friends. Both of them were out in the cold of the world alone right then. Sarah in a haunted hotel room, braving the night almost a thousand miles from home. Fitz walking a dark river path to a wooded clearing, and then to a cave darker still.

A--P--E, I whispered.

Tap. Tap. Tap.

A--P--E. Tap Tap Tap.

Not A--P--E. That's not right at all. It's not about a giant monkey. It's something darker, like the darkness of the cave in the deep wood.

E-A--P. That's the order of the letters.

Tap tap tap goes the Raven on my windowsill.

And we all know who wrote the poem I'm getting at.

Edgar Allan Poe. E-A--P.

I GOT OUT OF BED AND WENT TO MY DESK AND STARTED WRITING THIS JOURNAL ENTRY, MY HAND SHAKING SO BADLY I HAD TO STOP AND TAKE THREE OR FOUR DEEP BREATHS. SOON, I HAD THE RAVEN PUZZLE BEFORE ME, AND THE WHOLE THING FELT SUDDENLY DRENCHED WITH MEANING. THE GOTHIC MADNESS OF EDGAR ALLAN POE WAS SMEARED ALL OVER IT.

I UNDERSTOOD. THERE WOULD BE NO NEED TO VISIT THOMAS JEFFERSON'S OLD HOME AT MONTICELLO. I'D FIGURED THAT OUT, TOO. THE DRAWING SAID TO PUT THE LETTERS IN THE MIDDLE, BUT IF YOU TOOK THE MIDDLE OUT OF THE HOUSE ON THE BACK OF A NICKEL, IT WASN'T A BUILDING AT ALL.

IT WAS A TOMBSTONE.

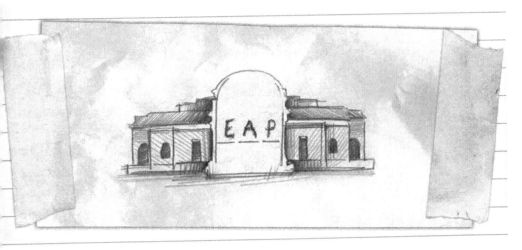

That part of the puzzle was meant as a clue, not as a place to visit where something might be found. No, where we would find what we were looking for is a hundred and sixty miles away in Baltimore, Maryland.

Edgar Allan Poe's tombstone.

It's where we're going to find the very end.

Email from Sarah, sent three hours ago.

Ryan,

I got your note first thing this morning when I woke up. Chilling, to say the least. But good, too. Baltimore is one step closer to home, and it's only three hours from the hotel near Monticello where I'm staying. I'll wrap things up here. I didn't make the post yesterday, so I'll get the black vial in the overnight to you before I leave Savannah, then hit the road. (By the way, you SO owe me for postage. These packages are crushing my dining budget — Slurpee for lunch, here I come.)

New password for you with a documentary I made about room 204 and the Apostle footage: theredroom1849

A note on the documentary: After staying a night in room 204, I'm of the opinion that it is, in fact, haunted. You know me — I'm a debunker by nature — but I'm telling you, something is in that room, and it's not of this world. It's angry, sad, not at rest. Needless to say, I didn't sleep at all last night.

A note on the Apostle video before you watch it: It's the last one. We've reached the end of the journey.

If I have time, I'm going to work up a documentary on Edgar Allan Poe. He's more important to all this than I thought.

He's been here all along, hasn't he?

Sarah

THAT'S EXACTLY WHAT I WAS THINKING, THAT POE HAS BEEN HIDING IN THE SHADOWS FROM THE START. ALL THE WAY BACK TO THE VERY BEGINNING, WHEN I WAS LAID UP IN A HOSPITAL, MY LEG SHATTERED AND MY HEAD POUNDING — HE WAS THERE. HE'S ALWAYS BEEN THERE, HAUNTING MY DREAMS AND FILLING MY MIND WITH WILD IDEAS. IF EVERY WRITER HAS THE SPIRIT OF SOME PAST, DEAD WRITER LIVING INSIDE HIM, THEN EDGAR ALLAN POE ISN'T BURIED IN A CEMETERY IN BALTIMORE — HE'S BURIED IN THE DEEPEST, DARKEST PART OF MY SOUL, DIGGING HIS WAY OUT IN MY WORDS, TRYING TO FIND THE LIGHT OF DAY.

SARAHFINCHER.COM
Password:
THEREDROOM1849

TUESDAY, JULY 19, 7:02 P.M.

THE APOSTLE HAS VANISHED LIKE VAPOR IN THE AIR.
HE'S GONE, AND I REALIZE NOW THAT ONLY ONE
REMAINS: THE RAVEN. I HAVE A FEELING, DEEP DOWN IN
MY BONES, THAT THE CROSSBONES IS ALL BUT WIPED
OFF THE FACE OF THE EARTH. THEIR THREE-PART
MISSION FEELS LIKE SOMETHING SITTING AT THE BOTTOM
OF A BOX IN AN ATTIC, LEFT OVER FROM A TIME LONG
PAST WHERE SUCH THINGS HAD A PLACE IN THE WORLD:

1) PRESERVE FREEDOM.
2) MAINTAIN SECRECY.
3) DESTROY ALL ENEMIES.

ONLY ONE GUY LEFT LIVING BY THAT CODE, AND
HE'S GOT HIS SIGHTS SET ON ONE ENEMY.
ME.
TODAY, I HAVE WANTED THE COMFORT OF MY
JOURNAL AND NOTHING MORE. ALL DAY I WISHED FOR
A PEN AND PAPER, TO FEEL THE SECURITY OF WORDS
TRAPPED ON PAGES. I PUT THEM IN, THEY CAN'T GET
OUT. AND THE WORLD CAN'T GET IN. THESE WORDS
ARE A PRISON WITH BARS TO KEEP THE RAVEN AWAY.

I'm being followed. I have very little doubt about this fact. It's a feeling that probably eludes anyone who lives in a big city. But out here, where there are a thousand trees for every person, I can feel when someone or something is moving toward me. I don't have to see them. I could be blind as a bat and I'd know.

I spent part of my day running errands for my dad. To the post office, out for lunch, to the grocery store for bottles of water and Clif Bars. Every time I left the safety of the fly shop I felt it, like ice on my neck: The Raven watching me.

Sarah will reach Monticello by nightfall. She'll check into her hotel — the last hotel before returning to Boston — and she'll call her parents and say something like, "Yeah, all tucked in for the night. Can't wait to get home tomorrow. Miss you, too." Then she'll get right back in her car and drive three hours up to Baltimore. There, she'll examine Edgar Allan Poe's grave site. I can't say that I'm thrilled. For once, I wish it were me standing at a

GRAVESTONE AFTER MIDNIGHT. I THINK STANDING AT POE'S GRAVE MIGHT BRING ME A SENSE OF RELIEF, OF HAVING COME FULL CIRCLE.

I KNOW TOO MUCH ABOUT THIS GUY. FOR EXAMPLE, I KNOW THAT THE GRAVESTONE SARAH IS GOING TO SEE IS NOT THE ONE THAT WAS ORIGINALLY PREPARED FOR MR. POE'S BURIAL PLOT. THAT ONE WAS MADE, BUT NEVER PUT TO USE. INSTEAD, IT WAS STRUCK BY A TRAIN RUN OFF ITS TRACKS, BROKEN INTO A THOUSAND PIECES. THIS KIND OF THING WAS ALWAYS HAPPENING TO EDGAR ALLAN POE: THINGS SNATCHED AWAY WITHOUT WARNING OR REASON. EVEN IN DEATH HE COULDN'T ESCAPE THE RANDOM CRUELTY OF LIFE.

AND SO HE WAS BURIED IN AN UNKNOWN PLOT, WITHOUT A HEADSTONE OR A MARKING. THIS FOR THE MAN WHO INVENTED MYSTERIES, SCIENCE FICTION, AND HORROR. LIKE VAN GOGH BEFORE HIM, POE WAS AN ARTIST REVERED IN DEATH, NOT THE LEAST BIT APPRECIATED IN LIFE.

SOMETIME LATER, A CHEAP SANDSTONE MARKER WAS PLACED OVER THE BURIAL PLOT WITH THE NUMBER 80, NOTHING MORE. AND LATER STILL, MONEY WAS RAISED IN ORDER TO BUILD A PROPER GRAVE SITE.

Unfortunately, even this effort ended in a final offense that remains to this day. Poe's birthday is engraved as the 20th of January, but he was born on the 19th. Insult piled on top of insult. After all he's given us, we can't even get the man's birthday right.

Maybe that's why I don't show anyone the stories I work on. I'd just as soon skip the part where nobody cares and I die in obscurity without having someone from some magazine say my stories lack depth or my character development is weak. No thanks.

Later on, long after I'm gone, someone will find my stories and be like — wow, I totally would have read this guy when he was alive, what a shame. But I know the truth. Nobody would have cared. Critics would have ripped me apart. They'd have been cruel.

I love to write, especially when I'm feeling miserable and paranoid.

This was fun.

THE CALL CAME IN, ONE MINUTE PAST MIDNIGHT, SARAH STANDING BEFORE THE POE GRAVE. IT SITS INSIDE A CHURCH GATE, OFF IN THE GRASS, AWAY FROM THE MONUMENT. THE HEADSTONE IS SUPPOSED TO DENOTE THE LOCATION WHERE POE WAS ACTUALLY BURIED, WHICH IS SEPARATE FROM THE MONUMENT ERECTED CLOSER TO THE STREET.

"THERE'S A RAVEN ON THE TOP," SHE WHISPERED, BECAUSE IT WAS AFTER HOURS AND SHE'D CLIMBED OVER THE STONE RAIL INTO THE CEMETERY. "AND THE WORDS 'QUOTH THE RAVEN, NEVERMORE.'"

I HAD TO TELL HER IT WAS THE LAST LINE OF THE EIGHTH STANZA IN HIS MOST FAMOUS POEM, A HEARTBREAKING EPITAPH.

BUT THAT'S NOT THE INFORMATION SHE WAS THERE TO GET. THE RAVEN PUZZLE HAD MADE IT CLEAR: LOOK ON THE BACK RIGHT CORNER, DOWN BY THE GRASS.

"I DIDN'T SEE ANYTHING AT FIRST, BUT THEN I DUG A LITTLE INTO THE GRASS RIGHT AT THE BASE OF THE HEADSTONE," SHE SAID. I WAS, AS USUAL, AMAZED. WHO DIGS AROUND THE EDGE OF EDGAR ALLAN POE'S GRAVE IN THE DARKEST PART OF THE NIGHT?

"I don't think you're going to like what it says."

I had already been wondering about this. In my heart of hearts, I'd always known. I knew it before she said it, knew it from the start.

All roads lead to Skeleton Creek.

"Are you ready?" she asked me.

"Nope."

"Too bad."

And then she told me what she'd found. She couldn't say whether it was part of the original carving in the stone or if someone had carved it after. But there it was, filled in with mud, which actually made it easier to read with a flashlight.

"SC: Plot 42"

We both knew what it meant. For some reason, when she said it, I laughed. It all felt so right, like every part of our effort had led to the only place it could lead in the end. SC: Skeleton Creek. Plot 42: the old cemetery on the hill. There were two cemeteries in Skeleton Creek, the newer one at the far end of town, and the old one on the hill. No one had been buried in the old one for a while, like a hundred years, and it was in poor condition. All those headstones were numbered, that much I knew. It was the way things were done in a small town long ago, just like the number 80 on Edgar Allan Poe's gravestone.

And how about that number, 42? Everything all coming together like a puzzle now, the same number as the dredge.

Whatever final secret the Crossbones was hiding, it would be buried under headstone number 42. I'd need a shovel and a load of courage. The shovel I could get easy enough. The courage was another matter entirely.

"You can do this, Ryan." Sarah could sense my deep hesitation in the silence that hung on the line. "And you have to do it now, not tomorrow or the next day. Right now. Waiting isn't going to make it any easier. And more important, waiting is going to mean someone else could find it first."

She was right, of course. For all I knew, Albert Vern had already tapped into my phone or figured out a way to put a tail on Sarah from back at the Washington Post. What would happen if he figured this whole thing out and beat us to the location? I could already read the headline in the paper: Reporter Uncovers Deepest Mystery Yet in Skeleton Creek, Outdoes Local Hero.

I can live with that. The problem? Sarah can't. After all she's done, she'll never forgive me if I don't get my sorry self out of this room and up on that hill before dawn.

"Remember what we talked about before," she said. "How you gotta get out there or life will pass you by? Those journals aren't going to give you a life. You have to go out and take it."

I think she's wrong about that. Minus Sarah, I think writing is the best part of my life. It makes me happy. So sue me.

"I'm going back to my hotel now," she said. "And tomorrow I'll be going home. The end is up to you, and I'm glad for that. I tell you what — dig the grave and I'll come out and see you. How's that for incentive?"

It _was_ a strong incentive. And I figured she could do it. She'd talked her parents into letting her drive across the country once, why couldn't she do it again? Or better yet, make it easier and take a dang airplane this time.

"Call me when you land," I said, thinking of an airplane but meaning when she landed in her hotel. "I'll get it done."

I sat in my room for ten minutes.

Then I thought about how much Sarah would want to see what I was doing, so I took a roll of silver duct tape out of my desk drawer. A guy can make just about anything out of duct tape. I fashioned a little pocket for my phone and held it against one of my baseball caps. Then I wrapped duct tape around the pocket and the hat and put it on. Now I could run my phone's video camera and dig up a grave at the same time. It was a very Sarah thing to do.

I PULLED OUT THE GHOST BOOK AND WISHED I KNEW
WHAT IT MEANT, WISHED FITZ HAD NEVER GIVEN IT TO
ME IN THE FIRST PLACE. I TOOK OUT MY COLLECTION
OF POE STORIES AND TURNED TO THE END OF "THE
PIT AND THE PENDULUM." I'D READ IT TEN OR TWELVE
TIMES AND FELT ITS POWER.

HE SPOKE TO ME THEN, DOWN THROUGH TIME, ONE
WRITER TO ANOTHER. AND I FELT AS HE MUST HAVE
FELT ALL THE DAYS OF HIS LIFE.

THERE WAS A LOUD BLAST AS OF MANY TRUMPETS!
THERE WAS A HARSH GRATING AS OF A THOUSAND
THUNDERS! THE FIERY WALLS RUSHED BACK! AN
OUTSTRETCHED ARM CAUGHT MY OWN AS I FELL,
FAINTING, INTO THE ABYSS.

I FEEL THAT WAY NOW, AS IF I'M FALLING INTO AN
UNMARKED GRAVE, ALREADY FORGOTTEN BY ANYONE
WHO EVER LOVED ME AND EVERYONE WHO NEVER
KNEW ME. I AM FALLING, FALLING, FALLING INTO THE
ABYSS.

I WON'T RETURN UNTIL I DIG UP THE GRAVE
MARKED 42.

WEDNESDAY, JULY 20, 3:19 A.M.

I'M NOT DEAD.

SARAHFINCHER.COM
Password:
THECLAUSE

WEDNESDAY, JULY 20, 3:39 A.M.

SARAH KNOWS EVERYTHING NOW. SHE'S SAFE, WHICH MAKES ME HAPPY. PRETTY SOON SHE'LL BE SLEEPING, AND AFTER THAT SHE'LL WAKE UP AND DRIVE HOME. I'LL BE HAPPIER STILL WHEN I KNOW SHE'S OFF THE ROAD FOR GOOD.

SHE IMMEDIATELY TOOK WHAT I SHOT AT THE CEMETERY AND PUT IT UP AT HER SITE. I WANTED HER TO SEE IT FIRST, TO KNOW WHAT I KNOW BEFORE I WRITE IT DOWN.

SHE SAID I SOUNDED LIKE I WAS IN SHOCK. SHE SAID I DIDN'T SOUND LIKE MYSELF. I HAVEN'T SLEPT IN A LONG TIME AND EVERYTHING ABOUT WHAT HAPPENED AFTER MY LONG WALK TO THE OLD CEMETERY IS A BRAIN MELTER. I'M STILL PUTTING IT ALL TOGETHER.

EVERY STORY, FACT OR FICTION, HAS ITS OWN WAY OF UNFOLDING. THERE IS PURPOSE TO THE WAY WE CRAFT THESE THINGS. SO SARAH HAS THE IMAGES, BUT I'M STILL GOING TO WRITE WHAT HAPPENED.

WEDNESDAY, JULY 20, 3:45 A.M.

MY LEG BEGAN TO FAIL ME AND I STARTED TO LIMP AS I WALKED DOWN THE STREET WITH THAT SHOVEL IN MY HANDS. I'D PUT THAT LEG THROUGH A LOT DURING THE PAST FEW DAYS — RIDING DOWN TO SEE FITZ, CROSSING THE RIVER, MOVING THROUGH THE WOODS — AND IT WAS FINALLY SAYING, HEY, DUDE, ENOUGH ALREADY.

A DOG WHINED OFF IN THE DISTANCE AND I IMAGINED IT WAS HIT BY A CAR, WOBBLING OFF INTO A DITCH TO DIE. OTHER THAN THAT, IT WAS A STILL NIGHT IN SKELETON CREEK AS I APPROACHED THE HILLTOP GRAVEYARD. I LOOKED BACK OVER MY TOWN AND HEARD THE DOG ONCE MORE. IT WASN'T LIKE STARING OUT OVER A CITY AT NIGHT WITH ITS SEA OF LIGHTS. SKELETON CREEK, FROM UP HERE, LOOKED AS SECRET AND HAUNTED AS IT ALWAYS HAD. A PORCH LIGHT HERE AND THERE, A DARKENED MAIN STREET, THE SHADOWY OUTLINES OF TREES AND HOUSES.

I SEARCHED THE GRAVEYARD IN SILENCE AS A SOFT WIND DRIFTED OVER THE HILLTOP. WITH A FLASHLIGHT IN ONE HAND AND A SHOVEL IN THE OTHER, I CREPT CLOSE TO EACH STONE AND FOUND THEY HAD NO ORDER. I WOULDN'T FIND HEADSTONE 42 NEXT TO 41

789

NEXT TO 4̶0̶. WHOEVER HAD ENVISIONED THIS PLOT OF LAND HADN'T BEEN IN POSSESSION OF AN ORDERED MIND. MORE LIKELY THEY'D DUG A HOLE IN WHATEVER OPEN SPACE THEY COULD FIND, DROPPED THE COFFIN INSIDE, AND PLANTED THE HEADSTONE. MAYBE THAT WAS THE WAY THINGS WERE DONE A HUNDRED YEARS AGO, OR MAYBE THE PERSON IN CHARGE JUST DIDN'T CARE. EITHER WAY, I SEARCHED FOR A WHILE BEFORE I CAME TO NUMBER 42.

THE NUMBERS WERE ON THE BACKS OF THE HEADSTONES, AND COMING AROUND THE FRONT, I HAD AN UNFORESEEN MOMENT OF TERROR. BECAUSE THERE IT WAS, THE NAME I SAW ON HEADSTONE NUMBER 42:

ALBERT VERN.

I STARED AT THE WORDS, AND, LIKE MAGIC, THE LETTERS BEGAN TO MOVE IN MY MIND. WHO WAS ALBERT VERN, IF NOT THE MAN HE'D CLAIMED TO BE?

THE FIRST LETTER REMAINED, HOT AND GLOWING IN MY BRAIN.

A

ALL THE REST OF THE LETTERS IN HIS FIRST NAME FELL AWAY, LIKE WHITE BONES OVER A CLIFF, TUMBLING INTO A BLACK SEA.

The last name remained: VERN.

And then the letters started to move, rearranging themselves as I wished they wouldn't and my grip on the shovel grew tighter.

The man had never been A. VERN.

He had only ever been the RAVEN.

There was a brief moment where I started to scream, or tried to, at least. My throat had gone dry and nothing but a whimper came out. Too bad, Mr. Mayor. There is no reporter from the Washington Post. Only a man with a black ax searching for answers.

I knew then that Albert Vern had been following me all day. He'd been following me all week. He knew I had the ghost book. He knew who'd given it to me. And what was worse, he'd arrived in the cemetery, black as night, drifting in through the trees.

The Raven approached with that same inhuman motion I'd seen before. The ghost of Old Joe Bush moved like that. Far away, then somehow standing right beside me.

And then he spoke.

"I've been following you."

He held the great ax in his hands, spun the blade, examined me carefully. Would I run away? Would I scream someone awake in the dead of night? He need not have worried: I was still like one of the tombstones, turned to stone with fear.

"I know what you stole from me."

I held the shovel as if it might protect me from the swinging ax.

"I know the Apostle led you here."

"I know what lies beneath the grave."

The Raven moved harrowingly close then, his face almost knowable, but still bathed in shadow. I wanted to point my flashlight in his eyes, but my mind and my hand wouldn't cooperate with each other.

"Step aside, son. Or meet your maker."

The Raven raised the ax over his head. If ever I needed to move, now was the time.

But I couldn't. Or at least, I didn't.

THE AX HOVERED OVER THE RAVEN'S HEAD, AS IF HE WAS SEARCHING FOR A REASON NOT TO SWING. AND THEN A NEW VOICE BOOMED INTO THE GRAVEYARD.

"I INVOKE THE CLAUSE!"

THE RAVEN TURNED IN THE DIRECTION OF THE VOICE AND LIGHT FLASHED OVER HIS FACE. THE RAVEN, ALBERT VERN, FITZ'S DAD — THESE FACES WERE ONE IN THE SHADOWS AND THE GLOOM.

I COULDN'T TAKE MY EYES OFF HIS FACE. WAS IT AN HOUR, A MINUTE, A SECOND THAT I STARED INTO THOSE EYES? TIME HAD NO MEANING UNTIL I FINALLY DID TURN TO SEE WHAT THE RAVEN SAW: FITZ, SHADOWY AND BIG, HOLDING THE CLAUSE IN ONE HAND AND A FLASHLIGHT IN THE OTHER. THERE WERE WORDS ON WHAT WAS ONCE AN EMPTY SHEET OF YELLOWED PAPER, BROUGHT BACK BY WHATEVER HAD BEEN IN THE VIAL I'D GIVEN HIM.

WITH A VOICE OF AUTHORITY I HADN'T HEARD BEFORE, FITZ READ THE CLAUSE.

"WE BELIEVE IN THE EVERLASTING SUPREMACY OF ONE GENERATION AFTER ANOTHER.

WE BELIEVE THAT THE WORLD IS EVER CHANGING."

793

THE GREAT AX LAY AT THE RAVEN'S SIDE, AND HE
BEGAN READING ALONG WITH FITZ, THEIR VOICES
DRIFTING TOGETHER OVER THE STONES OF THE DEAD:

"WE GIVE POWER TO THE FIRSTBORN SON OF THE
LAST MAN STANDING.
WE TRUST IN THE PASSING OF TIME AND THE KNOWING
OF ALL THINGS.
THE DUTY TO PRESERVE FALLS NOW IN THE LINE
OF ALL GOOD MEN."

THEY WERE BEAUTIFUL WORDS, STRONG AND
MEANINGFUL. THEY HAD AUTHORITY. THE RAVEN FELL
SILENT, AS IF HE'D WAITED HIS WHOLE ADULT LIFE TO HEAR
THOSE WORDS, WONDERING WHEN THEY MIGHT BE SAID,
KNOWING THEY WOULD HAVE POWER OVER HIM IN THE
END. I WONDERED IF HE'D SAID THE WORDS HIMSELF A LONG
TIME AGO, WRENCHING POWER FROM A LONG LINE OF MEN.
FITZ READ THE LAST OF THE CLAUSE ALONE
WITHOUT EVEN LOOKING AT THE WORDS HE WAS SAYING.

"I TAKE THIS OATH
TO PRESERVE FREEDOM.

To maintain secrecy.

To destroy all enemies.

I appoint these three:

To protect: Sam Fitzsimons

To record: Sarah Fincher

To treasure: Ryan McCray

We are the Crossbones now."

Fitz paused and I looked back and forth between the two. And then the son spoke the last of the oath to his father, and there was a sadness in those words I didn't see coming.

"Your time has passed."

The Raven never did take the hood off of his head, but he did drop the ax. He left it lying there in the cemetery and Fitz picked it up. I had a strange sensation, seeing my friend there with a weapon of some size. Was Fitz to be the new muscle of the Crossbones? And more

IMPORTANT, WAS I TO BE ITS HENRY, AND SARAH ITS APOSTLE? THE VERY THOUGHT OF THESE THINGS LEFT ME FOGGY IN THE HEAD, AFRAID OF WHAT WAS TO COME IN THE MONTHS AND YEARS THAT WOULD FOLLOW.

WE BOTH WATCHED AS THE RAVEN — OR WHAT ONCE WAS THE RAVEN — DISAPPEARED INTO THE TREES. AFTER AN AWKWARD PAUSE, FITZ SPOKE.

"DID THAT JUST HAPPEN LIKE I THINK IT DID?"

I DIDN'T THINK ABOUT MY REPLY. I SIMPLY SAID IT, WHICH MADE IT FEEL TRUE EVEN IF IT WASN'T.

"I THINK WE'VE BECOME WHAT WE WERE FIGHTING ALL ALONG."

I LOOKED AT THE TOP OF THE GRAVE SITE AND I KNEW WHAT I SHOULD HAVE SAID.

STAND BACK. I'VE GOT SOME DIGGING TO DO.

BUT I DIDN'T, AND I CAN'T SAY EXACTLY WHY.

FITZ DIDN'T KNOW THERE WAS SOMETHING TO FIND AT GRAVESTONE NUMBER 42. HOW COULD HE? THE GUY HAD BEEN COOPED UP IN A CAVE FOR A WEEK. HE DIDN'T ASK FOR THE GHOST BOOK, WHICH SEEMED TO HAVE SLIPPED HIS MIND JUST THEN. HE simply said it was over, we'd ended the Crossbones.

"I think he wanted it to be over," Fitz told me, holding the ax in one big hand like a man of the woods. "Give him a few days chopping trees and I bet we'll be back at the trailer. It'll be like old times. I might even get my old job back at the fly shop."

I nodded, smiled weakly, let the words hang in the air. All I could think about was what lay under the ground I stood on.

"I need to go home," I said. "It's late."

"Yeah. I should probably follow my dad, make sure everything's okay."

Fitz said something about the clause and shook his head, hardly believing what had happened. But I felt it — we both did. Fitz's dad knew about the clause. He knew its power over the Crossbones, knew his time really had come and gone. The clause had achieved its cruel duty.

I walked maybe five minutes toward town as Fitz went the other way, then I stopped and

TURNED BACK. I WASN'T SCARED THIS TIME AS I STOOD OVER THE GRAVE. I WAS EXCITED.

As I STARTED TO DIG I REALIZED WHAT I WAS DOING, WHAT I'D BEEN DOING MY WHOLE LIFE.

I WAS KEEPING A SECRET.

WEDNESDAY, JULY 20, 4:03 A.M.

It took about five minutes to find what I was digging for: a metal box a foot belowground that clanged when my shovel hit. There was a lock — not a very good one — but it didn't matter. It was a cheap sort of metal with crummy hinges that popped free with one blow from the shovel.

Inside was another wooden box, shaped like a coffin, only much smaller. It fit in my hand. When I opened the coffin and pointed my flashlight inside, there was a vial like the one I'd already given Fitz. Like the one Sarah was supposed to mail me right after she got it, but missed the deadline for overnight by an hour.

The black vial Sarah finally did mail that would arrive in Skeleton Creek in a few hours.

But this vial was different. Inside, white liquid, thick like Elmer's glue, and on the vial a short poem.

One part black, three parts white.
Make the Crossbones fear the night.

799

I PUT THE METAL BOX AND THE SMALL WOODEN COFFIN BACK IN THE GROUND AND BURIED THEM. THEN I MADE MY WAY HOME WITH THE VIAL IN MY POCKET, QUIETLY SNEAKING UP THE CREAKING STAIRS.

AND NOW I'M SITTING HERE, WIDE AWAKE WHEN I SHOULD BE SLEEPING. I'M WAITING FOR THE BLACK VIAL TO ARRIVE, SO I CAN MIX IT.

ONE PART BLACK, THREE PARTS WHITE.

AND THEN I'LL USE A BRUSH AND I'LL PAINT THE PAGES OF THE GHOST BOOK. AND IN THE GHOST BOOK I KNOW WHAT I'LL FIND.

SOMETHING SCARY.

Just got off the phone with Sarah. She's on her way home. I told her everything. At first she laughed — yeah right, you and me, Crossbones, that's a good one — but then she fell silent. Like me, I think she's wondering what that means, if anything.

I couldn't keep the white vial a secret from her. I even told her I'd kept it from Fitz.

"Good," she said. "I've never even met him. Let's wait and see what the ghost book tells us. No sense spilling the beans to the Raven's son just yet. Could be a trick."

I hadn't thought of that, but it didn't really add up. Fitz was a good guy, a friend. All he wanted was a normal life and a normal family. I could hardly begrudge him things like that.

"I guess this is the end, huh?" I said as we were wrapping things up.

"Either that," Sarah ventured, "or the very beginning. I mean, hey, we run the show now, right? Could mean a lot of things."

I couldn't help thinking it meant the three of us would be at war with one another one day.

I'm starting to wonder if I have trust issues.

Sarah left off by saying she'd been getting more and more interested in Edgar Allan Poe. The fact that this entire thing led to his tombstone really got her wheels spinning. So, in typical Sarah fashion, she's working on an Edgar Allan Poe documentary.

This girl acts more like the Apostle every day.

WEDNESDAY, JULY 20, NOON

Mom's working, dad's at the shop, I just ran out to grab us some lunch and stopped at the house. There was a small package at the door, as I'd hoped.

I have the black vial.

WEDNESDAY, JULY 20, 6:45 P.M.

SUSPENSE IS KILLING ME! I WON'T BE ABLE TO SNEAK OFF TO MY ROOM UNTIL LATER TONIGHT, PROBABLY NOT UNTIL THE SUN GOES DOWN. I WOULD HAVE PREFERRED TO OPEN THE GHOST BOOK WHEN THE SUN WAS STILL UP, BUT THAT'S NOT TO BE.

THE NEWS BROKE ABOUT HENRY. SOMEONE BLABBED, OR MAYBE IT WAS SIMPLY TIME FOR THE NEWS TO GET OUT. EVEN IN A TOWN KNOWN FOR KEEPING SECRETS, HENRY'S DEATH WAS A HARD ONE TO KEEP. SARAH IS BACK IN BOSTON, SAFE AND SOUND, SO EVEN IF THEY DO QUESTION HER ABOUT WHERE SHE WAS ON THE NIGHT THE BODY WAS FOUND, IT WON'T MATTER THAT MUCH. SHE'S VERY GOOD AT COVERING HER TRACKS. AND SHE'S OUT OF DANGER, SO I DON'T THINK ANYONE IS GOING TO DIG TOO DEEPLY INTO IT. HENRY WAS SICK AND DYING. HIS BODY HAD SIMPLY LOST ITS ABILITY TO CARRY A SOUL AROUND. IT HAPPENS. ESPECIALLY WHEN YOU'RE WALKING ALL OVER KINGDOM COME, BLEEDING ON THE INSIDE.

IN ANY CASE, THE TOWN IS BUZZING TONIGHT. THE MAYOR HAS HIS UNDERWEAR IN A BUNCH, AND ALL OUR NEIGHBORS KEEP STOPPING BY TO SEE WHAT WE THINK.

Even Gladys Morgan, who doesn't get out much, sat on our porch and spent an hour trying to convince my dad to run for office. She kept saying Skeleton Creek was turning into a theme park and it had to stop and Paul McCray was just the guy to do it. My dad kept shaking his head, and my mom couldn't stop laughing. The idea of her quiet, unassuming husband running anything other than a fly shop, let alone an entire town, made it impossible to keep a straight face.

Time passes on the porch in Skeleton Creek. It's not as interesting as it sounds.

WEDNESDAY, JULY 20, 9:57 P.M.

Now that it's after dark, I have a mind to wait until midnight. Things seem more meaningful when one day is turning into the next.

So I'm waiting.

I couldn't do it. Four minutes was all I could stand before I had the ghost book open to the first page. I had a cereal bowl from the kitchen and an old watercolor paintbrush and the two vials.

At first, things went very badly.

I did like I was instructed: one part black, three parts white. It made a thick, pasty gray goop, and when I tested it on the corner of the first page, the page began to sizzle. The whole corner of the page was eaten away before my eyes.

Whatever sort of alchemy or chemistry was going on here, the two substances mixed together were way too potent for paper.

I sat there for a few minutes all bummed out. My first secret as a Crossbones member was a total dud. It was the watercolor brush that got me thinking.

Watercolor.

That kind of paint starts out thick. Add water and you get the result you're looking for.

807

I GOT A CUP OF WATER AND POURED IT INTO THE CEREAL BOWL, MIXING THE GRAY GOOP INTO A BUBBLY BROTH.

"CORNER NUMBER TWO," I SAID, FEELING LIKE I WAS TALKING TO THE BOOK. "TRY NOT TO BURST INTO FLAMES."

IT DIDN'T IGNITE OR SIZZLE LIKE BACON IN A FRYING PAN. INSTEAD, THE PAGE CHANGED COLOR. IT TURNED A SMOKY BROWN, LIKE IT WAS A PANCAKE THAT HAD JUST BEEN PERFECTLY COOKED.

I FILLED THE BRUSH AGAIN, AND THIS TIME, I RISKED PAINTING THE WATERY CROSSBONES BREW OVER THE FIRST PAGE OF THE BOOK.

MY BREATH CAUGHT IN MY THROAT AS THE ENTIRE PAGE TURNED TOASTY BROWN. BUT IT WASN'T ALL COLORED. SOME OF IT REMAINED AS IT WAS: PAPER YELLOWED WITH AGE.

WORDS. AND NOT JUST ANY WORDS. WORDS WRITTEN BY THE MASTER HIMSELF.

"NO WAY," I WHISPERED.

I'D SEEN HIS HANDWRITING BEFORE. AND BESIDES, HIS NAME WAS PLAIN AS DAY.

E. Poe — January the 4th, 1849
    They're after me now. What an indignity!
    I might have thought twice before bringing them
into my confidence.
    A mistake, no doubt. But this! Thrown to the dogs,
left to rot.
    It anguishes me, this deceit.
    And so I shall make them pay all the days of their
sorry lives.

THERE ARE NO WORDS TO DESCRIBE THE WAY I
FELT WHEN I BEGAN READING THOSE WORDS. DON'T GET
ME WRONG — MILLIONS IN GOLD AND A LIBRARY OF
LOST BOOKS ARE NOT BENEATH MY INTEREST. BUT THIS
WAS SOMETHING ALTOGETHER DIFFERENT.

THESE WERE WORDS NO ONE HAD EVER SEEN
BEFORE.

THIS BOOK — THIS GHOSTLY BOOK ON EMPTY
PAPER — IT WAS FILLED WITH EDGAR ALLAN POE'S
WORDS. WORDS HIDDEN FROM THE WORLD ALL THESE
YEARS. FOR A WRITER, THIS WAS THE GREATEST OF
ALL PRICELESS TREASURES.

ONCE I CALMED DOWN AND READ FURTHER, I BEGAN
TO REALIZE THERE WERE TWO UNFATHOMABLY
IMPORTANT THINGS ABOUT THE GHOST BOOK.

THE FIRST:

EDGAR ALLAN POE WAS A MEMBER OF THE
CROSSBONES. TO THINK THAT SOMEHOW, DOWN
THROUGH THE YEARS, I, TOO, WOULD END UP A
CROSSBONES MEMBER — WELL, IT'S JUST UNTHINKABLE.
READING HIS WORDS AS THEY RAN DOWN THE
FIRST TWO PAGES, I FELT TERRIBLY SORRY FOR HIM.
THE CROSSBONES DIDN'T LET POE IN BECAUSE
THEY LIKED HIM. THEY LET HIM IN BECAUSE THEY
FEARED HIM.

Words are my weapon. They want to take them from me. I won't let them!

HE GOES ON TO DESCRIBE A COURTING PERIOD,
WHERE A SECRET SOCIETY INVITED HIM TO SECRET
MEETINGS TO TALK ABOUT SECRET THINGS. BUT HE

KNEW, AFTER A TIME, HOW THEY REALLY FELT. THEY
HATED HIM. THEY WANTED TO CRUSH HIM. THEY WANTED
TO BURN HIS BOOKS AND SHUT HIM UP. HE WAS BAD FOR
AMERICA, BAD FOR THE CHURCH, BAD, BAD, BAD!

*They don't know what bad is, these fools! They don't
know what it means to suffer.*

DECEIVED AND AFRAID, ONLY A FEW MONTHS SHY
OF HIS OWN DEATH, POE BEGAN THE GHOST BOOK. HE
LEFT NOTES AND SENT LETTERS, TOYING WITH THE
CROSSBONES.

*There is a book, a book without words. This book, it tells
your secrets. Your crimes!*

AND SO IT WAS THAT EDGAR ALLAN POE MADE
THE CROSSBONES THINK HE'D BETRAYED THEIR

SECRETS, THOUGH WHAT SECRETS HE ACTUALLY KNEW ARE HARD TO SAY. MEMBERS OF THE CROSSBONES ARE PARANOID BY NATURE, AND HE SUCCEEDED (OR SO HE SAYS) IN DRIVING THEM HALF MAD WITH FEAR.

FROM BEYOND THE GRAVE THE BOOK WAS FOUND, BUT POE WAS NOTHING IF NOT GOOD AT BEATING THE CROSSBONES AT THEIR OWN GAME. TO ONE HE GAVE THE WHITE VIAL, TO ANOTHER THE BLACK, AND A THIRD THE GHOST BOOK. HE WHISPERED TO THEM EACH — THE OTHERS CAN'T BE TRUSTED — AND SOON AFTER THAT, EDGAR ALLAN POE WAS DEAD.

THE CROSSBONES, EVER WARY OF THE TRUTH IN THE BOOK, RIPPED THEMSELVES TO SHREDS IN ITS PURSUIT. IF ONLY THEY'D KNOWN THE KEYS WERE ALL HIDDEN WITHIN THEIR OWN RANKS.

LIFE LESSON: DON'T MESS WITH MASTERS OF WORDS. THEY'LL ALWAYS GET YOU IN THE END.

THE SECOND SECRET OF THE GHOST BOOK, A SECRET A THOUSAND TIMES MORE IMPORTANT THAN THE FIRST, IS ONE I CAN SCARCELY BRING MYSELF TO REPORT.

HERE IT IS — SOMETHING REMARKABLE, SOMETHING GRAND.

THE PLOY AGAINST THE CROSSBONES LASTED
ONLY TWO PAGES. THE OTHER FORTY PAGES WERE
SOMETHING ELSE.

IT BEGAN ON THE TOP OF THE THIRD PAGE.

> I have a dreadful fear. Of my own death? No, not <u>that</u>
> death. It comes for me either way. Fear will credit me
> nothing. I fear the death of my words. I fear they'll find
> them, burn them, hurl them into the abyss!
>
> Here I keep them safe. Here they can't be found.
>
> Drink, world, drink! These secret words I write
> for you.

AND AFTER THAT? WORDS. MANY OF THEM. I SAT
IN MY ROOM AND PAINTED THEM INTO EXISTENCE. IT
WASN'T ONE LONG STORY — NO, IT WAS SOMETHING FAR
GREATER THAN THAT. PAGE AFTER PAGE OF IDEAS,
STORIES HE WANTED TO TELL BUT DIDN'T HAVE THE TIME
FOR. EVERY PAGE IN THE GHOST BOOK WAS THE
SKELETON OF A NEW STORY. AND THE MOST AMAZING
THING OF ALL — A HUNDRED YEARS LATER, I WAS

ENTRANCED BY EVERY IDEA. EACH OF THEM WHOLLY
ORIGINAL, EACH OF THEM GHASTLY, GOTHIC, MYSTERIOUS,
OR FANTASTIC. STRANGE CREATURES AND CHARACTERS
IN PLACES STRANGER STILL, THE MASTER IN HIS
LABORATORY, BUILDING A MONSTER BEFORE MY EYES.

Thursday, July 21, 6:30 a.m.

I've decided to keep the ghost book. I know what you're thinking: That's a crime. You can't keep it all to yourself. It belongs to everyone, not just you.

I suppose you're right. But I'm still keeping it.

I've been giving a lot of things back to the world lately. I'm just not ready to let this one go. I feel like Gollum in The Lord of the Rings. The ghost book is my precious. I wonder if it will make me live a thousand years and move into a cave and eat raw fish for dinner? Somehow I doubt it.

Hear me out before you judge me.

Edgar Allan Poe didn't have a rich family to lean on or a job to fill his bank account. He believed his writing would be enough.

Poe failed in the end, and part of that failure was his own. No one is saying he didn't dig at least half his own grave. But the world dug the rest, and the crossbones used a big shovel. One writer to another, I feel like a secret torch has been passed from a master to an apprentice. I feel

LIKE THESE IDEAS WERE HANDED DOWN TO ME, LIKE HE

REACHED HIS HAND INTO THE WORLD FROM THE GREAT

UNKNOWN AND MADE THIS HAPPEN. HE PUT THE GHOST

BOOK AND THE WAY INSIDE IN MY HANDS. I'LL ALWAYS

BELIEVE THAT, NO MATTER WHAT ANYONE SAYS.

I'M GOING TO FINISH WHAT HE STARTED.

SARAH WILL PROBABLY LAUGH AT THIS, AND THAT'S

OKAY. BUT I WANT TO HANG ON TO THESE WORDS FOR

JUST A LITTLE WHILE AND TRY TO TURN THEM INTO

WHAT I THINK HE WOULD HAVE WANTED. I'M NOT GOING

TO USE HIS WORDS, I'M GOING TO USE MINE. AND I'VE

DECIDED SOMETHING ELSE.

I'M GOING TO TELL SARAH AND FITZ ABOUT THE

GHOST BOOK.

THE THREE OF US ARE GOING TO DO THIS

TOGETHER. WE'RE GOING TO TURN THE CROSSBONES

ON ITS HEAD. WE'RE GOING TO MAKE IT INTO

SOMETHING NEW. THIS CROSSBONES WILL NOT BE

ABOUT THE BUSINESS OF KILLING IDEAS AND STORIES AND

BOOKS. IN A TWIST OF FATE ONLY POE HIMSELF COULD

HAVE ORCHESTRATED, THE NEW MEMBERS OF THE

CROSSBONES ARE GOING TO GIVE THE WORLD MORE

OF HIS STORIES, NOT LESS.

I CAN'T HELP WONDERING IF A DAY WILL COME WHEN FITZ IS FORCED TO TAKE UP THE GREAT AX AND PROTECT THE CROSSBONES FROM SOMETHING I CAN'T YET SEE. OR IF SARAH WILL LEAVE SECRET VIDEOS AND PUZZLES FOR TWO CURIOUS TEENAGERS TO FIND. I WONDER IF WE'LL BE AT ODDS WITH ONE ANOTHER SOMEWHERE DOWN THE LINE, IF WE'LL FIGHT FOR POWER. I HOPE THAT WILL NEVER HAPPEN.

IN OUR OWN WAY — A WAY ONLY WE CAN UNDERSTAND — I HOPE WE'LL BE TOGETHER ALWAYS.

WWW.SARAHFINCHER.COM
PASSWORD:
RESTINPEACE

Made in the USA
Columbia, SC
06 June 2019